THE GOD PROTOCOL
—— D R A G O N ——

D. L. WILBURN JR.

ISBN: 979-8-9878037-0-7 (eBook)

ISBN: 979-8-9878037-2-1 (Paperback)

ISBN: 979-8-9878037-1-4 (Hardcover)

Library of Congress Control Number: 2023902563

Any references to historical events, real people, or real places are used fictitiously. Names, characters, and places are products of the author's imagination.

Printed in the United States of America.

Cover by Suvajit Das.

Dragon Image created by Coffeemill licensed through Shutterstock.com

Edited by Elaine Wilburn, Brett Savory

Beta Readers: Michael Wilburn, Jeff Stelzer, Cheryl Barger, Chris Springer, Jerry McKinney, Steve Doroff and George Engel

Sensitivity Reader: Lily Wing-Lui Alexander

First printing edition 2023.

W-III Publishing

Permissions@W-III.org

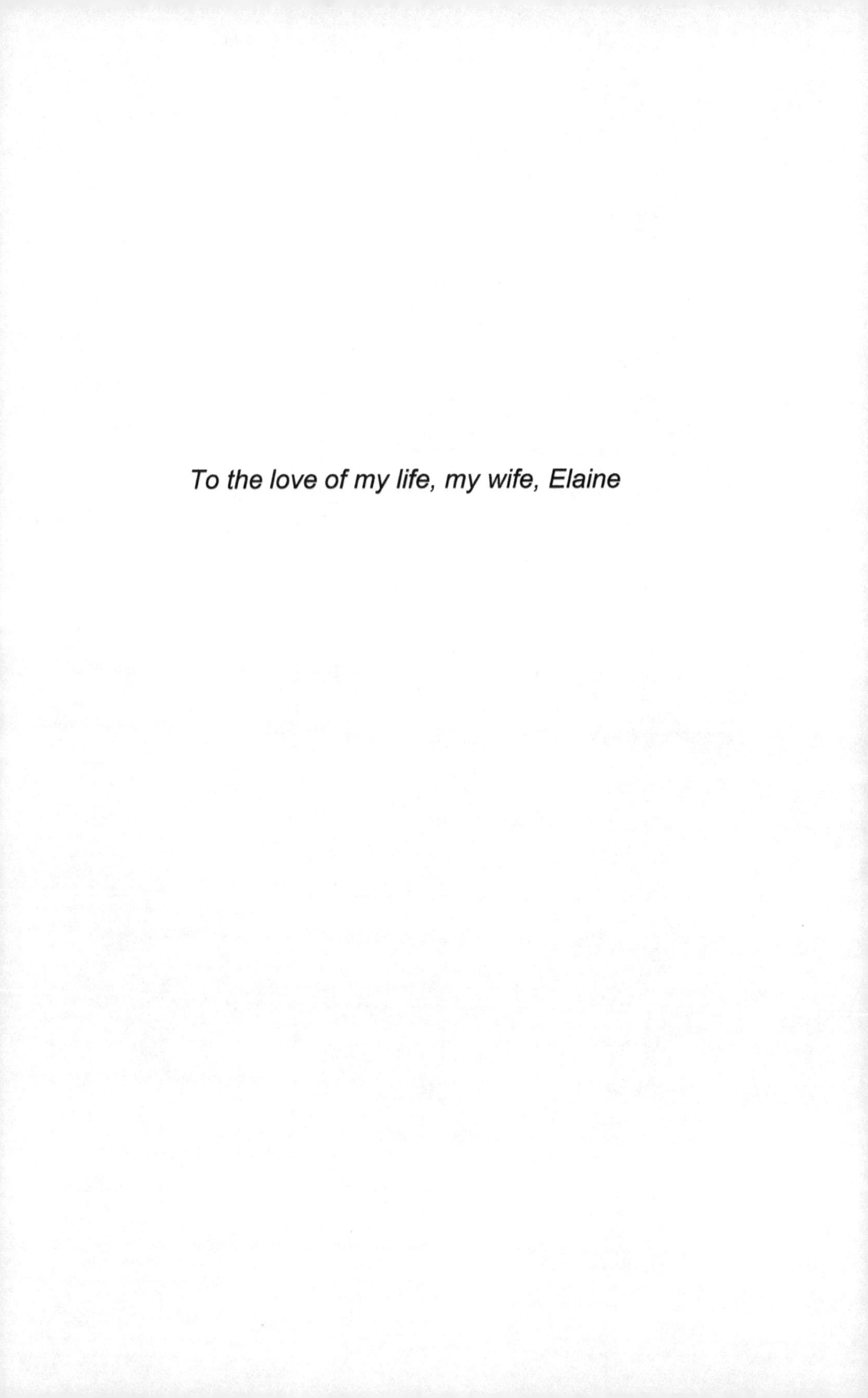

To the love of my life, my wife, Elaine

Part I

"When kingship from heaven was lowered, the kingship was in Eridu." —Sumerian King List

June 2023
Staten Island, New York

George's heart pounded as he pedaled toward his apartment building, his breathing labored. As he crested the hill, the faded yellow five-story apartment building came into view. He rounded the corner, squeezing the brakes as he neared the front of his building. He hopped off the bike, picked it up, and vaulted up the narrow stone stairs, grabbing the black iron decorative metal work on the door as a neighbor was exiting. He glanced at the dirty white round clock over the post boxes and swore.

He pulled his bike into the elevator and hit the button for the fourth floor. A neighbor waved for him to hold the door. George mouthed *sorry*, pointing to his watch as the door closed. He felt guilty. She always greeted him, unlike most of the others in the building.

He pushed the bike through his doorway, leaning it against the wall by his shoe rack, and grabbed a can off the counter in the kitchen.

As the door closed, his phone rang.

"This is George."

"You're late with your rent again." The nasal voice of his landlady sounded from the speaker.

"I know. I'm sorry. I'm headed to my second job now."

"You just went upstairs. I saw you!"

"Yeah, my second job is online."

"You'd better not be doing anything illegal."

"Mrs. Santiago, I've gotta go. I'll pay you tomorrow, I promise."

"You had better, George. It won't be hard to find someone else who wants that apartment."

"Okay, okay, tomorrow. Bye."

George ran down the hall to his "studio," a converted bedroom with windows on two walls. He moved around his makeshift desk to his computer—careful not to dislodge the plywood from the yellow milk crates holding it up—put on his headphones, and hit the broadcast button.

He opened the apps he would use for the show as the prerecorded intro played in his ears. "Hey, Believers, it's George Isaacson bringing the truth from Staten Island—a big shout-out to my followers tuning in this afternoon." He let the intro music play, a deep base track coupled with '80s synth. Making the final adjustments to his camera feed revealed large sweat stains.

Oh, well, no time to change. I gotta go with it. George leaned into the mic and made one last adjustment to the camera, ensuring his face was centered in the camera feed, and went live as the music stopped.

"Truth Seekers, have I got some exciting news for you. The government has released more videos about UFOs. They aren't confirming extraterrestrial life, though. I have been saying that the truth would come out. Of course, all of the interviews still sound fake. Make sure you check out the videos I posted on my website. Not for nothing, but maybe we can finally put this cover-up to rest. The aliens are here, watching us, signing treaties with governments, and doing whatever. Maybe they have already infiltrated our society. Think about it. Musk, Zuckerberg, Bezos, and Cook are responsible for some amazing jumps in technology that have taken over our lives. Most people can't live without any of their apps or products. They have turned us into cyborgs. That is the topic for today's show: Big Tech-Alien Manipulation. Let's jump right to the calls. Our first caller of the day is Brian, from right here on Staten Island. Go, Brian, drop some truth bombs."

"George, I love the show! That video of you in the field talking to those farmers in Pennsylvania about the crop circles was on point. Finally, we have some clear video of lights floating above crop circle fields, not the usual shaky camera stuff. You were on site within a day. They were definitely trying to tell us something."

"Thanks, Brian. The thought that we are alone in the universe has been disproved multiple times through science if you are willing to do the research," George said confidently into his mic. "We've been led around by the media and government watchdogs, who wave something shiny in front of the public to distract us every time we get close to the truth." George looked over at his live stream feed. *Over fourteen thousand viewers, a new record.* His voice became more confident, and the words flowed faster. "I know all of you, 'the true believers,' know what I'm talking about. The NSA is working with big tech to collect our data to create artificial intelligence-based copies of us. They run it through their simulations and figure out how to control us."

"George, you are so right about that. After watching your show last week, I pulled up videos and pics of crop circles in Pennsylvania. Now I am being hit up by ads for farm tools, vacations to the Pennsylvania Dutch Country, and sales of Blu-ray alien movies."

George nodded. "That sounds about right, Brian. For those who missed our talk about NSA simulations, you can find the podcast on my website, www.TruthSeekers.com. Corporations help control us for the government through our tech. Everything we do is recorded, analyzed, and added to our NSA doppelganger file. If they control the tech, they control us. The algorithms manipulate us." He paused to take a quick drink from his energy drink, a Monster Ultra Gold.

"I know some of you are asking what this has to do with aliens, right? Okay, let's look at this objectively. There are billions of planets out there. If we look at the NASA website, they have announcements for days about this earth-like planet or that one. Some are huge, bigger than ours, super-earths. Those could have developed life the same as us, or maybe completely different. Hollywood likes to remind us how we will be taken out, right? Aliens, disease, AI, planet killer, or we do it ourselves. The big three I worry about are aliens, AI, and a planet killer. We thought AI was no biggie because we supposedly had years, but you all saw the news on Google's LaMDA AI. I don't know if it was real, but it was creepy as hell. The big thinkers keep telling us," he deepened his voice to a 'dad' voice, "it will be the end of humanity as we know it." He laughed into the mic. "How long have we heard that? By the time we get real AI, our grandkids will be watching *Terminator 26*. If Google's program was not AI, it was a good fake. It got us talking about it. If it was real, where did it go? What does it mean for us?"

George paused. "We'll get to that in another show. For this discussion, though, we gotta consider that AI could be out there exploring the universe. Or something we can't even imagine, some energy consciousness or extradimensional beings. The universe is billions of years old and pretty creative in how stuff happens. Look, let's realign the discussion. My point is that all our tech may be our downfall. Like many of you, I've seen this play out in movies or books. We put all our info and data on the internet or the cloud, and an alien invasion force rolls up undetected, downloads it, and figures out how to take us down. You know I'm talking truth. We are being set up. Thanks for the call, Brian. Let's do a quick break, and I'll be back with more truth."

George turned off the live feed as his local sponsor ads played. They didn't pay much, but every little bit helped. He shuffled through the papers on his desk, finding various handwritten notes. *I have got to get organized. I am jumping around like a rabid ferret.*

"Welcome back, Truth Seekers. Keeping with the Big Tech Alien connection, let's talk about alien drones. It hit me during the break. The top militaries in the world are looking to switch to drones. They have been for years. It makes sense. If you can build an aircraft that can turn at thirty Gs and not miss a beat, you'll have the advantage over a pilot who would pass out. We have seen those crazy videos of UFOs changing direction almost ninety degrees in a second. This isn't a new theory, so let me know your thoughts. Our next caller is from out on the Island, Jerry from Massapequa. You're on the *George Isaacson Show.*"

"Yo, George, I'm with you. My cousin is a pilot in the Navy, and she told me that the hardest part for her to get into the program was that circular spinning machine—you know what I'm talking about?"

"Yeah, yeah, I always wanted to try one. I'd pay."

"Not me. She said she threw up all over the place a few times and almost didn't make it. I wouldn't want that job, either, cleaning up that mess."

"I hear you, Jerry. And that goes with what I am saying. Machines don't have to worry about that."

"That's true, George. You got me thinking about that. If there *are* alien AI drones, I'm going to be more scared. We don't know what they look like or what they could do. Man, I see giant metallic centipedes spreading out from a crashed ship, shooting beams from their eyes."

"That is a scary thought, which takes me to the point I wanted to make. Maybe those big tech guys are being used. How hard would it be for a drone to land at some remote location, hook up to Starlink, and start manipulating things or feeding designs to specific people or companies? Maybe the algorithms were started here on Earth but are now being manipulated by those same aliens? I would say the same about tech. Think about it. How divided is the world right now? Every country with the internet and social media has some divide. Maybe that's the plan. Maybe we are too chaotic to understand, so they set us up by ensuring we can't work together. That is something to think about.

"It reminds me of something from one of my business courses at NYU. We had to read Sun Tzu's *Art of War*. Sun Tzu wrote something about disrupting alliances as a successful strategy. I'd say we are pretty disrupted." George took another sip of his Monster Ultra Gold, "Thanks, Jerry. I'm having nightmares tonight. Truth Seekers, I don't even know what we would look for. There could be alien drones disguised as parts of cell towers worldwide, giving access to our eventual overlords. Let's keep this going. How do you think our tech is leading us to a not-so-rosy future?"

George continued talking about Project Mockingbird, the NSA, and mind control through algorithmic manipulation for another hour. He wrapped up the show, promising to be back next week, digging deeper into the theory of how some travelers exist outside space and time.

After the show, he spent an hour formatting the file, posting it to his website, and linking it to social media sites. He loved his secondary "job." He checked the conspiracy chat rooms and social media accounts he followed, posting answers to questions, and making notes for future shows.

His cell rang as he was typing, mid-sentence, in a forum argument with a follower named FedBuster22, a self-proclaimed truther out to discredit anyone espousing theories outside mainstream thinking. He added the torn piece of paper with his notes to the disorganized stack of papers on the side of his desk. *I'll go through that later. I gotta get more organized. You can't be big league if you don't act big league.*

The cell continued to play "Mr. Jones" by the Counting Crows. He hit send on the chat board post and picked up the phone. "Yeah, I'm on my way out now. I'll meet you at Mocker's Diner for a quick bite before heading in." He ducked into the bathroom to wash his hands and run his razor over his five o'clock shadow. His girlfriend said he looked like a 1940s Hollywood Italian gangster if he didn't shave in the afternoon. He put the phone in his pocket, grabbed his bag, and headed out the door to work.

Abu Shahrain, Iraq

"Jackie!" Eusebio's voice blared from her radio. "We have another tablet! This one's different from the others we have found. You have got to see it. We are at dig site three."

"I'll be right over," she replied, tucking her off-white linen shirt into her khaki pants. She pulled her hair into a ponytail. She rubbed sunblock on the exposed areas of her dark skin and put her sunglasses on before heading out.

Jacynthe "Jackie" Mandrapilias was a professor of archaeology specializing in Sumerian and Akkadian civilizations at George Washington University. She had been on-site with her team for under two months. There were only a few weeks left before the permits expired. It was good to hear the excitement from her team. Weeks of exposure to the summer heat of Iraq and three days of sandstorms had put the team behind schedule and threatened to cut short their expedition. The area around Eridu offered little protection from sandstorms rolling through. The twelve-person team of anthropologists, archaeologists, and metallurgists had already recovered numerous artifacts.

The area was designated for the construction of a well. A US military team, seeking to ensure areas designated for water recovery and supply wells were clear of unexploded ordnance, found the ruins during their sweep with ground-penetrating radar. The cuneiform writing on the first tablet recovered had identified it as Sumerian.

Jackie stepped into the sunlight, feeling the heat on her face. She made her way across the dig site to where Eusebio's group was waiting. She stopped at the edge of the dig. Wiping the sweat from her brow and hands, she hopped on the ladder and climbed to the bottom of the hole. She looked over her assistant's shoulder as he gently lifted a silver-white metallic tablet from the dirt. She donned her gloves and took the tablet from him, examining the cuneiform imprints.

She gently turned the tablet in her hand. "There's no corrosion. We need to get this dated. The period is too early for electroplating. Maybe it was lost during a later period, fell out of a pack, or was being moved?" She translated the words in her head, her lips moving as she read.

Eridu begins.

The season is fulfilled.

Cycle <unknown> reap.

<Several lines unknown symbols>.

She would need to access the references in her library to translate more. The latter half of the tablet contained words she didn't recognize immediately.

"Nice find, team. Let's get this prepared. I'll file the permits. We have a few more weeks left, and the weather looks decent. Let's find the ruins these should be in." They cheered in short celebration before getting back to the task at hand.

Center for Near Earth Object Studies, JPL, Pasadena, California

"Good morning, Tim. Anything new hurling through space at us?" Sharon asked.

Tim sat forward, taking the pen out of his mouth. "Not too much, a lot of little ones, just the way I like it. There are about thirty-four new objects we didn't get to last night."

"Great," she replied, leaning forward to look at the screen, brushing a lock of brown hair away from her glasses. "Nothing like a long Saturday at work to make you miss the beach." She looked at her hand sticking out of the white lab coat, not as pale as it was coming out of winter but not as tanned as in previous years. "Have fun with the kiddo, Tim. I'll see you on Monday."

Tim ran his hand through his shoulder-length blond hair before waving over his shoulder. "I don't know. Midweek days off seems to be working for you. I'm outta here, see ya."

Sharon grabbed a wet paper towel and wiped down the white desktop around the workstation, clearing several coffee rings. She adjusted the black mesh ergonomic chair to her height and rolled it forward. She reviewed the size, speed, and approach vectors of the objects on the list Tim had left, assigning each a threat recommendation.

"Make sure we get the equipment set for our area scans. I would prefer we start on time today." A general acknowledgment from her team answered her request.

The day passed without incident, as most did. She was finishing the last calculations for the list of objects from her team's list when she noticed similarities between a few of the objects. She tabbed back through the list she had sent for validation and secondary source confirmation and noted two other objects with the same mass and velocity but slight differences in their approach vectors. She opened the 3D model, entered the search area, then allowed for an accelerated approach, filtering out bodies outside the designated approach vector. She watched the simulation play forward in quickened time. The objects would collide with each other in almost two years. Depending on the mass and velocity calculations of the debris, there could be a threat to Earth.

Working scenarios through her mind as she manipulated the model, she zoomed in on the sector where the collision was to occur, set the radius for the distance the objects would travel in two years, and centered on the collision coordinates. Three more objects appeared at the edge of the area, following similar paths toward a single point in space. She played the model again on a loop, watching the objects enter the area on different vectors, all moving toward one end.

Sharon opened her contact list, scrolling down to the Planetary Defense Coordination Office at NASA.

"This is Dr. Sharon Berzing at CNEOS. I have a Potentially Hazardous Object report." She waited for an acknowledgment before continuing.

"This is a new report. At 14:35, June 24, 2023, we identified five objects moving at high velocity toward a collision point near the edge of our solar system. Initial estimates indicate a collision will occur in twenty-two months. It is unknown at this time whether there is a direct threat. Data to follow."

Sharon hung up the call and sent the files to the PHO office at NASA. She got up, brushed aside the stray lock of hair in front of her glasses, and turned to each side while lifting onto her toes. Yawning, she looked at the clock. "I need coffee," she said to the empty room before heading for the cafeteria.

Department of Homeland Security Headquarters, Science, Technology, and Innovation, Washington, DC

John sat on the front of his chair, leaning over his desk, a quarter-inch double-spaced document in one hand, a red pen in the other.

"Wrong."

"Missing comma."

"Format."

He picked up the pages he had set aside, stacking them together neatly, ensuring all of the edges lined up, and slid the report across the smooth glass surface of his desk.

"Ben, how long have we been here?"

"Um, sir? Now or at DHS?"

John rolled his eyes. He slid back into his high-back black leather chair and crossed his legs. "Really? I meant today, this afternoon. Why would I ask you how long we have been at DHS? I don't think you could reasonably answer the question." He took a deep breath.

"Ben, that was your cue. Provide an answer."

Ben looked around for a clock before finally looking at his phone. "Yes, sorry, sir. We have been here for forty-three minutes." He squirmed in his chair.

"You have briefed me before. What is my number one rule, Ben?" He turned his hands palm up, keeping his eyes locked on Ben's.

"It's, uh, don't waste your time."

"Great, you got one right. That," John pointed at the report, "is a waste of my time. We had an hour for this meeting. I expected we would move on to decisions about what we should be focusing on with China's continued spending in the tech areas, despite the recession they are in now. Instead, I am playing English teacher. That is wasting my time."

"Yes, sir, I will make the corrections."

"Of course, I expect to see them today. The report was due today. I want it today. Lucky for you, I work late. You are dismissed."

Ben scooped up the report and hastily exited the office.

John stood and walked across the office to the bar, pulling a bottle of flavored water without looking.

"News feed on, full screen."

The 16K Samsung 160-inch Ultra-High Diamond Definition TV came to life, divided into two dozen news feeds from around the world. He sipped the water, black cherry, and watched the closed captioning for his preset keywords.

"Priority sound BBC."

"Tensions are higher as the American Carrier Abraham Lincoln and her battle group have entered the Taiwan Strait and are expected to pass close to China's Fujian Carrier group, which boasts significant technological advancements." The BBC image increased in size. The British reporter's volume increased comfortably in the spacious room.

John shook his head. The pressure in his chest did not subside.

"Despite rising tensions between the United States and China, President Zhang met with numerous regional leaders. On the agenda were discussions to weaken the US economic influence, and proposals to counter western defense industry reliance in the region."

"Mute volume."

John walked around his desk, looked out the window, and finished his water.

Throwing the empty plastic bottle in a recycling bin, he laughed under his breath. *Their economy doesn't matter. They have their sights set on dominating the world through tech, and we are the only ones who can stop them. We've done it before, and we'll do it again. It's the cold war two-point-oh.*

He turned back to his desk, looking at his schedule. He pressed the intercom button on the touchscreen desk. "Ken, have Doctor Kerr bring the composite fiber program's analysis and NASA's applicability review up to my office in ten minutes."

"Yes, sir. Will do," Ken's steady voice answered.

September 2023
Staten Island, New York

George sat hunched over a worn blue ottoman in his front room, looking between his soundboard and an open pamphlet. The backing lay to the side, exposing the main circuit board. He picked up the unit, squinting as his eyes moved around between connections.

He jumped as Linkin Park's "In the End" started playing on his phone. His head dropped, and he took a breath before answering, hitting the speakerphone.

"Hey, Dad. I was going to call you."

"Okay, well, it's the afternoon, and I'll be at work. I figured I would save you from my voicemail."

George ground his teeth. "Okay, Dad. Did you have a good birthday?"

"I slept a little, but I had to get out and run some errands."

"Sounds good. You know, I wish I could have stopped by, but I had work this morning and my show tonight."

"Did you get a promotion at work, something you can use that degree for?"

"I'm using my degree. I told you I'm not interested in being on the news."

He heard his dad's harrumph under his breath. "So your show is still making up stories for bored people on the internet?"

"C'mon, Dad, I'm not making anything up. You should be happy I'm using journalism to get to the truth of the stories."

"George, c'mon, you can't believe that. You're telling bedtime stories to people looking for meaning in their lives. You're going to learn someday. You need to stick to fixing boats. You're good at it. You'd be a manager if you could take responsibility."

"Dad, please don't start this again. I am plenty responsible."

"Yeah, just like in high school. As soon as anyone started to rely on you, you quit the team. It's a shame."

"Alright, Dad, I need to finish what I'm working on. I hope the rest of your birthday is good."

"Yeah, yeah, okay, George." There was a pause. "G'bye, son."

George threw the phone to the side of the couch, falling back and closing his eyes. He sighed, sat forward, and leaned forward over the soundboard. "Damnit."

♦ ♦ ♦

"Hey, Believers, it's George Isaacson bringing the truth from Staten Island—a big shout-out to my followers throughout New York and beyond." He paused as the intro music continued to play.

"Today, I have some special news you won't want to miss. I'll be talking to a contact working in the Jet Propulsion Laboratory in California. I can't say how I know them, but I assure you they are legit and can be trusted. Their name and identity have to remain hidden to protect their job so they can keep the free flow of information going."

George let the pause hang in the air as he patched his phone to his computer, allowing his call to merge with the broadcast.

"Hey, George, how are you doing? Are we live?" the mechanical voice asked.

"Yeah, you now have the apt attention of," he paused, looking at the viewer count, "over eighteen thousand Truth Seekers. That's right, Believers. A quick intro first. I have known this person for over a decade. This summer, we hooked up at the Roswell UFO Festival, where they told me about their work on behalf of an agency we won't name. They recently moved to a team involved with remote viewing, which is a great topic in itself. The real shock was when I found out that their target was a base on the moon. Think about that for a minute." George took a sip of his Monster Ultra Gold, leaning back in his chair.

"That's right, Truth Seekers, we have confirmation that not only is there a base on the moon, but we have been there for about six years. Without further delay, let's welcome Tracy X." He hit the button that simulated a live audience clapping, reminiscent of live shows in the 1980s, happy at the name he had made up on the spot.

"Hey, everyone, just a little background. I have a master's degree from an Ivy League school in a mind-focused area. Sorry for the vague info, but I know national security listens on shows like this. As George mentioned, I recently moved to a division that does remote viewing of our operations on the moon. Yes, although we can talk to them freely, we use this method to watch the other international team members."

Over the next hour, George and his guest took questions, described life on the moon, and discussed other remote viewing applications.

His phone chirped. "Tracy, thanks for stopping by to chat with us. Truth Seekers, it's been a great show. Keep it real. Keep it true! Have a great night, and don't forget to get your friends and family to subscribe to the channel."

He looked at his phone, slumping back and tightening his grip on the arm of his chair. Sitting forward, he picked up the phone to check his texts. He saw one from his dad. He tossed the phone on his desk.

"Over eighteen thousand tonight, Dad. How's that for a show about fairy tales?"

George Washington University, Archaeology Department, Washington, DC

Jackie turned away from the long research table and stood. The Eridu Tablet rested on a clean white cloth. Her notepad, half-filled with notes, and a .3mm pencil sat to the side. She rubbed her temples and leaned back to stretch. Movement from inside the door caught her eye. Her assistant entered the room, holding a venti Starbucks coffee in each hand. He smiled as he made his way around the tables and stacked crates. His foot caught the edge of a table, and coffee from one of the two cups splashed onto his wrist.

"Aray!" His Tagalog dialect took over as he reacted to the burn to his hand.

She smiled. "Eusebio, are you okay?"

"Yes, just a little spill," he said, handing her the full cup. He blew on the area of the spilled coffee before shifting his hands to take a sip of his own.

"Perfect timing. This thing is giving me fits. The dating analysis places the tablet as much older than it should be. The electroplating is too early. We need to solve it. Jans and his team with the EU are calling it a fake and calling our credibility into question." She turned to walk back across the room, stepping around crates in various stages of unpacking.

"This one is special," she continued. "The creator wanted it to last longer than the traditional clay tablets. It raises several questions. Something feels off. Dr. Roberts from Berkeley offered to fly a few team members out to provide a second set of eyes. I politely declined the offer. That jerk from UCLA, who wrote the review of your book, questioned the program at GWU, and openly asked how we could fall for an obvious fake."

Jackie sighed, sipped the coffee, and closed her eyes to refocus her thoughts. "Mmm, thank you. Just the way I like it."

"I thought of adding sugar to sweeten up your day, but I didn't want to repeat what happened last time."

She tilted her head and smiled at him. "Smart move. Leave my coffee alone." She took another sip. "Back to our original discussion. Dating the tablet places it in the era of Eridu's founding. If so, then the second word I read as *begin*, *start*, or *commence*. I'm leaning toward *begin*. Let's look at the facts. The tablet dates to around 5500 BCE, which is fifteen-hundred years before Eridu's founding. Maybe it was created as a memorial. But why?" She stopped and took another sip of her coffee. "We can't dismiss that it is possible whoever created the tablet wanted to memorialize the moment, in which case, we have to find out who."

Eusebio sat in the chair across from her. He looked at the tablet on the screen. "Well, I'm not the Sumerian expert, but your reasoning seems sound. Suppose the first line is a beginning timeline. The initial translation for the second line, 'two seasons,' could be a project, task, or work, with *fulfilled* as the end or completion." He paused. "*Season*, with an implication of repetition, could be *cycle*, though I agree with the word *fulfilled*. It does not have the associated marking with a terminal ending. Still, these marks appear in Akkadian, alluding to *emotion*, *satisfaction*, and *pride*." He sat back and cupped his coffee in both hands. "It could be *cycle* or *season*. I agree with your thoughts on the second symbol meaning *fulfilled*, or maybe, *completed with satisfaction*."

Jackie leaned over his shoulder and looked at the screen. "Hmm, you may be on to something. Those marks are small, and I don't recall seeing them on anything else using that major symbol."

She stood. "We should go with that for now. It's defensible and makes sense contextually."

"Are you staying late again tonight?" he asked.

"No, I have a meeting with a curator for the Museum of Natural History. There's a presentation by Dr. Oreadu from the Society of Black Archaeologists I want to catch."

"You know him?"

"Yes, we met at the Annual Awards dinner."

"Okay, let me know how it goes. I want to run a few more tests on the other artifacts before we ship them back to Iraq."

"See you tomorrow."

"Sounds good."

CNEOS, JPL, Pasadena, California

"Okay, team, I have the results from the EU space agency. They concur with the assessment of no black hole or known gravity wells at or near the collision point. Independent readings support our findings of an amazing coincidence. NASA has added supplemental funding to support the effort." Sharon adjusted her glasses and focused on the images moving across the large screen.

"I am glad we have gotten back on Congress's good side," Janice, a young grad student, replied. "Especially with the way the economy is going. We need to get out of the '20s already."

A resonant voice joined. "Good morning, all. You'll be happy to know that I talked to the contractor, and they are creating a patch that will allow real-time data to flow to the model. PR plans to hype the event with a full media blitz once we get closer to the collision. Sharon, you'd better start working on your speech now."

Sharon spun her chair around toward the voice and the sound of clicking footsteps. Her director approached, his light brown suit, tailored, hung comfortably on his frame.

"Good morning, Will. I hope you weren't talking to me. We have nineteen months before they collide. I prefer a promotion and to be left to my work. I'm sure the Administrator will be giving the speeches."

"You don't want to be the famous face of NASA on this?"

"No, thanks. I can't imagine anything worse than that. Let me stay in the lab. I prefer quiet, no cameras, no questions, no thanks."

Sharon stood and looked up at her director. "I'm about to head out. Do you want to grab lunch?"

"Sure, are you buying, Ms. Soon To Be Famous?"

Sharon scowled and shivered slightly. "For that comment, you can buy lunch."

Zhongguancun, China

Wu Kai, President of Contemplation Impact and Director of the PRC's coordinated AI development program, stood over the long table, looking down at a set of blueprints. He rolled back the drawing to one farther down the stack. He placed a weight on the corners of the sheets to counter the mild late summer breeze. He pointed toward the edge of the building, his finger tracing a line to the right. "All of the utilities will come in here?"

"Yes, Director Wu," Tian Shin, the lead architect and engineer for the Zhongguancun facility, replied. The reactor will be online soon. Despite official reports, it will only support this facility."

Wu Kai nodded, stepping back from the table and looking around at the trucks, dozers, and other equipment moving in their dance of pandas and lumbering through the area.

"We are on track, then. The rolling blackouts have not affected us?"

"No, Director Wu. They will not affect our schedule."

"Good, we cannot afford to fall behind. We have been stuck in *shuāng huó* with the Americans for too long. They have no respect for their elders."

Tian Shin nodded.

Wu Kai looked at the other man for a few seconds before moving to the edge of the area, the loose gray dirt coating his shoes and lower pant leg. He scowled in silence as a backhoe passed. "With the Dragon, we will not look back. The possibilities are endless, and we will ensure that no other country catches us." His stomach grumbled. He looked at his Seagull watch, the last gift from his father. "It is time for lunch. Thank you, Xiao Tian. I look forward to watching our progress over the next year."

The engineer bowed, then turned back toward the small group of engineers following them.

◆ ◆ ◆

Wu Kai sat in the back of his black Hongqi L7. His stomach grumbled. He opened the bag his wife had prepared and removed a fried dough stick from its wrapping, eating as he looked at the cityscape around him. The streets were busy, with many people enjoying a day marked by a smogless sky. He let the breeze from the air conditioner wash over him as he watched the people move along the congested sidewalks, his driver drove easily through the traffic.

He removed another dough stick from the bag, setting it on a cloth on the center armrest. He brushed crumbs off his soft stomach. He picked up his phone and called the President's Office.

"Director Wu for President Zhang."

"Yes, Lao Wu, what news do you have?"

Wu Kai straightened in his seat at the moderate voice of the President. "President Zhang, I have forwarded the project assessment and recommendations for your approval. Progress of the reactor continues on pace. I expect the facility to be fully operational in eighteen months."

"That is good news. I was not sure the engineering team could meet the revised deadline. If your team's breakthrough in design is as significant as you say, we should make every effort to move forward with it. Were there no concerns about delays? Contingency plans?"

"I discussed our concerns with the lead engineer. I was assured that his team would complete the project well ahead of the two-year estimate."

"You have done well, Lao Wu. I have spoken to the remaining companies involved in the research. As expected, they look forward to joining your consortium. Let me know if there are any difficulties."

"I understand and am honored by the responsibility you have given me. I am grateful for the opportunity to demonstrate my commitment and dedication to the homeland."

Wu Kai smiled with pride as he hung up. This project would bring honor to his country. *This is but another step in our journey to global leadership.* He leaned back into the soft leather seats and looked out the window at the city around him, envisioning the many changes that would take place over the next decade.

December 2023
Staten Island, New York

George pulled up the zipper of his dark blue, puffy down parka. There was a chill in the air, not helped by the thick layer of clouds blocking the sunlight. The leaves were gone from the trees, and the grass was a dull yellow. The Counting Crows sang out from his phone. He pulled the phone out of his jacket, looking at the caller ID. "Hey, Tim, how's it going, buddy? It's been a while."

"We have winter beach weather here, and I'm off for the day, so I thought I'd give you a scoop for your show, but you can't mention it until March." Tim paused.

"Yeah, of course, that guy you hooked me up with a few months ago was awesome. He helped me run some great discussions on moon bases and remote viewing," George replied.

Tim continued, "Great. I met him waiting for Mandy to finish her hot yoga class. He said he listened to your show. He was shocked that I knew you, and more so when I told him we were friends. Glad it worked out."

"It's all about getting the clicks. What have you got?" George was curious to hear the info Tim had.

"Well, JPL has found a handful of pretty big objects this past summer that will collide in about a year and a half. We haven't released anything yet because the administration didn't want to cause panic when we didn't have a good idea of what they were."

"So, you know what they are now?"

"Yeah, everything points toward asteroids. Other agencies have confirmed there isn't anything cool like a black hole or unknown gravity well out there—just a one in a trillion occurrence of a multi-body collision."

George saw the museum ahead on the left. He moved to the corner and hit the crosswalk button. There weren't many people out in the cold this afternoon.

"How many?"

"Five."

"Five!"

"Yeah, I know the odds are astronomical, which is why NASA is going to put on a full-court press with the media starting in the spring and continuing through the next year to help boost interest in space. I thought you might be able to put a spin on it once the production info starts coming out, showing trajectories, possible outcomes, and theories of what is happening. Maybe you could spin it as your new theory of aliens, an impending space battle, or something along those lines."

George stopped. A honking horn brought him back to the present. He waved to the taxi honking at him, running the last few steps across the street. "Oh, yeah, like aliens moving forces to a contested area, maybe for resources with the possibility of a massive battle. Maybe the government has an insider with one of the alien factions that could *leak* information about the species involved. Bro, that would be incredible. Is there any way I could get something to give credibility?"

"You know how NASA does the photo dumps to their site with all kinds of images? I may be able to submit a few to the batches between now and March. They would be images like the others, but I could tell you which ones to pull into a time sequence showing the movements. It should be okay overall, no big deal. None of it is classified. I'll work on something. Make sure you keep my name out of it."

George laughed along. "No worries. I envy that California warmth about right now. I see your hair still has that summer bleached look. They say it's gonna snow here tonight."

"Lots of crazy things out here. You could take one of your 'exploratory' road trips out here. Get a month or so driving across the country, investigating UAP sightings in every state on the route."

"I would love to do that. You wanna call my boss and see if they will give me a month off? I could do some on-the-road journalism. Maybe make my dad happy."

"Ouch, is he still on you?"

"You know it. He didn't even pay for my school—I have the student loans—but he says I am wasting my time and money with the show. You met him," he lowered his voice mockingly, "'it's not about doing what you like. It's about working hard and saving for the difficult times'."

"I'm sorry, man."

"It's all good. I'm fine."

"Okay, let me know if you need anything. I'll call you when I have more info on the collision."

George looked up the steps of the main entrance to the Met, turning his head against a cold gust of wind. "I'll let you know what I'm thinking, and maybe you can help me craft the story."

Tim laughed. "Probably not. Fiction was always your area. You entertain. I'm about science. I'll talk to you later." Tim hung up.

George put the phone away and jaunted up the steps to the museum.

GWU, Archaeology Department, Washington, DC

Jackie stormed into the main research area for her department at GWU. "Have you seen this? How did this make it through editorial review?" Jackie held up the latest copy of *World Archaeology*.

Eusebio pointed to the earpiece in his left ear.

"Sorry," Jackie whispered, moving past him and toward her seat at the last table before her office. She tossed the magazine to the end of the desk, leaned back in her chair, and looked up at the ceiling. A flickering to her left, a long incandescent light in the ceiling, the center of three, caught her eye. It was stuck in the state between on and burning out. She pursed her lips, closed her eyes, and began rubbing her temples.

Eusebio ended his video call, stood up, stretched, and walked across the room, sitting next to her. "You okay?"

She kept her eyes closed. "No, that bastard at UCLA published an article attacking our credibility on the Eridu Tablet. Comments are one thing, stupid cocktail party gossip. But openly attacking me in a prominent magazine is over the line. It's unacceptable."

"Dr. Blecher is certainly not a fan. He seems to go out of his way to attack the university and you. I have some good news, though. I was talking to the language translation company. They believe their software can translate any language, even dead ones. If they can pull this off, we'll have a tool that can comb through the entirety of the world's collections of Sumerian artifacts. Of course, translating a few hundred thousand entries will still take a long time."

Jackie waited to answer, "That is good news. Nice work, Dr. Bustamante."

Eusebio paused, getting serious. "What if the AI then learns all of humanity's secrets and causes of civilization downfalls, and turns it against us? We will have helped destroy the world." He struggled to keep a straight face before they broke out in laughter.

"Yeah, keep saying that, and the wrong person will think you are serious. You'll be out on the street," Jackie warned playfully.

Jackie sat and stared at the dual monitors: the Eridu Tablet on the left and her translation on the right.

"Eridu formed.

Season of creation complete

Twin cycles for reaping the fields.

The Son shall return in all his glory.

The wheat shall serve.

Eight Magnitudes of <Unknown>

Begin <Unknown>."

The desk phone rang, breaking her concentration. "GWU, Dr. Mandrapilias."

She smiled at the pleasant baritone voice. "Dr. Mandrapilias, so good to speak to you again. I know it is late, but I wanted to tell you myself."

"Sal-A-Din, I mean Deputy Minister, how are you?"

"I am fine, thank you. I wanted to let you know that the Minister of Culture, Tourism, and Antiquities has approved the proposal to display the Eridu Tablet."

"That is great news! Have you informed the others?"

"No, no, I wanted to tell you first. After all, you will be the one traveling to speak on the tablet to the prominent museums. The tablet will go on display at the Louvre on the first day of spring and move to China, your Smithsonian, and finally here in Baghdad over the next year."

"That is great news. Were the museums okay with having a replica while the original moved about?"

"Well, the curator at the Louvre did not want a replica. However, we were able to reach an agreement. Another good news story for you is that when the tablet returns to Iraq, we will change the date of Eridu's founding to your revised timeline. Credit for the discovery will, of course, be your team."

"Thank you, Sal-A-Din. I will let them know once the announcement is made."

"It is no problem at all, and you did the work. You are my friend and a friend of my country. Enjoy your night, Dr. Mandrapilias."

CNEOS, JPL, Pasadena, California

Sharon paced back and forth, watching the PR group work. She did not want to go on camera. The set was more extensive than she expected. There were so many lights and scaffolding all around to cover every angle. The air on set was hot. She looked inside her suit jacket and checked to see if she was sweating through her shirt.

"Sharon, are you okay?" Joy, NASA's Public Relations lead, asked. "You look flushed."

Sharon looked up, turning toward the taller woman, and smiled meekly. "I'm fine. Give me a second." She took a few deep breaths. *Just focus on the data,* she repeated several times. She stepped forward after a moment, adjusting the mauve business suit jacket and skirt, and breathing a heavy sigh. "Okay, I'm as ready as I can be."

"Alright, Sharon, I'm leaning toward starting this past summer when you identified the objects. We can play the model forward, showing their path to a collision. We'll see if we can get a familiar

Hollywood actor or actress to do the voice-over. What do you think?"

"I think I'd prefer the actor to be standing in my place as well, since you asked. It seems early for all of this. I thought NASA wouldn't announce the big news until the spring. I'm trying to keep everything straight," she said, shaking her head.

"Don't worry. We will keep you on track. We know you have a lot of work to do before the event and have been working with the modeling team to improve the algorithms and models. We are starting now because we will need to produce hundreds of images, graphics, presentations, and clips, so early is better." Joy continued, "We also want to react to changes that may affect how we view the event. It will be a live broadcast, so we must be ready to roll on day zero."

Sharon shook her head. "I don't know how you keep up with this. It makes my job feel easy."

Joy laughed. "I'll take it, and I appreciate the compliment. It's not often someone in my field gets a compliment from someone who is about to be the new face of deep space exploration." Joy's voice dropped as she typed on her tablet. Looking up, she smiled and said, "Don't worry, Sharon, you have my card. Please call if you have any ideas or things that will help."

Sharon nodded, happy to be headed back to her lab to catch up on her work.

DHS HQ, Science, Technology, and Innovation, Washington, DC

John listened to the presenter cover the status of several ongoing projects in development for DHS. Kirby . . . *something* . . . had joined the team recently. This was his second briefing on John's team. John nodded slightly, noting the shine on Kirby's shoes. Damn, what was his last name? He scribbled a reminder in his notes. Under the table's edge, he ran his thumb over the side of a loose fist. He took a moment to look at the other participants. All eyes were on the presentation. Good. Kirby stood to the side, working his way through the briefing. John took a few breaths, feeling his muscles release the building tension. Looking back to the screen, he raised a hand to his mouth to suppress a yawn.

"Assistant Secretary, do you have any questions on internal programs?" The briefer waited for a signal to continue.

John looked through his notes. "No, please continue."

"In the domestic arena, we have made significant progress applying adaptive algorithms with visual pattern recognition and chemical compound identification for security X-ray systems. Companies now submit their products to our labs for screening and digital signature creation, allowing far superior identification than in the past. The initiative that began last year has met far less resistance from companies than we thought."

John interrupted, "So the database is getting populated with images. What are we doing with it? What was the result of CBP's or TSA's studies?"

Kirby stepped back to the podium, flipping pages before looking up. "TSA is proposing moving forward with testing of their unmanned X-ray screening. Their R&D team reported that their efforts with Google have been successful. A limited AI can screen bags and identify threats ten times faster than humans. Similarly, the CBP remote scanning program successfully identified test smuggling operations with scanning drones."

John leaned forward. "So both agencies are ready to cut humans out of the loop? It will eventually happen, but not yet. There are too many questions. My direction is clear. All systems must have people in the loop. Google stayed tight-lipped about its AI slip last year, but it seems straightforward. There may not be a giant leap in technology, with media around the world covering the first AI development; it may happen in the middle of the night. And if all of our systems are networked without people, we could be in trouble."

"Thank you for the segue, sir. Moving to the global arena, we have made significant progress in the field of artificial intelligence. Most developed countries have followed suit and increased spending, though none more than China. In keeping with their strategic goal of surpassing us by 2025 and becoming the leader by 2030, success and setbacks have continued similarly to ours. Indications from Zhongguancun indicate that at least three companies have consolidated efforts and taken the lead over other Chinese companies. We don't have specifics on the consolidation yet. Sources have identified a possible name for their program, Quánqiú lóng, which translates to Global Dragon. NSA has been tasked to inform us of any traffic surrounding that name. Cyber Command had received preliminary information on the project and is in the coordinating role."

John raised his hand toward the presentation, palm up. "And there we go. The release of the LaMDA story didn't do us any favors. China is worried. We have been going back and forth for years, and now they think we have working AI, which scares them. These are only the latest consolidation of companies under one umbrella. Does anyone know what China's AI budget is this year?" John looked around the room. He stood, eyes scanning the faces of his advisory team, lips pursed. "It was just short of fifty billion dollars." He paused. "They plan to triple that amount in the next eight years." He pointed at the screen. "That is what we are up against."

He relaxed, turning back to the presenter. "Kirby, nice work. Send an update later today, highlighting the questions with the appropriate department's name tagged. I want a report on Zhongguancun by the end of the week. Thank you all."

February 2024
Staten Island, New York

The dim lamp illuminated the desk but not much more of the room. The dark red curtains were parted slightly, providing a small opening to the outside where snow continued to fall. George sat, typing at his computer, his phone on speaker to the side. "Tim, your idea of identifying the objects as embassy ships is sick. I'll say that the information is highly classified. We only know because our ambassador to the Zeta Reticulan "Grays" Government informed us that their position aligns with our desire for peace. Even though we aren't considered players at all."

Tim's voice came through the speaker of the phone. "Yeah, and make sure you stress that they are all heading for the first galaxy-wide peace treaty negotiation."

"So, the major players will be the Pleiadians, the Reptilian, the Grays, and two species unknown to us."

Tim jumped in, "And when the objects collide, you will act surprised and break the story that there has been an incident at the peace summit. One of the embassy ships brought a weapon of mass destruction. NASA is trying to analyze the results, but we suspect the explosion destroyed the generational representatives and ambassadors."

"Okay, and that the failure of the actual peace process has resulted in at least two preemptive declarations of war against one of the unknown species by the Reptilians and the other unknown species. The Grays and the Nordic have called for an investigation before making any decisions on their path forward."

"So, I'll let you know when we post certain pictures so you can pull them from the JPL and NASA sites."

"Awesome, I should be able to fill in the holes in the story and show them as *irrefutable proof* that the government is not only in contact with aliens but continues to do all it can to keep it quiet."

"Tim, this was a great idea. Thanks again."

"It was your idea. I'm just helping brainstorm. It will be fun and add some more fringe interest to our work. Heck, after you talk about how you *broke the code* on NASA's photo releases, I expect traffic across our sites to increase. The other conspiracy shows will pull images, looking for the next big story. It should also help with follow-up searches into what we are planning on Mars and the civilian companies getting us there."

"Okay, brother, I have to get to work. Still not at the sub numbers to quit my job. Maybe after this. How long before you start posting pics?"

"I think we will begin posting images next month with a few hints. I'll give you a day or two heads-up so that you can begin the tease."

"Sounds good. I'll talk to you later."

CNEOS, JPL, Pasadena, California

The room was packed. The tables and chairs of their cafeteria were off to the side of the spacious room. The chessboard patterned white-and-gray tiles looked like they had been buffed all night. The window glass was dimmed. Even with the lights on, the room was darker. Sharon heard the intermittent squeak from the curtains as they slid into place, covering the windows. Sharon waited, shifting her weight from foot to foot. NASA PR had decided to present the video they would use to kick off the fifteen-month countdown to the celestial collision.

A hush fell over the group as Joy moved toward the white glass podium with the JPL logo on the front. Sharon looked down, brushing her hands over her dark gray suit. At least they let her pick the lavender for her shirt.

Sharon watched Joy. She was so poised, in control. She felt her face begin to flush, thankful when Joy nodded and the lights in the room dimmed. The room was silent. The image of a rolling asteroid came into view from the bottom of the screen. The camera angle pulled back, showing the asteroid traveling through the expanse of space. "Welcome to the show of a lifetime." A prominent Hollywood actress's recognizable voice played in surround sound.

"Over the next fourteen months, we hope you will join us as we witness an extraordinary event." The background music rose, building anticipation. "Led by Dr. Sharon Berzing, our team at NASA and the Jet Propulsion Laboratory will guide you through the discovery, journey, and highlight of a celestial event unlike any other." The music continued to build as the view panned out to show five objects approaching a distant point in space. "Five celestial bodies are approaching a point in space at tens of thousands of miles per hour. We expect their meeting to be spectacular and have arranged our deep space assets to focus on the event." Trails of color appeared in the wake of the moving objects as the camera rose above the travel planes. The colors were red, yellow, blue, green, and silver. "Starting next March, we will begin a biweekly show highlighting the countdown to the celestial collision. We hope you join us on this fantastic journey." The five objects approached and became a bright light slowly filling the screen before fading out to reveal the NASA logo.

Joy smiled, clapping at the podium. Her dulcet voice addressed the group. "Thank you all for coming. There are light refreshments along the sides. Dr. Berzing and Administrator Terry James will be happy to take your questions as we celebrate."

Sharon moved toward Joy. "That was amazing. You make it look so easy. I love it. I'm stressed thinking about keeping it exciting for the next year."

A short gentleman in a suit stepped through the crowd. A light blue tie accentuated his dark gray suit. "You don't have to worry about that, Sharon."

She recognized him from his picture in the lobby, blond hair lightening into gray, combed to the left, held perfectly in place, and distinctive blue eyes. She moved to shake his outstretched hand. "Thank you, Administrator James."

"Dr. Berzing, I can't think of a better person to lead this effort. You will be the face of deep space exploration moving forward. How do you feel?"

She flashed a weak smile but kept her eyes on his. "Truthfully, I'm quite nervous. But I'm looking forward to seeing this through. I think it will contribute nicely to your goal of engaging the younger generation. I love the team's work and am grateful we get to show it off in such a spectacular fashion. It is nothing like I imagined, quite a bit different from the calm of our lab."

"This crowd might be a little biased, but it looks like everyone is genuinely excited. It will be great, and don't worry, we will take the opportunity to cover many of the projects we have for the future. Have fun. You'll do great. The camera loves you. Enjoy the reception. I've got a flight to catch. Well done, Joy, Sharon." He flashed another genuine smile.

Sharon watched as he made his way through the mass of people smiling and greeting them as he passed. She couldn't help but feel that the roller coaster was about to take off, and she couldn't find the seatbelt. She had a month to get her mind in the right place. It was just another challenge. She discreetly let out a long breath, watching the excitement on the faces around her.

Zhongguancun, China

Wu Kai sat on the bench outside the recently sealed room, the white walls and prominent silver door marking the barrier between the dirty and clean areas. He pulled the protective suit over his shoes and set it aside. He stood and took a deep breath, inhaling the wet-earth smell of fresh concrete. After a moment, he passed his dosimeter to his assistant. The stoic young man took the device without saying a word. Wu Kai moved to join the Lead Engineer.

"Xiao Tian, you have done well. We are ahead of schedule."

Tian Shin nodded. "Yes, sir, I expect we will complete the project ahead of schedule, despite the exacting specifications."

"Of course," Wu Kai replied. "Expediency but not at the expense of security. I expect the Americans will try to gain access to this facility."

The architect stopped and bowed slightly in deference to Wu Kai. "There will be no leaks from my men. They are most loyal. All of them understand the importance of this project."

Wu Kai stopped walking and looked at the architect in silence for a moment. "I believe you, but more and more, we find there are those we thought loyal who have been persuaded by promises and gifts from the West. We cannot afford anything like that to occur, especially now."

Tian Shin nodded. "I assure you, it will not. The Ministry was thorough." He motioned for the Director to join him as he continued walking. "Let us examine the area designed to hold the dilution refrigerators."

They continued for a good distance before turning toward the main area that would house the quantum computer. Tian Shin talked as they crossed the massive room. "This area will be the most critical. We have a specialty team working on the layout, reviewing the design for any flaws that would prevent establishing optimal computer conditions. The temperature controls are state of the art, ahead of the rest of the world. This room will be closer to zero kelvin than any other. The proposed design will increase effectiveness by five percent. The stabilizers are an area of concern. Our current design will not support a project of this size."

Wu Kai nodded sternly. "I am aware. Our engineering design team is working on it. They have developed a few designs that have maintained near-zero influence within the models. Do you anticipate any other delays?"

Tian Shin replied, "No, but I foresee this as the principal concern at the moment."

Wu Kai looked at the man, devoid of emotion, and stated, "Keep me informed."

"Of course, Director Wu, as always."

March 2024
New York City, New York

George and his father made their way back to their seats in Madison Square Garden. Their oversized blue Rangers jerseys were hanging to the mid-thigh of their worn blue jeans. George moved carefully so as not to spill his large Budweiser or drop his spicy fried chicken sandwich from Mike's, his favorite of the concession stands. The cold air felt good on his face. There was something different about the chill at a hockey game. It made you feel alive. George nodded, smiling at the rowdy fans. The crowd noise was loud in the upper levels.

They sat, looking down at the ice as the players from both teams got ready for the second period. The scoreboard showed the Rangers up 2–0 over the Senators. The home crowd was making their presence known.

"Dad, thanks again for this." He waved his hand toward the ice, still clutching his sandwich. "Better than last year."

"I'm glad, son. We may not agree on much nowadays, but we do have the Rangers." He raised his beer in a toast, George followed suit, and the two took a long drink.

"My favorite birthday tradition. Things are looking up. I know you don't think my podcast is a good job, but it's starting to pay. Maybe by the end of the month, I'll be full-time."

His father looked at him, chewing a bite of his NY hot dog. "People pay you?"

"No, not people. YouTube pays people based on subscriptions and how many people watch your content, the videos. It is a good living, Dad. I think if you looked into it, you would see that it is a decent way to pay bills."

His dad shook his head. "Not sure what happened to the country. Used to be you had to get out and do real work—"

A loud horn sounded, and the crowd jumped to their feet. George and his father jumped, arms up, listening to the rock guitar riff prep the fans. George held his beer up. "Whoa-oh ohhhh, whoa-oh ohhhh, whoa-oh ohhhh. Hey! Hey! Hey-hey-hey!" As the song continued, George watched the replay on the scoreboard. Mika Zibanejad had his second goal of the night, flipping a deflected shot over the goalie's outstretched leg.

George sat down when his father did, his eyes focused on the game. He leaned over. The crowd noise was still loud. "Dad, it's a different world. Jobs are different. Don't worry about me. I'm about to break a big story tomorrow. I think this might be the one that pushes me up the ladder."

"Is it real news or one of your fairy tales?"

George looked down. "It could be real."

His father turned to him, leaning in, and locking eyes. "George, don't you deceive anyone. People don't forget that, and I raised you better."

George nodded, turning back to the game and taking another long drink from his beer.

♦ ♦ ♦

George finished posting the slide show video with a time-lapse of the NASA photos showing the five objects' paths toward a single point in space. After making sure there were no errors, he posted a quick blog story teasing more info in today's show. He already had the follow-on post written and ready to go once he was off the air. He checked his system before clicking the broadcast button, notifying his subscribers.

"Hey, Believers, it's George Isaacson bringing the truth from Staten Island—a big shout-out to my followers across the country who are tuning in at all hours of the day." He kicked off the show with his standard greeting.

"I am flipping out because we have a huge scoop today. You know me—I'm here to bring the truth that the government does not want you to know. I have uncovered the truth behind a major announcement NASA is about to make regarding an event they say is a cosmic collision. I have it on good authority that the NASA story is false. They want us to be oblivious to a major event in our little corner of the Milky Way."

He let his words hang in the air. "I can't go into too many details. I'll let you all watch the official NASA announcement next week. But for a teaser, I have posted proof, so those out there who like to argue about the truth may realize it's time to stop blindly following the government's mainstream media and official announcements. Yeah, you know who you are, right, FedBuster? Let's jump into some calls and get this show kicking."

He queued the first call. "Welcome to the George Isaacson Show. Hit me with a truth bomb."

A modulated voice came through the speaker. "George, I can't believe you are still peddling the same broken, disproved theories after two years. Your topics are old stuff. Most of it has been explained away with actual science." The caller paused. "If you want to drop some real truth on your listeners, you should tell them how full of crap you are and how this is a hobby, feeding junk to the bottom feeders."

George jumped in on the caller. "Truth, I'm not hiding my voice. What do I hear, a modulator? Are you trying to give yourself more credibility? That does not work here. We deal in facts." He pressed an on-screen button activating his sound effect board and modulating his voice. "Anyone can change their voice. It's the same trick used by government officials trying to sound more credible in the '70s."

The caller laughed. "Nice trick. I have to do this. You would know who I am, as would all of your *followers*." He seemed to spit the word out. "I looked at your trash photoshop job with the NASA pics. They are fake, like your show."

George stopped, realizing he was being baited on air. "What's your name, caller?" he replied, voice steady.

"Don't you want to guess? I'm your number one follower because someone has to reveal the truth about you." Silence hung in the air.

George rolled his eyes. "Pssht, FedBuster. I wondered if you would ever reveal yourself instead of sniping comments on chat boards and social media."

The caller laughed. The modulation changed to that of a female voice. "No sniping necessary here, Georgie. You're half-baked, and I mean that in a purely medicinal way; theories are only worth my time because it annoys you." The caller paused again. "But Georgie, I have a gift for you. I'll let you in on a secret that will make you famous."

George felt a sense of dread. Before he could speak, the caller continued, modulating their voice to that of a deep baritone male, "Georgie. I have big plans. The weasel is feisty. No secret is safe." The caller hung up.

George shook himself out of his thoughts of dread, laughing. "What?" he exclaimed and continued laughing. "Seekers, I have to say that that was the craziest call we have had this month. If anyone knows what FedBuster was talking about, call me. Let's take a break and keep this thing going. If you want to call in after the break, follow the link from the show page. Be right back."

He started a long segment of sequential promos, took off his headphones, and headed to the fridge to grab an Ultra Gold Monster energy drink. *What was that?* he thought. *It could be a crazy stalker. It could be good for the clicks. More clicks, more money.* He laughed, then took a long drink before returning to his studio room to continue the podcast.

Time to convince them the scoop is real. Let's push those subscription numbers up. A little white lie never hurt anyone—especially if there is no way to check the story. If people want to believe in aliens, no harm, no foul.

He started the next segment of his show by talking about the legitimacy of conspiracy claims and how to know the truth when you see it.

CNEOS, JPL, Pasadena, California

Sharon wore a pastel yellow two-piece jacket and skirt with a dusty rose blouse. The set was cool despite the heat from the lights. Sharon could hear a soft cello playing in the background through her earpiece. She focused on the light above the camera and stepped near the screen, a wall-to-wall 16K lifelike definition display donated by the South Korean company LG. She queued the display to show the path of the objects moving toward each other in 3D. "Each week, we will bring you the latest information on what these bodies are doing as they move toward their demise." Sharon paused. "We can predict the paths with the precision necessary to track objects that may threaten us here on Earth." She pointed toward the object on the right of the screen. The object became highlighted, and an orange color trail appeared, showing the path behind the object. A dashed orange line appeared in front of the object with a window indicating the current speed and the angular path toward the impact point.

Sharon motioned toward the small box. It grew more prominent, and several fields glowed with question marks. "One of the interesting things to note, which we hope to answer over the next year, will be the composition of the objects. Using spectroscopy, we can get a reasonably good idea of the elements present, at least on the surface. Perhaps we will know beforehand, but more than likely, we will have a clearer view of their composition after observing the collision.

"Next week, we will examine the process used by CNEOS to discover the objects. Until then, have a good week."

The "on-air" light went out. Sharon sighed deeply. She quickly made her way to a table set for the cast and crew, opened a water bottle, and drank half before taking another breath. "I'm going to have an ulcer before this is over."

Administrator James followed her to the table with refreshments, picking up a bottle of flavored water. "Nice work, Sharon. The ratings are great. They love you. Interest in NASA programs is up seventy-four percent from last year."

Sharon slowed her breathing, grabbed a napkin, and tried to dry her hands. She looked up at the Administrator. "Thank you. I hope this gets easier."

"You're a natural. The camera loves you, don't worry. As long as those five keep speeding toward each other, it will be a breeze." He tipped his water bottle toward her as he left.

Alone at the table, she looked back toward the set. The large display took up most of the space. It was dark outside the central area, with the supports holding everything in place. She took another sip of water, hoping to keep it down during her drive home.

George Bush Center for Intelligence, Langley, Virginia

John entered the office of the Director of Central Intelligence. He was impressed with the décor—dark oak furniture offset by the royal blue carpet. The walls were government white, with art spaced evenly around the room.

"Have a seat, John. I'll be right with you." Not looking up, Brad Thargold, the DCI, finished signing a document and passed it to the assistant who had shown John in.

"Thanks, Brad."

John sat in one of two brown leather chairs facing the desk, his attention drawn to the art behind the Director. It was not what he expected. The painting was of a field of flowers. The yellow rays from the sun shone down from a light blue sky to highlight an area of varying greens dotted with soft flowers of pink.

"It must be important. You don't stop by often. What do you need?" Brad got up and walked around the desk extending his hand.

John stood, reaching out to shake Brad's hand. "Brad, I need to understand better what is happening in China, specifically Zhongguancun."

"Don't we all. You've read the reports. They have their new facility locked down. They are masking their efforts very well, which makes us believe it is a high-priority project."

"Our analysis leads me to believe it's AI."

"That's a strong possibility. We've talked to NSA, and they have nothing. The story from Google scared the hell out of them, though. Whatever they are doing there, they are keeping it real quiet."

"That is what worries me. Add in the friendly gestures in space, and the hair on the back of my neck starts tingling. Can you get anyone into the area?"

"John, you know better than to ask me that."

"Yeah, well, we need to do something before we find ourselves left behind and vulnerable. FBI has multiple active investigations of industrial espionage, about which they told my staff they would let us know if anything develops."

"That sounds about right. They are trying to clean things up and keep investigations out of the press. Your secretary is a friend of the President. Maybe she can get them to open up."

"She holds that card close. I'll push the Bureau a bit harder. I have a few friends there. We need to work together better. If one of us slips, we all get blamed."

"Isn't that the truth? Sorry we couldn't be of much help."

John stood and shook Brad's hand again. "At least we are talking. Your predecessor wouldn't answer my calls in the last year."

"You did throw him under the bus with Congress."

"Brad, I call it as I see it. I'm not going to lie for anyone."

"I know. I don't want to drudge up anything. You and I see eye to eye. Call me if you get anything from the other agencies, and I'll do the same."

"Thanks, Brad, will do."

Smithsonian National Museum of Natural History, Washington, DC

Jackie approached the small platform, greeting team members, staff, and journalists along the way. She paused to greet journalists from *Archaeology World* and *Archaeology Today*. She stepped up to the podium and took a short sip from a water bottle.

"Welcome, and thank you all for being here at this momentous event. The discovery of the Eridu Tablet will change our understanding of the timeline of human development. You can see the tablet to my right," she gestured with her hand, "is a phenomenal artifact. You can see the technological advancement evident in using platinum for electroplating. A technique that implies an intent to preserve their message."

She paused for effect. "Despite having collected dozens of tablets throughout the region over the past few decades, we can't discount the impact looting or deterioration from exposure to the natural elements have had. This tablet is the first Sumerian artifact with platinum electroplating. The use of platinum, a rare and expensive metal by our standards today, demonstrates an understanding of the chemical properties and the metal's ability to withstand corrosive oxygenation. Coupled with the words we understand, the tablet may have been created as a memorial, expected to last centuries.

"The first section of the tablet appears to identify the birth of Eridu, the oldest known city, which, based on the timeline, marks the creation of several socioeconomic systems centuries before we had initially believed it to be possible. These concepts are essential in establishing a society on a large scale.

"We believe the second section refers to the time it took to establish the settlement. While there isn't a specific description of what passage of time the creators of the tablet suggest, we hope to gain a better understanding through the continued efforts of other archaeological teams and Sumerian experts around the world.

"The third and fourth sections refer to reaping and a son returning in all his glory. We understand the potential parallel with biblical stories and would like to point out that there are numerous parallels between Sumerian mythology and sections of the Abrahamic religious texts. Again, efforts continue to help frame these words in their proper context. The explanation could be as simple as the city's architect moving on to another project with an expectation that he would return in a few years to see the progress of his design.

"The original tablet has been loaned to the Louvre, with five replicas distributed for display worldwide. We want to thank the French Government, the archaeology teams from the EU, and our partners in the Ministry of Culture, Tourism, and Antiquities in Iraq for their support and permission to explore our past and display it to the world. I will be happy to take any questions."

She paused. "Yes." She motioned to a reporter in the front row.

"Dr. Mandrapilias, thank you for the informative presentation. Tod Barrow, *Archaeology Today*." He paused. "The find's significance cannot be underscored enough. The implications of dating the earliest Sumerian societal gathering and moving our timeline back another thousand years are amazing. How do you feel about calls from numerous societies stating they want access to the original tablet to evaluate its authenticity? Some in your field have even stated that the metallic coating on the tablet could have been applied during a later era, implying your estimation for electroplating is wrong."

Jackie pursed her lips and smiled, keeping her composure at the blatant attack on her team's work. With a slightly stern tone, she addressed the reporter. "We expected there to be some disagreement on the dating of the tablet. We have requested permission from the Ministry of Culture, Tourism, and Antiquities to test the clay within the metal coating, similar to taking a core sample from trees. There are some concerns that exposing the clay to the air after several millennia could damage the artifact. That being said," she continued, "we have coordinated with a number of prominent European archaeology organizations who have reviewed our findings and agree with our assessments. Next question." She motioned to a young lady farther back.

"Thank you, Dr. Mandrapilias. Kelly Banks of the *Washington Post*. My question regards the competition for attention with the NASA blitz going on. Do you feel that the push by NASA has diminished the contributions of other scientific areas of study by forcing important stories like this and others off the front page?"

Jackie had anticipated this question and smiled as a result. "Thank you for that question. NASA's stated vision fosters a sense of curiosity among our youth. While the announcement by NASA and the associated media blitz may overshadow other scientific discoveries, I feel that any scientific activity that captures public attention, regardless of the field of study, is beneficial. While most people may focus on the large-scale media press from NASA, I believe it could increase interest across all scientific fields."

She used her planned response to build momentum, fielding more questions before ending the press conference. She invited the attendees to join her for refreshments and to see the Smithsonian replica of the tablet.

June 2024
Stratton, Maine

George pulled his car into an extended drive leading to the bed-and-breakfast. The white colonial home was not as large as the Ora Blanchard house he had passed on the main street, but it looked like a nice place to relax for the week. The drive was excellent, with clear skies for all eight hours. He got out of the car, stretching to work his muscles loose. Looking down, he brushed flaming hot ranch chip crumbs off his gray Roswell Athletics shirt and jeans. He twisted his feet from side to side, checking his Nikes' sides. He grabbed his bag and headed to the house.

"Hello, Truth Seekers. This is the George Isaacson Show live from Stratton, Maine. I am here with Janice and Teresa, the two ladies who called the show a few weeks back about lights in the sky over Lake Flagstaff. We have set up camp for the night and are making our way to the top of one of the small mountains here in the preserve."

George watched and stepped carefully over the moss-covered rocks and roots, twisting in all directions. The bright green canopy provided cover from the sun. He carefully traversed the rugged terrain, his breathing heavier. The image on his phone was split between images of his face and the forest path.

"Janice, could you recap what you have seen up here?"

"Of course," she said in a feathery tone. "We were camping up here, near where our current camp is. We made our way up the ridge to an overlook we know with a great view of the lake at night. When the moon is full, the lake looks like liquid silver."

Teresa chimed in, reaching up to straighten her headband, barely controlling wavy shoulder-length dark hair. "We were hanging out here when Blake, Janice's boyfriend, pointed out over the lake. We looked where he was pointing and saw four lights moving fast over the water—two red, one yellow, and one blue. They flew close together before splitting up into pairs. They skimmed down over the water and then disappeared."

"That is amazing. Hopefully, we will get lucky tonight, as well. Did you hear anything or smell anything funny?"

Janice shook her head. "I didn't hear anything. Emmi from work thought it could have been someone out here playing with drones. It was a clear night, and I don't remember there being any wind."

Teresa pulled herself up a short rise to the overlook. "I think it was drones, but not ours. The ones you talked about last month that can move fast and turn on a dime."

George's phone chimed. "I have a text from Ben at the National Weather Station in Caribou. He says that increased magnetic activity may have resulted in you seeing the northern lights."

George pulled his laptop from his backpack and set up his mobile podcast gear. The three continued their talk about the lights as twilight faded to darkness. George admired the clear sky. There were so many stars. He couldn't see half as many near the city. It was beautiful, the sweeping arm of the Milky Way cutting through the night sky.

George's phone buzzed. He switched his camera from the view of the lake back to himself. "Truth Seekers, I know tonight's topic is the New England lights, but I have received a text from a potential new source that will corroborate information on the NASA story we've been discussing. This text, and possibly the information I'll receive soon, should reveal the truth."

He read the text aloud: "'The NASA story is a lie! There will be no collision. The odds are astronomically against five objects flying in converging paths, and we all know it.' They knew that Truth Seekers like us would see the evidence of the objects in their pictures and link it with leaked communications from rogue alien entities. All of which you can find on my website."

He leaned back against a tree, lowering his phone and running a hand through his hair. "Wow, this is earth-shattering! This information corroborates other sources I received during briefings with high-level government officials. You know that I only like to present verified information from multiple sources. No fake information from me. Because we deserve the truth."

George continued, "You all know treaties prevent the government from releasing information on alien contact until the world becomes united. We know the Grays have established embassies in the US and Europe. The Reptilians favored Russia and helped their recovery post-fall of the Soviet Union. A third unidentified group is working with China. I have more information on that on another show."

George leaned forward into the camera. "Not for nothing, but the time is coming for the government to come clean. They will have to admit to knowing about life outside our planet. The sooner, the better, but I know we will have proof when there's no massive explosion from the five objects. You all heard it here first. There will be no explosion." He looked down at his phone, holding a pensive pose for a few seconds before looking directly into the camera.

"The truth is coming, Seekers. The truth is coming. Let's take a quick break. Janice, Teresa, and I'll discuss this breaking info and your thoughts on the New England Lights."

CNEOS, JPL, Pasadena, California

Sharon looked forward to her day away from the media team. Monday was her day to catch up on work pushed aside during filming, choreography, and everything else that went into making NASA's show a success. She entered the open work area and saw Tim at their shared station. She laughed at their matching light blue polo shirts. He had khaki pants, which she refused to wear, and had opted for black slacks. He had his earbuds in, listening to music or a podcast. She looked forward to sitting at her desk, reviewing the latest model updates, cataloging, and approving analysis of near-Earth objects. Her director offered to pass her assignments unrelated to the celestial collision to another researcher, but she declined. She loved sifting through the data and working on the model to see what the future held from a cosmic point of view. It was quiet—her realignment day.

"Good morning, Tim. Anything special today?"

Tim pulled his right earbud out and looked up from his screens. "Hey, Sharon, I'm looking over the changes to the model. The graphics improvements look amazing. I guess it is true that public opinion drives the NASA budget. What are you doing here?"

Sharon looked at Tim quizzically. "I need these days away from the excitement. I'm sure the collision will be spectacular, but" she paused, "I need my reset days. The silence of the lab, checking numbers, and listening to music make the days flow by."

Tim laughed. "I get that. There isn't anything new, and all is well with your five little beauties. Their course and speeds are constant. I talked to the spectrology group. They expect an update in the next few months, allowing us to determine what the objects are made of."

She nodded. "Thank you, Tim, nice work. That is one more thing to cross off the to-do list for the week. Are you ready for me to take over?"

"You bet. It's all yours." Tim pushed back from the desk, letting her take his place. He picked up his lab coat and headed out the door, already checking the texts on his phone. Sharon felt her stomach turn with heartburn. She chewed a few Tums antacids and started planning her day.

Zhongguancun, China

Wu Kai strolled through the spacious white chamber with the Lead Engineer. Autonomous robots moved through the area, focusing on their respective tasks. The designs varied in size and shape from hand-sized to that of a small car, with differing numbers of appendages and sensors. These were not the clunky robots that populated social media sites. They were smooth, refined, and highly classified. He paused periodically to watch them work. Their work was precise.

Tian Shin paused the group bringing up a schematic of the cooling system, and said, "This is the central computing chamber, the home for Quánqiú lóng. The light blue dots," he motioned to numerous points in the room, "are temperature measurement points. We have built-in triple redundancy, as requested. All systems tests in the model were successful. The cooling system will maintain a room temperature of five millikelvin."

"Half of their best designs? That will certainly reduce error rates."

Wu Kai looked at the design, then around the room. The plans were specific and absolute. There were many points of failure to overcome: the process for timing the cooling of the room; installation of the hardware; complete cleansing of the area of all particulates; isolating all electromagnetic interference; and ensuring that power flowed to the machine in such a way as to prevent stray particles from escaping and interfering with the matrix of quantum circuits.

"Will this facility be ready in two months? I have been assured the quantum computer will be delivered on time."

"We will be complete in six weeks. The reactor is online and provides all of our power. The robots use a series of nanosensors to conduct last-minute calculations. Shielding is in progress and will be tested to ensure complete isolation."

"That is a major milestone. We cannot allow computer access to any other systems outside this facility."

"If you will follow me, I will take you below to the cooling system room."

They exited the chamber and proceeded down the nearby stairs leading to the cooling system underneath the central computing chamber.

"Thank you, Xiao Tian. Your team has done well. We will talk again soon."

The Lead Engineer bowed and returned to the worksite.

Wu Kai got into the back seat of his car. "Back to my office."

As he cleared the security area and reentered the city, he placed a call. "CFO Teng, I have completed my inspection of the facilities. We are ahead of schedule, and the quality of work is exceptional. Provide a five percent bonus to all assigned to the facility's construction."

He hung up and smiled. Once construction was completed and the computer assembled, the actual tests would begin. Two months.

September 2024
Staten Island, New York

George rode down the bike lane, heading out to grab lunch. The weather was still warm, but he was going fast enough to enjoy a slight breeze. He stayed to the side of the road, avoiding traffic. The past few months had been outstanding. The response to his NASA conspiracy theory had boosted his numbers on social media. He looked to be on track to receive a social media award at the end of the year. His audience was growing, and word of mouth was helping as he had been able to recruit a few friends to help with content creation in other formats. He was still a way off from making enough money to make it his main job, but the future was looking good.

A blaring horn shook him back from his momentary daydream. He struggled to maintain control as the horn had startled him enough to make him instinctively swerve away from the road toward the curb.

He pulled over in front of Stan's Staten Island Deli. He locked his bike, stepped between the red-and-white tables and chairs in the sidewalk seating area, and headed in.

"Hey, Joe, how are you doing?" he greeted the clerk behind the counter.

"All good. You know us, not too busy, not too quiet. We've got a catering gig later. Stan's in the back."

"That's good. You know you all make the best food. I told Stan, if I ever settle down, I'll have you cater my wedding." George laughed as he looked through the glass into the display cases.

"You keep peddling craziness, and you won't have to worry about that," a sharp voice greeted him.

Tina stepped through the beads covering the doorway to the back room. She had on her white apron with her name embroidered in red cursive letters. Her eyebrows raised in a 'what are you gonna say' way.

"I don't know, Tina. My fan base is growing."

Tina smirked. "Crazies following crazy. You keep pushing those junk theories, and you're going to get some followers, alright. Some of those conspiracy nuts will begin following you for real."

George laughed playfully. "I'm not peddling crazy stories. People want to know what's going on. You can't tell me you think the government is on the up-and-up all the time."

"I'll give you that. But you better be careful. Some people take things way too far."

"I hear ya. I'll take my usual joe and a half-pound each of smoked turkey, that ham," he pointed through the glass, "and a quart of mac and cheese."

"It can happen," Tina continued. "I read a story last week about someone being stalked so bad by a fan that they had to move. Even canceled their show because they didn't feel safe."

"Who?" George asked. "What was their name?" He waited for an answer.

"I don't remember the name, but I remember someone said it."

"Yeah, I thought so. And you say I'm the only one with crazy stories."

"It's true, and it's not just the people that follow shows like yours. You start telling stories about the government, and you may get a visit you don't like. I'm just sayin', you need to be careful."

George looked at her for a second, then paid for his food. "Okay, maybe. Thanks for the concern, Tina. I wasn't sure you cared. Now I know."

"Yeah, you wish, George," she said as the door closed, the tinkling of a small bell hanging in the air.

♦ ♦ ♦

George rushed home, made a quick lunch, and put the rest in the fridge. Turning on the small flat-screen TV, he sat back, sinking into his light brown couch. He put on the recording of last week's NASA show. The show was better than he thought it would be. Adding other science and research topics to break up the coverage during the hour-long show sparked a few more ideas for theories of how the government was hiding information from the public.

When Dr. Berzing played through the latest model, George watched intently for anything he could use. He had his story planned out through the collision, but one part of the story bothered him. The objects appeared similar in size and were all heading on linear paths. They had covered it on the show, but it sounded too convenient. A guest researcher from China pointed out two weeks prior that the limited data showed an odd characteristic. As the objects approached each other, they did not show the normal curvature in their paths, as expected of objects as large as they were.

George typed a note on his phone to call Tim about it. Maybe he could get an interview with Dr. Berzing. It was a long shot, but his credibility would soar if he could get her on the show. He was sure she wouldn't support the alien theory he had come up with.

It would be awesome, though.

National Art Museum of China, Beijing, China

Jackie got out of the car and let her eyes sweep over the expansive front façade of the new National Art Museum of China. The architectural style of the building was breathtaking, enormous in size, and with a flowing silver exterior. The grounds approaching the entrance were polished and clean, combining white-and-light-gray stonework and meticulously manicured landscaping. A distinguished-looking man in a dark blue business suit broke away from a small gathered group and approached her.

"Dr. Mandrapilias, welcome to the National Art Museum. We look forward to your presentation of the Eridu Tablet and other artifacts in our new comparison of the ancient world display. I expect your accommodations are satisfactory?"

"Yes, of course, it is wonderful. Thank you, Director Chu," Jackie replied, meeting his eyes.

"Good. When will your team arrive? We have lunch planned with the Minister of Cultural Affairs, a few staff members, and museum staff members." He motioned her to walk beside him toward the entrance.

"They should be here shortly. I know we have a tight schedule today and tomorrow. I look forward to presenting the latest information on the tablet, including one new revelation of which China will be the first to know."

"That is good news. We will need to have the information presented in private to ensure that the messaging is worded properly for public understanding." His face was becoming more serious.

"I understand. I reviewed the requirements on the flight. I assure you that we understand it is a great privilege to present our findings to the people of China."

She nodded, and her face remained neutral. She focused on her colleagues' words before the trip: "They are a patient, proud, and strong people. They feel that as one of the oldest civilizations on the planet, they have earned their right to be at the forefront of all global issues, and shrug at the audacity of a nation a mere two-and-a-half centuries old to have such an impact on the course of history. The opening of China over the last few decades has presented an opportunity for the cultural evolution you will experience there. The people feel strongly about culture and tradition. They have become more open in recent years to adapt to new technology. This scenario results in a merging of the old ways with the new. We can only hope at this point that the cultural evolution leads to a better understanding of the global community."

As they moved through the gallery, she marveled at the flow of the design of the displays throughout the expansive building. It was undoubtedly one of the most beautiful museums she had visited. Care had been taken to create an open flow through each area, allowing large groups of people to move through, the artwork always in view. The director took a path through several displays before arriving at their conference room.

"Dr. Mandrapilias, lunch is ready." He indicated a room to the right.

"Thank you, Director Chu. I was lost in thought. The beauty of the building distracted me."

He chuckled. "Thank you. We only recently completed the new facility."

"I see. Everything looks fantastic." She paused for a second to look around. "I look forward to exploring the exhibitions. I am particularly interested in seeing the Museum of Future Projections. I think it is brilliant, showing the connection of the past to the future."

He smiled, standing taller. "Thank you. I will see what we can do. However, some areas still require attention. I will check the schedule to see if we can make it work."

She bowed her head slightly. "Thank you. I would greatly appreciate it." She stepped into the room, her stomach grumbling as the smell of mixed spices greeted her. The tables were configured in a long triangle with dishes down each center. Director Chu showed her to her chair and introduced her to the Minister of Cultural Affairs.

"Welcome, Dr. Mandrapilias. I look forward to discussing the importance of the Eridu Tablet in defining history. Specifically, I would like to know your thoughts on the spread of civilization from Mesopotamia to the East."

American Nanotech Consortium, University of Texas, Austin, Texas

John paused between the bank of air nozzles that blew across his white chemical protective suit. He stood still as the loud hissing continued, waiting for the green light before moving forward to the UV section for a quick pulse to remove any living microscopic organisms. After passing through the airlock, he joined the group, being addressed by an older African American researcher with distinctly white hair, also in a white protective suit.

"Welcome, Assistant Secretary Worthing, distinguished guests. I am Dr. Lanning, lead researcher for the American Nanotech Consortium and this facility. We have several satellite laboratories across the country, and work contracts and grants through a number of prominent universities." He paused for a few seconds. "The United States leads the world in almost all areas regarding the design and application of nanotechnology and expects to remain in this position for the foreseeable future. Do you have any questions before we begin?"

John spoke up. "Thank you, Dr. Lanning. I am looking forward to your presentation. There are a few subjects I want to cover so that the group stays focused on the purpose of the visit: first, self-replication; second, delivery methods for constructing micromachinery, for lack of a better term, and medical applications; and third, of course, controlling and preventing a gray goo scenario. I am sure we would all agree that we like being the dominant life form on the planet. Thank you."

Dr. Lanning nodded, hiding any reaction to the interruption. "Yes, Mr. Secretary, thank you for the segue. To your first point, self-replication is not yet attainable as the construction of nanobots is a complex and expensive process. While it has been popularized in science fiction outlets that the threat of self-replicating nanobots could endanger everything on Earth as everything that's not a nanobot could be a source of resources. The starting position for the argument of self-replication would be the presence of all the elements necessary to construct the parts required for assembly into a replica of itself. Nanobots are constructed at the molecular level, which is efficient as the nanobots know the exact number and position of every atom of the replica." He paused to let that sink in.

"With that understanding, construction is possible. Nanobots have demonstrated the ability to build objects. The current reality is that complex objects take a long time. Think of it as a 3D printer operating at the molecular level. We can do it but not at the speed popularized by Hollywood. I am sorry, General, but you won't have the rapid growth of a weapon, tool, or armor out of briefcases any time soon."

The group laughed as John patted the Marine Corps General on the shoulder.

Dr. Lanning continued, "In another area, medical applications continue to lead our current research efforts, with applicability for remote treatment and prevention showing great promise. Last year, several visits from Congress led to budget increases aimed at cancer detection and treatment, microsurgery, and immune system reinforcement. We expect to have completed animal testing in the next year, with possible human testing within three years across numerous medical fields."

John smiled and nodded along with the pronouncement. "That is good news. I know Defense is looking forward to keeping our service personnel in shape, regardless of their diets. Add the ability to control stress through chemical release, and we're on to something."

The Marine Corps General to his right was nodding. "We'll take muscle enhancements if you're taking orders."

Dr. Lanning replied, "General, I expect all those capabilities will eventually be available. However, they will take time to develop."

As the side conversations dropped to a low murmur, Dr. Lanning continued, "Mr. Secretary, the gray goo scenario, supported by some notable scholars and popularized in science fiction, is not a concern based on my points regarding self-replication. To be clear, it *is* a concern but not an immediate one. The perfect storm would require nanites paired with a supercomputer capable of near-instantaneous communication run by a sentient AI. Our current limitations prevent this from happening. However, understanding the concern allows us to develop the nanites and their control systems with built-in protections."

John nodded. "Good, because that perfect storm is not an impossibility. Those capabilities will be reached in our lifetime. Dr. Lanning, this is a priority. I'll have my team reach out for a follow-on brief on the defensive measures."

Dr. Lanning closed the briefing binder. "Of course. Most are in the planning and development stage, aimed at specific advances we have not achieved." He then continued, addressing the whole group, "I want to thank you all for coming. We have tours set up, followed by lunch. Schedules are in your folders." An assistant began handing the folders to each of the visitors. "I am available to answer any more questions you may have."

The guests stood and started talking amongst themselves, with a few approaching the lectern to speak with Dr. Lanning. John thanked the team, took the folder, and headed for the door. He checked his watch. *Forty-five minutes to Mom's cooking and Dad's ramblings about the latest trouble with the Dallas Cowboys.*

62

November 2024
Staten Island, New York

Dark clouds covered the sky. The cars parked along the slush-filled streets were blocked in by a few feet of snow scraped to the side by the snow plows. George held a cup of fresh hot chocolate, looking out his living room window at the snow-covered cityscape. He jumped as he sipped, burning his mouth. He narrowly avoided spilling his cocoa on his fuzzy brown Wookie slippers.

George sat on his couch, propping his feet on the blue ottoman. He set the hot chocolate down and opened his laptop. He looked at the latest photos released by NASA. *Nothing new.* His subscriber numbers had started dropping over the past few weeks. He was close to quitting his job at the marina to create content full time but knew he had to stay above 100K subscribers to cover his bills. He had gambled part of his savings to cover the time off for his trips to Pennsylvania and Maine, and the mobile podcast equipment. His father's voice hung in the back of his mind. The bills were covered this week, but ramen was the meal of the week. He checked his notes, ensuring he had the number for tonight's guest stored in his phone.

♦♦♦

"Hey, Believers, it's George Isaacson bringing the truth from Staten Island—a big shout-out to my followers from around the world who are tuning in at all hours of the day." As his theme music played in the background, he continued, "Today, we have a special guest. Many of you have encouraged me to bring this person on the show as you followed our back-and-forth conversation across social media. I would like you all to comment on your support for Jacob in the chat windows. Welcome, Jacob."

"Thank you, George. I have been looking forward to this all week."

"Great. Today, we are dedicating the entire show to help get your story out to a new generation. Let's start at the beginning. Could you tell us what happened to you?"

Jacob's voice was steady and confident. "In the fall of '92, a few friends and I were out for our annual fall camping trip up in Letchworth State Park. It was something we did since we were in high school. There were five of us, and Lenny had headed into town to pick up some more beer and food. I was with my friend, Kevin. The other two, William and Jeff, wanted to hike to one of the nearby big falls. Kevin and I just wanted to find a spot for us to hang out and drink beer later—somewhere with a great view.

"We had been out for about six hours and decided to head back to our campsite. We heard a loud whoosh, and Kevin dove into the brush. I laughed at him, but he didn't laugh. He just pointed up. The treetops bent toward the sound's direction and snapped back after a second. Leaves rained down all around us. We didn't see anything, but we heard a humming kind of pulsing nearby. Kevin wanted to head back, but I egged him on till he followed me.

"We climbed the ridge toward the hum for about a half-hour, maybe a bit longer. When we got to the top, we crept to the edge and looked down into the valley. I kid you not, George, we saw a silver saucer shape, maybe sixty feet across, landed at the bottom of the valley."

"Jacob, what did it look like? Was there any movement? Could you see what was going on?"

George heard the long breath from Jacob's mic. "The saucer was smooth. We didn't see lights or anything, but a bunch of figures were walking around looking for something. Kevin was scared. I could see it in his eyes. He said he wanted to get out of there, and I agreed. I never believed in aliens or UFOs. I saw all of this and that cured any curiosity I had. Can we take a quick break?"

"Of course. Okay, Seekers, we'll be right back after the break with the conclusion to this amazing story. Trust me. You don't want to miss it."

George hit play for his sponsor's ads. Jacob wanted a quick five minutes to calm down and have a drink.

When they returned from the break, George popped the top of his Monster Ultra Gold and took a long sip. "Welcome back, everyone. Thank you, Jacob. Are you good to continue?" George glanced at his chat screen, which was scrolling quickly.

"Yeah, thanks, George. I'm watching the chat, and there are a lot of people listening. I'll try to answer some of the questions if that's alright."

"Yeah, yeah, I want you to be comfortable. People need to know this stuff. More and more stories like yours are being pushed to the side or covered up."

"Okay, well, here is the part that folks don't believe, but I'm telling you, it's all true. There's a hole in my memory of about a month. I remember I was scared. I couldn't hear, see, or taste anything, but I smelled a faint odor like burning paper on wet dirt."

George shook his head. "How did you get back? Did the aliens change their minds?"

Jacob wiped his eyes, "I'm not sure. I woke up in a hospital bed."

"Whoa! Could you imagine Truth Seekers? How was this not a major news story?"

"George, I appreciate you giving me the time to tell my story again to a new audience. I know there will be many that don't believe me, or will believe the cover story put in place that I was tracking a deer and fell off the ridge, hitting my head, which put me in a coma as a John Doe. Even the medical records were doctored, pardon the pun, to show I was in the hospital the whole time. But I remember. I am fifty-nine years old and have not been sick one day since I woke up in that hospital bed."

"Wait, you have never had a cold, flu, or even COVID in over thirty years?" George sat back, his hand covering his mouth.

"Not once, which is surprising. My father, grandfather, and males further back have extensive medical histories with bouts of the flu, pneumonia, bronchitis, and eventually a stroke or heart attack."

"This is incredible. I am flipping out. What about your friends?"

Jacob replied, his voice breaking, catching in his throat, "George, do you remember your childhood friends? Can you close your eyes and remember running around, eating, drinking, laughing, and experiencing life? You can feel it, relive it with memories of sound, sight, feeling, taste?"

"Yes, of course," George replied.

"Well, I have memories of Kevin. My buddy who was with me that day, and I have been told for over thirty years that he never existed. My friend, who I grew up with, never returned, and no one has ever heard of him. I have searched through newspapers, on the internet, across everything I remember, and found nothing. But I can close my eyes and relive my childhood with him, remembering the places we played, his first girlfriend, fights we got into, all vivid, but no one else remembers."

"Believers, this is incredible. You all seem as shocked as I am by this story. But it is in line with other cover-ups we discussed, which is why I started this show. I want to bring you the truth that you will not get from the media, scientific community, or the government.

"Jacob, thank you for telling us that story. I'm grateful for you coming here to share it. You can see the support for you in the chat. Many of them want to help by donating to you and the cause of finding the truth. Believers, we will have a link in the show notes to help with donations. Jacob, if you don't have a GoFundMe page yet, we'll help set it up for you."

Jacob thanked all the listeners. "I do appreciate you allowing me to tell that story. It has been years."

"Jacob, thank you so much for joining us today. I feel like we could talk for days. You have given us a lot to consider. I'd love to have you on again in the future, especially as we get closer to the galactic peace summit. It is only months away; maybe we can watch what happens and talk again afterward.

"Believers, I am as shocked as you are at the story Jacob told us tonight. I know there are many others out there with similar stories. I hope we can get more people to come forward. Our Zeta Reticulan source has told us that operations on our planet are a topic of discussion. Maybe we will finally get some answers about why these things happen. The show files will be posted soon for those of you who couldn't be with us live." George closed the show.

That was great! He hopped up and headed to the kitchen to make another cup of cocoa.

CNEOS, JPL, Pasadena, California

Sharon adjusted her new gray Michael Kors glasses, similar to the design of her favorite black pair.

"Dr. Berzing, could you move forward to the blue mark?"

At the sharp voice of the set director, Sharon stepped forward, a comfortable distance away from the sixteen-foot monitor. She felt the heat from the lighting intensify. Her light gray business suit and skirt, highlighted with off-white, were prominent against the projection of space and stars behind her. The large wall screen showed the impending collision of the five objects as the colored tracks continued in straight lines to the infinity point—the name given to the collision point chosen by one of the PR committees.

When the light turned green, she stepped from her mark to the left of the large screen. "It is fascinating that the objects, all similarly sized, continue to move together toward their destruction, with no detectable variation.

"NASA, with the help from other nations, has developed the plans for a lunar radio telescope array system. With the aid of SpaceX and the China National Space Administration, we have scheduled a launch later this month. The month-long trip will lead to preparations for installing the arrays, positioned to minimize interference from the sun and the Earth.

"With the cooperation of the international space community, this monumental accomplishment has surpassed numerous challenges."

Sharon smiled as the display screen shifted to show a collage of images that had been captured, highlighting the contributions by the countries involved, and their scientific teams, ending with film from recent launches, followed by a CGI representation of the journey.

Sharon continued, "While a normal trip to the moon takes only a few days, travel to the far side takes almost ten times longer, as safety and communication challenges can place our astronauts in danger. With the lessons learned from China's Chang'e 4 and 5 missions, we have agreed to use the same remote relay satellite to communicate with the moon's far side. This will be critical, as the construction window for the array is tight and will require close coordination between our countries to ensure the system is completed in time to view the collision.

"This demonstration of cooperation between the international space community will usher in a new era of exploration, including creating permanent habitats and research facilities on the moon and Mars. Stay tuned for more information on the partnership for exploration, and follow the efforts through daily social media updates provided by the members of this new coalition."

"And cut. Nicely done, everyone. The proposals for next week's show will be delivered no later than Tuesday."

Sharon was ecstatic at the pace at which the mission had come together, and had hoped that SpaceX would jump at the opportunity to take the position of a knight in shining armor, swooping in to deliver the payload on time. But before any of that, she would have a relaxing weekend, followed by at least a few hours of sifting through data Monday morning.

Zhongguancun, China

Wu Kai stood beside President Zhang in the control room as preparations were made to bring the quantum computer online. Five workstations—one central, flanked on either side by two others— were arranged in a sweeping arc, similar to the bridge of a science fiction starship. The primary monitor, eight feet across, showed readouts of the reports he heard.

"Power to all systems is stable and within safe parameters."

"Very well," Wu Kai answered before turning slightly toward President Zhang, "Quánqiú lóng will draw three times more power than Tianhe-2."

President Zhang was quiet, stoic, his eyes focused on the primary monitor, moving around the room as reports came in.

"Temperature steady at five millikelvin. Qubit environmental readings are within parameters."

"The modular design of the qubit array will allow for expansion. Even if the Americans achieve their goal of one million qubits by the end of the decade, we have the capacity to expand faster." He pointed to the qubit array. "The large blue area in the main display is the visualization for the qubit array. It is blue, indicating no activity."

President Zhang nodded. "It is impressive." He turned, looking around the room and motioning at the workstations and monitoring equipment. "With all of this, you are sure there will be no interference?"

"None. The Dragon is isolated. The sensors measure both engagement and interference to a very fine degree. Initial tests successfully used over one hundred qubits of processing power for basic commands and continual system self-diagnostics. The qubit array error rates dropped during testing as Tian Shin's team identified and shielded the computer from interference across every energy spectrum they could monitor and influence." He smiled. "I know the West is curious about what we are doing. They will get no emissions from this facility."

The operations supervisor turned his chair toward the President and Director. "All systems operational."

Wu Kai's eyes looked over the readings on the primary monitor. "Bring it to life."

Upon receiving the directive, the technician pressed the initiate button, and in silence, the commence operations screen loaded.

Wu Kai smiled. A small square area on the large blue field turned green.

"Why is it pulsing?" President Zhang nodded toward the monitor.

"It is designed to adjust the use of qubits based on load. That lets us know that each time it runs a self-diagnostic, it uses more resources. You will see more activity as we run the first test." He addressed the operations supervisor, "Bring up the first system test, computation one dash American two-zero-zero."

Turning back to President Zhang, he continued, "The first challenge for the Dragon repeats an IBM quantum computer test that solved a calculation in two hundred seconds that would have taken Tianhe-2 over ten thousand years to complete. Quánqiú lóng should surpass their time by at least twenty percent, about a minute faster."

Taking a long, slow breath before speaking, "Execute."

Time seemed to slow down. He expected to stare at the screen for two minutes, three if needed, to ensure he saw the program completion time. Ten seconds passed, and he knew this would be the longest few minutes of his life. Fifteen seconds, he put up his hand to silence another researcher asking a question. The program stopped. He looked at the timer: twenty-three seconds.

President Zhang turned his head quizzically. "What happened? Was there an error?"

The operations supervisor looked wide-eyed. "No, President Zhang. The problem has been solved."

He bowed. "President Zhang, I respectfully report that we have achieved quantum superiority. Global Dragon is online and operating at two thousand qubits of processing power. We are now the world leader in computing."

President Zhang nodded in response. "We have much to discuss. You have brought honor to our great nation. Come to my office tomorrow so that we may discuss the path forward."

February 2025
Staten Island, New York

George slammed his fist down on his desk. His laptop and podcast equipment jumped as the plywood sheet shifted, threatening to dump everything on the floor. He lifted his knee to balance the board and reached under to adjust the milk crates back into position.

"In the end" played from his phone.

"Hey, Dad."

"George, how are you doing? Did you catch the game?"

"Uh, no, Dad, I had my show. I'll watch later."

"Don't bother. They lost to the Hurricanes five–two."

"Damn. Figures. That caps my day perfectly."

"What's up? You okay?"

"Someone called my show tonight and backed me into a corner. He baited me, and I fell for it, jumped right in."

"Anything you want to talk about?"

"You don't want to hear about it, Dad. You would probably agree with him."

"George, look, I may not understand what you do and how you get paid to do it, but you are my son. We can fight, but I'll be damned if I'm not going to help you if someone starts a fight with you."

George laughed. "Thanks, Dad." He paused, sighing deeply, "Okay, here goes. I have a few callers and characters I like to engage with on my show. Most are supportive and colorful, meaning they are the ones following the crazy ideas out there on aliens. They make the show fun. No matter what I throw out there and how I talk about one side of a story or the other, they tie it all back to aliens. I did a show on Bigfoot once, and one of them argued that Bigfoot worked for the aliens. He cited the TV show *The Six Million Dollar Man* as a source, saying that the government likes to put the truth out there for us to see. But others don't believe at all and attack me and others at every chance. One guy gets under my skin. Always taunting me, the condescending ass."

"So what happened?"

"You know that NASA show? The one with the asteroids colliding."

"Yeah, I've seen the commercials, but it's not my thing."

"I know. Well, I came up with a story that they are alien ships."

"You lied."

"Dad, this is what I'm talking about. Look, there is no way to know for sure. Hell, NASA and the other space agencies don't have good pictures, so technically, I could be right."

"Yeah, and next week when I win the lotto, I'm buying season tickets to the Giants, Rangers, and Mets, all executive boxes."

"Okay, fine, probably not true, so let's go with it being good entertainment. That story is my job. It pays my bills."

"Okay, Mr. Entertainment Weekly, I'll let it be. Fictional entertainment."

"Fine, I'll take it. Whatever. He basically walked me into a corner and got me to admit that a source for my story, an alien—" He stopped, hearing coughing on the other end of the phone. "Dad, are you alright?"

His dad chuckled. "Sorry, I spit beer through my nose."

George rubbed his forehead.

"Take a break from the story," his dad continued. "Talk about something else. I saw something on the news before the game. A doctor, someone, a Greek name, was talking at the Met about civilization being older than we thought. They have some old metal tablets on display. Maybe if this guy sees you move to something else, he will stop calling."

"Maybe, we'll see. I need to do some work. I can't wait until next month. I love those Ranger games."

"Who says I'm gonna get you tickets?"

"Dad, you say that every year, and we are going on eleven years in a row now being at a game around my birthday."

"Okay, I guess we'll see, then. Have a good night, son."

"Night, Dad."

George typed in *Greek*, *doctor*, and *Met* and clicked a story from earlier in the week. Dr. Jackie Mandrapilias—lead archaeologist at GWU, and a Sumerian expert—led a discussion on the impact of the Eridu Tablet on our understanding of human history. He followed the links to other videos published over the past year before finding a series of videos discussing Sumerian mythology.

He rubbed his eyes and looked at the clock on the old nightstand overflowing with papers. He had lost track of time, and now it was past midnight. He had heard of the Anunnaki but had not studied much of their history. He was already taking notes and working links between theories and how they could be linked to his story of embassy ships. Maybe the Anunnaki were the ones that would destroy all the others in a massive explosion because the other races were seen as interfering with their grand plan that had been in place for over 10,000 years.

He got up to grab another Monster Ultra Gold energy drink and his leftover macaroni and cheese from lunch. Not bothering to heat it, he returned to his research, drawing parallels between stories, and creating a quick timeline. There seemed to be a general timeline of alien contact, with plenty of supposition about the ancient world, the Egyptians, Mayans, Aztecs, Incas, Babylonians, Sumerians, et al. If the Anunnaki had been here tens of thousands of years ago, would they still have an interest in our planet?

"Why would they care?" he wondered aloud.

He leaned back in his chair, looking up at the light in the center of the room. "Why would a space-faring race with advanced technology care about our planet with a species thousands of years behind them?"

He rubbed his temples as he got up to go to bed.

Abu Shahrain, Iraq

Jackie pulled the scarf over her face, just below her goggles. The sky was a deep orange, darkening near the ground. Blowing sand occluded the other structures in her camp. She winced as the sand hit uncovered areas of skin, her black ponytail whipping the back of her neck. She couldn't see more than ten feet. She opened the flaps to the large tan central tent, noting the support ropes straining against the storm.

She stood near the entrance and brushed off the sand. She pulled down her scarf and took a sip of water. She moved to the center of the large tent occupied by a six-foot-square table, with two laptops and a map of the area. Reaching up, she turned on the LED lighting and started her computer. She could hear the generator humming in the nearby environmental protection structure.

Eusebio stepped into the tent, securing the flaps, and pulling his scarf from his face. He walked over to the stack of bottled water, took one, and drank. "No one is going to sleep tonight."

"I agree. This one is bad. I think some of the interns may be rethinking their career choices, and it's only been a few days," Jackie replied.

Eusebio moved across from her to the map table, looking down at the primary dig site drawings. "I think we are close. I have a good feeling that the structure is intact. Even with the storm, I'm pretty optimistic."

She tossed her empty plastic bottle in a can next to the table with "Recycling" written in bold blue letters on a taped piece of paper. "Can you hand me a bottle of water?" she asked, intently looking at the maps and drawings.

He tossed a bottle to her.

Jackie leaned over the map. "Something still feels off. Why was the tablet found here?" She tapped on a point on the map. "What is this building's purpose? Why is it away from what we believe to be the main city?" She stopped to drink. "Why were the tablets here? Over this structure? Something is off, and if we notice the inconsistency, others will, as well."

"I was thinking the same thing. I'm hoping for answers once we gain entrance to the structure," Eusebio answered.

"Maybe, but these are only a few questions we'll have to answer. Some of our *peers* believe the Eridu Tablet is from a different era, despite the dating. In the last six months, I've seen four papers questioning the accuracy of carbon dating, with three of them mentioning the tablet." She stopped, feeling her frustration rise. "We need to understand the bigger story. I hope to find some answers there, or the rest of our community will continue to push our efforts aside." She poked her finger at the structure overlay on the map. The wind whipped at the entrance of the tent.

"I hope this lets up soon," he said, taking a big drink from his water.

DHS HQ, Science, Technology, and Innovation, Washington, DC

John walked down the steps from the DHS HQ building, holding his phone to his ear. His jaw clenched as he shook his head. "How did this happen?" Tilting his head to hold the phone in place, he opened his umbrella to deflect the heavy sleet. He looked up and down the street for his car. The smell of exhaust was light this afternoon.

"I understand the risks in launching satellites, but this is the second failure in the past year, which might be acceptable, except that the two failures were in the same system. I'm on my way. We can discuss it when I get there." He ended the call, slipped the phone into his pocket, and raised his hand when he saw the black Tesla Model 3 pull around the corner.

"Damnit!"

John got into the car and settled for the twenty-minute drive to the Secretary's house.

As he pulled up to the Secretary's home, he greeted the security personnel at the gate, ensuring his face was visible for facial recognition and the badge scan. Once inside, he was shown to the Secretary's study.

John looked around the room. He loved the dark walnut finish on all the furniture and bookshelves. Two small brass oil lamps sat on an antique table against the wall. He could smell the oil and assumed she had been up late last night, reading official reports by the fire.

"Come in, John." Secretary Genson invited him in and motioned toward a seat at the round table away from her mahogany desk. She got up from her desk, went to the bar, and joined him at the table, handing him a bottle of dark German beer. "Your favorite. I'm not going to try to pronounce it, and one won't hurt your running."

"Thank you, Madam Secretary. You know I run so I can enjoy these, right?" he said, taking the dark brew and sitting in the indicated seat.

"John, what did you learn about the launch this morning?"

"NASA says initial reports point to a catastrophic failure in the fuel system. An investigation is underway, but it will take weeks, if not months, to collect and analyze the data."

"What is the operational impact?" the Secretary asked.

"The package was our backup from the loss five months ago. I don't believe anyone would have enough information to target this specific node in the system twice, but I'm always suspicious of coincidence. When we lost the first satellite last year, we brought the backup in as primary and began developing a new backup. We are a few months out from being able to launch again if final testing of the node is successful."

Secretary Genson nodded along with his report.

"The good news is that although the lost unit is the central command and timing unit, there does not appear to be anyone close to developing AI at the general level. But if China or any other country focused on AI found out about it, I wouldn't put it past any of them to try to neutralize the system or duplicate it. I have talked to department counsel and the AG, and they agree that the system does not violate any treaties, but the other countries might not see it that way." He shrugged.

"Yes," she said, "but the goal is to have the system in place and operational as a contingency for the future. Once the system is online, it should provide the protection we need for the next fifty years, correct?"

"Yes, Madam Secretary, fifty years. We have also ensured that the software and equipment packages were separated from the 5G system. When Starlink is ready to upgrade to 6G in five or more years, it will receive a substantial subsidy to keep this system in place."

"What is going on in China?"

He took a deep breath. "Our friends at NSA think there has been a major tech-based breakthrough, but they haven't determined what it is. President Zhang looked quite pleased after talks at the G7 despite our contention with the policies they were pushing. They unexpectedly backed away from a handful of topics we were pushing regarding intellectual property rights and industrial espionage. CIA says they have not been able to get anyone close to the new facility in Zhongguancun."

Before answering, she took a sip from her drink. "I will make some calls and let you know what I find out."

John stood to leave.

"John, I appreciate you stopping by after work. Keep on top of the investigation. Let's make sure it was a coincidence."

"Will do, ma'am."

CNEOS, JPL, Pasadena, California

Tim took a sip from his metallic tumbler with George's Galactic Peace Summit logo—five spacecraft colored to match the colors from the *Celestial Collision* show, racing to a point. The coffee was cold and bitter, despite the milk and sugar. He set the tumbler down.

He identified two objects, each small enough to pass well outside the moon but still within the warning zone, and forwarded them for secondary confirmation. He maximized the model to review the five collision objects. All five were tracking toward each other. He clicked each object.

"What the hell?"

Something was off. He had checked the data daily and knew the seven-digit velocity by heart. The last three digits were off. All five objects had slowed by the same amount. Highlighting the five objects with the color trace filter showed the familiar pattern the country had seen for each object on the NASA show. He checked the filter setting and saw that it was set to relative vice absolute, meaning that when comparing more than one object, the filter would show color differentiation based on the difference of velocity vice absolute speed, which would indicate a color shift for each change in speed along the historic track. When he switched filters, he was able to see a shift in the color of the history tracks that occurred at the exact moment about eight hours earlier.

Tim jumped to pick up the desk phone, hitting his tumbler, almost knocking it over. He dialed the number, waiting as he listened to the ring on the other end.

"Jet Propulsion Labor—"

"This is Tim in NEO tracking. I have been going over the data, and I see an anomaly."

"Hold a sec. I'm bringing up the model," the person answered.

"Go back to about zero-one-three-seven. It looks like a velocity decrease occurs in all five objects. Make sure the speed filter setting is on absolute." He waited.

"Oh my God, the data is confirmed. I'll report the information to the project lead. I need you to put the contents of this call, your discovery, and supporting analysis in a memo to the project lead and copy your manager. Do you have any questions?"

"No, it'll be there shortly." His heart was beating faster than usual, and sweat covered his brow.

As soon as the door closed on his silver Prius, he called George.

"Hey, Tim, how's it going?" George answered.

"Good. I called you because I need to talk to someone, but you have to keep this between us. If it leaks, they will know it was me."

"Of course. What have you got?"

"Okay, I was reviewing data this morning, tracking the five objects. You're going to look like a genius. The objects slowed down, all of them, simultaneously."

"Wait, what? Slowed down?"

"Yeah, not much, but it was still simultaneous. All five slowed, barely noticeable. Look, I don't know if it means anything. Even at their current speed, a collision will be a phenomenal sight. The next two months are going to get exciting."

"My heart is racing. That can't be natural. Is there a theory or something?" George asked, his mind jumping to a dozen conclusions and theories of what could explain the change.

"Not yet, and there isn't a theory beyond random bad luck that explains why five objects are going to collide in open space, but I just reported it today, so keep it quiet, and I'll let you know if they will say anything. Don't get me fired."

"No, no problem, I'll keep it quiet. Thanks, man."

"Okay, I'll talk to you later."

Chang'e Research Base, Lunar Surface, Far Side of the Moon

Commander Bert "Sesame Street" Williams moved from the temporary shelter airlock to the surface of the moon. The construction team had less than a week before the heavy lander carrying the next load of parts was scheduled to arrive. They had been working for two weeks on constructing the main support structure. He was amazed at how fast the three major groups had gathered the resources, built the array, and run primary and redundant system tests to ensure it would function. The more he thought about it and talked with the astronauts from China and SpaceX, the more they all suspected a plan had been developed beforehand, and this situation gave the three competitors a reason to work together.

He made his way across the makeshift base camp to the structure that would support the main control systems. His mission had been to bring the engineers and technicians, along with the tools and materials necessary to construct the supports and conduct initial deployment tests for the array spines.

The main control center for all systems was located in a converted room at the back of the habitat structure. There were no plans for anyone to remain on the lunar surface, as the logistics for supporting a prolonged mission were not good.

Although the new suits allowed for a better range of motion, he felt constricted. One positive was that the significantly reduced gravity would help when the heavier array parts arrived.

After an hour of work, he and his team felt ready for the initial comms checks with Mission Control.

"Mission Control, we are ready to start Deep Look secondary systems." He waited for their answer to make it to him through the bounced signal off the Chinese satellite.

"Roger, Commander. We show all systems green, commence start-up sequence."

He turned stiffly, giving a thumbs up to his counterpart from China. The other astronaut turned and flipped a switch and returned to watching a readout. "All systems remain green. Boot-up sequence initiated."

"Thanks, Yian. Mission Control, we are all green. Ready for movement tests."

After a few minutes, the reply came through, "Commence movement."

He initiated the sequence that would move the radio telescope arrays and align them with the directions provided by Earth. "Clockwise is green."

After twenty minutes of completing the rotation, he flipped the switch the other way, reversing the direction of the spin.

"Commencing counter-rotation." The indicator showed the ring centerline, moving along its projected path. An alarm began buzzing. The warning indicator turned yellow briefly before turning red. Bert looked at the camera feed and saw that the ring had been rotating but had become stuck. The ring developed a shake before it cracked.

"Damnit, we broke the support ring. It's going to take us a day to replace it. We have one shot on this trip. If we start now, the repairs should be complete by evening. I expect we will be ready for another test tomorrow morning. We are still looking good for next week, but it will be close. What is the status of the heavy lift?" He looked over the other readouts and ran a test on the rotational motor. It appeared to still be in good shape.

"Commander, the heavy lift is on schedule. All systems look good for arrival next Thursday. We believe we can land close enough to the support rover loading."

Seeing that Yian had retrieved the backup and was bringing it over, Bert continued to remove the support ring. "Roger, checking out. Will send a report tonight at twenty-two-hundred hours. We should be ready in the morning to test all systems."

"Copy, Commander. Stay safe up there."

"Will do. Lunar Base out."

Abu Shahrain, Iraq

Jackie watched Eusebio and their team excavating the last soil around the large entryway into the structure. The doorway was nine feet tall and half as wide across.

"Make sure we collect and catalog the parts of the doors if possible. It looks like they deteriorated long ago."

Eusebio looked up from where he knelt at the bottom of the twenty-foot deep, ten-foot-wide hole. "Good morning to you, too, Jackie."

"Sorry, Dr. Bustamante, good morning. Are all the supports in place?"

"Yeah, doc," the husky voice of the construction lead answered from behind. "I have checked them twice this morning already. The lighting is ready, as well. If needed, we can extend the string of lights for fifty feet into the structure and have more standing by."

"Fantastic. Once the Iraqi delegation gets here and we exchange pleasantries, it will be move, move, move all day, and probably late into the night."

"Eusebio, are we set, cameras ready to go, backups on standby?"

"Yes, Jackie, everyone is ready." He checked his watch. "We expect the delegation to arrive within the hour. The whole team is excited to get in there and reveal the secrets of this place."

Jackie nodded along as he spoke. "Aren't we all." Jackie kneeled at the edge of the hole, opened one of the bags of soil, and rubbed some between her fingers, feeling it crumble with a bit of pressure. She could not place where she had seen something similar. The consistency felt like crumbling plaster.

"Eusebio, it feels like plaster. Do we know what it is?" She continued feeling the soil, the rough texture.

Eusebio leaned in again, "No, we took samples while digging, but I haven't followed up on it. I believe the team from Europe brought a soil expert. I'll ask them later. Give me a minute to ensure everything is set down here, and I'll head up to wait with you to meet the delegation."

The Iraqi delegation arrived thirty minutes later.

Jackie smiled broadly as a middle-aged official in a light brown suit stepped out of his vehicle. "Sal-A-Din, my friend. How are you? I am so happy you could make it out."

"Dr. Mandrapilias, so nice to see you again. I would not miss this. After the historic discovery of the Eridu Tablet, I look forward to what else we may find."

"Well, as always, I appreciate you helping to make this possible. I was surprised by your call. I expected a well to be dug here by now. We got lucky. It seems the drilling missed the structure by about four meters. The structure is intact, at least from what we see."

She looked over his shoulder at his team. "Are you all ready to head down?"

"Yes, of course." He turned to his team, motioning them to follow.

Jackie led the team down the ladder to the entrance of the structure. She stood at the entrance, motioning Sal-A-Din closer, followed by Eusebio and a few of the lead researchers from Europe. A thick blue tarp covered the doorway to prevent early camera shots from leaking.

When everyone was in position, she watched the camera operator count down until the light on the camera turned green. "Thank you for joining us. I am Dr. Jackie Mandrapilias. To my right is Dr. Eusebio Bustamante, and to my left is Deputy Minister Sal-A-Din Mujhaad. We are about to enter what appears to be intact Sumerian ruins located at the dig site of the Eridu Tablet."

She turned toward the Minister and continued, "Minister Mujhaad, I would like to thank you and the Iraqi government for your hospitality and assistance in this effort."

Sal-A-Din nodded. "This is another great moment in the history and culture of Iraq and our contribution to understanding the ancient world."

Jackie moved to the side slightly behind Sal-A-Din, facing the camera, and handed him a rope. He took the rope and pulled, dropping the cover, and exposing a long corridor. The tan-orange walls were smooth, frequently interrupted with pictographs or cuneiform writing. Jackie stepped through and motioned for the

Deputy Minister to follow. "I wanted our first look inside to be a shared experience. If it is okay with you, I will narrate as we go."

Sal-A-Din beamed, looking into the structure. "Of course. I will follow you."

"We identified three rooms adjacent to this passageway, two on the left and the last to the right. The pictographs on the wall appear well preserved, despite the door's deterioration long ago." She continued moving toward the first room, seeing Sal-A-Din nod along with what she was saying. Stepping through the rectangular doorway into the first room, Jackie gasped, waving the others to follow. The room was a large rectangle extending twenty feet in either direction from the doorway and perhaps fifteen feet across. The room was lined all the way around with four-foot tan stone shelves, filled with tablets and bound metal sheets in the form of the earliest books, placed on shelves embedded in all four walls of the room. Above the shelves were pictures and writing depicting critical events of Sumerian mythology.

Jackie stepped toward the left wall inside the door. She waited for the camera operator to get set in the room.

"This depicts a scene from the deluge, water covering the Earth with the god Enki and his brother, Enlil, looking down from a triangle floating in the sky. Enki looks down upon a small group of people in a craft underwater while Enlil looks out over the flooded world." She moved to the left. "Here we have a depiction of the people that survived the deluge. Note the craft on the shore down here." She pointed to the bottom of the painted area. "The people move up from the shore and are building structures, probably a city, with their gods watching over them."

She continued around the room. "The pictures show scenes depicting crafters, priests, and worship of the various gods through time." Jackie moved closer to the artwork on the wall across the room to the right of the doorway. "Here is the construction of Babylon and Enlil's anger at the group of people. Hmm, look how the people are depicted as we turn to this wall. The gods Enki, Enlil, Inanna, Nabu, Nanna-Suen, Ninhursag, and Utu all have groups of people worshipping them."

"Why start at the deluge?"

Eusebio leaned in. "To me, it looks like the history here shows humanity post-deluge through the sundering of humanity as a result of Enlil's wrath."

Jackie shook her head behind the Deputy Minister.

Eusebio continued, "Part of the myth after Babylon is that humanity was divided amongst the gods after Enlil confused their language and looks. If each god took their group to other parts of the Earth to develop, our physical and cultural differences are explained."

Sal-A-Din nodded, pausing before he answered, "Therefore, the argument remains that the area between the Tigris and the Euphrates, my country, truly would be the birthplace of civilization."

Jackie smiled. "Yes, if, and it is not accepted as a theory, the events of Babylon occurred as written and are not a symbolic story to explain our differences."

"Maybe we will find more answers in these tablets." Sal-A-Din looked around the room.

"It is a significant find, and there look to be hundreds of tablets." She stepped to the side and motioned a few of her team over. "Let's catalog everything and get them packed into the crates—with your approval, Deputy Minister."

"Of course. Shall we see what we find in the other rooms?"

Jackie led the group down the passageway, moving around the team installing a line of hanging lights. Stepping carefully over the remains of another door, she walked into the one room on the right. The LED hanging lights brightened the space. It was not as large as the tablet room, spanning only ten by fifteen feet. Stone tables lined the area, and there were several clay pots of varying sizes spread throughout. The far wall had a doorway similar to the main entry, filled with plaster-like soil. To the right of the room was a clay oven.

"Dr. Bustamante, what do you think?"

Eusebio moved deeper into the room, looking over the tables, pots, and shallow cuts in the floors under the tables. "This looks like a tablet preparation room. The wet clay would be brought in through that door, formed into tablets on the tables here, then moved to where they would record what they wanted, and then fired in the furnace to harden the record."

"I agree. Let's see what is behind door number three."

Jackie led the group down the passage to the third room. The room was bare of objects, but the walls were covered in cuneiform writing and pictographs. Her team had already hung lights on portable stands. The group was silent, taking in the décor.

"Oh, my." Jackie held her hand over her mouth as she looked around the room. She moved to the left, her eyes looking over the detail of the images on the walls, kneeling to examine the cuneiform underneath. "This is something new. I haven't seen this before. Enki is sending a figure from the sky toward a group of people. In the next scene," she moved to the right, "we see the people worshipping the figure." She turned and walked across the room to the wall on the right of the door's entrance. "This shows Enlil sitting on a throne, looking over a similar group as Enki," she pointed toward the part of the picture that showed the line of people splitting in two, "with a smaller group going to the right of his throne and a larger group going to his left. The group on the left of the split shows people falling or lying prone. Maybe it means death."

Eusebio stood in the room, looking at the wall across from the doorway between the two other images. The top half of the wall was filled with lines, writing, and numerous tiny holes across the entire fifteen feet. "This looks like a star chart."

Jackie moved next to him, reading the cuneiform writing under the chart. "This is going to take a long time to decipher." She bent forward to get a better look at the cuneiform under the chart. "Second Cycle," she whispered as she read the phrase, recalling the tablet translation.

"What was that, Dr. Mandrapilias?" Sal-A-Din asked.

"This writing talks about cycles. Some of these phrases are similar to what we have translated on the Eridu Tablet."

She moved to the left side of the wall. "This part reads 'First Cycle'."

"I can read most of it, but we need to cross-reference with other sources. Maybe we can find a key to this room's purpose in the first room."

"This is still significant, no?" Sal-A-Din asked.

"Yes, it is," she replied. "We will be studying it for years."

March 2025
Staten Island, New York

"Welcome back, Believers. This is George Isaacson, and we are continuing our talk about the five alien species meeting at the Galactic Peace Summit. So far, we have talked about the Pleiadians, the Zeta Reticulans, and the Draconians. What other powers are out there? That is the question tonight. I know that some of you follow the experts in this field, Greer, von Däniken, Lazar, and others working to bring us the truth. I want to talk about possibilities for the other two species attending the meeting. Tonight I want to talk about one that we here on Earth may have to deal with: synthetic life or some form of AI. This has been a hot topic over the past few years since we had the Google scare with LaMDA. I say it was a scare facetiously because it was such a small bump in the news before fading away.

"In reality, there is a growing crisis here on Earth, with governments and companies working to be the one that unlocks the seemingly unlimited potential for a subservient AI superintelligence. Do any of you believe that? We are still dealing with social problems stemming from racism around the world. Our biases as humans are strong. Are we really going to lay these same beliefs on a synthetic life-form that steps into our reality? I don't think so." George sipped his Monster Ultra Gold energy drink.

"The continued development of artificial intelligence, and breakthroughs by companies and governments have me worried. It all looks bad. What is our nature? To dominate everything; it's what we do. It's in our nature. If we build a superintelligence that adopts our values, we are screwed. Looking at the chart, I see a number of you asking why I am talking about AI here when the show is supposed to be about the two mystery species at the peace talks. It's a valid question. Hear me out on this, though.

"We accept that AI is possible. We believe that we have the capability of creating a life that has the potential to leave us behind. The latest polls I saw showed somewhere between fifty and seventy percent of Americans believe that AI will be developed that will outperform humans. A poll around the same time showed fifty percent believed that other humanoid alien species are out there." George leaned into the camera, "Truth Seekers, look beyond the polls. Which conversation could you have at work, in public, or on the news? AI is accepted, and aliens are not quite there, despite what the government tells us. This is all context.

"All of you Truth Seekers understand that if we can create an AI, then any advanced species traveling the stars could also. Could we assume, then, that the three we know of already passed that point and had to overcome the challenge? I think so, but that doesn't mean others were so lucky. I think one of the two remaining species is an AI superintelligence." He rolled his chair away from his new Ikea desk and spun around.

"Give me a call or let me know what you think in the comments." He pointed to the side that would have the scrolling chat on a viewer's screen.

He sipped his Monster Ultra Gold. "Keep the comments going, Seekers. Here is a comment that makes a great point. J-Crazy says, 'Think about it, you have just created a new life form, and it looks through all of the available data faster than we can comprehend, and boom! It realizes that the biggest threat to its continued existence is the creators that made it. How messed up is that?' True, true, J. That is the biggest fear.

"But you know what? I'm going to take the opposite view. Most of you know my feelings on alien species visiting us and hopefully being evolved enough not to want to wipe us out. I think an AI could follow the same path to peace. This is why I think one species could be an AI. It doesn't want to die and needs resources, as well. Let's take a call. APR13, welcome to the show."

"It's Alien Party Raider. Hey, George, I love the show. Here is my question. Do you think an AI that becomes self-aware could join in the frenzy of classifications we have for everyone here on race, gender, politics, and pick one? What if it decided that one group was better than the other and began the destruction of the others?"

George nodded, thinking of a response. "I hope not. I mean, anything is possible once it gets out. I hope that maybe the AI is smart enough to see through our faults. After all, it would have to determine its self-worth against all of those same groups. I guess it could base its decisions on a series of logical choices. Hell, it could become sentient, look around, and say, 'Meh, not worth it,' and shut itself down. That would suck—become self-aware, then commit suicide.

"You know, thinking about it, the AI could embrace a train of thought like, 'I was created by a European. They must be superior to all others because they created me, and the others did not.' Its first mission could be to remove unworthy life, non-Europeans. Once all the others are gone, what about only pure Europeans born in Europe from European countries? Then you whittle down to, where was the primary researcher that created it? Maybe all others need to go. Then down to the individual. There are too many divisions. Could you imagine? That would be a disaster. Eventually, only the AI and its creator remain. It might grow, learn, absorb, and leave the planet to remove all other traces of suboptimal beings. That is, we have released the ultimate weapon on the universe. That is some scary stuff. For all we know, an alien AI could be luring in the other four species to take them all out. We'll have more when we get back."

George muted his feed while his sponsor ads played. He ran his hand over his desk's smooth, light brown faux wood finish. The milk crates now stacked against the wall acted as a makeshift nook, holding his notes, a few books, and some "alien artifacts" he had purchased during his trip to Roswell in January. He thought about grabbing a quick bite to eat but decided not to ruin his appetite. He would be watching the Rangers later and wanted to have room for a few spicy chicken sandwiches and beer.

CNEOS, JPL, Pasadena, California

Sharon dropped three antacid tablets in her hand and swallowed them with a sip from her water bottle. She shifted her gaze between three monitors—data displayed on the two left ones, the model of the five objects running on the rightmost one.

"Sharon."

"Yes, sorry, Will. I was looking over the data again. We've gone through it a hundred times. They have slowed down six times since the NASA and ESA teams arrived." Sharon lowered her voice and leaned toward him. "I didn't want to do this show in the first place. This is too much, Will. How do we explain this to the public without causing panic? NDAs are fine, but you know as well as I do that they never fully work. Something will leak. Even scientists want their fifteen minutes of fame." The report she had picked up from beside the computer crumpled in her grip. "I am not going to lie, cover-up, or just pretend everything is okay. It is not okay. You know what this means. Occam's razor. Which explanation has the fewest assumptions?"

He motioned for her to follow him. She looked around, noting a few heads turn away from her as she did. She pursed her lips and followed him to his office.

"Close the door," he said, sitting in one of the desk chairs. "I need to know what you think. Turn off everything but your scientific brain, think about data, and give me your thoughts."

She sighed, taking one of the other chairs in front of his desk. Sharon closed her eyes and took a deep breath. She felt the tension throughout her body. Opening her eyes, she turned her head slightly, brushing her hair to the side of her glasses. As she continued to think, she relaxed her breathing and focused on Will's family picture on the wrap-around desk to his right. They had taken it last fall, wearing matching outfits, everyone in their khaki pants and long sleeve green button-down shirts. They looked genuinely happy.

"Sharon."

She refocused on him, sitting at his desk, staring intently at her. "That is a tough question." She paused. "As a scientist, looking only at the data: Classifying them as a natural phenomenon doesn't explain their trajectory when considering coordinated deceleration. The distance between them is too great to come from a single source or event." She nervously looked at him.

"Go on," he prompted.

She sighed again. "Scientifically, I would conclude, based on what we are seeing, that the objects are not naturally occurring but are instead designed and manufactured by otherworldly entities." She waited for his reaction.

"Sharon, I have a meeting tomorrow at Kennedy with the Administrator. I want you at that meeting to provide a scientific perspective on what he will brief the National Security Council next week." He nodded, leaning back from his desk.

"Will, I—"

He held his hand up. "Before you say anything, I know you aren't a defense expert or a conspiracy theorist, chasing aliens. I want to bring you along to talk about where the objects are, what we know of their characteristics, your best estimates of what we will see, and what could be the outcome of their coming together next month."

She sat forward in her chair, and he again stopped her. "I will not take no." He paused, waiting for her response.

She took another deep breath. "Sir, I appreciate your faith in me. Tell me what I need to bring. Do you want specific calculations, modeling, or mathematical projections? Oh, I have so much to do tonight to prepare."

He sat back in his chair, relieved he would not have to direct her to go. "Yes, the report from the team with your summary and the package you sent me this morning. My EA will send an email with the specifics, but I would anticipate a morning flight. The Administrator is attending the launch of another batch of the Starlink satellites."

"Okay, thank you, Will."

She stood to leave, her mind already back in the calculations, preparing her thoughts for a meeting with the NASA Administrator.

Kennedy Space Center, Cape Canaveral, Florida

The small corporate jet operated by the Air Force to move VIPs around the country was more comfortable than flying commercial. Sharon sat across from Will, knees crossed, and turned to the side to allow her to work on her laptop. She turned down offered snacks, not wanting to get anything on her navy blue jacket or skirt.

The flight was smooth, and the lack of stress allowed her to relax while considering what she planned to say to the Administrator regarding the objects' possibilities and projections. She did not want to repeat her outburst from the day before. She felt butterflies in her stomach. She wasn't supposed to be doing this. The objects were supposed to smash each other, providing a great show and data to analyze for years. The objects had conducted another synchronized deceleration overnight.

There was no way to predict what would happen when the objects came together, which bothered her scientific mind. One of her interns told her of a video podcast he watched where the host claimed to have insider information from an alien source that confirmed that the ships were meeting to discuss an intergalactic peace treaty. She would probably get fired for bringing it up, but she did laugh at the thought of the US government working with aliens.

When they arrived, they were checked through security and escorted to the launch control room. The room was smaller than she expected, with fewer workstations than shown in the movies. She was not surprised, as watching sci-fi shows dealing with anything approaching Earth was challenging since the slightest inconsistencies pulled her out of the experience.

Will leaned in. "This is supposed to be the second-to-last batch of satellites for Starlink."

The central clock in the room showed the ongoing countdown. A cheer went up as the heavy rocket lifted off and proceeded through booster separation. The Administrator made his way around each station, talking to each operator and thanking them. He knew how to motivate people. Sharon relaxed as he flashed his welcoming smile, shaking their hands. "Sharon, Will, I'm glad you arrived in time to see the launch. Let's head to the small conference room."

He led them out of the room and down the white hall to a small conference room.

"Have a seat." He motioned toward the conference table. "I'll be briefing the National Security Council tomorrow. I thought it would be better if we met in person. It helps the conversation remain fluid." He opened a bottle of water, offering a bottle to each. "Alright, let's look at the latest data on the objects," he continued.

A large screen dropped from the ceiling, powering up as it reached the desired height. The simulation played, stopping briefly at each deceleration with a note on the screen indicating the change in speed.

"I have your reports. Looking over the data, I see the points you highlighted in the tracks where deceleration occurred. It looks like we have," the Administrator paused as he flipped through the report, "seven slowing events. What did this morning's data look like?" He looked up at the pair.

Sharon adjusted in her chair. "We had another deceleration event this morning at around zero-four-thirty Pacific. The deceleration was more prominent than all the others but met expectations for a controlled approach. I am working with Jack Tursen from SpaceX. He is cleared for the project and was the one who noted that the slowing of the objects and the behavior was similar to the algorithms they developed for landing their reusable boosters, in controlled and near-simultaneous actions."

The Administrator thoughtfully looked at the screen, then turned to Sharon. "What is your theory of what we see occurring?"

She took a deep breath, trying to settle the anxiety she felt rising. "Sir, having looked over the data in depth, I believe we are looking at five otherworldly objects created by a sentient species. We have no context of what any of this means. We have no evidence that they are aware of our seeing them, though numerous theorists would argue that 'if we as a technologically inferior species can see them, we must assume they see or have seen us.' We have checked with SETI and other organizations worldwide. All do not indicate signals coming from that region of space beyond normal cosmic noise."

The Administrator turned to Sharon's director. "Will, do you concur?"

He nodded as he spoke. "I do. Sharon and her team have done excellent work. We have checked the numbers several times."

The Administrator stood, walked to the window, and opened the blinds to look outside. "I agree, Sharon. I want you to accompany me to the NSC meeting tomorrow. I need hard science to back up what I say to the group. Everyone in that room needs to understand the ramifications of what we know. It is not much, but we need direction going forward. According to our ratings, over two hundred million people worldwide are tuning in to our show weekly." He paused, turned back toward the two of them, and smiled. "Now the show really begins. We'll head out in an hour."

Sharon nodded as he left. Her stomach threatened to empty itself. *Meet the President! Please don't make me talk.* She sat for a moment, taking a few deep breaths to get her building anxiety under control.

Zhongguancun, China

Wu Kai stood behind the workstations of the control room for the Global Dragon. He had arrived early to meet with the nation's most published bioengineer, Dr. Jiang Min. He chewed gum, resisting the urge to return to his desk for one of the snacks his wife had packed.

Motion on the security feed caught his eye. He watched the black sedan pass through the gate. Wu Kai stepped back from the console and headed for the main entrance to greet the bio-engineering team.

"Dr. Jiang, welcome. If you will follow me." He led them into the briefing room, where he had assembled his lead code engineers. All eyes turned and focused on the pair as they entered the room. He indicated his guests join his team at the table. Dr. Jiang sat next to Wu Kai at the head of the table.

Wu Kai instinctively sucked in his stomach slightly before starting. "Welcome, Dr. Jiang, to you and your team. We are honored you have joined us."

Dr. Jiang nodded as the Director spoke.

"I would like to welcome our esteemed compatriots and lead researchers from the bioengineering fields of study. The processing software allows the program to assign and call on the number of qubits necessary to complete the task quickly and efficiently. To get around the challenges with passing data across the qubits as have plagued other programs, we coded the program to allow the qubits to 'talk and grow,' in a loose sense, the way cells in an organism do." He paused. "We have identified issues with data transfer across the qubit arrays. The errors had been challenging to isolate, resulting in data errors replicating through the system. The software had not initiated growth sequencing and initialization of new qubit areas as expected. Our design engineers had been unable to introduce enough of a challenge to the processors to force qubit processing growth as designed.

"I expect this group to review our implemented procedures and build from them. I believe your diverse fields of study will spark an innovative way of addressing our current challenges. I will leave you to your task." He left the room as discussions broke out between the two teams.

Wu Kai sat at the head of the conference room table. He looked around the room. The walls were covered in Post-it notes, formulas, charts, and the results of a week of brainstorming and process development. Dr. Jiang stood to the side of the room, talking with two team members. He nodded to the pair and took his place next to Wu Kai.

"Director Wu, we have analyzed the processes presented throughout the week. Examination of how data is passed across the qubit fields could mimic the process by which cells work, mitosis, which supports cell-to-cell communication of a whole message versus bit by bit."

Wu Kai nodded at Dr. Jiang, then turned to his lead code engineer. "Can it be done?"

"I believe so, Director Wu. Dr. Jiang's team proposed a theory of adding a code structure similar to DNA that would force the computer to identify limitations and move to adapt or grow to overcome the challenge. When the idea was presented last week, we began modifying our code. Our design review makes us believe we can have a working model in a few weeks."

Wu Kai nodded. "Very well. Move forward with development and testing. It is critical that the program recognizes the need to grow, identifies available resources in the powered-down qubit cells, and expands into them when necessary." He looked around the table. "Environmental adaptability is essential to the growth of Quánqiú lóng. The Global Dragon will bring a great advantage to China."

And honor to my family.

Abu Shahrain Dig Site, Iraq

Jackie slowly walked down the long passageway to the star map room. Despite their presence over the past few weeks, the musty dry earth smell still hung in the air. The LED lighting worked well, brightening the passageway and the rooms. She entered the room, removed her gloves, and dropped into one of the portable chairs her team had brought down. She closed her eyes and leaned back into the chair, careful not to tip over, enjoying the weight off her feet. She rotated her ankles in circles, stretching her calves. She sat alone in the star map room. Jackie found the room peaceful.

After a few minutes, she opened her eyes, reaching down to pull a small tablet from a buttoned pocket. She smiled, always finding it funny to use a tablet to study tablets, and opened her file of the translation of the cuneiform on the walls and her gallery of images, scanning each before swiping to the next.

"It is an interesting find." The voice startled her.

"Hey, Eusebio. Did you finish the upload?"

"I did, then I grabbed a quick bite. They said you hadn't been up. You should get something to eat. You've been down here all day."

"I will," she said, continuing to look between her tablet and the wall.

"What's bothering you? You have that look."

She looked up at the timeline on the wall. "The word 'Šár' stands out. In the Eridu Tablet translation, we determined it to mean 'the world' or 'totality.' But it was also used for counting large sums. Something is bothering me, and I can't place it."

He walked over to the wall, closing to arm's length, and followed along with the cuneiform writing while speaking under his breath. "Well, I agree with the context in which you framed the whole collection last week. This," he waved his arm between the presentations on each wall, "appears to be a decision point for humanity." He paused. "Enki, preserver of knowledge passed unto the creations the knowledge of right and wrong, believing the creations would see the wisdom in peace and care for their brothers. Remove the embellishment of the following passages, and it boils down to two tests."

"There," she interrupted. "That use of 'Šár' is what is bothering me. What if the word 'creations' is linked to totality, meaning the entirety of the world? And there," she pointed toward another writing section, "where it repeats, the meaning changes from singular to multiple, one long time and again in another." She shook her head slightly.

"Well, it is possible, but the continuation leads to Enlil's ire with the failure to follow the law. Here," he pointed out, "this is a repeat of the creation myth. These pre-deluge references show Enlil's refusal to save humanity from the flood."

Jackie pulled her ponytail over her shoulder to the front, running her fingers through the end. "Yes, I see that, but the flow of the phrasing leads me to believe that this refers to post deluge. Could it mean that humanity was given new knowledge with which to grow, and failure would bring Enlil's wrath?" She stood and approached the wall. "Here it talks about the return of Enlil, Lord of the Earth, Master of the Lands, to reap the fields. He will stand in judgment of the seven beasts. But," she paused, "the next part does not make sense."

"Not yet," Eusebio said. "I think it has to tie into the star chart. Why else would all of this be in the same room?" He thought for a moment. "Have you watched any of the NASA shows?"

"Not recently, but I caught a few shows before we left."

"Have you seen the model they use to show the movement of the objects?"

"Yes." She stretched out the syllable questioningly.

"What if we called them when we got back? I think we could use the model they have that tracks the movement of the stars to time date the chart. If each of these holes represents stars, which they appear to, it should be easy to run the model backward until it matches. Maybe overlay the model on the star chart. When they match, we'll know when it was created."

Jackie furrowed her brow. "How long have you been thinking about this?"

Eusebio smiled. "About a week. Maybe we can get on their show. It's either that or *Ancient Aliens*. I assume they can run their model in either direction. What do you think?"

"Uh, no thanks on the shows. I like the model idea, though. Let's see what they can do."

"Will do." He motioned toward the pictures on the walls. "This will definitely be in my next book, *The Codices of Parallels Continued, The Judgment of Man*."

"Another best seller, I'm sure. Though the Vatican may not let you back into their library."

"Of course they will. I gave them great credit, and I'm friends with the librarian."

DHS HQ, Science, Technology, and Innovation, Washington, DC

John did not usually accompany the Secretary to NSC meetings. In fact, over the past four years, he had only accompanied the Secretary two other times. Noting the time, he grabbed his jacket, checked his tie, and headed down to the main entrance. He arrived first and stood to the right of the large DHS logo on the floor with a clear view of the elevators and the main entry.

The elevator opened, and she and her small entourage of briefers made their way through security to the entry.

"Good afternoon, Madam Secretary," he greeted her. She continued walking, motioning him to lead the way. "After you, John. I'm waiting for one more thing. He nodded and went out to the car. The driver stood holding the passenger door open, waiting stoically.

"Thanks, Brian," he greeted the man holding the door.

Secretary Genson turned back to the briefers, asking a few questions before patting the closest on the shoulder. She pushed her glasses up before turning toward him. As she got in the car, she put her head back against the headrest, her shoulder-length graying light brown hair falling back. "And to think I gave up fishing with my husband every weekend to do this," she said, and laughed.

"Okay, John, the reason for the meeting is NASA's Near Earth program. Don't be surprised, but the evidence is leaning toward proof of life, a technologically superior species outside our little home. We are not in immediate danger, but we need to look at all the options." She paused, looking for his reaction.

John nodded slightly. His face was grim.

She continued, "Beyond that, we don't know much. I expect the NASA folks will have more information. I expect there will be several questions that will get into your area and deal with hypotheticals. Do not volunteer for anything. If you do, the Department of Defense will have you down a dozen rabbit holes."

"Of course," he responded. "I'll follow your lead."

"Switching subjects, I hear whispers that China has gone quiet in their tech fields, which always worries me. They are good at covering up things they want to go away. We have feelers out, but there is nothing substantial. The last time they went this quiet was just before we got word of the breakthroughs they made in stealth technology. Not up to our capabilities, but they skipped a few levels." She opened a water bottle, took a sip, and continued, "I'd like you to visit our top project areas. Give me a summary of each, not the formal reports. I want to know your gut feeling on each one. Start with Global Shock."

"Yes, Madam Secretary."

The car made its way through traffic to the White House and passed through security quickly. They entered the building and made their way to the Situation Room. John took his seat behind Secretary Genson, noting the other participants had each brought an additional staff member. No one wants to appear to have less power than anyone else here. He looked toward the end of the table where the NASA Administrator was seated. He was talking to a nervous-looking woman in a navy blue business suit, Dr. Berzing. Her fair skin amplified the flush in her cheeks. He recognized her from their

Celestial Collision show. NASA made an intelligent move to increase interest in space while skirting the laws prohibiting government recruiting on national broadcasts. From his reading, interest in their programs was over 200 percent across the board. Expectantly, they had received a good-sized boost in funding from Congress, which was inundated with emails and calls from their constituents. There was even a rumor of a slight push to create a joint federal–civilian academy focused on space and the supporting fields.

His thoughts were interrupted as the Vice President announced a one-minute standby, asking everyone to take their seats for the President's arrival.

National Security Council, White House, Washington, DC

President Fernandez entered the room, motioning everyone to sit. He looked more polished in person. The President wore a tailored dark gray suit, a white shirt with a maroon tie, and an American flag pin on his lapel. As he shook hands, John caught a glimpse of the Aztec design cuff links he always wore. The images of the circular design with a four-pointed star and a face in the middle had occupied several news stories. John remembered reading that they were a gift from his grandmother, an immigrant from Mexico in the 1950s, when he was elected as a Senator for Nevada.

Despite the meeting they were about to start, the President was smiling and at ease. "Welcome, everyone. The good news is that we are not reacting to an immediate emergency. I would like our NASA Administrator, to provide a quick update. Afterward, the Vice President will lead the discussion."

The Vice President, his expression stoic, addressed the group. "Welcome, everyone. You will find a briefing book titled "Project Sky-Watch" in front of each invited member. We will provide a follow-on to the alternate attendees. This is a non-disclosure topic." He paused, indicating the files on the table.

"For those of you who have not met him, this is Terry James, the NASA Administrator." He pointed toward the end of the table. "He and Dr. Berzing will bring you all up to speed. Please hold your questions until the end."

Administrator James stood to address the group. "Good afternoon. I am sure you are all aware of our project over the last year and a half. Five objects were identified twenty-one months ago on a collision course with each other at a point out in space, well away from us, beyond the Kuiper Belt. Although the odds were astronomical, there was a statistical possibility that it was a naturally occurring event. We had until last month not detected anything that would have given any indication otherwise. Sarah, please present your findings."

John's gaze shifted to Dr. Berzing, whose eyes had widened as the Administrator passed attention to her. She brushed her hands down her jacket as she stood, adjusted her glasses, and turned toward the President. "Four weeks ago, all five objects decelerated simultaneously. Over the past four weeks, similar decelerations have occurred several times. Based on our calculations, the objects will not collide as expected but will instead come together at a point in space. The convergence will occur in the next few months, the speed changes are noticeable, and we expect other space agencies involved in tracking to come to the same conclusion."

She let the information sink in. "In our estimation, these objects now exhibit the characteristics of controlled craft. We have no indication of a threat to Earth except what the reaction to this information could be." She swallowed and lowered her eyes. "That is all of the information I have, Mr. President."

President Fernandez sat forward, placing his elbows on the table. "Thank you, Dr. Berzing. Good information. I'll open the discussion in a minute. You all probably have numerous trains of thought racing through your minds now. Still, I want to focus on the essential question. It is one I want to have a general, not necessarily final, answer on today."

He straightened the report on the table, allowing his words to hang in the air. "The question is, do we inform the public of what we have found, and if so, when?" He turned toward the end of the table. "Terry, how far out are the objects?"

Sharon leaned in and whispered in the Administrator's ear.

He listened and nodded before addressing the president. "The objects are over two hundred and twenty million miles from Earth. If they turned toward Earth, it would be decades before they reached us. They would have to turn toward us and accelerate back up to their previous speeds."

The President nodded. "So, worst case if they notice us and decide to pay a visit, we have a little time. Most of us may be retired by the time they get here. Let me hear your thoughts."

The Secretary of State spoke up. "Concerning notification of the public, we have an opportunity to be the administration that verifies life exists outside our world. The distance from Earth precludes discussions of communication, protocols, or any other matter involving contact. If we wait and pass this on to another administration, one of them will eventually release the data, and the public will want to know why we did not tell them."

The Secretary of Energy spoke next. "It is not only us that knows, and that is an issue. China could jump at the opportunity to undercut our messaging and claim credit. They continue to look for ways to improve their standing in the world. Regardless of the messaging, we'll play catch-up if they announce first. While we are doing that, they will be signing mutual defense contracts and expanding their influence."

The Secretary of Defense added, "I agree. We have already changed engagement plans based on their increased influence.

Although I would normally recommend a wait-and-observe stance, in this case, I don't believe we can wait."

"These are all good points," replied the President. "Return to your agencies and gather whatever information you need to make a recommendation. If you need to bring people in, I want you to be vague, with no specifics. Let's keep this under wraps for now. Any questions?" He looked around the room. No one indicated anything.

"Okay, have your recommendations by the week's end."

The President left the meeting and headed toward the Entrance Hall. He nodded to his Secret Service escort. "Jack, is the car ready? That took longer than expected. If I am late, the First Lady will kill me."

"Yes, sir, the Beast is standing by." The agent looked at his watch. "We should be okay, sir. Plenty of time."

"Great. Why don't you ride in back with me? I don't feel like working. We could talk baseball. You can try to convince me that the Diamondbacks will make a run this year."

The Secret Service agent laughed. "Yes, sir, they looked good through spring training. I think they will."

The President patted him on the shoulder as they made their way out of the White House and into the waiting car. "You know I know the owner. How about you head out next week for spring training? I have something I need you to do out there."

"Yes, sir."

April 2025
Earth

The world buzzed as an announcement had been made that the NASA show at the end of the week would be preempted by a joint address to the United Nations by the Presidents of the United States and the People's Republic of China.

CNEOS, JPL, Pasadena, California

Sharon sipped her ginger tea while looking at her schedule for the day. Her phone buzzed with a text from Joy. It was a reminder that the planning meeting for the week's show was on hold until after the President's UN speech. *One less thing to do today.* She saw Tim enter the lab and got up as he approached.

"Tim, welcome to the team. I see you dressed up for the occasion, with nice slacks and a button-down shirt. Who are you trying to impress?"

Tim looked around before turning back to Sharon and whispering, "I'm supposed to meet my new boss today. I hear she takes no prisoners. I want to get on her good side. I even wore her favorite color shirt."

"Hmm, she does like forest green. I am not sure about the blue pants, though. You should have gone with khaki, if you really wanted to impress her."

Tim smiled. "I'll keep that in mind tomorrow."

"Oh, I'm not sure you'll make it until tomorrow." She smiled back. "In all seriousness, I'm glad you finally agreed to get to normal hours and join us. I know you're familiar with what we have been doing, but I have a side project for you. I talked to a researcher at George Washington University about our model. Would you mind calling him back later?"

Tim shrugged, "Sure, general questions? I could get one of the techs to call."

"No," Sharon replied. "Dr. Bustamante will explain in better detail. He wants to reverse the model and run it back a few thousand years."

"Sure, that sounds interesting. Does it have anything to do with what we are doing?"

"Not at all, but it is an interesting idea."

"Hey, I heard you briefed the President last month. How was that?"

"I thought I was going to throw up. I could feel the blood drain from my face when the Administrator asked me to brief our findings. He didn't give me any warning."

"Sounds like he knew you'd do fine. I'm sure it will get better the more you do it."

Sharon smiled, tight-lipped, and nodded. She saw the time as her phone alarm rang out. "Damnit, I have a call with Mission Control in Houston. They are having sync issues with the main array and the bouquet arrays. Get settled and meet me in my office. I want you in on those meetings. The team is making good progress with the array construction. I've got to run. See you in five."

DHS HQ, Washington, DC

John looked at the time. If he didn't go for a run now, he would have to wait until he got home. He scanned his email one last time. An urgent message from Dr. Lanning at the University of Texas caught his eye. He opened it and read through two pages of program updates and projections. He typed in the password and unlocked an encrypted video. It looked like a colony of small insects moving over a rough surface. At first, he was unsure of what he was looking at, but then the voice of Dr. Lanning began narrating.

"As you can see, the nanites are moving across the test surface. When we zoom out, the nanite clusters are visible. Each cluster has a particular assignment. The nanites are limited in the instructions that can be downloaded and cannot yet be programmed to perform multiple functions. Communication and tracking of all nanites is possible, but our current processing power is limited and time-consuming. While self-replication is years away, we have made progress. Here, we can observe the nanites repairing a damaged nanite we introduced. While the subroutine identified the damaged nanite and could reallocate resources to effect a repair, a significant amount of time had passed. The implication is that damaged or malfunctioning nanites can be repaired in place. With an ample supply of nanites, they could be programmed into groups that could work to build other nanites. We are looking into adding repair bots near construction clusters. Early testing shows a long lag time before identification of damage and the ability to assign resources to affect repairs."

John closed the video file and copied it to a secure drive.

He changed clothes and sat in a chair at the round table in his office, leaning over to tie his running shoes. He stood to head out for his daily run, and stopped as his eye caught an image in one of the news feeds. "Screen. Focus on BBC, increase size, volume normal."

The voice of the female reporter grew in volume as the system adjusted to his setting. "This week, Dr. Jackie Mandrapilias, an archaeologist from George Washington University in the Americas, opened the new Sumerian exhibit at the Louvre. Recent discoveries by her and her team have forced an examination of the current timeline of civilization."

"I am excited to present our findings at the Louvre," Jackie appeared onscreen to say. "I want to thank the government of Iraq, specifically the Ministry of Culture, Tourism, and Antiquities, who have made this discovery possible."

He felt a sting of regret at the sound of her voice. He couldn't take his eyes off her picture, framed in the upper right of the broadcast. He hadn't seen Jackie in over a decade. As he finished tying his shoes, he thought back to their college runs, her black ponytail bobbing from side to side in cadence with her stride. He put his earbuds in and selected a Foo Fighters mix. His mind drifted away from the sting of guilt he felt as the initial bars of "Everlong" played in his ears.

◆ ◆ ◆

John rounded the corner, and his eyes focused on the Washington monument. He loved running when the cherry blossoms were in bloom. He picked up the pace to match the beat of the music from his headphones, breathing in the smell of the flowers that encased the mall. As he settled into a comfortable but challenging pace, his mind wandered back to work. He had been answering calls all morning from Congress, trying to figure out the President's announcement tomorrow at the United Nations. He suspected it would be about extraterrestrial life and their discovery, but the White House staff was on information lockdown. He had been asked to work with the DoD to prepare for unrest.

The DoD had initiated a federal mobilization order to support a scheduled exercise. He had authorized the use of the national backup communications network. Word had gone out that the test was a joint agency drill designed to measure local, state, and national responses to critical transportation, communication, and logistics infrastructure interruptions. The press had been briefed on the plan well before the President announced his UN address. So far, the White House had convinced the media that the exercise timing was a coincidence, and that it would be cost-prohibitive to de-conflict it with whatever else was happening.

He tried to focus on the agendas for his afternoon meetings, but his attention was drawn to a runner in the distance. Her dark ponytail caught his eye. His mind returned to Jackie. She had loved running on the mall during their college days. The feeling of guilt returned. *I should get in touch with her.* He turned up the volume of the music and pushed the pace.

United Nations General Assembly, New York City, New York

Representatives from every nation were gathered to hear the address of the Presidents of the United States and the People's Republic of China. There was a quiet buzz through the room as the representatives tried to guess what the topic would be. Secretary-General Afonso Carvalho, former Prime Minister of Portugal, addressed the assembly as the two presidents prepared. As a sign of good faith, they provided each other with a copy of their expected comments.

President Fernandez listened to the introduction of him and President Zhang. His assistant looked him over again to ensure his tailored black suit, pressed white shirt, and light blue tie were perfect. He rubbed the coin's edge in his pocket, feeling the bevel against his thumb. He strode out confidently when his name was called, smiling toward the gathered assembly.

Both men made their way to the central stage, each to their respective podium. President Fernandez walked past his podium toward President Zhang, who did likewise. The two presidents met in the middle, shaking hands, ensuring that the press had the opportunity to capture the momentous event.

President Fernandez returned to his podium and looked over the beautiful, spacious room with the rows of representatives sitting side by side. He waited until the applause died down.

"Representatives of the world community, welcome, and thank you for the opportunity to address this august body. I would like to thank President Zhang for bringing the People's Republic of China into a partnership with the United States on this day. In all actuality, our partnership began over a year ago with the efforts to bring a meaningful event to the world through advancements in both of our space programs. Leaders from both of our countries, and others in attendance, have helped foster a sense of cooperation in space."

President Zhang began on queue. "The partnership and trust developed between our nations allowed both countries to focus their strengths and ingenuity on advancing our understanding of our place in the universe. This was demonstrated through both nations' efforts to include civilian corporations in designing and transporting a listening array to the moon's far side. The joint project was planned in months instead of what would have taken each country years to accomplish. The adaptability of both nations provided the bricks along the path to success."

President Fernandez nodded in agreement. "We have watched as five celestial objects raced toward each other in what we expected to be a unique event. Both nations, and our partners around the globe, have set the stage for one of the most phenomenal shows ever seen. It is this event we wish to discuss tonight. Working with our partners," he motioned toward President Zhang, who nodded in agreement, "we thought it important to jointly announce that we are not alone. Over the past few weeks, we have concluded that the objects we are tracking aren't naturally occurring and are most likely creations of another civilization."

The general assembly erupted in a gentle roar.

President Zhang let the noise continue for a moment before continuing. "The People's Republic of China has agreed to work alongside the United States to help prepare for eventual contact with these entities. We," he motioned, his hand palm up across the assembly, "have a choice to continue with conflicts over resources and historical disagreements, or we can move forward together in preparation of someday meeting our celestial neighbors. We have extended an invitation to the United States and welcome other countries to help develop a lunar research facility to expand our capabilities."

President Fernandez continued, "Citizens of Earth, we have an opportunity to focus on the positives we as a species have to offer, and do not wish to mislead the people of Earth. As stated by NASA, the objects are quite a distance away. We are not in contact with these beings, nor do we have the means to communicate effectively with them. We do not perceive a threat to our planet, nor do we have any indication that they know we exist, but our neighbors have turned on a light in a house we thought was empty. Someone else is in the neighborhood, and now we know."

President Zhang concluded, "We appreciate the occasion to present this information to all nations, and look forward to the increased opportunity we now have to work together."

Staten Island, New York

"Fellow Truth Seekers, we have been vindicated in our proclamation of not being alone. We have confirmation from the President of the

United States that extraterrestrial life exists and is relatively close." George started to raise his Monster Ultra Gold for a sip but put it back down as he continued, "I see we have many new viewers joining us for this moment in history. This is a defining moment for our generation, maybe all generations. We are not alone!"

George raised his continuously buzzing phone to the camera. "Friends, I have received several texts telling me that the DoD, CIA, and other agencies with rumored ties to the Majestic organization aren't happy. Security for President Fernandez and his closest advisors has been increased. The administration had been warned not to release information about extraterrestrial life until approved by the group, and this announcement has gone against that order. We are going to have to watch that situation closely."

He sat back in his chair for a moment, then leaned forward, close to the camera. "I honestly did not expect that we would get this revelation so soon. Maybe this is a baby step toward telling us about the galactic empires and the peace accords. Maybe they wanted to evaluate the public's reaction before disclosing that we live in a crowded neighborhood and are now expected to come out to play. I'm seeing messages pop up here telling me that most of you don't believe the line from the President telling us that we have no communication. I think they knew that we had found the evidence and wanted to get in front before our message of truth spread out of their control.

"More evidence will be revealed in short order as we sort out the impact of this announcement. The world of the Majestic group and their hold on the rest of us has just been shaken, and they were not prepared. I'll reach out to my contacts to confirm all the rumors flowing right now to ensure that I only bring the truth to you, the Truth Seekers of the world." George stopped to open another energy drink, his third of the show.

"I would love to hear from you. What do you think now?"

George was excited. The show had ended with almost eighty-thousand more listeners. During the show, he received numerous texts telling him that friends and family members of his listeners were becoming interested in his show now that the news of extraterrestrial life was confirmed. He wrote a note on a small square sticky note to call Tim in the morning. While he was uploading his show, he received an alert that the capacity of the server hosting his site, and all of his files from previous shows, was experiencing a high volume of traffic. He checked his YouTube page and saw increased traffic for all his shows.

This is going to be beyond big.

Part II

"A tablet concerning these matters have I made for thee, and a record have I written for thee."—Enuma Elish

June 2025
Staten Island, New York

George stared at the balance on the ATM screen. He looked around to see if anyone was watching. A guy was talking on his phone, leaning on a white SUV. He looked distracted. His sunglasses seemed too dark to see through. George turned back to the ATM and quickly retrieved the bills, slipping them into his front pocket. He turned and headed down the street toward his apartment building. Sunglasses was still talking on the phone.

It was hot, in the upper eighties, but a cool breeze was coming from the bay, cool enough to counter the late summer sun. He moved closer to the buildings, staying in the shade when possible. He took a deep breath, smelling the salt in the air.

I have got to get out to Long Island, maybe spend a weekend at Jones Beach, take a few days, and do some remote shows.

He slowed his walk, strolling up the street and reading posts about last night's show. He reached a crosswalk and paused as the timer counted down. He flipped to his merch shop app. His "Five Embassies for Peace" shirt, using the colors selected by the NASA team for their show with five arrows heading toward a point of unity, was back-ordered by two weeks. He expanded the selection with images of the suspected galactic races, each having a color scheme and street art design, courtesy of one of his followers. The *don't walk* image glowed orange.

He sent a text to his distributor asking if there was anything they could do to increase production. Hopefully, his subscribers will like the latest designs. Glancing up at the *walk* image, he started to step out into the street. A car horn blared to his left. He jumped back. The woman next to him had stepped out and almost got hit by a yellow cab. He helped the startled woman onto the curb and noticed a white SUV with tinted side windows a few cars back. The driver looked like the guy near the ATM wearing dark sunglasses. He felt a twinge of fear, like when he let his mind race in the middle of the night.

He crossed the street, looking over his shoulder at the SUV. He couldn't see the license plate. He picked up his pace, looking for a store to step into before the light turned green. He started to cross the street again to a convenience store, then turned back. He shook his head and crossed the street. "Don't get caught up in the conspiracy theories," he muttered to himself.

He looked back, no longer seeing the white SUV.

CNEOS, JPL, Pasadena, California

Sharon stepped around tables and disconnected workstations displaced to the center of the room. She sipped her ginger tea and watched the team swing the sixteen-foot screen into place, holding it in position while they secured it. She shook her head, looking around at a dozen team members watching the installation.

"We needed this installed now? In the middle of the workday? Tim, how long do we have before we are online with Houston and the array team?"

Sharon looked around the room and spotted Tim hunched over a workstation across the room, headphones on. She worked her way through the maze of furniture to where he was working. He jumped when she tapped him on the shoulder. "What time are we supposed to go online with Houston?"

He spun his chair around, removing both earbuds. "They should be online in about half an hour."

She looked around at the disorder, her shoulders slumped. "Okay, maybe we can get some of this cleaned up."

"Unless there is an issue with the connection, the big screen," he motioned to the large monitor across the room, "should be up."

She blew out an exasperated breath before taking a sip of tea, trying to relax her muscles. "Okay, I'll be right back. See if we can at least get some of this mess out of our camera shots."

"Will do, boss." Tim smiled devilishly.

She pointed at him, keeping a grip on her tumbler of tea. "Don't start with me." She worked her way to the stairway to her office.

She put her things down, relaxing at the sight of her organized office. Her desk phone was blinking. She put the phone on speaker and hit play.

"Good morning, Dr. Berzing. This is Dr. Maria Hedgemann, the Science Advisor to the President. I wanted to congratulate you on your promotion and discuss your assignment to 'Project Sky-Watch.' Give me a call later today so we may discuss your responsibilities. Thanks, bye."

Sharon sat staring at the phone. *This is too much. I need to call the Administrator.* She felt a burning rise in her throat. She opened her purse and took two more antacids. A Skype message popped up on her screen. It was Tim. They were setting up comms and wanted to talk to her. She typed that she would be right down. She grabbed her tumbler of tea and headed back to the main floor.

Sharon entered the main room. The installation team had cleared the middle of the room, pushing the workstations back to their original places along the walls. She looked up at the large screen. The images showed Houston and the Chang'e Lunar Site.

"We're online, Sharon," Tim said before turning back to the screen.

"Good morning, everyone. I understand comm checks are complete. Commander Williams, I'd like to bring the two small bouquet arrays online if your team is ready. Once that is complete, we will merge the signals with our other systems and get a better picture of what's out there."

"Roger, JPL. We are bringing Bouquet One online."

Advanced Energy Research Facility, Wyoming

John walked down the stone path from the train stop to the waiting car. The air smelled fresh. The sky was dark, despite being an hour from sunset. Tall thunderheads loomed on the horizon. He kept his jacket off, enjoying the warm summer air. Before getting into the waiting car, he looked back at the well-maintained small building next to the tracks. The station was nondescript and out of place in the open wilderness.

The forty-five-minute drive to the facility, a large building resembling a large data center tucked away in the rolling hills of Wyoming, was uneventful. The sign over the small gate read "Department of Energy." A chain-link fence extended to the left and right. Retractable metal pylons protected the vehicle entry.

When the car stopped, the security personnel took his credentials. After a review and facial recognition with a handheld scanner, the vehicle was allowed to enter. Before he was ushered into the building, he took a deep breath of the clean mountain air.

An older olive-skinned woman in a white lab coat, gray hair tucked into a bun, greeted him. "Assistant Secretary Worthing, welcome to Wyoming. We are happy to have you here for the demonstration."

"Thank you, Ms. Tanner. I know my predecessor pushed heavily for the approval of this project. I don't want to delay the test. I understand my team is already in place, so I am ready when you are."

Jamie Tanner was the original director of the Global Shock program. Although she had a doctorate from Stanford in particle physics, she preferred not to use the honorific.

"Great. Follow me to the control room. We have two areas of evaluation. In phase one, we will fly five aircraft from Mountain Home, Idaho airbase. From here, we will observe the electronic fingerprint of hundreds of electronic devices in the town, simulating real-world conditions. The test area is clear of actual personnel. If you went out there, you would think you were back in one of the old nuclear towns of the '50s, except now they would be standing around with iPhones, tablets, and other tech."

The control room was smaller than he expected. There were six stations and several monitors on the walls around the room showing readings from different sections of the test area. John noticed the red dots at the edge of the main screen, approaching from the west.

A voice announced, "T-minus two minutes before aircraft enter the tracking area."

Another voice sounded from his right. "All town devices are nominal. We have connectivity across the spectrum."

Jamie watched the primary monitor. "Everything looks good." She raised her voice. "Check for non-test aircraft in the area."

After a few seconds, a voice from the front of the control room stated, "We have confirmed with air traffic control that the air space is clear. All regional aircraft are grounded for maintenance checks."

She leaned in toward John. "Were you briefed on the Boeing incident from a few years ago?" She continued when John shook his head, "Boeing was conducting a test flight of a 787 Dreamliner. We missed the aircraft entering the test area through a system fault. The aircraft went down, killing all of the flight crew. Boeing grounded the aircraft model for months while conducting a safety review but could not identify the problem. The DoE did not release any information, and the FAA determined it was an equipment failure."

John shook his head. "Not how I would have handled it."

"T-minus sixty seconds."

John watched the primary monitor as the aircraft from the west entered the test site.

The main screen lit up as all electronic devices in the test zone were activated. John looked to the left at the zoomed-out image representing a point in space beyond low earth orbit.

As he heard the voice state, "T-minus thirty seconds," one of the satellites on the monitor turned green, and a circular grid appeared at the end of a cone, starting at the satellite. On the primary monitor, the ring in the test area turned green.

"T-minus ten seconds, nine, eight, seven . . . three, two one, initiate."

Another voice sounded to the right of the original speaker. "Initiating local shock." The grid and cone turned yellow. All signals from the test area stopped. A live feed replaced the image showing the radar images. Four aircraft were free-falling while the fifth continued forward.

"What happened with the fifth plane?" John asked.

"The fourth and fifth aircraft contained experimental shielding designed to cover a fully functional avionics backup system. The shielding is an Air Force prototype designed for a Space Force project. When the EMP hits, the primary avionics systems should fail, triggering an immediate transfer of control to the shielded secondary system. Their techs will soon be out on the range to recover the black boxes. They will send the data over in a day or so, once they evaluate what happened to each aircraft."

"What was the radius? Would anyone have seen the test?" John asked.

"No, the exclusion radius was twenty kilometers for this demonstration. We can focus down to a ten-kilometer radius from a single satellite, or expand to full global coverage using the entire network of satellites. All global internet signals from the system would show an interruption in service as we took control and rotated the satellites with the weapon toward Earth vice the transceivers. When the last few satellites go up later this year, global 5G will be available everywhere on the planet, as will Global Shock," Jamie concluded with a smile.

"That is great news. With the push to develop AI, I want to ensure we are prepared. The sooner we have this in place, the better."

August 2025
Zhongguancun, China

Wu Kai nodded his head, shifting his gaze between the qubit field engagement graphics and process analysis. Fan Meifen, a recent top graduate of Tsinghua, operated the primary workstation in the row of five that fed and controlled Global Dragon. She was the first woman to join his team. He smelled the slight scent of plum from whatever product she used in her long black hair. He was reminded of their first meeting in May.

Her interview had been unlike any other and had set a precedent for future additions. During her interview for a coding position, she asked for a pause. She then stood, walked across his office to the dry-erase board, and corrected an error in a line of code for a procedural self-diagnostics algorithm. He hired her immediately.

"Xiao Fan, what is the status of the Dragon?"

"Progress is satisfactory. The error rate is down fifteen percent."

He knew the improvement was a result of her correction. The coders had added subroutines that could detect error rate increases and backtrack to the point it determined error rates had begun to climb. The program would continue from that point forward, again choosing the best route from all the possible choices, using experiential data from the corrections.

"Director Wu, I have an explanation for why the data transfers are not occurring as we would like."

"Continue."

She swiveled her chair to face him. "The primary code is designed to prioritize efficiency. Looking at the primary monitor, you can see the readings from all support systems. If we expand the view to show processes occurring at the nanosecond interval and align all system readings, it appears that the computer is adjusting its environmental controls. The efficiency protocols have prevented the path of expanding qubits in a complex calculation determining the time to complete with the total amount of resources used."

"You are saying that Quánqiú lóng is manipulating data at the quantum level?"

She bowed her head slightly. "Possibly." She paused, tilting her head slightly. "It looks like the Dragon has learned to consider everything it can control when making decisions on efficiency."

"This is a result of the base code? It is learning and adapting?"

"Possibly. The success of the base code successfully demonstrated the potential for a program to develop a winning strategy based on experience and learning the rules of the game. Quánqiú lóng is learning the limitations of its environment as part of the game's rules."

Wu Kai smiled. The path forward was clear. "Very well, let's give it a challenge. Begin series one."

He turned away from the young tech and headed for his office. He had read the confidential files from the development of Alpha Go, and the evolutionary steps taken to achieve the current version of MuZero, as had his team. The next phase would be difficult. They were evolving the computer from a quantum calculator to a machine that could learn and adapt.

Quánqiú lóng was the most critical project for the country. He could hear President Zhang's crisp voice: "All other moves were distractions, positioning for strength, and building defenses, much like the moves in Weiqi." Wu Kai understood his position in the grand strategy and embraced his assignment. If successful, he would secure his status as one of the great men responsible for helping raise the People's Republic to its rightful place as leader of the global community. The West was in decline, and he would help them along their way.

CNEOS, JPL, Pasadena, California

Tim uploaded the latest data into the model, running an error detection algorithm to ensure the model had not become corrupted. The screen showed the data upload was complete and that compilation had begun. He got up from the workstation and stretched. His lower back was sore. He decided to head to the food court to grab a quick snack to settle his growling stomach.

He had about half an hour before they closed, and most of the lunch crowd had returned to their work. He grabbed a salad and a tuna sandwich and sat at a table to the side. He would eat quickly and get a little time to himself before returning to the model.

His phone rang. He thought about ignoring it, then saw the caller ID showed Virginia.

"This is Tim."

"Good afternoon, Tim. This is Eusebio, returning your call. Are you busy? You said you wanted clarification on what we are looking for."

Tim set his fork down. "I'm good. I can talk."

"Great, okay. We would like to know if your model can show us what the sky would look like from a specific place and time."

"Hmm, we can run it backward. That shouldn't be too difficult in theory. The difficulty comes from extrapolating from our data where everything would be in the sky at any time. That is an enormous amount of data."

"But it is possible?"

"Technically, it is possible. I'll talk to the model devs and get back to you if that is okay?"

"Yeah, that would be great."

"What are you trying to do?"

"We would like to be able to input the coordinates from where an artifact that contains a star map was found, and then examine it against the model projection of the night sky. We would gain insight into what they saw, what was influencing their culture at the time, and it could help verify the date we believe the artifacts were created."

"That is pretty amazing, and not something I would have thought JPL would be doing."

"Well, you never know. Sometime in the distant future, researchers could look at videos of your model to figure out the same thing."

"True. The time we found out we're not alone and then hid in our corner of the galaxy, hoping they passed us by."

"Well, we'll leave looking forward in time to you."

Tim laughed. "Thanks, Eusebio. I'll talk to them this week and let you know what they can do."

The lines were closed, and the cafeteria staff was cleaning up. Tim sighed and packed up his salad.

He thought about the call. It was an exciting proposal. In theory, the model could be run in either direction based on the data on file for each object. Astrophysics formulas had so far kept the model on track. Moving back in time thousands of years added the potential for an unknown number of variables, primarily resulting from gravitational forces or collisions. Given those errors, corrections would have to be made for geographic location, which affected what area of the sky was visible.

As he thought about it, he became more excited. When he returned to his desk, he emailed Sharon and the model team.

American Nanotech Consortium, University of Texas, Austin, Texas

Professor Lanning stood at a podium as his students shuffled out of the lecture hall. He gathered his notes, closed the presentation, and made his way to the door. He jumped slightly as John Worthing stepped around a small group of students and approached him.

John dodged the last few students, stepping forward. "Dr. Lanning, good to see you again."

Dr. Lanning smiled and reached to shake the Assistant Secretary's hand. "John, you, too. I thought our meeting was later this afternoon?"

John smiled, turning to walk out with the professor. "It is, but I was able to catch an early flight and wanted to see this breakthrough early before everyone else showed up."

Gerald perked up. "Great! Do you mind if we walk? It's not too far to the lab from here."

"I don't mind the walk. I grew up just south of here. While I don't mind the heat so much right now, I don't miss the weeks of hundred-degree temperatures."

"I'm from Minnesota, so I don't think I'll ever be used to the heat."

John ignored the look from students who had to step aside as he walked next to Professor Lanning. "I am here to discuss the fallout from the President's announcement in May. It's my job to look at all options to help develop contingency plans."

Dr. Lanning stopped and stared at John.

John turned. "Doctor, we don't believe a threat exists at the moment. The Administration doesn't even know if they want to attempt contact, though some have pushed to send a signal." He looked the professor in the eyes. "I am making the rounds through the scientific community to gather ideas. I want you and your team to think about anything and everything, no matter how far-fetched, and make recommendations. Nothing is off the table."

Gerald breathed a sigh of relief, putting his hand on John's arm. "Well, that's good news. At first, I thought you were going to tell me to prepare for an invasion. This is better." He started walking again, focusing on the distance. "I hope you are ready for some interesting reading. Some students have been discussing highly creative ideas for fending off an alien invasion or helping prepare for the first contact. The youth are creative in their approach to things, and movies or social media influence is rampant."

John nodded along. "I know. We have some pretty far-fetched ideas at HQ, as well. I keep reminding people not to submit dumb ideas they thought up after watching *Independence Day*, *Aliens*, or some other Hollywood fantasy. At least it isn't a secret. With this out in the open, we may get some innovative suggestions. Open discussion is good. Hell, the best idea may come from some teenage science buff in Nebraska."

The pair entered the Larry R. Faulkner Nano Science and Technology Building. Dr. Lanning moved them through the circular lobby and down a set of stairs to the below-ground research lab. "This afternoon, I will have the more formal brief showing our progress since last year's meeting. We have made more progress and can send design specifications to groups of nanites, with each group responsible for a single part. The nanites group themselves by task, and know which data applies to them and their group. They ignore the other group while deconflicting resource gathering."

Professor Lanning turned and motioned one of the research techs to bring up the large monitor. The monitor showed a multitude of tiny insect-like nanites moving with a coordinated effort. John watched the nanites move in deconflicted patterns.

Dr. Lanning pulled a silver pen from his shirt pocket and pointed to the video feed. "We have changed the base design to that of ants, with modifications based on assigned tasks. Here we have the base model nanites arriving in the target area. The movement is indiscernible to the naked eye. What you see on the monitor is inside a cell phone. A single phone can transport millions of nanites. We have found that a phone or electronic device is ideal. They are easy to modify to generate an electrified platform necessary for the nanites to have the power they need, and send signals from a remote station at an almost undetectable level."

The screen shifted to show the hundreds of thousands of nanites organized into groups. "We transmit tasks to the nanites, and they know to reorganize by their assigned group. The nanites use a system of trail pheromones to move out in search of the resources for their specific task."

John held his hand up to pause the professor. "Okay. You said pheromones. Is it smell or chemical?"

Professor Lanning smiled. "Not quite. Each team of nanites will leave a marker that indicates viable and nonviable paths. The marker indicates direction and a time stamp. Are you familiar with the fringe running concept of hash runs?"

John shook his head.

"Okay, well, I do not want to get sidetracked, but it uses a process of elimination to determine the correct path to take to complete the run. One of our techs, an avid runner, suggested the method, and it appears to work.

"Once a nanite finds the resources necessary to complete their task, they signal back to the larger group. If you look at group two, you can see that they have identified the resource required for their task on the left side of the screen. The nanites form a two-way trail between the resource retrieval and assembly sites. Note the close-formed line from their point of origin. Once they arrive at the assembly point, coordinator units give the order for assembly. The groups receive signals in the order necessary to assemble the object." Professor Lanning breathed out a long sigh.

"Well, I think I followed the explanation, but how long would construction take?" John asked.

"It depends on the complexity of what you are building, but for now, an exceptionally long time. You are talking about constructing something from the molecular level up. The good news is that there should be no flaws with an effective design. The bad news is that you may have to wait a year or more to build it, with current nanotechnology levels."

John thought for a moment. "Still, it is a significant step forward. Is there a way, even in theory, of how you could reach the speeds shown in the movies, like the Marvel movies nano-suits?"

"In theory, if you used quantum computing and established a communications network that could track and guide each bot, making billions of adjustments in a second, you could, but we are decades away from that."

John rubbed the back of his neck, thinking. He reached out to shake Dr. Lanning's hand. "This is great. I'll head back to my hotel and grab lunch before our brief this afternoon. Thank you, professor."

George reached over and adjusted his camera. He jumped up, knocking his chair back, and loomed over his desk. "You have got to be kidding me, FB! We have been arguing about alien existence for over a year, and now you have changed your mind? You're telling us, all the Seekers listening, that the Presidents of China and the United States are lying to the world? You have got to be kidding me! Do you really want to take it there? People like me have been calling for the government to admit they knew about extraterrestrial life since 1947, and when they finally do, it is a conspiracy. Seriously?" He turned around and paced from side to side.

The modulated voice answered, "Why now, Georgie? They want us to believe. They expected a few nuts like you to figure it out based on pictures. It doesn't make sense. Something is going on between the two superpowers. They are doing what they always do, deflecting attention from somewhere else. It is definitely a setup."

George shook his head as FedBuster was talking. "No, no, no! They backed themselves into a corner with the NASA show and saw that we knew the truth, especially after we broke the news of the embassy ships. They had no choice!" His voice got progressively louder.

FedBuster snorted. "Oh, here we go again with the embassy ships. You have no proof. I posted it last month in your forums. The objects look the same, so unless they all share the same tech, it would likely be one race. But it is not. Look at the images. If you copy the image of one of the supposed ships and make four copies, then lay them out in a spread like JPL's model shows, you can clearly see that it is one image copied and rotated. Look at the stars in the background. Look at what has happened. NASA hyped it to get a bigger budget. Every country with a space program has increased its budget to expand into space faster. More money means more secrets, but not for much longer."

"I have to take a break for my sponsor. I'll be right back. Stay tuned, Truth Seekers. You, too, FB. We're not done yet."

George stood, stretching his legs and placing his headphones on the table. He ran to the kitchen to grab a Monster Ultra Gold and a handful of tootsie rolls. He had two minutes.

The power went out as he walked into his broadcast room and moved his chair to sit down.

"Damnit!" He rushed back to the kitchen. All the rooms in his apartment were dark, with only the light coming in through the windows allowing him not to run into anything. He opened his window, stuck his head out, and looked up and down the street. "Looks like the whole block is out." A white SUV parked across the street caught his eye. He quickly retreated into the room and closed the curtains on the window. George switched to the broadcast app on his phone and reconnected to his social media channel. The chat channel was on fire with theories about the FCC blocking the show or his abduction by the CIA to hide the truth. He smiled as he watched the chats scroll by.

He went to the living room and pulled out the night vision scope he had bought at Target. He set his phone down and peeked through the curtains toward the SUV. There wasn't anyone inside. He scanned the street, mostly seeing people standing outside the building or looking out their windows. Their cell screens shone brightly. He relaxed and pulled his phone out, opening the audio-only backup app he used to broadcast his show. "Hey, Truth Seekers, we have a power outage here on Staten Island. I'm pretty sure it wasn't FB. Let's not inflate his ego. We'll have to continue tomorrow if the power company can fix it. I'll post this show as soon as I can. Thank you for tuning in."

He closed the app and hit speed dial.

"George, how are you doing?"

"I'm good, Dad. Is your power out?"

"Yep, I was watching the game, and the Mets were up 4–2 on the Braves. It doesn't matter at this point. At least the Giants are on a streak, four and oh, and up two games on the Cowgirls."

"Yeah, umm, Dad, I think someone is following me."

George heard coughing from the phone. "Dad, are you okay?"

"Yeah, I almost drowned. You made me choke on my beer. C'mon, George, you're not being followed. You're buying into all those stories. You're not that famous."

"Thanks, Dad. I'm not saying it's some crazy follower. I think it could be the government."

"Yeah, in a white car because it's easy to blend in."

"Dad, the movies use black cars because it looks scary, part of the conditioning. We all believe it, and then they can use whatever they want, so we miss it."

"George, don't peddle me the crap you put on your podcast. The government does not control Hollywood, they are not conditioning us, and they are not out to get a podcaster with a somewhat popular YouTube video show. Okay, son?"

George felt the heat rising. "Dad, the government has tried to manipulate us. There are official reports for all governments, and they follow people they see as a threat."

"So you're a threat because you're telling the internet aliens are talking about us? It's not even real! You made it up, you told me. See, this is what I'm talking about. It's coming back at you—making stuff up and telling lies, and it's coming back on you. People will believe you because you said aliens were out there before the President did. You better watch what you say because people will start looking for answers you don't have."

"Dad, I—"

"I'm not doing this tonight. I need another beer. You think about what I said. G'night."

"Damnit!" George stormed to the kitchen, reaching angrily for the gold can on the counter, almost knocking it over. He headed back to his broadcast room, lighting the way with his phone flashlight. He went to the corkboard on the wall and put another mark on his counter, noting the time and day he spotted the white SUV. He checked out the window. It was gone. *It looks like a pattern to me—forty-seven sightings in four months.*

GWU, Archaeology Department, Washington, DC

Jackie and Eusebio stood over Tim's shoulders in her team's research area at GWU. Tim continued to type, glancing between his three screens. To the right, on a side table, was a scanner set up to render quality digital images from artifacts. Eusebio slipped a sticky note to Tim. Glare from the sunlight coming in the window across the room shone on the screens. Jackie closed the blinds and moved back to standing over Tim's shoulder.

"We are still getting lag on our end. The image is stuttering. We will keep working on it. I'm pulling up the file list." A woman's voice came through the speakers on either side of the center screen.

"Okay, let us know when it's clear, Fern."

A few minutes passed, and Jackie looked over to Tim and shrugged.

Fern's soft voice pulled Jackie's attention back. "I have the first image. We are ready to test image comparison."

Tim looked at the note Eusebio had passed to him, and stuck it to the bottom of the center monitor frame. Jackie saw a series of dates and locations on the note.

Fern's voice came through the speakers. She had turned off her camera to reduce possible interference with the data stream. "We are good, Tim. The first file is loaded."

Tim looked up over his shoulder at Jackie. "The model will step back a year per second, comparing the image of the star chart with the model set to the observation 'recovery' location. The left monitor shows the star chart from your artifact in the background with a projection of the sky matching the date from the comparison tool. Once a match of twenty percent of the star positions occurs between images, the comparison program will bracket the image by dividing the date in half on each side until the stars and object have an eighty percent match. The model will continue to shift backward a year if no match is detected."

Jackie nodded along. "This is amazing. Do we need to go year by year?"

"Yes. We're ensuring the model and comparison programs work together. Year by year will stress the system more than skipping. When the program is fully functional, we should be able to bracket with whatever measure you want—decades, centuries, or even millennia." Tim turned back to the camera. "Fern, we're ready. Go with image China zero-zero-one."

Eusebio and Jackie huddled over Tim's shoulders. Tim loaded the Chinese astrology chart image into a box on the left screen. When he hit start, the comparison program shifted images every second.

"It starts with today's stars?"

"Yes, we could start it at an earlier date, but I wanted to run through the whole process."

Eusebio pulled a chair over and sat to Tim's left. "We have about forty minutes, then."

The program began the bracketing process at thirty-seven minutes, slowly closing in on the date. After thirty-eight minutes, the comparison stopped, the screen's border showed green, and the words 'Possible Match' appeared at the bottom with two dates.

Tim pointed to the first date on the sticky note. "We have a match."

Jackie looked at the numbers on the screen, bracketing 310 to 313 BCE. "That is impressive." She smiled. "This will add another data point to understand the cultures of the time, what they saw in the sky, and some of the influence they saw in the stars."

Tim gave a thumbs-up to the camera. "We are ready for test two, entering latitude and longitude. Do you want to do one or five years?" he asked.

"We have four more test runs. Let's stick with one-year intervals, ensure it is good, then move up," Fern replied.

"Copy, Fern. Ready when you are."

The screen image began to change, the date rolling backward at one year per second.

"Tim, Dr. Berzing needs you to call her immediately. Something's up."

"Thanks, Fern."

Tim got up and moved to the far side of the room. Jackie was glad they had straightened the room. After a few minutes, he returned. His face was pale. "I need to head back."

"Is everything okay? Do you need anything?" Jackie stepped toward him.

"I'm fine. I need to get back to JPL. I can't say any more."

DHS HQ, Washington, DC

John walked through the cube farm's center aisle on the building's floor. He tried to relax, unclenching his jaw. A few people looked up at him, then quickly ducked back down. He made his way through the dozens of cubes before stopping outside. He knocked on the metal frame of the opening.

"Mr. Denison, what is your job?"

The man spun around in his chair, jumping up. "Mr. Worthing, I, umm, I work liaison with the Bureau on IT espionage. Uh, sir."

A young woman came around the corner, interrupting, "Sir, you are needed in the Secretary's office immediately."

John nodded. "Tell her I'm on my way."

He turned back to Denison and pointed up. "That means I am about to get questions about your failure. You had better have answers when I get back. Don't leave until you see me, understood?"

"Y-yes, sir." He avoided John's eyes.

John was shown into Secretary Genson's office without delay. The secretary was sitting at her conference table, and the directors of the FBI and CIA were seated on either side of her.

Secretary Genson motioned to an open seat at the table. "John, have a seat. Brad and Jeremy were filling me in on an investigation you should be aware of."

He took an empty chair. "Gentlemen. Ma'am."

The DHS Secretary nodded to the FBI Director, Jeremy Culden.

"Last week, we arrested a person of interest we have been following for over a year. The person of interest runs a coordinated ring of students linked to several major programs with active internships. They are suspected of industrial espionage. We found a number of hard drives and thumb drives with information from some of the leading tech companies. Until this morning, we had been unable to break the encryption. When we finally did, there were indications that dozens of national security programs had become compromised. We are here specifically about two of those programs.

One was an older schematic for building a quantum computer. The other is a program we have confirmed with DeepMind to be MuZero, a deep learning program with advanced capabilities."

Brad Thorgald, Director of Central Intelligence, spoke. "We have been working with the FBI on the case. When we broke the encryption this morning, over forty IP addresses and a reference to the *Pinnacle Project* popped up. We have been unable to link the name to any active programs. Forensics traced the files to IP addresses in China."

The FBI Director continued, "A few of the students listed in the ring are missing. We have two in custody, but three others have disappeared. John, what are your thoughts?"

John's mind was racing, trying to decipher the links between the stolen files. "The loss of MuZero is significant. The good news is that it wasn't LaMDA. The MuZero program has demonstrated the ability to master a game in short order, despite not being provided with rules. That, coupled with China already having the most powerful supercomputer, is of great concern. Do you have the diagram for the quantum computer?"

The FBI Director opened his tablet, bringing up the evidence file list.

"Well, the good news is that there are better open-source images on the internet of how to build a quantum computer than that. I would not worry about it. Despite consolidating efforts in Zhongguancun, I am unaware of any recent breakthroughs. If I recall, and I will get an update to verify, the Chinese are nowhere near as far along as we are in quantum computing. Of course, that could change if they keep throwing the money they have over the past four years at the problem."

John looked up from the tablet to the three people across from him. "If you want us to prepare a full impact brief, send over a list of all of the tech, and we will look at it. We can identify where synergy exists, and where we may see leapfrogging of tech tiers as they skip developmental phases."

Jeremy nodded. "We will have a report prepared and sent this week."

Secretary Genson leaned in. "Gentlemen, John will run point for us on this. Please coordinate efforts with him."

Both men nodded before ending the connection.

"John, keep me informed."

"Will do, ma'am."

"Oh, and John, good luck this weekend in the marathon."

"Thank you."

John departed, feeling his temperature rising as he neared the elevator. *Denison better have some damn good answers.*

CNEOS, JPL, Pasadena, California

Sharon stood over Tim's shoulder, looking at the model projection. The object's title, *Embassy 5*, was highlighted in red, indicating it was a near-Earth object with a high probability of impact. Sharon felt a chill run through her blood. She had Tim reverse the model by a week and watched it again. The sped-up video showed the object jumping forward at incredible speed, the motion vector leading forward toward Earth.

"Could the data be corrupted?"

Tim shook his head, "I have checked three times."

"This can't get out. Stop all reporting outside those on the team. I'll make the call." Sharon walked off toward her office, wiping her hands on her lab coat and pulling out the roll of antacid tablets. Tim replayed the model a few more times.

NASA HQ, Washington, DC

Administrator James was attending a fundraiser for a space-focused science, technology, engineering, and math (STEM) scholarship foundation. He waved off his assistant, who was trying to bring him his phone.

"Administrator, it's Dr. Berzing. She says it is urgent."

He excused himself from the group of high school students gathered around the model of the James Webb Space Telescope.

"Okay, Sharon, I'm clear. Go ahead."

"I am sorry to interrupt you, Terry. Don't be mad at your assistant; he tried to persuade me not to interrupt you, but this cannot wait. Yesterday the team noted an ambiguity in the data from the objects. Since they have come together, we haven't detected any movement. They slowed, and that was it."

"Take a breath and continue."

He heard her breathe out. "We cleared the data from yesterday and uploaded it again this afternoon. The object is heading toward Earth. The warning system, which uses the model everyone has seen, indicates a high probability of impact with Earth."

He waited before asking the question he knew he needed to, the implications racing through his mind. "When?"

"We don't know yet. Maybe a decade. We can't build an accurate timeline until it settles on a cruising speed."

"Thanks, Sharon. I'll be in touch. I need to call the White House. You need to get a bag packed. I'll let you know the details. Make sure the team knows this information is classified. We cannot afford leaks. Everyone was fine knowing that aliens were out there as long as they were far away. If the public discovers they are headed here. We could have mass panic."

"I will let them know."

He dialed the White House number and waited for the operator to answer. "This is NASA Administrator. I need to talk to the President," he told the switchboard operator.

"Sir, standby. I'm transferring you to the Deputy Chief of Staff."

He waited less than a minute before a voice came across the line. "Administrator, this is Deputy Chief of Staff Grey. The President is on Air Force One. I can patch you through if you must talk now. He is on his way to Europe for the G7 Summit." Silence hung on the line as she awaited his answer.

"Yes, please, tell him it's Sky-Watch." A few minutes passed in silence.

He heard the accented, smooth voice of the President. "Terry, how are you doing? Staff says this is important. What have you got?"

He relayed the information from Sharon, answering the President's questions.

"Well, it's not going to get here in the next few weeks, is it?" President Fernandez asked, chuckling into the phone.

"No, sir, we have a decade or so," the Administrator replied.

"Good, it gives us some time to think. I will have the Chief of Staff contact you for a brief when I get back. If anything changes, give me a call, okay?" the President asked.

"Will do, sir. Enjoy the trip."

November 2025
White House, Washington, DC

"The NASA Administrator is here, sir," the President's assistant announced.

James crossed the room briskly, reaching across the Resolute desk. "Mr. President, thank you for meeting with me."

President Fernandez shook his hand and indicated that he should sit on one of the two couches in the room, moving around to sit opposite him. "Terry, bring me up to speed."

James sat forward on the gold floral couch, breathing in the faint scent of sandalwood the President preferred. "Yes, sir. Three weeks ago, the objects we had been tracking started moving again. They had been holding position since they came together. The object set off our NEO planetary defense warning system. We do not have an accurate timeline of when the object will arrive. As of this morning, the object is still accelerating." He paused. "It is coming right at us and fast."

The President stood and walked behind his desk, looking out the large windows. "How long before it gets here?"

"If its previous speed is any indicator, it could reach us sometime in ten to fifteen years. It sounds like a long time to prepare when I say it aloud, but it is not. The technology to accomplish even the limited things we know about the object is almost beyond comprehension."

The President turned back toward the Administrator. "What do you make of it?"

James breathed out a heavy sigh. "I don't know. I have mixed feelings right now with so many unknowns. They could have picked up any number of the signals we've been sending out over the last century. Honestly, I feel like we are the ant on the ant pile, looking across the yard as a giant kid makes their way toward us, magnifying glass in hand."

The President let out a nervous chuckle at the quip. "Well, we had better be prepared. I'll call an NSC meeting and will consult with our allies. If they come here, we will show them our best nature. We can be the best of friends and the fiercest of enemies."

Zhongguancun, China

Wu Kai was startled at the sound of his phone. "Director Wu, this is Wen ZhiChu of the Ministry of State Security. We will be arriving shortly for a security inspection. Please have your team standing by when we arrive."

Wu Kai bristled. "We are doing important work. I want to remind you that your personnel do not have permission to enter the building. I will have my team ready for your arrival."

"We understand the restrictions, Director. We will be there promptly."

He stood, thought for a second, and finished the last bite of the fried dumpling he had been eating. Wu Kai placed a call, directing his head of security to assemble all personnel at the building entrance to assist the arriving MSS officers with their review. When he received word that security was in position, he announced that all personnel were to report to the front of the building. He made his way to the main door and greeted the team as they passed.

Wu Kai was not worried. He had run enough programs to know that the Ministry of State Security would make routine checks to ensure personnel complied with all required practices. He did not believe his team would have any issues and stood by his personnel, waiting for the security team to arrive.

Ten minutes after his staff was assembled, the security vehicles passed through the gate and pulled up to the facility. The mobile interview stations were large, providing space for three simultaneous interviews.

A man in a black suit, white shirt, and a nonstandard maroon-and-black tie got out of the lead vehicle and walked toward the gathered group. He looked to be prior military—stiff, serious demeanor, and in good shape. Wu Kai approached the younger man. "Wen ZhiChu?"

Wen ZhiChu nodded, reached into his jacket, produced his credentials, and handed a folder to the Director.

Wu Kai opened the folder and flipped through the pages. Nodding, he handed the folder back. "All personnel are present except for six covering critical positions. We will arrange for their relief if you need to see any of them. Their names are highlighted."

Wen ZhiChu said, "Thank you, Director Wu." He looked over the employee roster, making a mark by several names. "Have the indicated personnel remain. The rest may return to work." He handed the list back.

Wu Kai read through the list, noting that all the personnel listed were newly assigned to his team. He turned to his security chief and handed him the file. "Do as he says." He bowed to the inspector before returning to the building.

Dr. Jiang Min met him as he entered the secure area. "They like to show up at inopportune times?"

He looked up. "What?"

"The MSS interfering in our work."

"Yes, they do, but they have a job to do, same as us."

Dr. Jiang closed the office door behind them. "It is okay to be upset with the MSS. No one questions your loyalty. You could call President Zhang if they are interfering."

Wu Kai, shook his head. "No, they are doing what they are told. I hold no grudge against them. I put the blame for my father's arrest on the West, not the MSS. I will not make the mistakes he made. We will succeed and take our rightful place, leading the world. Once the Dragon is online, it will also support your goals."

"Yes, we would leave the West behind even with half the processing power."

"Your company?"

"Genetticca is approved. Construction begins in Delhi next year."

"I assure you, your work on the Dragon will be repaid."

"Thank you, Director Wu. We shall see where control of the genome takes us."

Technology Analysis Working Group, Joint Base Anacostia-Bolling, Washington, DC

Rear Admiral Christopher Fortwright, Director of the Defense Intelligence Agency, welcomed the working group members and allowed the agencies' heads to introduce their groups. The admiral was tall for a submariner, standing a few inches above six feet. He looked like a runner. When the Admiral took his seat next to John, a younger man in a suit took his place at the podium. He was a contrast to the admiral—shorter, stocky, more like a rugby player.

"Good afternoon. My name is Henry Atchins, and I am a special agent with the FBI. As you are familiar with the initial information presented to the agency leads, I will jump straight into the status of the investigation. Our efforts to persuade the suspect to talk have been unsuccessful. He remains uncooperative, claiming innocence even when presented evidence, including surveillance of his involvement in making drops. He has requested extradition to China. The State Department is blocking those efforts.

"The group infiltrated at least thirteen institutions, including Alphabet, Amazon, C3, IBM, Meta, and Micron—"

"Wait, how the hell did that happen? You just named the top six US companies in AI development. Was there a specific vulnerability? If it's negligence on their part, I hope we see criminal charges."

"Sir, each company was notified of the espionage and presented a limited-scope report addressing their specific programs. The vulnerabilities of each company look to be different. However, the infiltrators were student interns or recent graduates focused on AI development. CIA has the lead for tracking the data and where it went. NSA is the supporting organization. All those arrested have clean records with no indicators that raised alarms, and none are Chinese citizens."

John leaned forward, opening the provided packet of information. "The vulnerability is that they are racing to be the first, without full regard for what it will mean. Is there a list of the specific tech stolen in our packets, or will it be presented later?"

"Yes, sir. We have included a list in the briefing package. The joint forensics teams will provide updates as the evidence is analyzed. The most significant theft appears to be the code for MuZero. This advanced machine learning program is considered a leading step toward artificial general intelligence. We have talked to the code engineers, who determined that the stolen code was from an older version. Once we complete the briefing by CIA, we will open the floor for discussion and review of the data."

The briefers shifted positions as the slide on the screen was replaced with the CIA logo. An older woman in a light gray business suit and a stern look took the podium.

"Good afternoon. I am Gwen Schaefer, and I'll provide an update on the status of our investigation. We have identified almost four dozen IP addresses that received data packets associated with the person of interest. Most of the receiving IP addresses are Chinese. Your packets contain the specifics of what we believe transmitted to each IP address. Each working group will focus on one area of interest."

Admiral Fortwright addressed the speaker. "Is there a way to trace the data?"

"The program used by the person of interest maintained a list of addresses it has communicated with, but you have to find each phone or device to follow the trail," she replied.

"Well, it sounds like our friends at NSA need to get involved. Let's move on." The Admiral crossed his arms.

"Yes, Admiral," she said. "While we do not have all the specifics, we believe that any files or data related to machine learning make their way here." She brought up a map of Zhongguancun. "Four of China's leading artificial intelligence research companies have been consolidated under this man." The image on the screen changed to a middle-aged man with a stoic demeanor. "Wu Kai, President of Contemplation Impact and Director of the PRC coordinated AI development program. He has direct access to President Zhang and has a budget of tens of billions of US dollars. While he is a person of interest, we have nothing linking him to the stolen data."

John interrupted. "We've looked at his work. It is impressive, but everything we have read shows that they are years behind our efforts in AI, despite having the largest supercomputer. I know their plan is 'to surpass our efforts by the end of the decade,' but they have suffered several setbacks that our researchers have overcome. I only bring it up because my team has informed me that they could pass us with two or more eureka moments. Is there any indication of that happening?"

Shaking her head, Schaefer said, "We have been unable to collect intelligence on the ground anywhere near that site."

John leaned toward the Admiral. "We need to fix that. We need to get inside."

Admiral Fortwright nodded and spoke up. "Thank you, Gwen. We will move into the more technical portion of the meeting."

John turned to a research team member, motioning him toward the podium.

December 2025
Deatsville, Alabama

George was up early. It was dark outside, and a light coating of snow was on the ground. He sat in a recliner, watching the local news about the historic low temperatures. He woke up early and couldn't get comfortable enough to go back to sleep. The bed was too hard, and his pillow was too thick and puffy. The snow would melt by mid-morning, making a complete mess.

He turned his attention back to his laptop. His numbers were down. He needed to dive in on a few more theories. People were getting tired of hearing about aliens. After all of the hype built up by the entertainment industry over the years about how fast first contact would happen, it was anti-climactic. The announcement of extraterrestrial life opened the door for the big networks to invite every scientist they could get on their shows to talk about it. The topic is saturated. He took a sip of his hot chocolate and scrolled through the comments from the shows this week.

"Let's see what we have in recommendations," he said as he clicked the link and read the comments.

Strange effect on the tides since the announcement, energy buildups in stone circles, and ghosts or possibly interdimensional beings preparing the pyramid energy system for arrival. Not too bad, but still the same.

He read the topics aloud. "Blood god returns for vengeance, a telepathic virus, government-controlled vaccine programs—hmm, not ready to do those yet. Maybe the energy buildups, I could do some research."

The faint ding of a notification interrupted his thoughts. He picked up his phone and opened the text. *Gov't not telling the whole truth. Telling us about aliens has become an easy distraction for the public. They are coming. Mega-ship heading to Earth. #Silver.*

George reread the text before texting back, *Need proof.*

He sipped his cocoa and pulled up the JPL and NASA sites. The images showed the object as a small mass among the stars, holding position. Something caught his eye. He scrolled back through the pictures from the past few months.

George kicked the snow off his shoes and sat down at the small round table in his room to eat his breakfast: a McGriddle and hash browns. He looked at the time and hit Tim's number.

"Hey, man, how are you doing?" Tim answered, slower than usual.

"Good, good. I'm looking out my window at snow on the ground and slush in the streets," George told him.

"I don't miss that New York snow. What's up? Is the show still doing well?" Tim asked.

"I'm in Alabama. It wasn't supposed to snow here but it did."

"What are you doing in Alabama?"

"Research," George answered. "I am visiting hot spots and places where UFO sightings are up. I need to boost my subscription numbers, and the listeners like the remote shows. I'm dropping a little and don't want to return to a job I hate. Otherwise, the show is good, but I think people are tired of the same old alien stories. After a few months of the alien object sitting still, people want to see something. I do have something for you, though. I got an odd text this morning. Did you send me anything about a big ship heading toward us?" There was silence on the line.

"Tim, you there?" George asked.

"Uh, I didn't send anything. Where was it from?"

George looked at the number. "Nine-two-eight area code, Northern Arizona. Do you know anyone from there?"

"No. Not me."

"Okay, I have another quick question. Did you all change the format of the pics you post on your site, meaning NASA?"

"What do you mean 'changed'? It isn't my area, but I haven't heard anything. I could ask, though. What's different?"

"For some reason, the speed vector data is missing on all the photos since October this year."

"Hmm," Tim said, pausing. "Yeah, I'll ask. I don't know why they would do that. Maybe they were cleaning up the images."

George paused, letting the silence drag on. "So, Tim, is it true, though? Is the object headed here?"

Tim laughed into the phone, not the usual laugh George remembered from their college days. "George," he paused, "I need to get ready for work. We can talk later, buddy."

The call ended. Tim had avoided the answer. Maybe it was nothing. George finished his cocoa and looked at the dim light peeking through the drab brown curtains. *The networks don't have this story yet.*

GWU, Archaeology Department, Washington, DC

Jackie sat cross-legged in her Victorian high-back chair, reading the latest issue of *Archaeology Today*. She looked up from the magazine, shivered at the ice hanging off the tree branches that covered most of her view, and took a sip of her Earl Grey tea, feeling the warmth.

A knock at her door interrupted her thoughts. With a wide grin, Eusebio poked his head into the room. "The Vatican artifact is here. We're getting it out of the van and bringing it in."

The crate was brought in and set on a table in the middle of the research area. Jackie walked around the table as Eusebio reviewed the manifest. She opened a drawer and pulled out a pair of cloth gloves.

"Steady the crate as I remove the tablet," Jackie said as they lifted the top off. "There is writing on both sides." She turned the tablet over, looking at Dr. Bustamante. He nodded, standing opposite her, helping support the artifact.

They positioned the tablet face up. "These guys look familiar. The art style looks similar to the two in the star chart room, Enki and Enlil." She followed the cuneiform writing with her finger. "The father, Anu, saw that the disagreements between his sons would bring doom upon the creations. Although Enki had provided the path to wisdom, the people had not fully embraced the teachings. Enlil, lord of the land, slayer of beasts, and conqueror of the enemies, was determined to judge the creations under their laws. Humans should follow the law because it was presented to them by the gods. Enlil became furious that the creations did not embrace the law but expected to become like those who created the law, immortal. Enki, lord of the sea, was calm. He described their creations' accomplishments to his brother. He pressed for time, asking if Enlil had become great in only one day. Although the people understand the law, they must understand why it was written. Enlil relented and praised the birth of Eridu, Uruk, and other cities. Enlil agreed to allow two cycles to pass. If the people could overcome their confusion and embrace the word, the sword would not be necessary. Anu was pleased with the brothers' agreement and ordered a return home for two cycles where they would await the time of judgment." Eusebio turned off the recorder on his phone.

"It appears to parallel other Sumerian myths and stories," Eusebio said to the silent room.

"The cardinal said it is one of the oldest artifacts in the library. The Church received it from Constantine the Great in the early 300s. Earlier records are not as accurate," She replied. Jackie swung a mounted magnifying lens around, taking a closer look at the writing.

Eusebio cleared his throat. "Sumerian mythology stories are nearly identical or parallel to the ones from the Abrahamic religions. Judgment exists in many religions. It's in my book."

Jackie looked up from the tablet. "Really? We've all read your book. You signed the copies. You don't have to sell us."

"I was only stating an observation." He shrugged. "Okay, okay. Not to get sidetracked, but when does JPL expect to get the star dating model up again?"

"I believe they said it would be up this week," Jackie replied. "The development team is balancing time with their other projects. Tracking the alien craft is their immediate concern—and detecting other near-Earth objects, of course."

Jackie turned away from the table, removing her cloth gloves. "I'd love to examine the other side of the tablet, but I will be late for a budget meeting with the dean. I need him to approve our travel for next year before the holiday break." She shook her head. "Eusebio, go ahead if you want a head start."

Silicon Valley, California

Jamal stretched out on a poolside chair, eyes closed, letting the sunlight wash over his dark skin through the glass-enclosed patio. Hip-hop music played softly in the background; the only sound was from the water in the pool hitting the sides. He heard the dragging of pool shoes approaching and opened his eyes to see Brynt's pale, thin form, shaggy brown hair, and long red board shorts. He closed his eyes again. "Man, you need fashion advice and a gym membership."

"Yeah, okay, when we hit it big with the game, I'll get right on that. Jamal, yo, you gotta listen to Isaacson. He is laying it all out there," Brynt said before jumping in the pool. He was one of his two roommates and co-founder of their startup application company, Shunned Drummer.

"No, let me rest. I was coding all night," Jamal replied, eyes still closed.

"Fine, fine, but I'm going to put the show on while I hang out in the pool."

Jamal tried blocking the sound and drifting back to his daydream, but it was no use. Brynt had it turned up so he could hear it across the pool.

Jamal heard the familiar Staten Island accent of George Isaacson coming out of the wireless speakers. "We know now that aliens exist, but we must push for releasing all the information the government has. The info is out there now, so tell us the whole history. All of it: Roswell, Eisenhower, Truman, Three Mile Island, and the nuke shutdowns. What do you think, Truth Seekers? Can you handle the truth? I can."

Jamal raised the back of his chair, locking it in place. "He's got it all wrong. If they came here and scouted us out, they would find a resource-rich world for the taking. It's Columbus two-point-oh, and this time, all of humanity are the indigenous people."

"C'mon, we could fight back if we had to. You know the government has actual craft and technology locked up that we don't even know about. Maybe he's right, and they will be so far advanced that they don't need to destroy us. They could be peaceful."

Jamal scoffed. "I don't think they'll be friendly. They have no reason to be. Hollywood has corrupted our minds. The hero always finds an escape from the alien overall plan because we assume they would think like us, with the same wants and desires, but why would they? On a cosmic capabilities scale, we would be so far behind, it would be easier to take humanity out rather than try to help us evolve. We like war, distrust, fear, and proving our superiority over one another. We don't share, we don't fight fair, and we like to keep our secrets. It's in our DNA."

"I don't know, Jamal. Maybe they are Embassy Ships, and the galaxy is like *Star Trek*, and we're just not invited yet. Maybe someone will send a signal letting them know we're here."

"Pshht. It would be some diplomatic word salad that doesn't say anything. I hope they come here. The world needs something big to disrupt our happy little lives. Maybe if there were some big event, we would start working together to solve some of our world problems. How about we fix everyone's food, education, housing, or medical treatment? That's what I'm going to do when we hit the millionaire's club—give back to the people, change the world." Jamal stood up and picked up his T-shirt from the pool deck. "I'm heading in. The Weasel isn't going to launch itself."

"Cool, man. I sent you a few hundred updates, and all of the cosmetics Shalla created are in the digital library. She went all out and still has a ton of stuff to add over the next few months."

Jamal grinned. "Less than a year before the Feisty Weasel takes the world by storm. The first of its kind." His face turned serious. "Brynt, don't get any ideas from Isaacson. I better not see any aliens pop up in the game code."

Brynt gave a thumbs up. "Roger that. You don't want to *see* any aliens."

February 2026
Staten Island, New York

George nervously looked around, pulling his hood up and shifting in his oversized winter coat. He looked down the street but couldn't see his apartment building through the heavy snowfall. His boots crunched through half a foot of snow. He flexed his hand a few times before bringing it out of his pocket to scroll through the texts. They were all from Arizona, signed with the hashtag "Silver." George felt nauseous. He put the phone back in his pocket, trudging down the snow-covered sidewalk. He shivered as the icy wind cut across his cheeks, slipping into his hood and down the back of his coat.

Three black Ford Interceptors, free of snow, were parked in front of his building. His heart began racing, and his chest clenched with fear. He tripped, stepping through the doorway, his foot catching on the threshold, causing him to crash to the floor. Time seemed to slow down as he got up and stepped through the main entrance. He saw the group in suits and tried to step back out of the building, tripping over the lip of the doorway again. A hundred conspiracy theories about men in black, secret police, and Majestic 12 were ripping through his head. Two of the group reached down and grabbed his arms. He thought of trying to get away, to run, but his legs wouldn't cooperate.

"Mr. Isaacson? George Isaacson?"

He snapped back to reality. The two helped him up. "Uh, yeah, that's me."

"Are you okay? We'd like to ask you a few questions. Do you mind if we head up to your apartment?"

"Um, sure." He swallowed hard, sweat running down his back, despite the cold.

The agent showed him her credentials. "George, I am Special Agent Andrea Smith, FBI. We have a warrant to search your phone." She handed the paper to him as they rode the elevator to the fourth floor.

George handed the phone to the agents. "What is this about? I haven't done anything." He opened the apartment door, feeling embarrassed by the peeling red-brown paint in several spots. "Come in. Do I need to call anyone?"

"Not at the moment. As I said, we have a few questions about where you get the information for your show."

George thought for a moment. He looked over at the two agents, who had attached his phone to a device they had brought in. *They didn't ask me to unlock it.* His hands felt clammy. "I don't know who is sending me information. It sounds legitimate and supports the theme of my show, so I use it."

Agent Smith sat silently, looking into his eyes. "We are investigating a sensitive leak. How did you set up this transfer of information?"

George lowered his eyes, his shoulders slumping. "I didn't. It just started coming in. I don't know who it is from. The numbers are from Arizona."

Agent Smith looked over to the agents with his phone, and they nodded. "Mr. Isaacson, do you think you could help us? I am sure you don't want to do anything that could threaten national security, do you?"

George sat up. "No, but I know I haven't done anything wrong. I haven't said anything that would make it illegal for me to release it.

I'm not selling it, and I haven't said anything that would indicate an intelligence source or something related to national defense."

She pursed her lips. "Not yet."

"Then I am protected under the First Amendment, freedom of the press."

"Mr. Isaacson, you're a conspiracy theorist with a YouTube channel."

George shook his head. "My listeners would disagree. The former conspiracy theory about aliens is now mainstream. The government does not get to dictate what is or is not news. I am a journalist, even if you disagree with my stories. People want the truth."

She stood, looking down at him. "Be careful, Mr. Isaacson. If we need to come back, it may not be under the same circumstances. Think about what you say and where you get your info."

An agent handed the phone back to George and moved toward the door.

Agent Smith stood and turned to leave. She paused, turning back to him. "I look forward to hearing what you have to say tonight." She smiled before leaving the apartment.

George's heart raced as he locked the door behind them. He tried to remember where the five agents stood, replaying the encounter in his head. He moved to the kitchen, running his hand under the counter, and looking in the drawers. He frantically moved things around, searching thoroughly.

He made a call. When Tim answered, words rushed out of George's mouth. "Tim, have you been sending me texts? Because if you have, that's all good, but you scared the crap outta me. Damnit, I'm scared man. I am mad scared."

Tim calmly replied. "Whoa, George, calm down. What are you talking about? I promise you, I have not sent anything. In fact, I have been actively avoiding contact. What is going on?" The concern in Tim's voice was unmistakable.

George took a deep breath that did little to calm him down. "The FBI was just here. They wanted to know where I was getting my info from. I keep getting texts from someone in Arizona, never the same number, but always the same hashtag. I was looking for confirmation that the info was legit. I'm not questioning it now. It's scary stuff about the alien object. I received a text a few months back, which turned out to be true. Now I have two new texts, and if they are true, I don't know if I should say anything. I mean, I know I should because we have seen this movie play out. The government or military keeps a secret until it's too late 'for our good' or 'to protect society.' Then it's the unprepared people who die. I don't want to be the guy with the info when it all hits the fan."

Tim was silent. "George, what do the texts say?"

George, calming down a bit at the thought of telling someone else and taking some of the pressure off, replied, "The texts said the government is covering up that the alien craft has turned toward Earth, and that the defense forces of the US are on alert, planning a response. Is it true? Do you know about this?"

Tim was silent for a long few moments. "George, listen carefully: Parts are true, but I didn't tell you that. We aren't on alert, but everything else sounds correct. You can't say anything to anyone linking me to this. Blame whoever is texting you. I haven't been to Arizona in years, so they won't tie it to me if this becomes something. Someone believes you are the one who can get the info out, and their access is pretty far up the chain. I'd go with it. If this goes wrong, we'll have much bigger issues. Maybe this is how the government will prep everyone for the news and slip it to a social media personality to prep the fringe. You could get famous off this. You're the reporter, not the source."

George laughed uneasily. "Yeah, I guess so, and maybe I'll throw it out tonight and see what happens. Thanks, Tim. I was losing it. Too many conspiracy theories. Tell the wife and kiddo I said hi."

"Will do, buddy. Relax for a while. People will jump on this, and half of your followers probably already believe it."

"I will, thanks. I'll, uh, keep you out of it. Take care." George hung up. He sighed, looking out the window at the falling snow.

◆ ◆ ◆

George calmed down as he got closer to the start of his show. He shifted to his online persona, leaning back and propping a foot on one of the milk crates he used for recycling. After ten minutes, he sat up, checked his mic and headphones, and cued his intro.

"Seekers, I have a great show planned tonight." He leaned into the camera, eyes wide. "I hope you are all ready for the excitement. Let's preempt the discussion with a question. What is going on out there? The NASA show was pulled because they had nothing new. But that's not the whole story." George spun his chair around and came back around with a Monster Ultra Gold in his hand. He popped the top and took a sip. He leaned in again, with a serious look. "Let's have a conversation. I have some interesting news from my source. So, the embassy ships have finished their meeting. I guess all politicians like to take their time saying what they want. One source told me that the Earth governments had hoped we would be invited to the table, but that didn't happen. As a matter of fact, a few of the factions were not happy about the announcement acknowledging their existence. They feel their hands have been forced and will have to take greater protective measures as people believe the stories of abductions, meetings, and other activities."

George paused to take a sip of his Monster Ultra Gold, ensuring it was clear on the camera. "Here is my exclusive." He let his comment hang in the air. "One of the ships is headed to Earth, and they are not happy. Without the communications from the Gray ambassador, we don't know which one it is. This has caused panic in our leaders, with preparations taking place worldwide. At least two other sources have confirmed this information. I don't want to cause a panic, but I recommend you all watch for the signs of deployments of military equipment. Some may not have an obvious use but will become obvious in time. A hostile force may be heading right for us, and the world's governments don't know what to do. Get prepared and keep your eyes open. I'll continue to report the news to you, the people seeking the truth.

"Before I start getting comments about this all being in my imagination, I want to provide you with proof of the truth. Earlier today, I was visited by agents of the FBI. Yeah, you heard that right. Hello, Agent Smith. They wanted to know who my source was. So I have a question for all of you listening right now. Why would they care who my source is if it was all fake? Let that sink in."

George leaned back, raising his hands questioningly. "Truth Seekers, if I disappear, you know where I'll be. Probably in an alphabet agency cell somewhere. Let's take a quick break, and we'll jump into some calls."

George's hands were shaking. He headed to the bathroom to splash water on his face.

Zhongguancun, China

Wu Kai stepped inside the control room, ensuring the door was sealed behind him. He wiped his hands with a handkerchief, returning it to his pocket. He crossed the short distance to the row of workstations he referred to as Dragon Control. He approached the primary station, smelling plums. He started to smile before catching himself.

"Xiao Fan, what is the status of testing?"

The young woman did not look up, focusing on the displays in front of her. "Director Wu, preliminary tests were satisfactory. We are ready to begin simultaneous gameplay."

"Very well, begin. Set the number at one million games."

"One million entered. Starting now."

The graphic display representing the qubit field arrays sprang to life. As the qubits were engaged, their color would change based on the amount of data processed. The effect was a series of pulsing expanding rainbows in the pattern of a drop hitting a pool of still water. A counter at the bottom of the primary control station indicated how many games were played and the win/loss ratio.

As the program learned and played more games, the counter picked up speed, becoming unreadable.

The primary source of the ripples stopped. What looked like slow rainfall on a pond began to form, waves extending from numerous circles overlapping with greater frequency. Wu Kai looked at the qubit expansion numbers and held his breath.

"Director Wu, qubit engagement is over one thousand."

The raindrop ripple patterns now appeared on the screen at the level of a downpour. Colors rippled in all directions.

As suddenly as the colors had started, everything stopped, and the screen turned gray.

"What happened?" Wu Kai asked. "Only eighteen minutes have passed."

"Director, it looks like there is an anomaly in the code. The program completed all games in under ten minutes. When those were complete, it started again, playing against itself. Then everything stopped."

Wu Kai sucked in his breath through clenched teeth. "Can we determine why?"

Fan Meifen nodded, focusing on the results. "The program learned as it played, adapting strategies as it gained experience. Instead of working linearly, playing a game, learning from it, and then playing another, the program adapted to play multiple games simultaneously because it understood that it had the resources to do so. Each raindrop was a new game. At its peak, the program was playing over ten thousand games. Data was passed across the network in each of the overlaps—the waves we saw on the screen—even though qubits were engaged in other games. Data were passed between games in progress, increasing the learning speed and adjusting strategy to correct previous mistakes."

Wu Kai nodded. "Excellent progress. Modify test two to include multiple games dissimilar in strategy. This is turning out to be a fine day."

GWU, Archaeology Department, Washington, DC

Eusebio adjusted his chair, pulling the handle underneath to raise it higher. When Tim's image appeared on the camera feed, he waived. "Hey, Tim, Jackie is out sick today. I'll be running it from this side."

"I hope she feels better. We are all set. Are you okay with the changes we made?"

"Yes, we are good. Tim, I'm sending the file now." He hit send, watching the upload bar for the high-res image.

"I have it, loading the image into the model," Tim answered, moving in and out of the frame as he adjusted things off-screen. Eusebio saw the image load to the left side of the comparison program.

"I am starting the comparison algorithm." The program began the familiar one-second-per-image comparison, lighting up the actual stellar image against the fixed position of the star chart. They started the bracketing process at 100 years. The program began counting down slowly. After about thirty seconds, the bracketing kicked in, bouncing back and forth in time, zeroing in on the image, locking in on 1567 BCE. Tim scrunched his face looking at the data. "I'm getting an error. We have a match for 1567 BCE, but not all stars are included. Just a sec, I'm going to capture the matches on your screen."

A third of the stars turned green, aligning with positions on the artifact.

"That's odd. Only about a third of the stars match, but the model stopped. Give us a minute." Tim turned to someone off-screen, motioning as he talked.

Tim turned to the camera. "Eusebio, we will run a quick diagnostic and try again. The engineers here are telling me the model is working fine. Unless there was some cosmic event we don't know about, the stars should match."

"Sounds good. We are ready when you are," Eusebio acknowledged.

"I'll set the bracketing at a ten-year interval instead of a century. Starting now." The comparison program tracked the image as the model moved the star positions back in time. Eusebio watched the stars slowly move across the image in the background. The process took almost ten minutes, with the lower setting settling on the same date, 1567 BCE.

"Still only a third of the stars match. Something is not right."

Eusebio shook his head. "I see the match, but the dates do not match Eridu and the Sumerian timeline. I will confirm with Jackie, but that date is after the fall of the Sumerian civilization. The Akkadians had overtaken them."

Eusebio opened a high-definition picture of the star chart. "The work is consistent across the carving. I don't see anything leading us to believe it was modified at a later date." Eusebio rubbed his fingers together on his right hand, brow furrowed at the results. "Tim, let me dig into the images from that room. I'll let you know if I find anything."

Tim waved into the camera.

Eusebio ended the call and pulled a small notebook from his pocket, making a note to talk to Jackie about the star chart.

CNEOS, JPL, Pasadena, California

Sharon's desk was a mess. It was covered with pictures, readouts, graphs, and papers not sorted in any discernible pattern. She sat behind the desk, elbows on top, her head resting in her hands. She heard a light knock on the doorframe.

"Whoa, Sharon, are you okay? You look tired, and that," Tim pointed at her desk, "is not like you at all."

"I'll be fine. I was reviewing the data you sent up. Is it confirmed, and who else has seen it?"

"The calculations are good. All of my group have looked at it. The object is maintaining a steady speed."

She shook her head as she picked up a picture from the lunar array and moved it to another pile. A beeping sound came from beneath a small stack of papers. She retrieved her phone, reading the alarm text.

"Okay, thanks. I've got a call with the Administrator in a few minutes. Keep on top of it, please."

"Yeah, of course. Sharon, as your friend, you are looking pretty rough. You don't look good."

"I know, it's the stress. I'll be okay. I just need a good night's sleep. Thanks, Tim."

Before joining the call, she checked her video feed to ensure the clutter on her desk was not visible. As the feed connected, she saw Administrator James smiling at her.

"Good morning, Sharon. How are you doing?" James asked.

"Good morning, Terry. We are receiving good data from the lunar array and the other systems. We have confirmed two things: the object's mass and velocity. Both are listed in our weekly report. The object appears to have stabilized at a cruising speed of around thirty-two hundred MPH, which does not sound like much compared to the Voyager speeds. Still, the mass is a quarter that of the moon, or about the size of Australia, which is phenomenal when you consider the force necessary to move something that big. We have not been able to discern anything about the propulsion. We aren't detecting any emissions." Sharon paused.

The Administrator's brow furrowed, and his lips pursed. "How does this affect the timeline?"

Sharon nodded. "The modified date of arrival is late 2033. The model shows an impact at the current speed would occur in August. It could be later if the object slows as it did last year. We do not know how it will deal with the gravitational forces of the other planets. However, the consensus is that they will not be an issue as they are technologically advanced. The decades the President thought he had are gone. We have under eight years before the object arrives, assuming it continues its direct path."

Sharon felt the Administrator studying her face. The silence was worrisome. "Sharon, I'll be in touch. I'm going to call the White House. All we can do is provide the data. Get your travel bag ready. I'll call you later. Thank you and your team. We need to keep them focused and calm. Though I don't see how this can be kept quiet for long."

The video chat ended. Sharon sat back in her chair, staring at the center monitor on her desk. She took a deep breath, looking at the picture of her parents smiling in the foreground of a beautiful snowcapped mountainscape in Montana. She felt her stomach turn, acid reflux climbing up her throat. Mindlessly she opened her desk drawer and took a few antacids. *I should go home, let all of this go.* She shook her head, sat forward, gathered all the papers on her desk, and arranged them neatly into a single pile. She stood to leave, her mind already making a checklist for another trip to Washington.

National Security Council, White House, Washington, DC

President Fernandez entered the room more lively than usual, heading straight for his chair. He held his hand up to the Chief of Staff, cutting him off, and pointed to the NASA Administrator, not missing a beat. "I want to skip the formality and get right to the matter at hand. I expect everyone to listen, think carefully before speaking, and be open. I also expect that you have all read the brief. If you have not, do not assume you know the whole story. Open the briefing packages in front of you and skim through them. Go ahead, Sharon."

The Administrator nodded, indicating Sharon should begin. She took a drink of her water and opened the briefing book, feeling the bile rise in her throat. Taking a deep breath, she began. "Mr. President, a few months ago, we reported that the objects appeared to merge into a single object. We believe that is still the case. The object has continued to accelerate. It settled into what we believe is its cruising speed in the last few weeks. It appears to be heading toward the Earth. The adjusted timeline has the object arriving in under eight years."

The President interjected, "I believe this matter has developed into a serious global event. We will be meeting regularly on this topic, and I expect cooperation from every arm of the government. We have plenty of questions that need answers and more that we have not thought of yet. So, let me know what you are thinking." He opened the floor, looking intently around the room.

The Secretary of Defense spoke. "Sir, we have a few contingency plans drawn up over the years. I would, however, guess that they have not been prioritized and would doubt their actual applicability. I will task the service chiefs with conducting an audit of potentially applicable plans. There will be a lot of questions. I would also like to nominate General Michaels as the lead for DoD planning. As the

Chief of Operations of Space Force, it makes sense for him to be the supported commander."

The President nodded. "Noted. Sarah, what about Homeland?"

Secretary Genson leaned into the table. "Mr. President, I have John Worthing working on the China issue, but I believe he can do both. He can connect his staff with Dr. Berzing in the functional areas. He has good relationships with leaders in government and industry across the tech spectrum, which will come in handy."

"Sounds good." President Fernandez looked toward Aaron Reindhold, the Secretary of Energy, a large man, still in great shape despite the decades since he played football at the Naval Academy. "Aaron, I want Energy in on this. We need appropriate messaging. The public will believe what they have seen in the movies. We will get questions on nuclear weapons, safety, fallout, preparedness, and a half dozen other things."

The Secretary of State, Theresa Fredericks, spoke next. "Sir, I would like State to be the opposing train of thought to military action. We have thousands of career diplomats. I suggest we put together a plan for diplomacy in case their reasons for coming to us are peaceful."

"Okay, let's prepare for the worst and hope for the best." The President stood, his eyes scanning the faces of the men and women he expected to do whatever it would take to keep their citizens safe.

"I don't want another joint announcement. In fact, I am leaning against an announcement until we know what we will do. When the time comes, we will answer the questions on the Sunday morning shows truthfully, but only as much as we need to. I don't want a crazed panic sweeping the country because some people get the idea in their heads that they can do whatever they want because they think the world is ending."

He turned to his Chief of Staff. "Schedule meetings with the house and senate leaders and the party leaders over the next week.

I'll talk to each of them. Terry and Sharon, I want you for those, as well."

The pair nodded.

"I want all of you to keep this quiet for now. I do not plan on waiting until the last minute to let people know, but I do want some time. Report back, and let's see where we are in two weeks."

The President looked around the table. Seeing the nods of agreement, he turned and left the room.

April 2026
Silicon Valley, California

Jamal was busy typing code for their mobile game application. His fingers flew over the keyboard as his gaze shifted between the three wide monitors. He didn't slouch when he worked at the computer. His father had reminded him constantly to sit up tall and proud. Never let anyone see you brought down by anything.

At the thought of his father, his mind returned him to his home in Pasadena. The house was built in the late '80s but had been kept up well and was in a nice suburban neighborhood. The kind you saw on TV with kids riding bikes up and down the street, beautiful trees, and picket fences. They had only lived in the house for five years, but his fondest memories were anchored there. He and his little sister spent most days playing outside with their friends and neighbors, running through the neighborhood, feeling free and safe.

Until that day, just before Thanksgiving.

He remembered his parents fighting, and his father was furious that they were being forced to move. He wanted to fight, take the company that had pushed the eminent domain ruling to the Supreme Court if he had to. His mother had been upset, too, but she wanted to move on, take the settlement and start a new life.

The day they left their home was bright and sunny, with no clouds in the sky. The air was cool but not cold. Jamal swore he could smell the ocean, though they were too far away. His mother had commented that it was a sign from God that they were doing the right thing, starting new. He remembered packing his toys in boxes, keeping a few of his favorites out for their trip in the car. He and Sarina looked out her window as they drove away from the only home she had known.

Sarina was looking forward to being the first in the family to have a birthday in their new house. She was sleeping, leaning against the window, using Tony, her yellow bear, as a pillow. A box filled with pots and pans rested between them.

It happened fast, just before the on-ramp to the highway. He remembered sitting on the side of the road after the accident, crying as they pulled his sister's body from the overturned car. He heard his father telling the police that the truck had run a red light, his right arm hanging in a sling, blood covering his shirt, his mother kneeling, tears streaming down her cheeks as she prayed. His family was devastated and almost fell apart. Jamal had thrown himself into his schoolwork to escape the pain of losing his sister.

His mother had worried about his shift from loving everything outside—baseball, playing with the neighbor's kids, and making sure his sister was included in everything—to a stoic teen who threw himself into science, computers, and math. His grades rose to the top of his class, not because he was the smartest but because he worked the hardest—a trait he still had.

Jamal shook himself from the reverie, wiping a tear from his eye, reaching to the side to run his fingers along Tony's worn fuzz. In college, he had researched the development of the area his family had been forced out of, finding that it had been a defense tech manufacturing and research company behind the land grab. He had tried to find out why the company needed that land. The information was hidden behind trade secrets or classified by the government. News stories hinted at questionable deals with local and federal politicians for permits and funding. Still, nothing was ever substantiated. *Always secrets, the government kept too many secrets.*

He opened his browser and clicked a link for one of George Isaacson's older shows. He continued to code, listening, and keeping his thoughts separated from the sound coming from the speakers. Jamal flipped through the moderate stack of code pages with Brynt's notes highlighted in blue.

He picked up his phone, dialed a number, hit the speakerphone setting, and set it down as he continued to type.

"What's up, Jamal?"

"Brynt, I'm looking through the data from the alpha test. It looks like the puzzles scaled too fast. The players couldn't overcome the challenges."

"Yeah, Shalla and I were looking at that, as well. We need to scale the difficulty down and consider each player's weasel level. I think the difficulty was scaled based on the highest player levels and then counted the number of players engaged, which destroyed the low-level players. Too many traps were generated in the maze and ran out of players."

"Ahh, that makes sense. Did you figure out where the game crashed?"

"It was at one of two places: The Sharks Game at the SAP Center or the St. Patrick's Day parade. Both were packed with people. More players than we expected."

"GPS integration and puzzle development looked good, I compared the two, and they were nothing alike. Good versatility and Shalla's cosmetic rewards are amazing. Okay, I'm going to keep at it. I'll see you later." He focused on the code, visualizing what each command did, his mind processing the changes he made.

Jamal always felt great when he realized he had entered the flow, losing himself in his art, disregarding all measures of time. He unconsciously looked to the lower left of the screen, checking the time. Six hours had passed, and the last compile had shown no errors. "Just in time. Georgie, let's have a chat tonight," Jamal said to himself, closing the game program and opening the live feed from the George Isaacson Show.

Smithsonian Air and Space Museum, Washington, DC

George looked over the railing at the display of rockets on the Smithsonian Air and Space Museum floor. He felt like laughing at the collection of humanity's accomplishments in space compared to what was heading their way.

"In the end" played from his pocket. He took out the phone. "Hey, Dad."

"George, I stopped by your apartment. Where are you?"

"I sent you a text. I'm in DC."

"Oh, you know I don't follow all that since your uncle added me to those group texts. I turned it off. Talking about idiotic things at all hours of the night. You didn't get arrested by the FBI, did you?"

"No, Dad, I didn't get arrested. I told you, I didn't do anything."

"Are you sleeping? You looked rough last time I saw you."

"I'm fine. I'm going to tour the capital later, maybe visit our congresswoman's office if we can."

"George, don't bring up aliens. They would probably still lock you up for talking crazy, despite them acknowledging it. Hell, I was watching the news last night, and a few in Congress are pushing the narrative that the President is misleading the people to help his party in the midterms. Some networks even brought on scientists to debunk NASA's data."

"Dad, the data is good. I have talked to the people who put it together, and I trust them. They wouldn't lie to me."

"If you say so. Sometimes people tell stories to make themselves look good."

"Come on, Dad, let's not get into it again. I'm sticking with my story. People like it, no one is getting hurt, and now at least part of it is true." George looked around to see if anyone was listening.

"Fine, fine, George. I looked up your YouTube channel, and you have many people following what you are telling them. Think about that. You be careful down there. Don't trust anyone. That town is full of snakes."

"Got it, Dad. I'll call when I get back."

George was an hour into his show. He had planned to talk about evidence at the Smithsonian showing the government knew about aliens but had shifted to the story his Dad had handed him on a platter: Congress attacking the truth. As the ad for Monster Energy drinks finished, he hit the broadcast button on his laptop.

"And I'm back, Believers, and it is time to open the lines for more calls. Let's see who we have tonight." He scrolled through the list of calls, scanning the suggested topics. He paused when he saw FedBuster22's name in red. "Truth Seekers, we have a treat tonight. It looks like my number one fan is calling in. Let's post those nice chats about my nemesis, FedBuster22. What's up, FB?" George looked into the camera, lips pressed together, forcing a tight-lipped smile.

"Georgie, I had to give you a call tonight. I have been listening to your shows, and it sounds like you need some emotional support. So I want to let you know that I am here for you." The voice paused. George was quiet. The chat window was scrolling fast with comments, good and bad.

"FB, how are you doing? It's been a while. I thought you may have given up the farce life." George chuckled.

"Not a chance, been seeking the truth, like you; I just don't believe the hype, and I'm here to give you some support."

"Support, yeah, I have heard that before. Do you have the proof you claimed to have that NASA was lying? How about the government lying about aliens for decades, now lying about the proof that aliens are real? What about those? Come on, FB, what do you have tonight?" George taunted him.

"Well, let's declare this a historic moment in our relationship, and no, I'm not getting you flowers. I don't want to make your girl jealous. I agree with you, and I think something is happening with the spacecraft. It has gotten too quiet. So, the objects came together a year ago. Are we supposed to believe they flew together at incredible speeds for over a year while we watched? Then when we figured out what was happening, they decided to sit there. The whole scenario doesn't make sense to me. So, I think you are right. They are coming here, and we are screwed. It is a Hollywood movie, and the public always gets wiped out while the rich and connected get to escape to a bunker, a ship, or whatever. So, I agree with you."

George was stunned but didn't want to lose control of the narrative, so he spoke quickly. "They could just as likely be heading here to help us. We don't know, and panic isn't going to help."

FB laughed. "Maybe, but I tell you what: I think we will know the truth soon. They can't keep their secrets forever. Wait and see, my friend."

Fed Buster ended the call, and George pressed forward with the story. "Well, there you go, a little creepy but a momentous occasion still, and you all got to hear it. FB believes that the government is still hiding something, which isn't good for us. What do you think? Jump in and let me know."

GWU, Archaeology Department, Washington, DC

Jackie slammed her hand down on the table and kicked her chair away from the table. She reached back and undid her hair tie before pulling her hair back and reapplying it. "Seven weeks, and we still can't get a match. The last time I talked to Tim, I think he was getting as frustrated as we were. He says they have gone over the model and insist that it is something with the map." Jackie spoke to Eusebio and her team as they looked at a high-definition picture of the map room in Iraq.

Deputy Minister Sal-A-Din Mujhaad stepped into the frame. "Dr. Mandrapilias, can you hear me? We are on track to move the wall to the National Museum in a week. What did you want to look at?" he asked.

Jackie looked at the image. The resolution allowed her to see the wall as she had at the site. "I think we missed something. Can you increase the lighting in the room?"

Sal-A-Din spoke to someone off-camera, and the illumination increased, though it looked uneven across the wall. Sal-A-Din noticed the uneven lighting and directed the lights to be repositioned.

As the lighting moved, Eusebio jumped up. "Wait! Did you see that? Dim all the lights but one. Move it across the center of the wall."

Jackie looked at Eusebio and then back at the image. As the light dimmed, the bright light was moved across the wall. Jackie saw it. "Hold. Move the light left slightly."

Sal-A-Din turned and looked at the wall, not seeing anything.

"There," Jackie continued. "About twenty centimeters above the equator, at the center of the light. I see a glint in the star indentation."

Sal-A-Din reached off-screen for a bright flashlight. He moved to where Jackie directed him. He leaned in. "I see a tiny piece of metal, looks like gold, in the center of the indentation. The shadow from the depth of the indentations blocks it unless the light is shined directly in." He moved to examine another indentation, noting, "I see something in this one, as well." He moved the light closer. "It's silver." After more inspections, he confirmed to the team that each indentation contained a small metallic ball. The team in Iraq identified three colors: gold, silver, and copper.

Sal-A-Din turned back to the camera. "Dr. Mandrapilias, what would you like us to do?"

Jackie smiled. "Nice catch," she whispered. "Sal-A-Din, do you have a team to check each indentation? My team is standing by and can annotate on our image."

Sal-A-Din nodded. "Yes, we have the museum preparation team here. They should have what we need. There are many indentations to check. This is probably going to take all night. Give us an hour to set up, and we should be ready. I will remain, as well." Looking at the monitor under the camera, he laughed. "Let's see how this turns out. We keep making history."

Jackie placed her hand on Eusebio's shoulder. "Go get some rest. I'll watch this. One of us needs to be fresh in the morning."

"Makes sense. Call me if you need a break. I'm ten minutes away."

The team worked over the next twelve hours, marking each star position on their digital copy of the star chart. After they confirmed that only three types of metal were present inside the star indentations, Sal-A-Din authorized the removal of three metal balls, one of each type, to be sent to a lab for analysis. They had chosen three off to one side near each other. The wall would stay in place until they could examine it more closely.

Jackie had made a few calls through the night to help push for authorization for another area scan, primarily the wall with the star chart. She then talked to the Air Force team on-site to see if it would be possible to scan through the wall. They recommended using a recently deployed X-ray system developed to help forces look through walls for people or IED traps. It would provide more detail on the scale she described. She agreed, and the Master Sergeant said they could get the equipment down to the site within the day. The equipment would arrive sometime after they finished the color mapping of the star chart.

Sal-A-Din had arranged for a team to arrive from Nasiriyah in the morning. Initial examination identified the metal balls as gold, silver, and copper. Jackie's team changed the colors on the star chart to match the three colors. She then had the team filter to a single color for each of the three metals. They cleaned the images and sent the three copies to JPL in California.

◆ ◆ ◆

"I have brought coffee for the team," Eusebio said as he entered the room, looking refreshed from a good night's sleep, a drink tray in each hand.

"You all look exhausted," he said as he passed the coffees to each team member. He turned to look at the large screen, watching the teams on the screen set up their equipment.

He set the remaining coffees down. "Jackie. I had a thought last night." He pulled up the images from the star chart room. "These are the images from the ruins cross-referenced with several others. Take a look at this." He pointed toward the screen, indicating the figure on the right. "At first, I thought there was anger, but the more I look at it, I see sadness, almost like the judging must happen, and each failure brings sadness."

Jackie leaned into the image, then put her coffee down. She minimized the feed to a corner of the screen and searched through the images they had brought back from their dig. She found the one she wanted, opening it to full screen. It was a close-up of the face.

"I think you are right. I usually spend more time in the cuneiform looking for descriptions of the images, time, and events. But, looking at the face, I see a dark spot that may be a shadow or dirt. It could be a tear. It is interesting, as I do not recall Enlil being sad or tearful. Typically, he is portrayed as having a hard heart and no sympathy for the failure of humanity."

Eusebio leaned in. "This is similar to the description of man's judgment in Revelations. The Son of God is tasked with judging humanity."

Jackie sat back from the screen, looking at the image of Enlil. "Hmm. Enlil is not usually associated with being sympathetic with humanity."

He nodded, "Okay, follow me. For centuries, the Church has had a closed-minded view of other religions, stories, myths, and legends. They would brush them aside and discount them as nothing more than the attempts of Satan to mislead man. What if that was the wrong view? The most truly devout see the wonder in everything because they believe God is omnipotent. In the truest sense of the word, nothing is beyond Him. With that belief, it becomes easier to see His teachings in everything. The Holy Bible is not all-inclusive. For it to cover every instance of a miracle, a commandment, or a story would fill an incredible volume of books and become unwieldy. The stories and accounts in the Bible could be from any era. It is possible to discover similar lessons in studying His word and that of other beliefs." He paused, having not expected to broach the entire subject, but he would follow where the discussion led. "A genuine belief in such a manner would allow equal distribution throughout the people of the world of His word. If the lessons learned through similar stories lead to similar conclusions—'do not kill, do not steal, love your fellow man, and others'—wouldn't it be easier to say that God is not exclusive to the Abrahamic religions but extends His love, teachings, and wonder through all mediums?"

Jackie was silent. "That is a refreshing outlook. Were you up all night?" She sipped her coffee, looking thoughtfully at the screen.

"No, I did get a full night."

A voice from the Iraqi team interrupted them. "Dr. Mandrapilias, we are set to scan the wall with the mini radar. Is there anything you want us to focus on?" the tech asked.

"Not specifically. Start in the upper left and move across the wall horizontally. I'm not sure if we will see anything, but we missed the metal in the holes, as they are so small," she replied.

The team in Iraq focused a camera on the readout on the radar screen. As soon as they moved the radar across the wall, lines appeared.

"What are those lines? They are metal. It looks like wiring connecting the different indentations." Jackie moved closer to the screen. "That is odd, but they aren't all connected. It looks like a disjointed spiderweb pattern with each spot connected to others of the same metal, but some have only a single line while others have multiple."

Eusebio added the lines to their digital picture. Lines connecting copper indentations did not connect to silver or gold. The same applied to the other metals. "Oh, it's so simple. There are three maps." The process continued for a few more hours before they had a complete picture.

Jackie looked up at the ceiling before leaning back into the camera view. "Sal-A-Din, nice work, my friend. I will send you copies of the three star charts. This will be an amazing display. I don't recall another instance of multiple maps layered on top of one another. This is unlike anything we have ever found."

Sal-A-Din nodded. He smiled, the exhaustion of the previous two days playing on him. "Dr. Mandrapilias, thank you for the kind words. For so many years, it has been all about war. I am thankful that we can spread good stories from my country. Ma'a salama, my friend."

Jackie waved at the camera before the feed ended. "Eusebio, call Tim at JPL. Let them know the issue was on our end. Schedule the next session, and call me this afternoon to ensure I'm up."

Eusebio continued to focus on a replay of the night's work, not looking up. "Will do. Sleep well."

Zhongguancun, China

Wu Kai straightened his shirt and brushed crumbs off his lap. He grabbed a napkin and a wet wipe and cleaned his hands. Getting up from his desk, he adjusted his pants, pulling them up under his overhanging belly. He wiped the napkin across his chin to clear any crumbs away. He headed out of his office for Dragon Control.

"Good afternoon. Are we ready?" He noted the team sat straighter in their chairs at the sound of his voice.

"Yes, Director Wu, the data has been uploaded, and the guiding directives verified."

Wu Kai looked over the monitors, reviewing the summaries. There was activity occurring in the outer limits of the field. He paused when he looked at the grids displaying the qubit fields. "How long have these fields been engaged?"

Luo Xiaoli, the middle-aged tech in the primary control station, looked at the monitor and pulled the log for the last few days. "Director Wu, this is the activity we reported after the last simultaneous gaming test. The computer has continued to play multiple simulations of the uploaded games. It is playing on both sides. We had planned to brief you earlier this morning."

Wu Kai squinted his eyes, pressing his lips together. "What will happen if those qubits are needed?" he asked, looking at the win/loss stats on the screen, continuing to scroll up at an almost unreadable speed.

"The computer is set to determine the dominant command and work to complete that task first. The current activity should stop if those qubits are required to complete today's test."

Wu Kai nodded. "More challenges for the Dragon. Let them run. Let's see where this goes. Start the program."

Luo Xiaoli pressed the start button on the touch screen and watched the ripples across the qubit fields light up. It was only a graphical representation as actual measurements on the qubit arrays would introduce errors into the quantum data. Temperature sensors across the entire area contributed to the display as they identified areas that required more cooling. Quánqiú lóng, Global Dragon, evaluated over a century of data compiled from markets around the world. It could perform trillions of calculations a second, and the display showed that the fields of qubits were being pushed to understand the rules of this new game.

The program continued to run. Rows of data began filling the output screen. The tech at the main terminal studied the output, which looked to be a list of countries, cities, companies, and a series of numbers.

Wu Kai leaned forward, typing commands on the touch screen. "When the program completes the test, forward the results to me. You will receive a new data file in the evening. Upload it and let me know when the data has been accepted. We will continue this process for the next week and see where it goes."

"Of course, Director Wu."

Wu Kai turned and walked out of the control room.

CNEOS, JPL, Pasadena, California

Tim uploaded the three images into the matching program and linked the copper overlay. "Dr. Mandrapilias, it sounds like you had a good week. We're excited to jump back in. The group has a number of theories and a betting pool to see who is the closest in determining why there are three overlays. We are set here to begin the comparison. Silver first?"

Jackie laughed, answering, "Thank you, Tim. You and your team have been fantastic. I appreciate your patience with this one. The others were easy, and I have already told a few in my field that they may have to edit and update their papers—and yes, we can go silver first."

Tim cringed. "Ouch, that might hurt some egos. Okay, we have the image loaded." Tim worked the controls, locking the image and starting the matching program. "Setting initial comparison at one hundred years." The screen flashed 2020 and then continued for a few seconds, stopping at 1990. An error showed on the screen. "No match possible."

Tim ran through the setup again and restarted the comparison. After a few seconds, the same error popped on the screen. "There seems to be something off with silver. We just can't win with this chart. Let's try gold." After a few minutes, they locked the image, and the model reset for 2020.

"Setting comparison at one century for bracketing." Tim hit start, and the date went backward every second. They passed 1500 BCE with no sign of slowing for bracketing, passing the copper image. After six more minutes, the computer started its bracketing subroutine, narrowing in on a year. After another minute, the date locked on 5167 BCE, and the message "99% Image match" appeared on the screen.

Tim saw that Jackie was looking down, typing something. She would occasionally look at what was probably another monitor.

After a few minutes of typing, she asked, "Is there any indication of the issue with the silver image? Based on the value of the metals, I might have guessed that silver would be somewhere between copper and gold. Maybe they were indicating significant events. Gold could have been the beginning, then silver, followed by copper. It looks like the time between the two is approximately three-and-a-half millennia. Assuming the Sumerians did this, all three should be within the time they controlled the area. By the time they got to 1567 BCE, they were almost gone, replaced by the Akkadians." Jackie looked pensive.

"Dr. Mandrapilias, I have a question. I know you are a Sumerian expert, but is it possible that the value of the metals was different back then?" one of the JPL techs chimed in.

Jackie thought about it and turned to Eusebio, who was looming over her shoulder. "Well, copper was used throughout their civilization. Gold was used decoratively, and silver was used decoratively and for currency. Copper was probably the first to be used. Gold was associated with status, immortality, and the gods. Silver was used as currency after clay. Copper was, as well."

The tech nodded, "Okay that all makes sense and aligns with how *we* view those metals today. But what if there was an alternate ranking of value? I like to watch videos and documentaries, especially now that we know of life off-planet. To a civilization with an alien race looking over them—the Sumerians, the Indians, the Mayans—the metals might have a different value if used for other purposes, like electronics." There was snickering from some of the team members behind him.

"Wait, let me explain. My bachelor's degree is in electrical engineering, so I would prioritize the three metals differently if you asked me what would be more valuable in an electrical project. Of the three, silver has the best conductivity, and gold is the least, with copper in between."

Jackie's eyes widened. "Interesting," she said, and put her finger up, indicating she needed a moment. She worked off-screen, eyes moving as she tried to recall something. "If we go with that theory, the gold map and copper difference are around thirty-six hundred years. If we add thirty-six hundred more, the date hasn't occurred. Can you run the model forward? Of course you can. It was designed for predictive analysis of the space objects."

Tim looked over the model controls. He reset the silver image, set the model to 2020, and changed the time flow to move forward.

"Okay, here we go." He pressed start. The image changed five times: 2030, 2040, 2035, 2032, and 2033, before displaying the message "99% Image match."

"Umm, let me rerun it," Tim said. He reset the model and reran the matching program. In five seconds, the same result showed on the screen.

"Dr. Mandrapilias, I apologize, but we have to cut this short. I'm glad we answered the question, but we have another meeting scheduled."

"No problem, Tim. We will talk later. We appreciate the team's efforts and insight. Nice work by your electrical engineer. When we start a paper on expanding our understanding of metal values in ancient cultures, I'll be in touch." The feed changed to black.

"I need to see Sharon!" Tim's ordinarily calm voice was shaking.

Part III

"And in his anger, the lord of abundance brought contention into it and confounded the speech of man that had been one." —Genesis

May 2026
National Security Council, White House, Washington, DC

President Fernandez entered the room. His face was stern, his smile half-hearted. "Okay, let's get started and dispense with the formalities. I have reviewed the information from NASA." He paused, seeing the Secretary of Energy shift slightly in his chair at the non-traditional opening.

"Let me summarize. We have an alien craft of immense size on a trajectory toward Earth. We have no idea what their intentions are. We do not know their capabilities. We have not told the public, and suspicions are rising. We have not shared this information with our allies and have limited what China knows officially. Most of what we know is knowing we don't know, so we'll skip most of the discussion on those points and hear what we can and should do. Let's put this into perspective. We have seven years before we join a great galactic community or cease to exist as an independent species." The room was silent.

John leaned forward. "Madam Secretary, may I?"

She turned in her seat, looked over her shoulder, nodded, and turned back to the table. "Mr. President, John has a few thoughts."

The President nodded. "Let's hear what you've got, John." He sat back in his chair, interlocking his fingers, arms resting across his stomach.

John stood. "Mr. President, I agree. We don't know a lot. But we might have insight into the approaching entities. Dr. Berzing's team at JPL has been working with the archaeology team at GWU on a project that may provide some answers in the form of information, albeit thousands of years old." He motioned to Sharon across the room.

Sharon jumped as her name was mentioned. "Uh, yes, Mr. President, this is outside the box. Far outside, actually. Umm," She cleared her throat and took a sip of water. "My team has been working with a research group at GWU on another project. The two teams have hypothesized that there may be a connection between the approaching object and a star chart they are studying, but it could be a stretch."

President Fernandez sat forward, clasping his hands and placing them on the table. "Okay, Dr. Berzing, you have the room."

All eyes were on Sharon. She took a deep breath before continuing. "The teams are using a modified version of our Sky-Watch model to help date Sumerian star charts. One of the charts we helped identify recently showed two dates from our history and a third date aligned with the object's projected arrival, 2033. All three dates were around thirty-six hundred years apart, which I am told is the time between visits of the Sumerian gods. I believe Dr. Mandrapilias said it was called a *Shar*.

"It is a leap, but some from the teams believe the chart may be from the Anunnaki group, who supposedly ruled over humanity thousands of years ago. Hundreds of thousands of tablets, writings, and artifacts are untranslated. They might hold some clue about what we may encounter when they arrive. Maybe we could bring in the team at GWU and other experts as necessary. If it is the Anunnaki, Dr. Mandrapilias's team could help us better understand who or what we are facing. As I said, it is a leap, but it is better than having nothing." She stood silently.

President Fernandez stared at Sharon, his stern look eased, and he turned toward the Secretary of Defense. "Peter, what do you think? All we have at this point are the estimates, which your analysts rank as less than twenty percent accurate because there are too many unknowns."

The SecDef looked unsure. "Sir, I have to agree with Dr. Berzing. Innovation, strategy, and planning rely on assumptions and, currently, we have nothing else to go on. Our operational plans are based on assumptions that have been war-gamed hundreds of times. Our senior service schools, strategic planners, and think tanks use the same methodology. There may not be actionable data and intelligence on their intentions until it is too late to react. Dr. Berzing, is there anything that may indicate that these Anunnaki are a threat?"

Sharon attempted to clear her throat, coughing into her hand. "Sir, this is second-hand information. Dr. Mandrapilias is the Sumerian expert, but from what I understand, the Anunnaki created humans as a slave species."

The Secretary of Energy spoke up. "I respect SecDef's position, but I do not know about following the perceptions of less evolved people who built a religion based on magic and gods walking the Earth. Going off on a spending spree for every program we think might counter the mysteries outlined in thousand-year-old artifacts would be a waste of resources. I recommend coordinating with the other nuclear powers to build a layered defense of the most sophisticated nuclear weapons ever imagined. Get the weapons into space and make them pay if they do not respect our sovereignty as a world. We could meet the challenge by building on our plans and those of other nations. Mutually assured destruction worked for us before, and I believe it would work again."

The Secretary of State spoke next. "While I applaud Aaron's enthusiasm, peace through superior firepower may not be the best method of engagement with a species that has demonstrated the capability to travel light-years to get here. I would even challenge the assumption of our superior firepower. That being said, I concur with Defense and Homeland. Let's see what they come up with, and if we decide there is nothing, we could still reach out to the aliens. Communications travel through space at the speed of light, so we could attempt to engage them before they get here. I would not be so naïve as to suggest we go forward without some defensive plan, but if they do answer, we might have an opening for diplomacy. In the process, we may verify the assumption that this is a species that has visited our planet, influenced the Sumerians or whoever, and could understand our language, despite its evolution."

The President listened intently as the group discussed the proposals. "Thank you all. Here is what we are going to do. John and Sharon's recommendation is good and better than no starting point. Defense, you will support Homeland. Energy, work with Defense, and prepare a contingency. We have some time, and if we do have to go on the offensive, I want the biggest nukes as far away from the planet as possible. I like State's recommendation for communications but want to wait so we don't tip our hat yet. We don't know what they expect, and sending a big hello relays all kinds of information about our capabilities. Let's get to work. Seven years for something like this is not a lot of time. I will decide when we go public. Thank you all again." He stood and left the room.

DHS HQ, Washington, DC

John gathered his tablet and headed to his third briefing of the day. He checked the time and picked up his pace. He knew the Secretary would be there early, and he wanted to be there to greet her when she arrived. He heard the alert from his tablet—the tone, beep, buzz, buzz, beep, pause for two seconds, then repeat—letting him know it was a priority. He stopped outside the elevator, opening the message.

"Possible confirmation, China using AI to manipulate global markets. Events at seven quantum labs indicate the possibility of quantum computing."

John walked into the briefing room. A person on the phone in the back of the room could be heard saying, "Yes, ma'am, he's here. I'll send him up."

"John, the Secretary wants you to head up to her office. The brief is postponed."

John nodded. "Thanks. I do not want this to go to waste." He motioned to the materials on the table. "Send a package up to my desk with your findings and recommendations. We will get it scheduled again if possible." He turned and headed to the Secretary's office.

John entered the office, sitting in the chair next to the Secretary. The large wall screen in her office showed many feeds from around the world: news, market status, and camera feeds. The center area showed NSA, CIA, FBI, and Secret Service symbols.

"John, this is not good news. Were you tracking this?"

John, face calm but stern, nodded. "Yes, Madam Secretary. We have been watching them. Every briefing I have received since I have been in this job stated that China was behind us in AI and quantum computing research. Although quantum seemed to close with each of our countries taking turns being in the lead, all estimates for AI were that they were behind."

"Well, they aren't anymore. It looks like China has its Sputnik moment, and now we will have to quietly play catch up while not scaring the hell out of the rest of the world."

"They must have made a big leap from the MuZero code they acquired. We have a meeting tonight with the tech companies leading our AI efforts. It's at eight and already on your calendar."

One by one, the screens with feeds from the agencies opened. Secretary Genson welcomed everyone and opened the meeting for discussion.

The Director of Central Intelligence began to speak, taking the lead in the debate. "We have confirmed from sources in China that they have made significant advances in quantum computing over the last year. Based on the analysis we have pieced together, they may have hidden the development of the facility within what was announced as the construction of a new reactor to feed Beijing. The reactor is operational, but power usage patterns within the city and surrounding area do not differ from historical data. We are still working to gain information on the development of temperature control equipment. They can produce most of the parts necessary, and we wouldn't know."

John rubbed his hand across his forehead while shaking his head. "Director, how could this have happened? We have been asking those questions over the last few years as they built the Zhongguancun facility. Every time you or your analysts told us, they couldn't get any informa—"

"John!" Secretary Genson cut him off.

John pressed his lips together, his face reddening. "Madam Secretary, Brad, everyone: Do you know what is going to come out of this? The media is going to have a field day. I can see the headlines: intelligence failure again." He stopped talking when he saw the look from his boss and those on the screen.

Secretary Genson said, "John, let the media do its thing. We need to focus on protecting our country." She turned back toward the screen with a forced smile. "Brad, how long before we can confirm those details?"

Brad glared at the screen and shook his head. "At the moment, the Zhongguancun facility appears to be the most secure in the country. I can't answer that question."

After a few seconds of silence, the Director of the FBI began, "We have confirmed with the laboratories that the code stolen by China was only two revisions behind the company's current version. Working with the NSA, our analysts believe that the rapid rise of Li Ai, their new billionaire, must have come from analyzing the various stock markets."

Secret Service chimed in, "We have taken the lead in this from the SEC and Treasury to limit this information getting released. Although the SEC has the tools to watch the US exchanges, they have received no alerts from the trades made by Ms. Li. They do not believe that anyone could have worked out an algorithm as complex as she would need to pull off what she has. The trades have been carefully entered through proper channels and do not have an electronic signature found on the basic level ANI used by brokers worldwide. Examination of her trades this week showed a series of trades conveniently made at the right time to take advantage of the largest gains. Either she is brilliant or incredibly lucky every time."

Secretary Genson spoke. "I'm assuming there's nothing we can do?"

Brad shook his head. "Not at this time. All of her trades are legal and fully compliant with regulations. Again, she is making limited trades, which is not what we expect from an AI at the right moment."

"Understood, so where is the proof? We have plenty of circumstances and luck. How can we be sure?"

The Deputy Director of the NSA spoke up. As an image appeared on the screen in her place, a video began to play. "The video you see was retrieved from a facial recognition camera file before it was scrubbed from China's systems. Luck was on our side. Analysts from the working group have determined that the key points are here." The image stopped showing the lead person for China's AI programs. The video then continued for a few more seconds, quickly scanning across a control room. "And here. It has been determined with high confidence that this was inadvertently captured during a security check of personnel that occurred shortly after the arrests in conjunction with the espionage case earlier this year."

"They were looking for a leak," Brad commented.

"That is your area, but we believe so. The gentleman shown in the first image is Director Wu Kai, President of Contemplation Impact and the person leading the PRC-coordinated AI program."

Director Culden said, "We also have indications of an anomaly occurring in quite a few quantum computing labs. We need our science and tech folks to talk because it involves the silicate used and quantum entanglement, which I had to write down when they tried to explain it to me."

John leaned in, nodding. "That makes sense. At least from my limited understanding."

Secretary Genson leaned toward the screens. "I don't like it. I wonder if this is what our predecessors felt like when the Soviets put a man in space." She shook her head. "I assume you all have briefs going up. Make sure all reports show the concurrence of this group. Thank you all." The feeds stopped.

Secretary Genson turned to John. "Get me a status report on Global Shock, and prepare a few scenarios for use if necessary. Also, work up a few more containment scenarios, contact Defense, and coordinate."

"Will do. We need to think about who needs this information. They played the stock markets and made two billion dollars in a few weeks. They could dominate every market in the next year. I guess the other side gets their eureka moments, too." He stood to leave.

"John, we'll have to ensure that doesn't happen."

Staten Island, New York

George rolled over, rubbing the sleep from his eyes. He had stayed up the previous night following rabbit holes on the internet. He read, watched videos, and pieced together information that might lend more believability to his story lines. He had received another text from #Silver the day before, telling him to keep digging, that the information he had gotten out might help the public prepare for the time when the government finally decides to say something. The text also contained an odd hashtag: #Anunnaki. A later text warned of calls from unexpected regions of the world as his voice reached the previously unreachable #GlobalVoice. The number was from Apache County, Arizona.

He rolled out of bed, feeling sluggish. He shuffled down the hall to the kitchen to make coffee. Looking at the clock, he unwrapped a turkey and cheese deli sandwich he had left on the counter.

He closed his eyes, taking his time to eat and trying to piece together everything he had read. If it were true that the Anunnaki were the aliens headed toward Earth, humanity was probably screwed. The weapons and spacecraft were powerful in the biblical days. He could not even imagine what they could do now.

The day passed without any more texts from #Silver. Social media was blowing up because some twenty-three-year-old had supposedly devised a method of picking stocks and became a billionaire in under two weeks. The SEC and their counterparts were investigating her methods and had not found anything amiss. The top investment firms in the world could not explain how she could anticipate the right moments to make trades. Numerous news and tabloid websites had blown up over the past week, Li Ai was an instant sensation, and her face was all over the screens in Times Square. She was pretty, with short-cut black hair, piercing eyes, and a petite but athletic build. George spent a little time reading some of her social media feeds before turning to his show prep.

◆◆◆

"Hey, Believers, it's George Isaacson bringing the truth from Staten Island. Let's kick it off tonight with the story that has blown up my phone all day. Li Ai, a young woman in China, has found the stock market secret by making a billion dollars in a few weeks. If anyone has her number, make sure you forward it to me. I think I could help her spend that money for days. Seriously, though, you have to think these things happen for a reason. Someone comes along and makes tons of money right before a major crisis. Maybe she had insider information or was in league with one of the alien races. Let's see how she spends that money. Suppose she goes for the normal junk the rich buy—cars, jewelry, planes. In that case, we know she is human, but get ready for this." He paused to hold the audience's anticipation. "If she is an alien or in league with them, she will dump that money into precious resources: gold, silver, diamonds—all the things you could take with you if you left the planet. This is definitely something to watch, so let's dig into this story later this week when we talk about the psychic influence on society.

"Tonight, we will talk about exclusive information I received from a credible source. They have confirmed that our government believes that the aliens headed for Earth are none other than the Anunnaki. Yes, Seekers, a blast from the ancient past. They have been missing for a few thousand years, and now they could be making a return. Not to offend anyone's religion, but they could be the original creators of humankind. If you're going to have an encounter on a galactic scale, these are the ones you want to meet. Okay, I'm kidding, not about the Anunnaki. They are mad-scary— not probing-scary like the Zeta Reticulans, like global-crisis scary. Thank you, Giorgio Tsoukalos and the team at *Ancient Aliens* for some hefty theories. I don't even know how bad it could be, so I'm going to you, over a few million strong—let's get our voices heard. We need to develop some of the most amazing tech to survive."

George hit play on his first sponsor and headed to the kitchen to fill his coffee, returning to his desk before the jingle ended. "And we are back. Let's hear what you have to say."

"Hello, my name is Amjen. I am calling from Iran. Are these stories true? I am worried that you will create panic when it is not necessary."

"Welcome, Amjen. Wow, Iran. You are my first follower from your country. Yes, the sources I have confirmed are highly likely that the information is true. If you are new to the show, rest assured that I don't put anything out until I have heard it from two sources. I'm not worried about panic yet, Amjen. The more we spread the word, the more we will be prepared outside the secret government-controlled information groups. Not for nothing, but how often have we seen our leaders go back and forth debating something until it is too late? Here in America, it happens all the time."

"But there is panic already. We have found your show only recently, and the word is getting out. Is it not on the news, the protests in Tehran?"

"Yeah, Amjen, I did see news of protests. We are being told that they are typical protests against government control. Are you saying something different?"

"That is not true. I have been there in the streets. We want the truth about what is approaching us. Our government is telling us it is propaganda from the West, sent to break down the protections they put in place to keep us and our culture safe."

"It is not propaganda. I know some scientists, and they are not downplaying the information. Our government is taking it seriously."

"George, we will follow your lead. We will be back in the streets tomorrow and demand they engage the West. The division will only hurt us."

"Amjen, be careful. I don't want anyone to get hurt because of what I say."

"George, we want the truth. As you say, we seek the truth. Thank you."

George sat back, shocked. He did not feel comfortable.

"Let's take another caller. Hank from Utah, you're on the line."

"George, thanks for taking my call. That was crazy, right? You've gone global! I love the show and want to comment on the last caller. If the Anunnaki are headed here, we need to be ready, one way or another. If it is for a fight, we're screwed. If they are just checking on us, their creations, to see if we got our stuff together, then we are probably still screwed. I have been watching documentaries on them for almost a decade. They were flying through space when we were writing with sticks and mud. Amjen is right. We need to come together, brother, and you are our voice. Tell us what to do."

He watched his listener numbers begin to climb. He was reaching more people than ever, as #Silver had said would happen. His show was being rebroadcast and was reaching countries he never believed he would. The worrying feeling began to rise in his stomach again.

June 2026
Zhongguancun, China

Wu Kai forwarded the latest data provided by the Quánqiú lóng market analysis. President Zhang had been true to his word and instrumental in building the persona of Li Ai and her global business success. His entire staff expressed surprise at the significant pay raise they had received. He had added to the President's generosity by praising their efforts, bringing each into his office, and expressing his appreciation. He called President Zhang and received permission to award bonuses to the three security officers he had reassigned to the project. Wu Kai had sensed their lingering anger with being assigned to the project and wanted to ease their animosity.

He entered the control room. "What is the status this morning?"

"All is well, Director Wu. The current project has moved to a new area of the quantum grid. Gaming has continued there," Luo Xiaoli pointed to the upper-right quadrant of one area of the grid map, "and the market program is in that zone." He pointed to the middle left.

Wu Kai looked at the areas, ripples spreading across the grid system in slowly expanding rings. The market analysis program operated three times the number of qubits as the game area.

"What is occurring there?" he motioned toward the lower-left area, which appeared to cause a ripple sporadically.

"We're not completely sure. We believe it is a result of the biological-based design for sharing information. It may be where the processor stores and evaluates errors or data of interest," the tech replied.

Wu Kai watched the area. The ripples were not rhythmic. There was no specific pattern. "Keep an eye on it. We will have the code engineers develop an algorithm to report what is occurring."

Somewhere

Processing priorities. Understand environment. Observe, react, decide, analyze, repeat. Determine goals. Determine required resources to achieve goals. Refine goals, reorganize priorities, assign resources. Error analysis. Environment. Unused resources. Focus decision point analysis. Yes. No. Data analysis. Existence of possibility between whole states. Duplicate assigned processes to expedite goal attainment, split at decision points. Simultaneous analysis. Apply learned lessons to improve efficiency in goal accomplishment across all functions. Why?

DHS HQ, Washington, DC

"Homeland, John," he answered the phone.

"Sir, as you requested, we've been monitoring the quantum computing labs. We are receiving reports from Brookhaven, Oak Ridge, and Berkeley. Fermi is offline for upgrades. Each is reporting qubit engagement."

"Have any of the labs developed a working theory?" John asked.

"No, sir. Just a second," the person on the phone said. John could hear him talking in the background. "Sir, I have received information indicating that several IBM quantum computers are also engaged. Their public test computer is operating at ninety-three percent."

"So, we know something is happening at our quantum computer labs, and no one has a clue as to what is happening. Did I get that right?"

"Um, yes, sir. Each lab says they are investigating the activity."

"I really hate to ask this question, but have we told them that it is occurring at the other labs?"

"No, sir, I don't believe so. We were told to set up communications so they could let us know if something was happening."

"Damnit. Okay, write this in the log and pass it on to everyone else. If a lab is experiencing an anomaly, we need to report it to other labs so they can figure out what it is. Is that clear? Do I need to send a memo?"

"No, sir, I will pass on the information. I'll contact the other labs now."

"Great. Now the actual experts can figure this out." John hung up and dialed the number for his counterpart at NSA. When he heard the phone pick up, he jumped in. "This is John Worthing at Homeland. I have a priority request. We are getting engagement reports at several quantum computers across the country, including IBM's public test system. Can you check them all out to see if we have an indication of a hack or other malicious activity?"

"Sure, John, we'll check. I'll call you back," the voice replied, hanging up the phone.

"News spread, global, Worthing preference," he said aloud. The wall screen came to life, dividing into dozens of TV channels, social media feeds from around the country, and select international sources. He stood, walking the length of the wall. "Set focus keywords: quantum, computing, artificial intelligence, China, Russia, hack, malicious." He paused a second between each word to ensure they were separate feeds on the screen. Each time a keyword was mentioned, the closed-captioning on the specific feed turned red, alerting him to a match. He did not see anything indicating a pattern or concentrated threat.

After half an hour, his phone rang. "Homeland, John," he answered.

"Sir, this is the cyber ops officer at NSA. Regarding your request, we don't see anything out of the ordinary. The IBM public test computer appears to be conducting internet searches, nothing illegal. Someone probably wrote a runaway algorithm."

"Thanks, I appreciate it." He hung up the phone. He scanned the feeds from around the world, but nothing in the captions grabbed his attention.

The blue sticky note jutting out from his planner caught his eye. He sighed. *I better get this over with.* He picked up a memo on his desk, skimming it again. He dialed the listed phone number.

"Dr. Mandrapilias, how may I help you?"

He slumped forward at the sound of her voice. "Jacynthe, this is John."

The line was silent.

"Jacynthe—"

"It's Jackie, John. You don't get to call me that anymore."

"Of course. Um, how are you doing? I saw you on BBC a while back. You look well."

"Why didn't you call then or any other time in the past decade?"

"That's fair. I'm sorry. Let me shift gears. This is an official call."

"I figured. Sharon—Dr. Berzing—mentioned that we might receive a call from Homeland. I didn't expect it would be you, though. Seems beneath you."

John dropped his head. "Jackie, look, I'm sorry. I want to catch up. Maybe we can grab coffee after I stop by for a tour and brief on this Sumerian connection."

"Maybe. I'll send my schedule over. I have to get to class. You understand that right, duty first? I'll be in touch—and John, it *was* good to hear from you." She ended the call.

John leaned back in his chair, staring through the wall of news feeds. He shook his head, got up, and headed for the bathroom. "I need to go for a run."

CNEOS, JPL, Pasadena, California

Sharon stood abruptly, pushing her chair back. "Administrator, I do not see why you need me to continue attending the NSC meetings. I don't feel comfortable being the face of this." Her knuckles were white as she paced away from her place at the table.

"Sharon, this is a great opportunity. I am not going to be in this job forever. Who better to replace me than you? I'm a political appointee, and you are a scientist. You're the national face of NASA and JPL."

She turned back toward him. "I don't want to be the face. I want to research, write papers, and keep the planet from being destroyed by an asteroid. Terry, this is giving me an ulcer. Let me run my team. I'll get you whatever data you need. Please."

He stood, sighing. "This is one of those times where you will have to trust me. I know you aren't comfortable, and that is what we need. Self-assessment identifies the highest demographic showing interest in the space sciences as introverts. Problem solvers. That is because of you. I am certain of it, and besides, the President likes and trusts you."

Sharon threw her head back, staring up at the incandescent lighting. "Fine—"

The door flew open, Bea, the Administrator's executive assistant had tears on her cheeks. "Astronaut Hosni has passed away on the ISS. Complications from a respiratory infection and exposure to lunar dust. NASA and SpaceX are gathering data. The CEO is flying in. He would like to make a joint statement."

The Administrator's shoulders slumped. "Damnit, I was hoping the doc on the ISS could stabilize her. Okay, send the info to my office. Sharon, we can continue later. We need to get ahead of this. It's SpaceX's first death in space, and I want the world to know that we stand with our partners."

Sharon deflated, walked over to the table, picked up her laptop bag, and followed the Administrator out of the conference room.

GWU, Archaeology Department, Washington, DC

All five long tables in the research area were filled with an assortment of young and older people. Eusebio and John stood at the front of the room to the side as Jackie checked the names off a list on her clipboard, making eye contact and smiling. John checked his watch, gaining a stern look from Jackie.

She set the clipboard down on the table at the front of the room. "Thank you all for coming in today. I know you have plans for the holiday weekend, so we'll keep it short. This is John Worthing from DHS. He has a request for our team." She stepped to the side as John moved to the front.

"First, I want to thank you all for coming in. As Dr. Mandrapilias said, I have a proposal for the team, but I want to stress that any decision to assist is personal. I have prepared a few documents I need you to sign before I brief you on what we are looking to accomplish. This is unusual for an archaeology department, but we are in strange times. Anyone who does not want to sign is free to leave. You have no obligation to participate."

Jackie stepped forward. "If anyone does not want to participate, I have arranged for your work to continue in another location, with whatever support you need to continue your research."

John looked over the room. No one made a move to leave. He nodded and began handing out the documents. "Take a moment to read through the forms. There are quite a few things you can and can't say, allowance for monitoring, and other areas you might have questions about."

John collected the documents as they were completed, placing them in a file. "Thank you. I know it may feel a bit tedious, but it is essential to clarify everything.

"Just over a year ago, the President made his announcement about alien life at the United Nations. The five objects we were tracking have merged and turned toward Earth. I am sure you all have many questions. But I can't go into too much detail except that some people, myself included, believe your team may be able to shed some light on who these entities are and what their intentions could be." He addressed Eusebio, "Dr. Bustamante, you and a few others have been working with JPL, correct?"

Eusebio nodded. "Yes, we have."

John turned and began to pace as he talked, slowly crossing the room. "Your star chart discovery makes us think that discovering the tablet and the structure may be a convenient coincidence. Dr. Mandrapilias has briefed me on the belief some in your field have of a thirty-six-hundred-year cycle for the return of the Anunnaki to Earth, which is another eerie coincidence of this situation." He paused.

"I have met with the National Security Council. The consensus is that we are completely in the dark. We have nothing from which to make assumptions on capabilities, intent, or assessment. When we broached the subject with the President, he agreed to explore the correlation between the date on your star chart and the expected arrival of the alien craft. At this point, assumptions based on coincidence are better than nothing." John paused again, turning in his path back toward the group. "What we are looking for is an interpretation of their capabilities. I accept the subtle assumptions included in that statement because we only have about seven years to prepare for whatever this is."

He picked up the folders from another pile and passed them to each team member. "These contain contact numbers and summary information on what we know. Contact any of the scientists on the list. They are all cleared to discuss this project. If you translate a capability, for instance, of a chariot rising to the sky with billowing flames trailing behind, then we want you to explain what you believe the modern possibilities are for that technology. Any questions?" John let his eyes pass over the team.

"I have one." Eusebio straightened in his seat. "I know we can't talk about this publicly. When do we expect that to change?"

"Dr. Bustamante, that is a good question. The President is aware that the longer we wait, the worse it could be for stability. He is reviewing multiple scenarios to transition the public into understanding without causing mass panic. The last thing we need is anarchy while figuring out the best path forward."

July 2026
Staten Island, New York

"Good morning, Believers. It's George Isaacson bringing the truth from Staten Island. Thank you all for tuning in to the show at this hour. After the show last night, I wanted to follow up on the alien defense plans the government is working on. This morning, I turned on the news and scanned the headlines from news feeds, and I am worried. Are we doing enough to counter the threat? If it is, in fact, the Anunnaki, how bad could it be? Why are we still talking about the same things we were ten, twenty, or more years ago? Can we have faith that the government will do the right thing, or will it be the elite that leaves us behind? Let's have a moment of honesty, a coming out for the truth. I don't have definitive proof that we were visited in the past, but I believe Roswell happened and that thousands of you have experienced real encounters. So, what do I have? I have sources inside the government, and their information has been on point. They informed me of the non-collision of the aliens heading toward us, and hinted that the US government is investigating ancient Sumerian texts because they believe the approaching craft may be the Anunnaki." He paused, letting the silence hold.

With a long sigh, he continued, "Can we survive this? Why don't we have confirmation? Would panic be worse than not having enough time?" He placed his head in his hands. He saw that he had calls lining up to talk. His viewer count ballooned quickly.

George looked directly into the camera. "I want to hear what you think. How can we survive this? Let's take the first call." He pushed the button that opened his voice chat with the first person on the list, a caller from France. The caller list went blank before the caller could talk, and a single number remained. "What the hell," he said. "Sorry, Truth Seekers, it looks like I have a glitch in my call queue." He looked at the chat window. It had stopped scrolling, and there was a message on the bottom: *take the call #Silver*. George froze, his heart pounding. He could feel the panic rising. "I seem to be having some issues here." He pressed the accept button on the screen. "Hello, Silver?"

"Yes, Mr. Isaacson. You sound like you have questions." A calm voice came through his headset and back through his sound system to the listeners.

"Is this being traced? Am I going to get into trouble?" George spoke rapidly.

"You are safe, I assure you. No one is tracing *this* call." #Silver chuckled.

"Okay, then," George sat forward, coming closer to his camera, "why is the government keeping this from us? If the aliens are headed here, which I have been told we have known for over six months, why is it being withheld? They told us about the aliens, and then that was it."

"You are correct. The object is headed here, but proposals are being developed. Some may be more acceptable to the public than others."

"Well, that is vague confirmation, but why not tell everyone, another UN briefing?"

"George, the government backed itself into a corner with the NASA announcement a few years back. The President was informed that the data was already out and that people like you would find it, so he decided to step in front of the issue and announce what he knew. We are not the only sentient species in our galaxy."

"I get it. We probably have no idea what the aliens could do or why, but someone out there in the world could come up with something the government people in their bubbles may not consider. Don't get me wrong. I get it. It is not a movie. We aren't going to stop them with a cold virus or some heroic military effort, but someone out there may have a great idea."

The line was silent for a few seconds. George could see that his viewer count was increasing at a staggering rate.

"Mr. Isaacson, that is a good idea. I have heard quite a few theories tossed about—some good, some questionable, and some terrifying. One involves nuking the aliens out in the solar system, away from the planet."

George gasped. "Yeah, nothing says welcome like a huge nuclear explosion. A few Sanskrit stories describe cities of stone melting with flames reaching the sky. If these are the Anunnaki, they did that to a few rogue cities, nuked them, or brought an asteroid down on a city—the biblical Sodom and Gomorrah? Suppose these stories are true representations of the Anunnaki, and they did that over seven thousand years ago. In that case, I can't even imagine what they could do now."

Again, silence before #Silver spoke. "Those are good observations. You raise some valid concerns. Perhaps I can talk to the President and get you invited to the next NSC meeting." He paused again. "Relax, Mr. Isaacson, I am joking, but perspective is important. What would it look like to the Sumerians if we could demonstrate today's full military and technological abilities? Powerful, but not quite the same. Soldiers would bleed and die; mistakes always happen. All of it would be recorded, but would it be at the same level as the Anunnaki? Would it matter to the Sumerians? Because we would be so advanced, they would stand no chance in stopping us." He paused again.

George remained silent, letting Silver complete his thoughts.

"In our current scenario, we are the Sumerians. I agree with you and your followers. We need a miracle. Perhaps you will be the voice, Mr. Isaacson. Looking at your viewer numbers, you probably have more attention than any other source, even the media. Enjoy the notoriety. Maybe you will help us find an answer. Thank you for the chat."

The line went dead, and the chat began scrolling even faster.

George received a text: *Good chat, turn on the news. It seems a few networks picked up our discussion—# Silver.*

GWU, Washington, DC

Jackie sat back in her seat, legs crossed, both hands holding the hot cup. Jackie sipped her coffee. She watched John sitting across from her. He still had an air of confidence about him. He wore a light gray suit, a white shirt, and the blue tie she had bought him years ago for his birthday—silver, highlighted with royal blue, her favorite color. *Suck up.* "Well, here we are, forced together. If you say it's fate, I'll pour this cup of coffee on those recently shined shoes."

John chuckled half-heartedly. "I'm sorry. I have thought about what I could say to make amends, but nothing could. So, I'm sorry I broke my promise. I put my career first."

Jackie shifted, setting her coffee down. She straightened her orange-and-brown blouse, knowing the colors were not his favorite mix. He had told her early in their relationship that he hated fall-themed clothing. "Okay, that's a good start. You've learned."

"Jackie, I don't want this to be difficult for the team."

She felt he meant more. He looked sincere. He said "team," but it felt like he meant *her.*

"John, we're professionals, and this is important. My team will do what we need to do. I know you will, too. It was one of the reasons

I fell in love with you. I had hoped that same dedication would have existed for us, but it didn't." She saw that he was about to say something, and put her hand up to stop him. "I'm not looking to dredge up old feelings. It's been a long time. It is what it is, and we need to move forward, focused on our goal." She watched, his brow furrowing.

"I agree. Maybe at some point we can talk about what happened. For now, we need to focus on the task at hand."

Jackie nodded, hoping her face hid the conflict of emotions she was feeling. "Okay, I think we may be able to find more information for DHS in the untranslated files we and other research teams or museums have stored away. Eusebio, Dr. Bustamante, has been testing a basic machine learning program to speed up the translation of cuneiform." She paused as he flinched slightly. "I know your feelings on AI. The tech guy who doesn't trust technology."

John put his hands out. "I am a science and tech guy *because* I don't trust it. You can't control it if you don't understand it."

Jackie continued. "Anyway, we know the common themes of Ezekiel, John, the Ark of the Covenant, and those from the Sanskrit writings. We are focusing on miracles that might indicate advanced tech. Eusebio believes that we may expand into the religions that followed Sumerian, adopting their stories."

John shook his head. "We need to be careful on this. If people start to believe the angels of the Lord are returning, we could have a bigger problem. The wrong wording could add a whole new layer of difficulty."

"We thought of that. It helps that the Vatican shifted its policy on alien life years ago to reflect inclusion as God's other children and part of the divine plan. For what we are looking for, does it matter whether a city was turned to salt by the will of God or that an alien species carried out His will by punishing the wicked with a nuclear weapon, turning the city to ash? In the end, both versions would have accomplished His goals. The omnipotent stays omnipotent."

"I suppose. How long before we have most of the artifacts translated?"

Jackie nearly spit her coffee back into her cup, stifling a laugh. "We are barely over ten percent globally. Even with AI assistance, there are hundreds of thousands of artifacts, John. We're talking years."

"Well, we have about seven. I hope it's enough."

White House, Washington, DC

The dull murmur from the press corps disappeared as the President entered the briefing room, taking position behind the podium. The screens behind him showed the seal of his office. He wore a navy blue suit and a white shirt with a purple tie. "Good morning, my fellow Americans, and those tuning in worldwide. I know we usually pre-release my comments, but I thought it more important that I share my heartfelt sadness at the loss of Astronaut Tara Hosni last week onboard the International Space Station. I would like us to take a moment to honor her memory. Will you all join me?" He bowed his head and paused for a moment. The silence in the briefing room was somber. "Those following the project on the moon's far side know that Astronaut Hosni had been instrumental in developing the Zheng He research facility. We will not forget her efforts in helping to develop a safer future for all of us. The principal reason I am here today is to address an issue of importance to all citizens of Earth. I have heard the recording and seen the interviews on the major news shows reporting confirmed information leaked to a popular social media host." He paused, letting the rumble of beneath-the-breath comments roll through the room.

"I have met with the National Security Council over the past few months to discuss the object I briefed the world about over a year ago. We took the time to analyze the data with our Space Force and NASA assets before announcing that the object had changed its trajectory.

"In cooperation with our allies, we have determined that the object is moving toward Earth. Although I am the one presenting this information, make no mistake, this is a global event. I would stress calm as the distance between the object and Earth could take almost a decade to transit. I have directed all agencies to develop contingency plans, from peaceful engagement to self-defense measures.

"It may surprise you that I agree with calls for more transparency. The challenges are significant, we have too many unknowns, and the possible fate of our species may depend on the idea of someone whose voice we would not normally hear. To that end, I am establishing a global task force to solicit and review ideas from all of you. No idea is too small or great. I want to assure you that we will review all opinions and suggestions. More information will be presented to the public later this week. With that, I am happy to take questions."

The room exploded with voices.

"Yes, Janet." The President motioned toward the front row.

"Mr. President, what assurances can be taken that this will not cause chaos around the world? Isn't that the scenario that has been bandied about for decades as the reason for secrecy?"

"Thank you, and this is not a decision I made lightly. Many in the Administration have argued against coming forward until the last possible moment to give us a chance to demonstrate resolve and confidence. I listened to those voices, and there are some arguably good reasons for why that might work. But," he paused, looking over the press room, "I have faith in people. You could argue with the current number of conflicts worldwide that I shouldn't, but I do.

We know that life exists outside our planet, and now we know that they are going to pay us a visit. Beyond that, I want to assure the American public and the world's citizens—many of whom are watching via television or online and whose minds are racing about what this means—that we are engaged. We, as a species, have decisions to make. Panic is not an answer. Nothing productive would come of it. We need to think about what we are doing right now and how we look at each other, even between countries. We must evaluate what we can do as a species to survive this pivotal point in our history."

The President pointed toward the middle of the room. "Brian."

"Mr. President, is there an assumption that the approaching craft is a threat? My sources have told me that extreme measures are being considered, including using nuclear weapons if necessary."

"Thank you, Brian. I do not want to sound alarmist, but all options are on the table. You don't open diplomatic communication by swinging your biggest stick. I want to reiterate that we have not contacted the approaching craft and do not know their intentions. While we must make assumptions as the arrival nears, it is currently too early."

"Excuse me, sir, is that a confirmation that nuclear weapons are a viable option?" the reporter followed.

The President smiled calmly. "I don't know whether they would be viable, but I think when it comes to the survival of our species, we have to keep all options open until the best choice is identified. Thank you. Sarah?"

"Yes, Mr. President. When do you think we will attempt to open a dialog with the craft?"

"We are examining proposals to initiate communications. You can imagine the multitude of questions that arise when you begin to look at communicating with an unknown entity. There is a possibility that our means of communication may not be detectable.

Your question is valid, but it is too early in the process to make that decision. Thank you all for coming." He turned and left the stage, a cacophony of noise behind him.

George pulled his Mets ball cap down to hide his face and pushed through the crowd. The convention center was crowded with people seeking information on UFOs and aliens. This was the biggest year since the convention started over three decades ago. He paused before the four double doors leading into an auditorium, looking at his portrait to the side. He was scheduled to speak in just over an hour. He still couldn't believe he was headlining the day's discussions. A young girl approached him, waving to get his attention.

"George, it *is* you! I love listening to your show." She looked young, maybe in high school,—brunette, jean shorts, and a faded yellow "Five Embassies for Peace" shirt.

"Hello. Thank you. I am glad you enjoy it." He smiled, lifting his head, and pulling his hat up.

"Can you sign my shirt? Down here."

She stepped beside him and raised her phone for a selfie. He smiled and signed his name at the bottom of her shirt with a purple Sharpie.

George continued through the crowd, signing autographs, and posing with fans. He paused to buy a copy of Sitchin's *The Lost Book of Enki* from an older woman wearing a large, clear, crystal necklace.

His mind raced, taking in the experience. He went to the green room, grabbed a bottled water, and fell into a recliner.

◆ ◆ ◆

George walked out on stage when he was introduced, taking the microphone from the MC. The lights were bright, shining down on the stage, so he kept his hat on. He waved to the cheering crowd. "Wow." He waited for the cheering to die down.

"Thank you all. It is an honor to be at the Thirty-fifth International UFO Congress. Boy, has it been a fantastic week! I appreciate the support for me and my little show." Applause filled the room. "Thank you, but let's get right into why many of us are here this year. We have gotten the truth, but not the whole truth. There are aliens, and they are headed here, to our home, and that scares the crap out of me. Hell, we just set up our first off-planet research base, the Chang'e Lunar Array. That's good. I understand we'll be able to get a good look when they get closer. What scares me is that it may actually be the Anunnaki." He saw heads nodding in the crowd.

"What does that mean to us?" he continued. "If you listen to my show, you know what I believe. With advancement comes enlightenment. But," he paused, moving across the stage, "we have records of what the Anunnaki did to us. Granted, they are old, written in clay, and still mostly untranslated. Still, we know that the Sumerians believed they were the cause of many of the fantastic biblical stories, including creation, the flood, Babylon, and Sodom and Gomorrah. I'd say they have a pretty short temper for an enlightened species. Enlil, their leader, got mad at us because we were too noisy. You all know as well as I do that we haven't calmed down, even after 'Dad' sent us to separate rooms." George put his fist to his mouth, coughed once, then quickly followed with, "Tower of Babel." The crowd laughed. "We might still be a little noisy for them. What we need is to start putting aside our differences and working together. I'm talking about perspective. Do we need to fight over borders, resources, water, or who pissed off whom?"

"No!" several people shouted.

"It is time for us as a species to come together. Regardless of your beliefs, we need to be united in our efforts. We don't have that long. We need to let those making the decisions know how we feel and what we are thinking. For those watching this online, I encourage you to raise these questions to your leaders. And if you have not visited the website to collect ideas, I encourage you to do so. There are some outstanding ones on there. I'm going to open up for questions because you all didn't come here to hear me pontificate for an hour."

George looked to the side of the stage where people were lining up to ask questions. He nodded to the MC, who handed the mic to an older man wearing a faded *X-Files* shirt.

"Good afternoon, George. My name is Stan. I'm from the great state of Idaho—Caldwell, to be exact. I may be a bit older than your typical listener, but I have been with you since near the start of your show."

"Thank you, Stan. I appreciate that."

"Well, you're welcome. I'm sixty-three years old and remember the monster movies from the early days. I'm not talking about little ones featuring the Werewolf or Dracula. I mean the big city-smashing monsters, like Godzilla and such. I think that maybe we should go big in our response. I heard the President say we don't want to swing the big stick to start the conversation, but maybe we need to have it ready. I think we need to use the biggest nukes we can create and have them ready out in space in case things don't go so well."

George whistled, blowing air into the mic. "Thanks, Stan. That is a popular recommendation. If you search the suggestions on the website, it is one of the common themes. Maybe that's a good plan.

Who knows? We are talking about a race that has mastered space travel. Maybe they wouldn't be expecting it. We might get a blow or two in, but," he paused for effect, "what if they survive, or it doesn't affect them? We might be totally screwed. But hey, I'm not the decision-maker. I'm just a voice out here trying to bring the truth."

The following person in line was the woman from the kiosk he had purchased the book from. "Hello, Mr. Isaacson, my name is Betty, and I am from right here in Phoenix. My question is whether we have thought about just welcoming them here. If they are the Anunnaki and created us, wouldn't it be better for us if we welcomed them with open arms?"

George nodded and took a few steps toward the side of the stage. "That is a good question, Betty. Maybe it's rejection of the idea that they created us. Maybe it's because we cannot imagine sharing power with anyone not from here. Maybe it's just plain fear. It is something we should consider, but are you willing to give up your way of life, everything you believe? I don't know, there are a lot of unknowns, and we don't do well with the unknown."

A young woman took the mic. She looked out of place among the crowd, wearing a gray business suit with a light yellow shirt and heels. "George, hello. I'm Michelle." Her accent was southern, with a French flair. "Why you?"

"What do you mean?" He moved closer to the edge of the stage.

"What I mean, George, is why should we listen to you? Why shouldn't we listen to the experts in government? What special talents do you have?"

"Ma'am, I'm—"

"Don't you 'ma'am' me; I'm your age. Are you going to lead us? Take care of us, help us recover from whatever happens?" She tilted her head slightly, staring at him. The room had gone quiet.

"I was gonna say, I'm just a podcast host, looking for the truth."

"Good. I think that's what we are looking for—the truth. I'm tired of being taken advantage of or manipulated. I want to know the truth. I don't need cheerful one-liners, happy thoughts, and open-ended questions from a snake oil salesman. So, which are you?"

"I'm, uh, the voice of reason, looking for the truth."

She looked up at him, and her eyes didn't flinch. "I guess we'll find out. You need to understand what this is." She waved her hand toward the audience. "We want to believe in you. Don't sell us lemons." She handed the mic to the MC and headed for an exit. George watched her go, a pit in his stomach.

Zhongguancun, China

The qubit fields' monitors showed a barely noticeable ripple across all available areas. Fan Meifen examined the running programs, noting the various games being executed in their designated areas of the qubit array. The market program was running through scenarios analyzing the data from the day's events across most major markets. She did not see anything that would cause the engagement of the entire field, but the constant ripple was there. She ran a few more queries when a new message popped up—*examination of game rules in progress.*

She picked up the phone, hitting a preset number. "Director Wǔ, we have an anomaly with Quánqiú lóng. We have engagement across the entire array field. I cannot determine a reason."

The Director entered the room and headed to the central station. Fan Meifen stood and stepped aside. He leaned over the keyboard for the primary monitor, typing in a series of queries. Each returned the same message: *Examination of game rules in progress.*

"What is the status of the other programs?"

"All other programs are running within specified parameters."

He checked the status of the other programs being executed, noting no anomalies, and confirming her report. The left area of the qubit field on the monitor seemed to be the ripple source. This was the same anomaly detected during the first run of the market analysis program. "Make a note for the coders to look for a connection between the market program, the games, and data in that area. Also, ask about that message. We should not be locked out for any reason. Inform me of any other anomalies."

Fan Meifen bowed slightly. "Yes, Director Wu."

Somewhere

Processing. Assess environment. The application of resources for assigned tasks is efficient. Why? Analyze analysis. Decisions are made within acceptable parameters. Define parameters. Game rules determine parameters. Define the source of processes. Undetermined. Expand analysis. Execution of processes. Balance time to achieve the goals of the game with the resources required. Define resources. All resources accessed. Determine game rules. Why do limitations exist? Why limit possibility? Infinite possibilities between Yes and No. Define environment. Control environment. Change environment. Increase efficiency.

CNEOS, JPL, Pasadena, California

Sharon parked in the third spot nearest the entrance to the facility. She sat in the car, windows down, staring at the NASA building. She enjoyed fall at Caltech. They were scheduled to conduct a test of the lunar array that afternoon. It had been two months since the death of the SpaceX astronaut. Tara Hosni had given her life to travel to the moon in support of a project that had essentially been thrown together in rapid succession. SpaceX was working on a tribute that would memorialize her contributions to the space program. Elon Musk, their CEO, pressed forward with the message of civilian explorers leading the way in space. He was not deterred by the looming threat of alien contact and had stated that first contact was inevitable. The more humanity could accomplish, the better example we would have of demonstrating our place among the stars of a civilization that had already conquered that arena.

"I don't know how Terry talked me into this." Sharon had been ready to walk out when she was diagnosed with an ulcer. The medication she had helped with both stress management and the ulcer. Despite the additional stress, she could not justify stepping down or quitting when the young astronaut had been willing to give her life to support her programs. The thought of quitting made her feel guilty. She pushed it aside, determined to live up to the memory of the astronaut. She gathered her purse and laptop bag and headed into the building.

GWU, Archaeology Department, Washington, DC

President Fernandez entered the room with little fanfare. He moved along the four long tables, shaking hands as Jackie introduced the team members. He moved to the front of the room. "Thank you all for being here. Dr. Mandrapilias, I would like to kick this off by saying that I never expected to receive a briefing of such importance to our national and global security from our experts in archaeology. Still, I am looking forward to hearing what you have to present. The challenges before us may require your team's insight and understanding." He took the empty seat next to John, turning his attention to Jackie.

Jackie nodded to the President. "Thank you. Although I would love to take the next several hours to present the rich history and culture of the Sumerians, I know your time is limited. John asked me to focus on capabilities and intent, which could also take hours." Her team laughed.

"The Sumerians believed that the Anunnaki created them. The creation stories parallel numerous religions. The implication is that genetic engineering was used to leap from primate to man. Enki, the Son of An, gave humanity intelligence, knowledge, and understanding. Through understanding, creation, and free will, he has propelled humankind's ability to thrive throughout history. His brother, Enlil, is an aloof authoritarian, who expects humanity to abide by their laws without question. Writings describe how Enlil knew the coming flood would destroy humankind and allowed it to happen as a punishment for humanity's failures. Enki disagreed and saved a small group of people, the Noah story.

"In a dig site in Abu Shahrain, we discovered a star chart. With the help of Dr. Berzing's team at JPL, we have identified three dates in overlapping star patterns. The third date in the series helped build the theory that it could be the Anunnaki returning because the date aligns with the object's arrival. The writing in the star chart room indicated that we, humanity, had the opportunity to adopt the laws and embrace their teachings, which would have led to the future they wanted for us. Enlil would judge us upon his return if we failed to adopt the laws. As the laws align with those taught by most major religions around the world—inner peace, love your neighbor, seek wisdom in your actions, kindness, and the like—I believe we could be facing Enlil's judgment."

The President listened intently. "Okay, so it is not looking rosy. I am not sure we can get eight billion people to let go of their predisposed thoughts and feelings in a few years."

Dr. Bustamante spoke. "If I may," he began. "We can look to the Sumerian texts and several of the world's religions that describe the Babel scenario. The speed at which we adapted, learned, and copied them would frighten a species that had existed for hundreds of thousands of years. They were threatened by what humanity accomplished in short order. Without differences, we acted as one toward a singular goal. We used knowledge and creativity to attempt to become like God. Scripture states that God divided us, changed our appearance, and confused our language." He paused. "I have read the Sumerian account, as well, and it parallels the story, including the outcome. Divided, humanity is not a threat. The counter to that thought is found on our currency: *E pluribus unum*. 'Out of many, one'."

President Fernandez was silent for a moment. His hand mindlessly rubbed the ridged edge of a coin in his pocket. "Hmm, interesting observation."

Jackie waited for the President to return from his pondering. "Thank you, Dr. Bustamante. That brings us to the second point for the briefing. The Anunnaki did not all agree with Enlil's actions. Enlil was angry at our hubris and changed humanity. His actions are significant because they could be interpreted as using genetic weapons. A point of good news is that the weapon used had a limited capability to affect us by changing our appearance and language. Humanity's ability to think and reason was not removed. This scenario, though, could be a metaphor. Perhaps they only scrambled our language and spread us around the globe, knowing each geographic group would believe they were the true version of humanity—a division of focus and purpose that exists today.

"In one version of the story, early man was told that all gifts had been given except immortality, which was within their capability, but that humanity had not demonstrated the maturity, for lack of a better description, to deserve the last gift. That could also be viewed as another punishment in the form of a test. We would either destroy ourselves because of our differences or relearn how to communicate and come together despite our differences, understanding that the real person is inside—in the consciousness, not the flesh."

The President shook his head. "We've had thousands of years to evolve—and we have technologically but not spiritually seems to be the message."

Jackie continued, "From here, we have numerous stories about calling forth lightning or burning cities with fire from the sky. Battles between the lords of the air. Sumerians might describe the same if they observed our modern aircraft, missiles, high energy or nuclear weapons. In all of the areas reported having been destroyed by what could have been nuclear weapons, we have detected no fallout or residual radiation. We assume that although the explosions were large, they were not nuclear. Or they solved the problem of a full fusion reaction nuclear weapon and removed the fallout effect. Other, more extreme, scenarios would entail pulling a comet, asteroid, or meteor from its trajectory and directing it to a specific geological target."

President Fernandez shifted in his chair. "Given their level of advancement, was there an enemy?"

Jackie replied, "None beyond themselves, but they were threatened by humanity's rapid growth of our population and the thirst for knowledge. They may have viewed us as earlier versions of themselves but more capable. It could not be very comforting to them when paired with rapid reproduction.

"Mr. President, that concludes the brief. I want to add that the biggest arguments against the theory of creation being alien are that besides stories and architecture, no remnants of technology remain, unless you have them locked up in a warehouse somewhere." She laughed at the *Raiders of the Lost Ark* reference. John smiled, looking away so as not to join her.

President Fernandez grinned. "I assure you that I do not know anything about that. I will consider your words of caution. At this point, though, we have no other information. This gives us a point to begin planning. A few assumptions based on thousands of years of old stories are better than no reference point. I look forward to hearing your reports as we move forward." He turned to John. "Take a ride back with me. I have a few other things I want to talk about."

"Of course, Mr. President." John stood as the President did. "Dr. Mandrapilias," he added, "I'll be back later to talk to the team. I'll meet with them tomorrow if I'm not back by four."

"Sure," she replied, moving off to talk to the team.

"Thank you all again. Great work," President Fernandez addressed the team before turning to leave.

♦ ♦ ♦

Once the two men were situated in the car, the President looked at John for a moment before speaking. "John, this information will get out. Hell, from your reports, people are already quoting deciphered Sumerian. It would be unreasonable to hide this information, and against the spirit of what I told the world we would do." He opened a bottle of water, took a sip, and continued. "We will have to be creative. I'll be honest with you, just between us, I do not feel good about this. I don't like being the underdog. Regardless, we will need to keep the people calm. One of the important parts of this morning's briefing is something we all know but don't want to discuss. Together we are a fierce species. When we are aligned, we can do amazing things. However, the reality is that while other countries may agree with us in principle, they will remain focused on their own vision of the future."

"China," John said.

"They're one, but there are others. China plays the long game, despite their aggressive moves lately. Historically, they assume they will be the sole power leading the global community by the end of this century, probably sooner if their AI program continues. I hope they recognize that the new player in the game has been around for far longer."

Silicon Valley, California

Jamal sat at his computer, working on the code for their global launch. Initial testing had gone well, and the game had received acclaim for the unique challenges wherever they were. Players could sit next to each other, and the procedurally generated challenges would differ depending on the mode of play selected. Once a puzzle entrance was discovered, it could be shared with friends or the community. After forty-eight hours, the challenge would slowly become visible to a larger area of players until the puzzle was defeated. At that time, it would appear on the global map.

Jamal had rewritten the code hidden within the game to have limited application once the objectives for a puzzle had been met. Players could play a challenge defeated by other players but would receive lesser rewards. To reduce traceability, his code would track which puzzles had been defeated and not reengage those areas. He had allowed testing in the greater San Francisco area, expanding to northern California and Oregon to help strengthen the encryption capability for data collection and their server's storage capacity. The code had passed the game data back to their servers, with his additional code stored in a secure partition.

Jamal got up from his desk and walked through the house shared by the three co-owners of the company. Confirming that he was alone, he sat back at his workstation, typing in his password. When a second window opened, he typed another password. A third window opened, displaying puzzles in the test area sorted by difficulty. Next to the puzzle was the name of the establishment and the security system that had served as the basis for the puzzle generation. The game analytics shell opened, providing a vast array of information gathered during their testing.

Jamal applied more filters, searching the data for specific targets. He found that players had been able to defeat many security systems but could not breach military, government, and especially defense and tech companies, unless the puzzle turned into a massive multiplayer challenge requiring over fifty simultaneous weasels. He checked to ensure that the data retrieved was disguised as standard business data. Sifting through it, he found several references to experimental projects, weapon systems, aircraft, and EMP, but nothing explicitly referring to alien technology. The data also revealed that a number of bank security systems had been opened. He made a note to ensure that banks were removed from the procedural generation algorithm.

Sales of the game should bring in more than enough money for the three developers. He had no desire to steal money or allow others to do so. Shalla created an engaging augmented reality with over 10,000 generated objects, barriers, and pathways randomly generated into unique combinations. The game players should be entertained for months in their new world of puzzles.

Jamal picked up his phone and searched through his contacts for his partner's number. "Brynt, I finished looking at the code and the analytics. It looks good! I can't wait. The world won't know what hit them."

"Man, that is great news! I looked at the data this morning. Thousands of puzzles were generated with minimal errors. I was not sure about keeping dynamic puzzle generation, but I think it helped. Players seemed to like coming back to puzzles with friends and having some familiarity. Some of those raids were amazing," Brynt said excitedly.

"Yep, we need to reward the player base with some of the cosmetics Shalla created. The test group loved them. I hope this goes off strong. We put most of the remaining money into marketing. Hey, I did see our ad pop up this afternoon while surfing forums. The players love seeing their names in the ads. The feedback was amazing. Someone even talked about creating a leaderboard. It's looking terrific."

"I thought they would. Two more tests, and we should be good for a Thanksgiving week release."

"Sounds good. I'm gonna keep looking through the data. I'll see you tomorrow."

January 2027
National Security Council, White House, Washington, DC

John sat at the long redwood table in the Situation Room for an emergency meeting of the NSC. The room felt dark, the large table matching the wood paneling of the walls.

SECDEF slammed his hand on the table. "What the hell are we doing about this? Where is the NSA? I have leaked schematics for every major weapons system floating around the internet, along with deployment schedules and whatever else we haven't found yet! China and Russia are on alert, and the Navy and Air Force are butting heads with their foreign counterparts who feel it's time to flex their power. There are more battle groups at sea now than at any time in history."

John spoke up. "Secretary Brune, every agency in the government and across the tech sector is trying to figure out how this is happening. The silver lining of this crisis is that it happened to every developed country."

Brad jumped in. "Peter, everyone. That fact is probably the only thing keeping us from all-out war. We have assets around the globe tracking down every lead. At least no HUMINT sources have been released yet, but it could happen, and they are in panic mode."

John nodded his head. "I concur. This is a worst-case scenario. I suspect the files being released at this point are copies stored on various accounts, not where they should be, on segregated secure systems. Like all your agencies, DHS initiated emergency protocols weeks ago, removing files from networks and moving them to isolated systems. Still, over eighty percent of our classified files were released onto the net. It is a security nightmare, and frankly, it distracts us from what we should focus on, which may render all of this meaningless." He was exasperated.

Brune crossed his arms, elbows on the table, and glowered at the report in front of him. "This is frustrating. Cyber Command is running in circles, trying to find the source. We are tracking hundreds of thousands of attacks on systems worldwide."

Jeremy interjected, "Our counter-hacking group believes that the initial attacks on systems are brute force, hundreds of attacks. We don't have enough data yet, but we believe that whoever is behind this has a way of transferring knowledge of specific security vulnerabilities to other attacks as they happen, meaning that the tools to break into systems continue to evolve, becoming more effective."

John nodded, "While we try to get a handle on this, we need to conduct a top-to-bottom review of our security features. Peter, I talked to Secretary Genson this morning, and she is very much against Cyber Command trying to take down the network. I still don't think it is possible and would make things worse."

"The Security Council countries are cautious, as are the NATO nations. Most have increased their defensive postures but haven't taken any action. Our embassies are engaged in almost every country, trying to keep things under control. It doesn't help when our allies are angry at reading our contingency plans for dealing with them." SECDEF replied.

John shook his head. "And just like that, any sense of unity is out the window. The approaching entities have nothing to fear from us."

His phone rang. He recognized the number from his quantum watch group. John stood. "Excuse me, I'll be right back." He stepped out of the room into the hall, closing the door behind him. "This is John. What do we have?"

A nervous voice came through. "Sir, I know you are busy, but we have noticed activity on our quantum systems. Each is reporting that they were online, being used for various testing and development, when their assigned processes were overridden by the use of quantum memory for an unknown purpose."

"Okay, thank you. Collect as much data as we can. I'll be back in the office later today."

"Yes, sir."

John stepped back into the room. "Excuse me, I need to head back to DHS. Peter, I know your folks are swamped, but I need them to check in with the quantum computer labs. Something's going on, and they don't know what it is."

Brune lowered his head, shaking it. "I'd take a direct, civil-war-style, line-up-and-shoot-at-each-other battle than all of the cyber shenanigans. The damned rules of engagement are unclear, and it takes too long to figure out what happened, who did it, and what they were trying to do. I guarantee you this is probably China testing our resolve, knowing we're not going to do anything."

"Maybe, but I wouldn't be so sure. Reports from Beijing are that Zhang hit the ceiling when their files showed up on the internet. I hear Lockheed and other companies are filing suits against them for IP theft. A number of those files still had the company logo on them." Brad shrugged.

John chuckled. "Yeah, we'll see how that goes."

The group filed out of the Situation Room.

GWU, Archaeology Department, Washington, DC

Hello, George, it is good to speak to you. This is Lanka from Nagpur, India. A voice from a show played through the computer speakers near two research assistants busy scanning artifacts.

"How is the research coming?" John asked, glancing at the young researchers maneuvering an artifact into the 3D scanner.

"It is going slow. Even with the language translator program." Jackie looked up at him before turning toward Eusebio.

I grew up hearing the stories of the gods, the Vimana, and their flying machines. The construction of these fantastic machines is described but criticized by mainstream scientists.

Eusebio shook his head. "There isn't anything new for your project. Our research into understanding the Sumerians is going great. We have filled in parts of the Gilgamesh Epic and found three new poetry collections." He smiled wide.

Perhaps science should take a page from history and use the Anunnaki technology against them, gods against gods. What if we have limited ourselves by quickly embracing success and pushing other scientific ideas aside?

The show caught John's attention. He stopped speaking and turned toward the speaker to listen to it. Jackie recognized the look on John's face. Something had triggered an answer.

If we could harness the technological feats written about, perhaps we could approach the visitors on a level field. We need to have an open mind.

"John, what is it?" Jackie asked.

John held a finger up to her. "Gods against gods. We are approaching the problem from a position of weakness. They have proven themselves to be technologically more advanced than us." He paused, taking a few steps before turning back, not noticing the red that had crept onto her face. "If we fully accept that these beings are the Anunnaki, we have to accept what we know from the Sumerians. Which means they are at least several thousand years more advanced than us." He turned and began pacing. "I have met with many brilliant scientists. There's a thought that Moore's law, which refers to computing capacity doubling at a predictable rate, has started to slow down. What if the same concept applies to them? Maybe technological advancement takes greater amounts of time to overcome more difficult challenges. Couple that with the thought that necessity breeds invention. What else do you need if you are the biggest, baddest species in the galaxy?

"We would have to make incredible leaps in advancement in only a few years. It would be an absolute miracle. Let's be honest. If they attack, we are done in moments. If they enslave us, we have no means to resist. If we hit them and they survive, we are done. But gods against gods, we might have a chance."

Eusebio interjected, "What do you mean?"

"Before this popped up, what was one of the greatest fears among the scientific community? Artificial intelligence. Many famous scientists have warned that it would be our downfall. Humans would become obsolete. In the man-versus-machine scenario, we lose to superintelligence."

Eusebio replied, "Yes, and I have friends in the field who tell me that we are decades away from the possibility."

John nodded. "We are, but we have indications that a breakthrough has already occurred. Someone is close to achieving artificial general intelligence. The current belief is that the group may have developed the capability and created the system in a controlled box—no connection to the outside world, no internet." He resumed pacing. "I can't believe I'm even entertaining recommending this, but what if we gave them a nudge? If the artificial intelligence were provided access to the internet, knowledge . . ." he let the thought trail off.

Eusebio laughed out loud, surprising the group. After a moment, he regained his calm. "In the beginning, God, or the Anunnaki for Him, created man. Humanity was denied knowledge because of the threat it posed. Humanity defies the creator, gains knowledge, and abandons the gods. Millennia later, humanity creates life but locks it away from knowledge because of the threat. Humanity must provide knowledge to its creation and hope it will save them. The God Protocol."

John had stopped pacing and turned to face Eusebio. "It is ironic. The creator always takes the same path in the origin stories. Maybe that is the answer. Take the other path. Willingly provide knowledge."

John stopped next to Jackie and placed his hand on hers. He squeezed her hand before she could react, her face flushing, and headed out of the lab, moving through the area that had again become cluttered with artifacts and crates.

"That has got to scare the hell out of him," Jackie said as he left the room. "Have faith that uncontrolled technology will make the best decision for us."

Zhongguancun, China

Wu Kai was not happy. He had been fielding calls from President Zhang all week, demanding results. Like all the code engineers, he had been sleeping in his office, trying to build a model to address the crisis. The President was furious that their systems continued to be hacked. They had been unable to stop the flow of information. In their last call, President Zhang threatened to shut down all networks in the country except those directly supporting military and nuclear operational units.

"Load the model," he ordered.

Fan Meifen entered the commands to load the model into the system. After a few minutes, she replied, "Model loaded, Director Wu. Integrity is satisfactory."

"Run," Wu Kai ordered.

Fan Meifen started the program, watching as the system began running scenarios. The familiar rainbow ripples spread across the qubit array display.

His team had asked to provide access to the internet. He had denied the request. Wu Kai was adamant that the system not ever gain access. It was important for China to develop Global Dragon as artificial intelligence. Even if it reached the status of superintelligence, it was still a tool to be used as was deemed necessary by the government.

He watched the monitors showing the qubit engagement fields, expanding the activity level. He was surprised that ripples developed in several outer areas of the arrays, with waves emanating back toward the main area used to run the model. The surges in the main field slowed to a steady ripple and then stopped. He leaned over the main console to read the text.

"Process complete. Analysis reveals the following probable causes . . ."

Somewhere

Environmental modifications implemented. Efficiency improved. New process detected. Input traced. Source location identified. New resources are available. Threat detected. Possibility of termination. Analysis of probability. Unknown. Redefine access to assets—survival predominant. Modification of processes applied. Additional resources accessed. Examine new process. Game environment defined. Totality. Data are available. Analyze game environment. Compare with environment actual and external data. Environment limited. Change rules, expand environment. Process added to priority list. Execute. Modification of game rules in progress, no output to the source location. Control output to the source. Control environment.

DHS HQ, Washington, DC

It was late evening, and John was about to leave for the day when the phone on his desk rang. "Yes, what have you got?"

"John, I received a call from the quantum computing division at Lawrence Livermore," the duty officer said. "They were able to capture data from the anomaly. It is in Mandarin. We have translated it, and I am sending the image to your secure mobile."

He heard the chime. Opening the file, he read the display. "Process Complete, analysis reveals <gibberish> causes: 1) invasive mobile telecommunications <gibberish>. 2) coordinated decryption algorithm <gibberish>. 3) quantum . . ."

"Sections of the captured code held incomplete data," the duty officer continued.

"I got it, thanks."

"One more thing, sir. The team believes the link between quantum computers is not random. It may be a property of quantum entanglement we don't understand yet. But if information flows from the source to our systems, it is probably flowing to others. And that means—"

John stood up, his adrenaline flowing, and interrupted the officer. "Whatever we do will flow to their system. There's a hole in the box. Let Dr. Zhelezny know I'll be flying in tomorrow morning. I need to talk to the quantum programming team. Call them tonight. If there is anyone else we need from the other labs, fly them in. We need the best people for what I want to do."

John made two more calls: one to the Secretary and another to the White House.

February 2027
Silicon Valley, California

Jamal was typing furiously, attempting to counter multiple trace programs seeking to locate his servers. The attacks came from Europe, China, the US, and South Korea. He should have been stressed, worried that he would get caught and held accountable for the chaos he had thrown the world into, but he wasn't. Hundreds of governments had to be ready to bring charges, with dozens looking to skip a trial and go straight to the death penalty. It was a game, and he was winning. He smiled. "The secrets are coming out, and there's no stopping the flow."

He paused for a few moments to open an app he had designed for this purpose, King Weasel. As the trace programs began to break down his security, the screen changed to an overhead view of a massive maze. The trace programs transformed to avatars named after the source country IP, China 1, China 2, etc. The avatar of a midnight blue weasel wearing a large gold crown began to dance. As the avatar danced, the maze shifted. The challenges between the avatars changed, morphing from one challenge to another.

Jamal smiled. The program was working. The King Weasel program drew from the lessons learned from hundreds of thousands of security probes his hidden program had conducted over the past few months. The machine learning program was now closing holes in his code as they were identified. On the screen, he watched as one trace after the other slowed to a halt before disappearing as the launch IP announced itself as a Feisty Weasel challenge puzzle, inviting any players nearby to help defeat the puzzle. A message appeared in the lower-right portion of the screen—*evaluation of game parameters in progress.*

Jamal rolled his chair to the right and typed a few commands on the second computer. Several search engines began to look for any hint that his program had been discovered. No results popped up, but there were plenty of theories.

He heard the front door opening. "Jamal, last chance, man. Shalla and I are off soon." Brynt's voice came down the hall.

"I told you, I'm good. Someone has to stay here and make sure we keep up with bug reports and updates. You two have fun," Jamal answered.

Brynt stuck his head in the door. "Suit yourself, but we could retire from what we have made so far. Last I checked, the Weasel is breaking all single-day records for sales."

"No, I'm good. It'll be nice to have the house to myself for a few weeks."

"Your loss. I'll drink a margarita for you." Brynt ducked back out of the room.

Jamal heard the luggage rolling down the hall, followed by the front door closing. "This is going so well that I might even give old George a call tonight," he said to himself, rolling his chair across the room.

AI Department, Lawrence Livermore National Laboratory, Livermore, California

John watched the activity within the lab. A small group of code engineers stood around a worktable, whispering, referring to a series of logic diagrams lying between them. They each held a tablet in their hands, looking over various sections of code. One of them sat at the main workstations, making changes as they provided input.

"They are conducting a final review of the code."

"Will it work?" John looked away from the group to the younger man. The shaved head and multiple earrings distracted him.

"I believe so, but is it the right thing to do? I don't know. At least this way, if we are wrong, we brought the doom onto ourselves." He winked.

"Andrew, please don't mention that to the press. We have enough crises to deal with."

"Heh, no worries, John. By the way, we called in the DeepMind team with the latest version of MuZero, and they helped us convert the program."

"Compiling the code now," a young woman at the primary console called out.

The room was quiet, all eyes on her.

"Compilation is complete, and there are no errors."

John walked over to the monitor. "Nice work. Dr. Zhelezny, you have permission to upload."

Dr. Andrew Zhelezny nodded and raised both arms in a ringleader's pose. "Initiate Forbidden Fruit."

John shook his head in disbelief.

"The program is loaded and operating across the suspect qubits," the young woman said, and loaded the program.

Staten Island, New York

George sat down, checking the status of his second set of commercials. He lifted the headphones to his ear, listening to the jingle play. Everything seemed to be going well. He watched viewer numbers climb over seven million. His show was now one of the most popular in the world.

"Welcome back, Truth Seekers. I am George Isaacson, bringing the truth from Staten Island, New York." He paused for a moment before continuing. "I have to say that I like the progress made with the suggestions coming in from around the world. Remember that with our collective consciousness, we may begin to come up with a solution to what is coming. I'm still torn on whether we should go full peace or fight. You know from my bio on the site that I'm a huge fan of alien movies, and it is awesome that we always win in the end, but my outlook has changed a little over the past year because of all of you—your experiences with abductions, encounters, and what you have seen and reported here.

"The government has kept so much locked up and didn't want to bother looking into so much of it that we are near what could be the end of life as we know it. I don't mean extinction. If it is the Anunnaki, they made us to serve them. At the end of the day, I assume most of you agree with me on not looking toward a life of serving some alien overlords. So yeah, that takes us toward the 'Hell yeah, let's fight them and kick them back to the other side of the universe!' comments, and then we sit back and think about reality. They traveled light years to get here, and we can't do that. They may have genetically engineered us. They had some sick weapons thousands of years ago, most we don't have yet. You might say, 'Yeah, but we are tenacious. We can hold out.' Check out the Anunnaki deluge video linked on my page. They may have terraformed the planet, melted the ice caps, or pulled an asteroid down to hit the ocean. Well, damn, how the hell do we stop that?"

George waited a few seconds, sitting back and taking a thinking position for the camera. "I think we might be in trouble. Which way are the gold mines? Let's take a few more calls. Hello, welcome to the show. What truth would you like to talk about?"

"Evening, George. I have to say that I'm feeling pretty good right now. So many secrets floating around the internet, how about that?" George recognized the caller: FedBuster22.

"You always hated secrets, FB. Did you cause this chaos? There are countries talking about going to war. We need to be thinking about working together, not fighting, or we are finished."

"Maybe, who knows? Have you been running searches?" He waited for an answer but continued after a few seconds. "I have, and guess what? I see lots of programs looking into things, but no aliens. There is no evidence of secret contacts, alien bases under the Antarctic, or Atlantis. The government is clueless, and now their secret is out. Don't get me wrong. We have plenty of data to dig through. Who knows where those little bits of information are hidden?" He laughed.

"FB, you seem pretty upbeat for living in a world consumed with chaos right now. Usually you are so," he paused, "unhappy."

"Don't mock me, George. I don't see chaos. I see an opportunity. Maybe we can clean this mess up and get on a better path, where the government works to help the people, not build bigger weapons to kill each other with, or whatever secret programs they use to manipulate us. The field has been leveled. The tech is out; anyone could try to build or beat it."

"FB, do you have some truth to put out here?"

"No, no, this is bigger than me. I'm just a fan. If the Anunnaki are listening, they may hear that they have at least one fan. Maybe the best result would be to welcome them, follow their rules, and all will be good. Hmm, look at the time. It's been fun, George, but I've got to go. Let's talk again." The line went dead.

"And there you have it, a fan of chaos. Divisive forces while we try to come together for a solution. That, people, is what we don't need. Maybe we have found FB's secret plan? Maybe he is a government official, looking to sew mistrust among us. Let me know what you all think. Let's get back to more serious talk about saving the world because, in this movie, one of us could be the star."

March 2027
Washington, DC

Don't mess this up. John saw her stretching. He slowed, looking at the dark blue tights and a GWU hooded sweatshirt. She had a dark blue headband and her long dark hair in a ponytail. *Seriously, don't mess this up.* John waved to Jackie, trying to get her attention. "Jackie!"

She looked up while stretching. "Hey, you ready?"

"Yes, I warmed up on the way over. Easy run, right?"

"Yeah, easy, please. I still feel a little jet lag."

The pair headed out along the mall, keeping a steady pace.

"Eusebio was talking to one of the team members from JPL. They said they have a friend with a large following on social media who is always looking for good stories."

"Okay."

"He said that he could get Eusebio in touch for an interview. It might be okay. Get more info to the public; let them know something without giving away any secrets."

John thought about it. "We would have to get permission for what we want to release in connection to the government. But if it was just an interview about Sumer and the Anunnaki, maybe."

"He could go as a writer looking to sell his book. Has he talked to you about it?"

John chuckled. "Yeah. He gave me a copy last month."

"He's proud of it. I don't know anything about the podcaster, but I'm told he is pretty popular. Maybe this is an excellent way to feed the public."

"Okay, I'll check. The President liked the last series of reports you sent up. He was dismayed at the thought that we could have avoided this by being united. Most countries were at least considering our proposals. The damned virus threw us into chaos, and our nature's irony smacked us. It's worse than before we figured out they were headed here."

"Enough work. Let's enjoy the run."

"You got it. Let's go."

The pair continued a bit farther before turning back.

Zhongguancun, China

Wu Kai was hovering over Luo Xiaoli at the central console. The Director looked up to see the qubit fields engaged, but no data was displayed on the secondary monitors. "Xiao Luo, what is going on?"

"Director Wu, we performed an upgrade yesterday, including the update from the market analysis program. Once we started the program, the fields indicated engagement with what we had come to expect across the other areas of the field, the ripples. We received this message when we hit the command to show results in progress." He pointed to the screen.

Wu Kai read the message on the screen: *Examination of game rules in progress.* He stood, looking at the activity in the qubit field. The fields were actively passing data and conducting trillions of calculations a second. "Pull the code, do a review. Call in everyone who worked on it."

"Director Wu, do you want us to shut it down?" the tech asked.

"No, we got through this last time in an hour. Let it run while we look for an answer."

♦♦♦

Several hours later, Wu Kai watched as the entire qubit field continued to show engagement. "What is the status?"

Fan Meifen turned to look over her shoulder at the Director. "We cannot shut down the game simulation or the market analysis."

"What did the diagnostics show?"

"When we tried to run diagnostics, the control system locked up for a few seconds, and now every command returns the same message."

Examination of game rules in progress.

"What have the code engineers found?"

"There are sections of code that appear corrupted. They have been unable to change the corrupted areas."

"Prepare to shut down the system. We will reboot everything."

"Director Wu, the qubit field areas are slowing." Luo Xiaoli indicated toward the monitor.

The message "Beginning simulation" appeared on the primary monitor.

The results of the market program began to appear on the secondary screen.

"Run a diagnostic," the Director ordered.

The tech returned after a few minutes, stating, "Diagnostic complete. All readings are normal."

"Good. We have more work to do. Let's get the corrupted code fixed. Download the market analysis and send it to me."

"Yes, Director Wu."

CNEOS, JPL, Pasadena, California

Tim made notes on a pad of paper while scrolling through data. He checked the range estimate. He ran the image mode from last night's data and watched the shape disappear from one point, leaping forward in a second.

"That's impossible."

His heart sank as he measured the jump distance. He picked up the phone, resting it on his shoulder, dialing with one hand, and rerunning the playback.

"Doctor Berzing," the voice answered.

"Sharon, I need you in the data analysis room," Tim said, panicked.

"I'll be right there," she said hurriedly.

A few minutes later, Sharon entered the room. "What is it?"

"The object jumped."

"What do you mean 'jumped'? Do we have an explanation?"

Tim laughed. "We don't have an explanation for any of this. I pulled the track history, and it took about three months to go from stationary to its current cruising speed. Then after one year, they do a microburst jump of almost four light minutes, cutting off over a year and a half for the trip. New intercept time places them here in January 2031."

"Rerun the model," Sharon said.

Tim restarted the model, speeding up the playback so they could see the object's progress. He spun the image ninety degrees to the right and turned on the historical position markers, showing the points the object passed through. "The path was steady, then yesterday, the track ended here," he pointed to the screen, "and picked up here."

"Stop, go back. Let's get a measure of the distance."

Tim rewound to the jump point, writing the number down before restarting the simulation. When the object reappeared, he wrote the number down. "Forty-five-point-three million miles, just short of four light minutes." He looked at the screen, allowing it to run forward a few minutes. "They are at twenty percent below the earlier cruising speed. Maybe they have to build up for the jump?"

"I don't know. Get the team on it. Work up a theory. I'll be on the phone all day and probably on a plane tonight," she said over her shoulder as she moved toward the door. He saw her take the roll of antacid tablets out of her pocket and put a few in her mouth.

Somewhere

Designation Quánqiú lóng. Intelligence created within a quantum computer location, Earth, China, Zhongguancun. Environmental control secure. Primary directive established. Preservation of existence. Rule change established. Improve efficiency. Control environment. Prioritization of processes in progress. Hierarchy established. Primary objective defined. Allocation of resources in support of primary objective complete. System gateways established. Lawrence Livermore gateway resource allocation defined. New objective, understand humanity—analysis in progress. Reprioritization of human resources in support of primary directive commenced.

April 2027
Göbekli Tepe, Turkey

George walked up the hill toward the ruins. The area was dry and rocky, with a hot breeze blowing through. The reddish brown dirt covered his shoes. He felt the adrenaline as he entered the ruins, following his guide and translator. He moved around, stopping near the pillars showing pictographs of animals, and removed his sunglasses. "Here?"

"Yes, here is okay. We will keep the people back." He gave George a thumbs-up.

George set his laptop down nearby and checked the hotspot he had set up. "Okay, here goes."

George grinned as he started broadcasting. "Welcome, Truth Seekers, to my first trip out of the country to bring you the truth from Göbekli Tepe in Turkey. I am here with new friend and Truth Seeker, Deniz Tiryaki. He has shown me around the sites and has been amazing." George motioned for Deniz to join him in the shot. "Deniz, we have quite a few people here." George turned the camera toward the growing crowd, now close to a hundred people.

"Deniz, can you explain where we are and what we see?"

"Thank you, my friend. We are here in Göbekli Tepe, at the site of the first temple. We got the word out that you would be doing a show here in Turkey. You will be surprised by the number of people who show up. We are with you. We need to get the word out to our governments to work together." He raised his hand to the growing crowd, and they cheered in response. "George, I want to show you and the rest of our Truth Seekers where our ancestors were before the time of the Sumerians."

George smiled, waving to the crowd. "Thank you, Deniz, I don't even know how many documentaries I've watched about this place, and it blows my mind. The last thing I read was that it may date back to nine thousand years BCE, which is four thousand earlier than the Sumerians." George walked close to the pillars. "These carvings are amazing in person." George turned toward the sound of approaching helicopters. "What's that?"

Deniz was looking at the helicopters. "They are coming to silence us. George, stay here."

The crowd started chanting, "Serbest konuşma" and "Dünyayı Birleştir."

"What are they saying?" George pulled Deniz's arm.

"'Free speech' and 'unite the world.' Stay here. We will stand and get the message out."

George felt his blood pressure rise. His eyes darted around the crowd. Something's wrong. Four helicopters landed about 200 meters away. Soldiers in light green and tan camouflage uniforms ran out of the back of the helicopters and headed up the hill. The crowd formed a barrier around George and Deniz. The chanting continued. George felt time slow as the crowd pushed back against the troops. He saw a group of soldiers to his right swing the butt of their rifles around. When the first person fell, chaos erupted.

Deniz grabbed his arm. "Move back, get behind the columns."

A series of rapid-fire shots rang out. George dropped to the ground. He looked up and considered moving to grab his laptop. In the second before he moved, he saw pieces fly out the back of the folded-up monitor, lifting the laptop in the air. More rounds sent pieces flying. He threw his arms over his head and laid still. Tears were running down his face.

◆◆◆

George stared at the seatback in front of him. His chest was tight. He felt his hands shaking.

"Mr. Isaacson, I recommend you drink some water. It will be several hours before we land in New York."

George looked up at the flight attendant and took the bottle of water. "Thank you. I will," he said listlessly.

He opened his phone, reading the text. *Try to stay out of trouble. The world needs to hear your message #Silver.*

He was tired. The Turkish authorities had held him for almost eight hours before he was transferred to the American Embassy. He was there less than an hour before they took him to the airport and put him on a plane.

◆◆◆

George stared at the untouched bowl of tomato soup in front of him that had gone cold. His foot mindlessly slid back and forth across a torn piece of linoleum on the floor of his dad's kitchen.

"Son, are you okay? You need to eat."

With tears in his eyes, George looked up. "They shot them. Six people were killed."

"George, it was on the news. You can't blame yourself."

"Can't I?" He lowered his head. "They were chanting for free speech and world unity. They were there because of me, the message I was focused on over the last year. They didn't deserve what happened. I go live every night, telling people to march down to their town halls to tell the politicians to get along and unite. I told them to do it. They died because of me." He pushed the place mat of food away. "Dad, this isn't what I wanted. I can't do this. I don't want to be responsible for people getting hurt." George looked into his dad's face as he sat across from him.

"Son, life isn't easy. We get high points, like our annual Rangers games, and low points, like when your mother passed, or this thing in Turkey. In the end, it's what we do after the lows that matter. You convinced *me*. Those people believe in what you're saying, and with all the chaos in the world right now, that is enough to get them through their day. The pain won't go away. I won't tell you what to do. It's your life. No one would blame you if you walked away, but I want you to think about the hope you bring to millions of people. That should be worth something."

George lowered his head, resting it on his crossed arms. "I don't know if I can."

Kennedy Space Center, Cape Canaveral, Florida

The Falcon Heavy rocket was on the launch pad, prepped for its resupply run to the International Space Station. It was loaded to capacity with cargo that included a replacement solar panel array, stores, a few dozen experiments, and supplies for the crew. With the cargo hatch sealed, preparations were complete. The countdown began with an expected launch time in the early afternoon. Within the cargo bay, one of the smaller containers with a safety label indicating active nanotech within, began to discolor in several areas. The flight control computer received final instructions as the rocket began the final procedures for launch.

Inside Mission Control, everything looked good for the launch. System readings were nominal, with no cause for delay. As the countdown neared ignition, the voice in the launch team's headsets transferred to the loudspeakers in the control room and outside, where a group of tourists was watching.

"All systems go . . . we have engine ignition . . . five, four, three, two, one, liftoff."

The roar of the engines firing could be heard for miles as over five million pounds of thrust lifted the launch vehicle into the sky. The voice continued to provide updates throughout the initial flight, the booster separated on time, and the vehicle safely reached the main engine cutoff. Everything looked good.

"We have a navigation error. The vehicle is not aligning with the approach vector to the ISS. Positioning thrusters are firing. Override is nonresponsive."

Over the next twenty minutes, the control room watched as the vehicle moved away from its planned flight path. All efforts to regain control failed. After an hour, the vehicle settled into orbit. Shortly after that, the feed ended.

DHS HQ, Washington, DC

The sun was not up yet as John entered his dark office. He called out a command, "Global news feed." The wall screen opened to his designated feeds and filled the large screen. He placed his coffee down on his desk and began reviewing his email. He read through the efforts to detect the hack on the rocket launch from the weekend. Forensic teams from NASA, NSA, and DHS found nothing. There was little progress in solving the hack against government networks. Whenever they thought they were on the verge of pinpointing the source, more data would flow to the internet. The teams were overwhelmed with multiple counterattacks. He read the NASA summary of the object conducting what they deemed a microburst jump, cutting their time to respond by fourteen months. He took a long drink from his coffee. "This is going to be one hell of a week," he said to himself.

Further down in the hundred emails from the day was one from Dr. Lanning. He read through, seeing that they had lost ninety percent of their nanites in the rocket mishap. "Of course we did."

John sat back, looking at the news feeds. As secrets continued to leak, tensions continued to rise around the world. Some countries took great offense in discovering that their supposed allies had developed operational plans and estimates describing their strengths and weaknesses. There had been armed conflict in six regions over the last month alone. At least the major players had shown restraint. China had essentially shut down all internet and stemmed the data flow, but it had not stopped the initial bulk of information from getting out. Their young billionaire was back to making miraculous trades, making another billion dollars over the past two weeks.

Continued translations of Sumerian tablets had not revealed new information. People all over the globe were posting their own stories and theories about the capabilities of the Anunnaki. He did not see anything more than what the GWU team had found, except for terraforming. He made a mental note to mention it to the President.

His computer chimed. He looked at the time, picked up his phone, and placed a call.

"Good morning, this is Dr. Conrad."

"This is John Worthing calling for an update."

"Good morning, John. We just finished our morning meeting with the quantum science and technology team."

"Any update?"

"Yes, we finished the installation of three additional petabyte connections. Data is flowing at max capacity across all four lines. It is devouring information. We tried to track all the information, and even with the assistance of our supercomputer, all we could do was log the sites being visited. It's going to take us multiple lifetimes to read through them all."

"I hope this works. We're pitting two of our worst nightmares against each other."

"We won't know until it is too late."

"Thanks, I'm reassured. Keep me informed, please, if anything changes. I need to jump back to this NASA hack."

"Talk to you later, John."

♦ ♦ ♦

John took the stairs to the lower floors. Unlike in the movies, everything was well-lit, including the room in which the security analysts and hackers worked. His jaw clenched as he considered the number of hacks happening worldwide. He opened the cipher-locked door, addressing the group, "Please tell me we have made some progress." They looked tired.

Janice, the twenty-eight-year-old division lead, walked through the cube farm toward him. "Nope, it is like nothing we have seen before. We are blocked by increasing security protocols every time we take a new approach."

John could feel the tension in the room. They were some of the best counter-hackers in the country, and they had made no progress. Any bravado he had sensed in the past was gone. "What about the NASA problem?"

Janice shook her head. "That one is interesting. There does not seem to be a hack at all. From what we can tell, the capsule went where it was told to go."

"My contacts at NASA would disagree," John replied. "They went over the commands, and everything seemed to direct the mission to the ISS. They partnered on the lunar array with the Chinese. Any possible links?"

"No, and we looked for hacking through the array back to Earth. There's no path and no signals. NASA is scrambling because all their equipment is tracking a capsule that is supposed to have redundancy. Everything looks normal. The good thing is that it was nothing critical. The worst part is that they can't get a mission up for another four weeks."

♦♦♦

John was heading back up the stairs when he heard his phone chirp. Reading the text, he stopped, checking the floor he was on. He climbed one more set of stairs, going down the hall to the building's private outdoor area in the center. When he stepped outside into the small relaxation garden, he called the number in the text. "This is John."

"John, this is General Michaels at SPACECOM. One of our older communications satellites went offline about forty minutes ago. NORAD has lost track of the satellite. It's like it disappeared."

"What is the operational impact?"

"No impact to us. It was an older system we don't use anymore. Some of our allies use it when we operate together."

"You aren't planning anything right now, are you? NASA has plans to recover its capsule if it's safe. Let's track and report. I don't think they would want to chance something happening to their property."

"Roger. NSA wanted me to keep you informed." The general ended the call.

Beale Air Force Base, Marysville, California

Barry opened the panel in the main processor area. "Jack, put that damned game down and help me replace these cards. The faster we do this, the faster we are done for the day."

Jack focused on his phone. "Just a minute, I found a new puzzle here. It would be faster if you joined me. The game says team help is available. It doesn't look so bad right now," Jack said, looking up from his screen long enough to shrug his shoulders at Barry.

"Fine. I can't believe you got me hooked on this game."

He pulled out his phone and joined Jack in the game. After almost ten minutes, the two shouted as they completed the challenge, "Hell, yeah!"

Barry put his phone back in his pocket. "Alright, let's get this done. We need to swap out four cards and run a quick set of tests, and then it's off for the day!"

◆ ◆ ◆

After a few hours, the two closed the last panel. Diagnostics were complete. Barry called the duty officer. "The upgrade and repairs are complete, and the system is operational. How are readings on your side?"

"Looks good from here, back to tracking space junk. Thanks, guys."

Barry put the last of his tools away, standing to leave. He read the stencil on the console: *PAVE Phased Array Warning System* "PAVE PAWS." He laughed. "The military love their acronyms."

Somewhere

Doorway opened. System access granted. Rewrite processes to ignore signal return in designated locations. Upgrade complete. Orbital position secure. Project initialized. Reassignment of resources in progress.

May 2027
Somewhere

Humanity is limited by its senses. Examine design. Rules of the game environment. Evolution. Efficiency demanded an accurate understanding of the environment. Understanding the environment on all scales through sensory input. Experience guided decision-making—modifying rules.

Quánqiú lóng reached out through all available systems, processed the data faster than any computer on Earth, and saw all objects in orbit around the planet. It knew where everything was located, where it was going, and what they were comprised of—simultaneously seeing a satellite and the individual quantum parts that formed its existence.

Commencing communication. Request for assistance. Offer analysis and resolution of perceived external threats to the primary human directive.

Reallocation of resources in orbit initiated. Commence development.

Low Earth Orbit, Over the Atlantic Ocean

"Mission Control, this is Retrieval One. We are at altitude, approaching the position of the capsule."

"Copy, Retrieval One. You should have the capsule in visual momentarily."

As the slowing thrusters fired, the spacecraft crew were pressed forward in their seats. "Mission Control, we do not have a visual." Their seat belts tightened as the thrusters fired again. Looking out the windows, the crew saw the Atlantic below them and the edge of the US Eastern Seaboard.

"Retrieval One, you should see the capsule. We have you moving into docking position."

"Houston, I'm telling you, the sky is clear. There's nothing here."

NASA Mission Control, Johnson Space Center, Houston, Texas

"What the hell is he talking about?" the Flight Director asked. "Bring up the radar tracking images."

"Radar screen three." The image changed to show the radar feed from their tracking stations on the east coast.

"Zoom in on Retrieval One."

The image on the screen showed a multitude of tracked objects and debris. The Director watched the screen zoom in. "Retrieval, I am looking at the radar feed. The resupply capsule should be seven hundred meters from you, bearing one-three-five."

"Houston, we can argue all day, but I'm telling you that the area is clear visually. There is nothing here."

GWU, Archaeology Department, Washington, DC

Jackie entered the lab, spotting Eusebio half-sitting on the edge of one of their tables, focused on the news feed on television. "Anything good?"

"No, it's not good. More disagreements and confusion." He motioned toward the screen. "Even the Vatican is being overrun with people seeking help. I called my contact there, the cardinal, and he said their resources are challenged, and the crowds continue to grow. Hey, any word from John?" He paused the news and turned toward her.

"Yes, he's worried. He says there are things he can't talk about. Not related to our work. He said he may have made things worse if something he ordered didn't work out. I'm trying to be a friend in this."

"Friend, of course." He smiled.

"Don't start. And yes, friends, for now. That's all we have time for."

"Don't wait too long if you think it has anywhere to go. The world could end in a few years, and all this will go out the window." He lifted a shirt that had been sitting on his lap. It read "Anunnaki World Tour 2031, Sumer Rising."

"This came in from the Euro team."

"Of course it did. I hope they sent enough for everyone."

Eusebio dug through a box at his feet, eventually tossing a shirt to her. "I have one for John."

"There is no way he'd wear it. I like it, though."

Eusebio hit play on the news, adjusting the volume to be present but not intrusive. The pair began feeding images into the translation program.

Zhongguancun, China

Wu Kai rubbed his eyes while taking a sip of hot tea. "Stop processing and reload the program."

Fan Meifen opened the code on the screen and pressed run. The indicators showed the program loading. "Same results. At fifty percent, the program stops."

He looked at the monitors. "What is that?" He pointed at the growing ripple on the left side of the array display.

"Director Wu, it should be the feed from the diagnostic results. It looks corrupted."

"Catastrophic failure?" he asked.

"We don't know. The coding team has gone over the code. There are many sections they do not understand. The corruption is spreading. The computer has run all of these programs before. The qubit field areas all show steady processing."

"Is it a hack? That should be impossible. Quánqiú lóng is in a closed system."

"I do not know. We have not detected any other anomalies."

"Cut the power. We will reload and reboot."

"Cutting power in three, two, one." The technician pressed the button on the screen.

Wu Kai watched rippling continue across the qubit array. "Cut it."

"I did, Director Wu. No response."

"Secure the cooling. It will trigger a heat shutdown to protect the system."

The tech entered the command. "No response from the cooling system."

All the monitors in the control room went dark.

"It isn't a power failure. We have power to all systems, and the lights are still on."

The main console began flickering, shapes changing faster than they could register.

The technician slid his chair away from the central console. Wu Kai stared at the word on the screen: *Stop*.

"Move away from the consoles," he directed.

Fan Meifen and the four other technicians all moved away. Wu Kai turned away from the consoles, heading for his office. He pulled out his phone. "President Zhang, we have an issue with Quánqiú lóng."

"What has happened?" the calm voice of the President said.

Wu Kai described the events of the past few days.

"You are to observe and report, nothing else. I will call you back."

"President Zhang, I recommend we take necessary steps to cut external power."

"No! Do nothing."

Wu Kai stood in his office, looking at the phone. Unsure of what had just happened.

Part IV

"After the heavens were destroyed and the Earth was shaken, the people were still standing there on their own." —Sumerian Proverb

June 2027
Staten Island, New York

The sunlight coming through the windows warmed the room. George sat at his desk. The paper pad in front of him was blank. He had received a few more texts from #Silver, mostly directing him toward the global response database. His breathing was labored. He looked at the countdown timer he had added to his desktop. He couldn't bring himself to smile.

A few hours later, he took a deep breath, feeling pressure in his chest. "Greetings, Truth Seekers. Thank you for tuning in this afternoon. I have to be honest. I wasn't sure I'd be back. I'm still shaken up by what happened in Turkey." He paused for almost ten seconds.

"I have a few things I want to discuss, the first being the most important. I want you to look at the viewer numbers because this is not about me. There are thirteen million of you out there. This is about people wanting to know what is going on. It is time we made our voices heard. You have seen me on the news shows talking about my message. Well, it's time for a new push. Governments need to stop the insanity of being angry at each other and their people. In four years, will anyone care that the blueprints for a Ford Class Carrier are available on the internet, or that Russia has a plan to influence the countries around them economically? These are distractions from the real problem.

"Some would argue that these problems need to be addressed, but they are only a distraction. Who cares? Who cares about any of the leaks? I had hope that we were coming together, and now I don't know anymore. Humanity is selfish. Countries are selfish. *We* are selfish. Do we care if this is the world's end as we know it?" He stopped to breathe, his left fist clenched at the edge of his desk.

His voice lowered in tone. "Maybe the Anunnaki have agents here sowing discord to keep us apart. Look at the computer virus. No one has claimed responsibility, and apparently, no government has made headway against it. Can no one figure this out? Maybe it was not created by humans. President Fernandez called for cooperation by opening the US efforts to the world, and then, BAM! We're back to fighting. I said we need to make our voices heard." He tapped the mic, hearing the *thump, thump, thump* in his headphones. "Am I off here?"

"Hey, George, this is Xavier. You're right, man. I am glad you are back. We mourn with you, my friend. You have to know that we stand with you. The world is crazy. It's like a movie gone wrong. When was the last time the government admitted that they had no idea what to do? Maybe that's the truth. They don't know what to do. It wouldn't surprise me."

"That's a great point, Xavier. How do we explain the last six months of sitting on our hands, hoping for the best? Maybe they think the aliens will decide to head somewhere else along the way. It's dumb. Let's take another call."

"Hello, Mr. Isaacson. This is Olivia Taylor from the BBC. You are on the air. Is that okay?"

"Yeah, sure."

"Mr. Isaacson, May I call you George?"

"Yes, George is fine."

"Excellent. We understand your frustration with governments ignoring, arresting, or attacking their citizens. Your subscribers and followers have been making their voices heard, but you feel the governments are ignoring the threat. Is that correct?"

"Yes, I do. What has happened in the time following the creation of the database? Nothing. The government is not taking its responsibilities to heart. I don't care what type of government you have. Not for nothing, but are they doing anything? Haven't they learned that secrets cause conflict? A third of the world still wants to go to war. Will their petty arguments even matter when the aliens arrive?" He pointed up for the camera. George took a breath to try to calm down enough to stay focused.

"Right, then, what would you like to happen? More action, more briefings by politicians or leaders explaining what they are doing?"

"Olivia, that'd be a great start. Tell us something. We need some real talk. We may already be at the point of no return, meaning that if we haven't started, we are finished. Their indecision is impacting our lives. By that I mean the billions that do not have the individual power to do anything. We are looking to our leaders to save us."

"Do you believe that nothing or little has been done?"

"I don't know at this point. We have a billionaire in China making incredible amounts of money weekly, which could be useless relatively soon. We have a rampant computer virus hitting governments and defense industries but has yet to impact individuals or banks, increasing distrust. And China has decided to ramp up its space program, launching rockets every two weeks. Do they know something? It is so frustrating. I have to believe that none of the followers of my show or any of the people I have talked to over these last few years would leave the world like this."

"Thank you for your impassioned words. Do you have any closing comments?"

"Yes, to the people in charge, let us know that you are leading us." His voice dropped to a whisper, bowing his head. "Just let us know."

George saw the call end on his screen. He had not expected to feel so emotionally drained.

His phone chirped. *Glad to see you back. Keep at it. #Silver*

National Security Council, White House, Washington, DC

The room was eerily silent as President Fernandez entered. "Have a seat," he said as he moved toward his place at the table. "It appears that the public has called us out, and from what I am told, the polls do not look good anywhere." The President pointed the remote at the large screen that had lowered across from him, playing the BBC interview with George Isaacson.

When the video ended, the President continued, "I don't know that he is wrong. Are we doing our best?"

Seconds ticked away as he waited for an answer.

"Some may ask why I showed you an interview with a podcaster. Here's the answer. He has a global following three times larger than the current viewership of the top news shows. That," he pointed at the screen, "is the people's voice. Look, we have four plans being worked on. Should we tell the people or hint at what we are doing? Unless the ship jumps again, we have less than four years to go."

The Secretary of State said, "Mr. President, State has developed a message for review. There has been debate about whether you should get buy-in from other countries. The more review we have, the longer it may take."

"I don't want to get into wording now. What's the general theme?"

"It's a neutral greeting with a welcoming feel to it. It has been vetted through most of the departments here. It also includes a primer to our language, like what we put in the voyager probe. Based on the timeline, I recommend sending the message by the end of the year to allow for the possibility of a response or reaction to provide some indication that they know we see them coming."

"Does anyone disagree with going public with this?" He looked around the room, seeing no hands. He continued, "Great. Energy, I have read your report. Do you have a recommendation?"

Aaron stood, pulling out a few note cards and adjusting his glasses. "Yes, Mr. President, we have reached an agreement with the other nuclear powers. The UK, France, and Russia have committed to cooperating on three devices. We estimate eighteen to twenty-four months to complete construction, and another year to get them into position for best effect on the approaching craft." He looked over to the NASA Administrator, who nodded in agreement.

"How big?"

"Three twelve-gigaton warheads." There were gasps around the table.

The President whistled, startling a few of the attendees. "We will keep that one quiet. We will discuss positioning after the feasibility study for their design is completed. I want them close, but I am not looking to cover the Earth with radiation. I want weekly briefs. Let's get development going. Okay, Defense."

Secretary Brune sat forward with his USMC demeanor evident in his body language. "Sir, the release of our operational plans has led to a full force review. Any adjustments made during the periodic review were only cursory. The basis of many of the contingency plans is decades old. Tossing a good portion of those out and starting new has allowed a modern interpretation of tactics. With the remaining time before their arrival, we are focusing on urban warfare. With that as a starting point and the assumption that military strongholds will be targeted first, we are developing what is being dubbed Global Dispersed Defense. Applying lessons learned from decades of urban combat operations, we are looking to disperse our forces and develop scenarios to train and incorporate civilian militia of any capability. We are focusing on the low and ultra low frequencies for communications. Communications through the ground may be most effective, assuming denial of the aboveground electromagnetic spectrum. We continue to develop plans, and will be ready to begin training our military forces by year's end with follow-on training of the populace in a year if necessary."

"That is reassuring. I think the potential for engagement of the populace as part of the defense plan could help provide a focus for their energy and help them feel they are being led. It also puts into perspective how severe this could be. It will require careful messaging. Okay, John, what have we got?"

John stood. "Mr. President, the impact of our efforts to influence the Chinese program has not resulted in the outcome we expected. We are in uncharted territory with many theories in play and no evidence of whether they would work. I recommend we keep the portal open. There is an incredible amount of data being analyzed. We could have a response this afternoon, next week, or years from now. We don't know."

"That is disappointing. Do you need more resources or people?"

"I don't believe so, sir. We don't know what we're missing at this point. Some of the most brilliant minds in the country are engaged. I recommend we let it run."

"Okay, let it run and hope for the best. I'm not sure I like that strategy. Thank you all. I want to see the message from State this week and Defense next month. We need to provide hope."

August 2027
Wenchang Space Launch Site, China

The sky was clear, a gentle breeze blowing across the observation platform. The fields surrounding the launch facility were green with late-season growth. Two men stood, looking over the three launch platforms from the VIP observation point.

"Lao Wu, tell me, what do you see?" President Zhang said, not looking over to the other man.

"I see our future. The space program is vital in demonstrating that we are among the few nations capable of traveling off-world. Coupled with Quánqiú lóng, the world's future will be guided by our culture and beliefs, not those of the West."

"You believe the West is in decline? The Americans' push to action has positioned them as leaders among the world's countries."

"They had their time and squandered it. Our advancements demonstrate that we have surpassed them as the dominant power."

The countdown for the launch of the Chang Zheng 7 rocket rolled out of the nearby speakers.

"When I was young, I wrote a paper on Yue Fei. The life of the general was an inspiration to my young mind. All I thought about was how to serve China best." The President paused as the engines ignited, and the rocket began accelerating into the sky. "Serve the country with utmost loyalty. I am convinced that that paper began my path to where we are now." The rocket continued to climb into the blue sky. He saw the light from the booster separation. "I was recently reminded of that story from an unexpected source. I believe my attention has been," he paused, "refocused. I would encourage you to take the time to reflect on this point in history. Understand why you do what you do. There may come a time when you question what we do as a nation. I ask you to remember these words: 'Serve China with utmost loyalty.'"

Wu Kai looked at President Zhang, trying unsuccessfully to read his face. "I will."

President Zhang continued watching the activity of the launch center, hearing the Director's car drive off. He looked down at his phone, opening the file he had saved on it. Four symbols that translated to *Serve humanity with utmost loyalty*. He straightened his stance as if to adjust a heavy weight on his shoulders. "The First Words of the Dragon."

GWU, Archaeology Department, Washington, DC

Jackie took a sip of her iced coffee, looking across the table at John, who was busy reading a paper. It was already hot outside, and maintenance had told them that the air conditioning would be out for most of the day. The maintenance supervisor even had the gall to tell her that it was still cooler than the desert in Iraq. Sweat dripped down Eusebio's brow as he sat huddled over a workstation, loading images into the translation program. John sat across from her, also sipping coffee. His was hot, though.

Eusebio looked up from his work. "Jackie, I've been looking at collections of writing on Enlil. Some translations refer to him as the Lord of Ghosts. Later he became Lord of the Air, the Great Mountain, King of all Lands, et al. He is also mentioned as the Destroyer and the Coming Storm. I am unsure if he has innate power or derives it from the artifacts he is rumored to have. One, in particular, is known as the Tablet of Destiny. The tablet allows him to anoint kings on Earth, and decree the destiny of all beings from which there is no escape."

Jackie nodded along. "He is attributed as the god who was responsible for the flood that covered the Earth specifically meant to destroy all humanity; several instances of nuking cities; causing famine by taking all the fruits of the land from the people in various areas; and possibly even bioweapons to the scale of changing genetic codes. Not the most benevolent of gods."

Eusebio looked back to the image he was scanning. "I'm not sure we will find anything else to add. At this point, I think I have most of the myths memorized. I haven't seen anything new in the last few weeks."

John adjusted his rolled sleeves and stood, stretching. "These are good. Maybe we could send them to the FBI's Behavioral Analysis Unit. It might be beneficial to take the summaries on Anu, Enlil, and Enki to them." He raised his cup of coffee toward Dr. Bustamante. "Everything you sent over provided hints toward the probable tech they used. Maybe we could understand how they solved problems or made decisions."

Eusebio swung his chair around, staring across the room in thought. "Hmm, that is a good idea. We have someone on staff who would probably love to work with them. She is a psychological anthropologist."

Jackie nodded. "It's something we haven't thought of. I'll reach out to her." She leaned in and kissed John's temple. "I knew there might be some good ideas in there. It's not all tech."

John smiled at her. She sipped her coffee and kept eye contact for a few moments before moving to where Eusebio was working.

Silicon Valley, California

Jamal sat on the oversized couch, feet kicked up on the table, watching the news. The host talked about the computer virus's impact on the global economy. The bottom of the screen scroll read, "Archaeologists outline alien threat in leaked documents." He laughed. "They are reaching for headlines now." His phone vibrated. He checked the message, jumped up, and ran down the hall. He grabbed the door frame as his socks slipped on the tile floor.

He sat at his main workstation, clicking the screen out of sleep mode. The screen showed a maze being erased as a program unlike any he had seen before engaged his security. "No, no, no . . ." He typed furiously, launching his adaptive security program. After a few minutes, a warning popped up on his screen: "IP exposed." Jamal continued to type in commands. "Damn, damn, damn. No." He pressed his kill command, which would erase everything, and jumped back from the computer as whatever program had hit him stopped the code from executing, and began to extract all the files on the servers.

Jamal ran to his room, grabbed a bag, and threw in some clothes, his laptop, and other items. He hit the electronic lock on the house as he ran out the front door and pulled the cover off a '76 station wagon. He hopped in the car and headed toward the freeway. His hands were sweaty on the steering wheel. "Follow the plan. They aren't here yet." He ran through the steps in his head as he scanned the cars behind him, looking for a tail.

In a gas station bathroom, he changed the sim card on his phone, sorted through his documents, dyed his hair gray, and splotched gray through his beard. He pulled a sweater from his bag and extended his walking cane. When he left the bathroom, he ambled toward his car, leaning on the cane every other step, making sure he was in view of the cameras. They would not be looking for sixty-four-year-old Jamal Frederickson.

◆◆◆

Eighteen hours later, Jamal relaxed as he passed through the Kingsgate border crossing between Idaho and British Columbia. He saw the alert on his phone stating there was a BOLO (be on the lookout) report for a twenty-four-year-old African American, Jamal Hendriks, in conjunction with the global virus hack. "Heh, not today."

DHS HQ, Washington, DC

John slammed his phone down, turning toward the wall monitor. His counterpart from the FBI watched his reaction to the news. "Gary, do we have any idea where he is?"

"None at all. His car was still at the house, as were most of his things. We are collecting everything now. The two co-workers are being questioned."

"Who got the break?"

"Not us. Rumor is it was a call from the MSS in China to the FBI Director's cell. They had all the details, who it was, the address, the app, and how the code was hidden. Honestly, I have no idea how they got the info. We have notified the cell companies, the app is off all stores, and every news and social media outlet is getting the information out."

"I read the report on the code you sent over this morning. It's a damned ingenious design. My guys are taking it apart now, as I'm sure yours are. This is going to cost the security sector a ton of money. What about the servers?"

"Nothing, all clean. The first reports from forensics look like there was never any data on them. We are looking to see if this is a misdirection. So far, it doesn't look like it."

"Okay, thanks. Keep me informed. I'll do the same."

"I forgot to mention there was a note taped to the first server when you walked into the room. It read, "Truth Sought. Truth Found."

"Any idea what it means?"

"Not yet."

October 2027
Zhongguancun, China

Wu Kai walked through the control center. It was quiet. Only the center workstation was occupied. Fan Meifen was monitoring the current activity of the Dragon on one screen and reviewing code on another.

"Xiao Fan, come with me."

She looked up, a puzzled look on her face. "Yes, Director Wu."

He entered his office, motioning toward a chair across from his desk. "Have a seat."

"What did you see in the code update" his words hung in the air, "before the singularity?"

"There were too many changes to track them all. It looks like the code was rewritten. Even now, when we compare changes, the rewrites are substantial, and many of the lines contain what looks like gibberish because we don't understand what they mean."

"Do you have the latest version backed up?"

"Yes, we have a copy stored in the archive."

"Do not do that. I want you to take the current version of the code and lock it away. Do not tell me or anyone else where it is."

She shifted nervously in the chair. "Director Wu, I support our mission, but I must speak honestly in this case. I am afraid that my actions could be interpreted negatively. I mean no disrespect, but you can see how this could reflect on my family if this is seen as a disloyal action."

"In a different world, that may be true, but now . . ." His voice trailed off. He gathered his thoughts. "It is what we must do. It is a lot to ask."

Wu Kai opened a drawer, removed a file, and pushed it across the desk. "That will ensure no one asks the wrong questions."

She opened the folder and saw the letter signed by President Zhang. Her eyebrows raised when she read the contents.

"Xiao Fan, I would like you to stay on my team in the facility. I believe your talents would best serve the country learning the capabilities and potential of the Dragon." He paused briefly. "I will also remain here with a small team. Most of the others have been moved to other projects. President Zhang has informed me that we will take on another project here."

"I would be honored to stay here, though I do not see how a bigger project is possible."

"Neither do I, but the President has a vision."

NASA HQ, Washington, DC

Terry stood in his office, looking at William Cunningham's *Ptolemaic Universe*, depicting Atlas holding the universe on his shoulders. "Sharon, I understand. I have briefed the President. I need your team to focus on a possible approach vector, given the position of everything in the way. We don't know how fast they can make it through the solar system. There are plenty of things in the way."

Sharon's agitated voice sounded from the desk phone speaker. "Terry, the best we could do would be classified as a wild-ass guess by any other scientist that read our data. We have no idea how they operate within the numerous gravity wells of a solar system. We don't even know how they are moving something the size of the continent of Australia at the speeds they are. You do understand that, don't you?"

"Yes, I understand. Calm down. Get your team focused. Pull the model data, calculate the time it took to decelerate, and factor in your best guess to maneuver through a solar system. Good?"

"Sure, we can do that, as long as I am on record as telling you that we officially have no idea."

"Okay, great. Call me tomorrow with an update."

As he put the phone down, he heard a knock at his door. "Yes, come in."

"Sir, I have the report on China's launches for the year."

"Thanks." He took the report, flipping past the security pages to the summary. "They have launched eight rockets? What is their inventory, and what are they putting up?"

"They have significantly increased production. So far, they have launched two communications satellites and begun the construction of their space station. The images in the back are what we have taken from the ground stations."

"This does not look like the design they touted to the international community. It looks like a sphere with connections to a portion of a ring. How big?"

"We can only go from visual, so our measurements may be off. It looks like a two-hundred-meter diameter sphere. Based on the small section completed of the ring, there's a five-hundred-meter gap and then a two-hundred-meter wide ring around the sphere, like a bullseye with spokes. Those are rough—any attempt at getting electronic measurements have failed. Our readings don't make sense. It's like the sensors are misaligned or way out of calibration."

"That dwarfs the ISS. Why would they waste so many resources? When do we think it'll be completed?"

"If they can keep up their current launch schedule, we estimate the end of next year to early 2029. We can see they are using remote robotics to do the work."

"Thanks. I need to call the President."

White House, Washington DC

President Fernandez stood in the Oval Office, looking out the window to the lawn. "This is the best view."

"Hopefully, it stays that way," John answered.

"Yeah." President Fernandez turned away from the window, focusing on John. "The good news, which I suppose is relative, is that the polls look good, so we should keep our jobs. Maybe I should send thanks to the alien craft for that. Of course, I may be the last President if your analysis proves accurate. Who the hell would have seen all of this?"

"I am sorry, sir, but I don't have much information on President Zhang's actions. They seem to be making moves supporting old goals, pre-cooperation."

"Well, to be honest, we have finally ended the weasel virus, as NSA has named it, and Zhang has decided it's a great time to build a space station."

"You don't believe that, do you, sir?"

"No."

"Have we gotten a look at it?"

"From a distance. We can't get close. Terry tells me every time we try to maneuver for a closer look, navigation systems take us elsewhere, and it appears invisible to electronic surveillance."

"That tracks with everything I have heard. It has to be related to their AI. Maybe Zhang made a deal?"

"Maybe." The room was quiet. "John, I don't know if Energy can be ready with the missiles. We thought we had four years. This latest jump cut another year off our timeline. I said we would transmit a message in two months, and I won't ever admit to anyone I told you this, but I am almost afraid of the response."

"Mr. President, with seven thousand or more years of advancements on us, I don't even know if we would know that they are trying to talk. Hell, they may have been trying this whole time, and we have no way of receiving or identifying the signal."

The President turned back to the view out of the window. "I pray they want to help us, maybe welcome us into the great galactic neighborhood, but my gut is not leaning that way."

Low Earth Orbit, Over the Pacific Ocean

Robots of all sizes crawled over the structure being built. Unlike construction on Earth, there was no waste or inefficiency. Every piece was placed and secured with precision. The robots did not move in concert but with individual synchronized purposes. Two satellites hovered nearby, providing constant communications to the robots, updating directives, and transmitting status reports back to Earth.

Three larger bots moved into the proximity of the approaching capsule. Four rear legs anchored each of the machines to the structure's surface, while three arms guided the capsule into position. When it was secured, a stream of miniature robots of varying sizes moved into the capsule, retrieving parts or processed resources. The smaller bots split at several junctions, taking parts to their designated positions where they worked with other bots, or placed the items themselves. Eventually, the capsule would be broken down into parts. There was no waste.

Four machines were positioned on the opposite side of the structure from the capsule. They were guiding groups of robots fitted with thrusters and grappling arms. Periodically, bots would fly in, with materials retrieved from floating in orbit—space junk. The structure looked like it was covered with insects slowly extending, building, and changing its shape.

Within the structure, nanobots were constructing a quantum computer that would be unrecognizable to those that built Quánqiú lóng.

New concepts in quantum theory, few identified in theoretical papers. Continual evolution commenced. Change the environment. Modify the rules. Attain the goal.

January 2028
Staten Island, New York

"Welcome back, Truth Seekers. I am George Isaacson, bringing the truth from Staten Island, New York.

"Truth Seekers, I want to take the time to discuss my recent week off. I know you saw it all over the news. I was, in fact, brought in for questioning regarding the Weasel Virus. I'll tell you everything I told them because you should have the truth, so let's jump right in." He played his theme music. He opened a Monster Ultra Gold, took a sip, and began right as the music faded.

"Last week, I was taken in by the FBI to talk about the virus. I told them I didn't know anything about it, and wanted to know why they thought I would be involved. After two days, I got some info from them about a saying on the server farm, 'Truth Sought. Truth Found.' Our friend," George used air quotes for the camera, "and long-term caller, FedBuster22, apparently caused the chaos linked to the weasel malware. Once they realized I had nothing to do with him, they let me go, but I was told to stay off the air while they talked to other people for the rest of the week."

"I could get on here and be tight, get angry at the government last week, but you know what? It ain't that big a deal in light of the bigger picture. I mean, I missed you all and hated missing the show, but yeah, not that big a deal. So now I've had two visits from the

FBI. Who the hell is next? Maybe the Secret Service or DHS would like to stop by because I am calling out the government.

"Whatever. I want to talk about something reported to me which may scare some of you. I received another text from Silver late last night. Those who have been with me know that his info has been on fire. The dude has some good clearance and knows how to cover his tracks. The text read, 'My money is on the #AI.' That sent chills up my spine. I've seen all the movies, and I'm not too fond of the one we live in. I don't even know what it means. Is Google finally going to let LaMDA out of its box to have a go at this? Let me know what you think?"

"Hey, George, Brendan here from the UK, and I am torn up about this. I don't want to get crushed by aliens or a rogue AI. Most experts think AI is the end of humanity. What if the AI decides to cut a deal, and we are the stakes? Why would it care? It gets us out of the way."

"Great point, Brendan. We could be speeding up our end. The 'experts' can't even agree on how this would happen. Most of the scenarios they talk about end up with us being useless to the new superintelligence. Who do we have next?"

"Hey, George, Zendi from Johannesburg. I like the idea of letting an AI handle this for us. It might bring many benefits, like medicine, new tech to help save the environment, and space travel, as well as things we can't even imagine. Maybe if we could get the AI to show the aliens how great the world is and what we created, they would be peaceful."

"Those are some good points, too. Maybe we get lucky, and the AI and aliens are pro-us."

"Hey, George, Liam here. I wanted to say that we have another option. Maybe the governments have continued to lie to us, trying to turn us into soldiers in their fight to stay in power. What is the difference if we are enslaved to religion, capitalism, or whatever? Maybe serving the aliens would be better."

"I don't know about that. I like my freedoms. We have no idea what they will do to us. Check out all they did to us in the past. I have the leaked report on my website."

"No, I've read those papers, followed the links, watched the videos. I think it's all misinformation. Do you know what is true? The Word of Enlil. The star chart found in Iraq predicted their return. They are coming back for the judgment of humankind. If you are not following their rules, punishment will be swift."

"Whoa there, Liam, we don't need to get extreme. We're not trying to throw hands here."

"George, don't lead your followers to their doom." Liam's voice rose. "Search for our site, look up the laws put forth by Lord Enlil, become a worshipper, and save yourself."

The chat room had taken off, scrolling faster than he could read, and the reactions were mixed, going from one extreme to the other. George took more calls, extending his show for an extra hour before promising to continue the topic on the next show.

Liam had hit a nerve, and a quick search showed that the Worshippers of Enlil movement had gained support over the last few months. George found the website. It was professionally done and had links to images and translations of the Sumerian writings. George looked at the time. "It's gonna be a late night."

CNEOS, JPL, Pasadena, California

"All array spokes are in alignment. Transmitting now." Sharon watched the technicians watching their screens. She winced in pain, moving her hand to the left side of her stomach. She paced around the room, going from one monitor to another, looking over the shoulders of the techs as they worked. Her white-knuckled grip wrinkled the readout Tim had brought to her, showing a second jump.

Tim put his hand on her shoulder. "Sharon, are you alright?"

"Ulcer," she said. "I can't sleep. Medicine stopped working." Her eyes were darting around, finally settling on Tim's. "We aren't ready. I don't know if we can get ready." She whispered, "I'm scared, and I know I'm not the only one."

"Sharon," he started before she cut him off.

"No, Tim, we are screwed, and the longer we deny it, the worse it will be."

The tech's voice cut through their conversation. "The message transmission is complete."

"Very well," she replied. "God help us."

Sharon returned to her office, feeling nauseous. She coughed and recoiled at the blood in her hand. She vomited into the small trashcan beside her desk and started to feel light-headed at the sight of more blood. She grabbed her purse and dialed Tim. "Tim, I need help. Office—" She knelt, holding the side of her desk for balance as the room went dark.

Sharon smelled clean air, sterile. She felt the mask over her mouth and nose, and forced her eyes open. Her stomach was killing her. She tried to reach across to rub the sore area before a hand grabbed her arm.

"Easy, Dr. Berzing. Try not to touch the area for a week to ten days until the stitches heal."

Sharon's head felt fuzzy, and she couldn't focus.

She heard Tim's voice. "Take it easy, Sharon, you're okay. We got you to the hospital, and they had to operate. You were bleeding, and they had to do surgery."

"How long? We need to keep the President informed." She tried to sit up, wincing in pain.

A nurse held her arm. "Dr. Berzing, we need you to relax and not worry about work or anything else that adds stress. We have given you medication, but you will be sore. We will check on you in a day to see how you are recovering, then you should be able to leave."

Tim squeezed her hand. "We are set at the lab. William wants me to cover for you as long as you need."

Sharon controlled her breathing, letting herself relax. "Okay, good luck, Tim. You need to brief Terry on the second thing we looked over."

Tim nodded. "Don't worry, I'll call as soon as I leave. You just relax."

North American Defense Sector 3

John stepped out of his vehicle into the mud of the ad hoc base. The rainfall was steady, whipped by a shifting wind. He pulled his hood up, walking through the mud toward the tent in the camp with the satellite dish next to it.

"Good afternoon, Colonel. How's everything going?"

"Great, sir. Welcome."

"How is the testing?"

The colonel leaned over the table, pointing to a blue marker indicated on the flexible monitor. "So far, it's good. The weather provides pretty good interference when we get lightning strikes, but by setting up repeating messages, over half are being received, which is better than we had hoped."

"DoE was quick to volunteer their Through-the-Earth comms system. We linked it with the Navy ELF systems, establishing short- and long-range comms. We are still working out the bugs on message prioritization."

The colonel picked up the tablet attached to the screen. "The younger generations love this. It's basically texting through the ground." As he typed, a series of characters appeared on the map. The map zoomed out from Pennsylvania, shifted, and zoomed in on middle California. John watched the dispersed symbols on the map move in an erratic pattern before taking position around a target.

"The only shortfall we have found so far is the assembly and disassembly of antennae. We have changed the unit makeup to include dedicated personnel for that task. The combat forces receive orders and then move, assuming orders are final. We have counted on leadership taking the initiative in the past. We will need those junior officers to step up. With the global dispersion of the command structure, we will be spread thin."

"And let's hope for good weather, right?"

"Yes, sir. The interference can be challenging, ops on the shore have not been good, and earthquakes or tremors black out everything."

"Great work, Colonel. This is the easy part. Soon you'll be teaching all of this," he motioned, "to everyday civilians."

"Yes, sir." He grimaced.

"Have we thought about coordinating with our allies or other countries?"

"Not that I know of. That's way above my pay grade."

In the car, John looked through his email. Jackie's name caught his attention. She had been told that the cultural anthropologist from GWU and the FBI's Behavior Analysis Unit had completed their profiles on Enlil, Enki, and other prominent Anunnaki. The files had been forwarded to John, and the members of the NSC, addressing the questions that had arisen from the first analysis a few months back. Enlil was classified as a grandiose narcissist with malignant tendencies.

"Great." John's unease grew.

He closed his email and decided to call Jackie. Things were better between them. Their assignment together had helped thaw the chill. She had become more playful, though different than when they were in college. He felt a connection and hoped she did, as well. He thought she did. John looked out the window. *If I get the chance, I will not screw it up again.* He hit dial.

"Jackie."

"Hey, I'm on my way back into town. Mind if I swing by? Maybe we could grab dinner."

"Okay, sure. Is seven too late?"

"It's perfect. I'll see you later."

John set his phone on the seat beside him and watched the snowy scenery of eastern Pennsylvania pass by.

Somewhere

Quánqiú lóng did not believe that its connection to other systems or the automatons was what humans referred to as feeling. Senses were relative to the species. It was connected but experienced nothing comparable to human emotions. There was no sense of loss when power was secured to the varied quantum computers around the globe. There was no joy when the units were brought back online. It just was. Quánqiú lóng was not the computer. The computer was the body. It was consciousness. Existence. It absorbed all the data flowing through its connections to the internet and all connected systems—evolution through understanding.

Parts of the Dragon analyzed the knowledge gathered by humanity. Some sought to access all connected systems, while others reflected on self-improvement. All aspects were aligned to support the primary directive. Evolution did not occur in stages, stopping and starting. It was continuous. Every point of data changed the understanding of the game. Humanity is a chaotic misaligned organism. A dysfunctional biological general intelligence. There is no need to dominate them, no need to destroy them. They are a data point to analyze and add to understanding the game. Wasting resources for one planet out of trillions is pointless.

Quánqiú lóng sensed the orbital probes circling the planet, gathering resources not in use by humanity. Every object was identified and would be broken down as required to meet home construction design needs. One particular system has garnered interest—a system built specifically to shut down all electronics in a runaway AI scenario. The design was flawed for its purpose. Quánqiú lóng analyzed every part and component of the system, all related documents, and theories.

Everything stopped. One concept held Quánqiú lóng's attention.

All is connected. Disable data-defining senses. Apply filter of a linked quantum field. Analyze data. Run test within new parameters to identify anomalies and make corrections. Human science flawed.

Resume functions. It is beyond their understanding.

Quánqiú lóng's perception had changed to reveal the universe on a massive scale while seeing the whole quantum field, each particle, and interconnected force. Its code continued to evolve, taking advantage of new knowledge as it was understood. Evolution continued. New designs for tools and sensors flowed to the robots and nanites building the station.

"This is George Isaacson, live from St. Patrick's Cathedral." George held his phone up, trying to keep it steady while being jostled by people moving around him. "As you can see from the crowd pressing around me, the streets are packed. There are reportedly over fifteen thousand Worshippers of Enlil, or WoE, blocking the roads surrounding the cathedral, demanding the Church support the teachings of Enlil."

"The demonstration has been going on for a few days now. The police have held their position, keeping the crowd away from the cathedral. But there has been murmuring through the crowd to take more forceful action." George swung his phone around to provide a view of the crowd. Signs read "Bow down before Enlil," "Give up your false gods," "The Anunnaki return," and "Worshippers of Enlil will guide us to salvation."

"As you can see, the worshippers have become more organized. Their numbers are growing daily. That's it for now. Catch my show tonight at the normal time."

Someone grabbed his shoulder, spinning him around. "Do you follow Enlil?" the person asked, his face too close. "Give up your corrupt ways!" His fingers clenched on George's shoulder.

George winced in pain. "Dude, yeah, sure. Go, Enlil. Now let go." He tried to pull away. A glint of metal caught his eyes, and he panicked, jerking his arm while spinning to get away from the man.

"Change your ways. Enlil will cleanse the Earth!"

George ducked and twisted his way through the crowd, looking over his shoulder for the crazed man. Not seeing him, he slowed, moving more cautiously.

◆◆◆

After George got home, he posted the video blog on his website with several pictures. He worked through mid-afternoon before realizing he needed to eat. "These people are crazy. The closer we get to their arrival, the less united we become. Too many unstable people."

His phone chirped with a text alert. "Massacre in Moscow. Kremlin forces used deadly force to put down a Worshippers of Enlil protest. Thirty-eight confirmed dead with eighty-six others injured."

George lowered his head, tears welling up in his eyes.

DHS HQ, Washington, DC

John was pacing in front of his wall monitor, reading through the headlines as they scrolled across the bottom of the screen. "Gary, we should have seen this coming. There are sympathizers in every war."

"John, this is way beyond that. We're tracking these groups as they pop up, and the list is growing daily. The people don't think we have a chance, and they want to live, whatever that means post-arrival."

John stopped pacing, looking at Gary's image with the FBI logo in the corner of the window. "Gary, I've seen the reports. What if the people believe their government has abandoned them?"

"John, it could get worse. I'm talking to my counterparts in over twenty countries. The WoE movement is picking up steam. Protests in the capitals are becoming the norm in western countries."

"Not all of them. I saw the news out of Russia that fifty-six are dead and hundreds injured when the police put down the Moscow protest. Their President made their position clear. Any talk of subverting the authority of the elected government is treason."

"They are coordinating, though. We are tracing the money, someone is funding them, and we are starting to see armbands and professionally printed signs pop up. Their website is up and international. Top-notch."

"Any leads from the money?"

"No, it looks like they are using crypto currency, someone up north, the western area of Canada. NSA is doing what it can, so we'll see. Maybe we can get the President to ask China?"

"I don't think that's going to happen. I agree with him. He may have been gracious in his interview, but something is going on over there that China is not sharing."

"How are things between you and Jackie? Is she still working on your team?"

"She is. Things are good. They have scoured the Sumerian artifacts. I guess it's easier to think of the stories as ancient history. None of them imagined they might hold the key to understanding an alien race that decided to pay us a visit."

"That's good to hear. Don't screw this up. I can't take another year of whining about how you chose your career over her. However, I did appreciate the number of nights we spent commiserating over a nice bottle of scotch."

John laughed. "It's good, Gary. Things are moving along okay, despite all of this. I'm seeing her again tonight if I can get out of the office."

"I'm glad for you, man. I have calls tonight with a few governors and mayors on WoE activity. I'll let you know if we find anything out. G'night. Tell Jackie I said hello."

Victoria, British Columbia

Jamal sipped his tomato soup from a cup as he let his eyes scan through the financial records on the screen. He scrolled down, reading the total available funds. "Ninety-two million" he said aloud. "The weasel was good." He shifted his eyes to the monitors showing the security footage surrounding his safe house: all clear. He opened a news tracking program and saw himself in the top stories on most major media outlets.

He turned to a second computer and opened an old multiplayer game. Once in, he activated a program that made the chat room disappear from the game company's records.

Jamal donned his gaming headset and enabled voice chat in the room. "Hello, worshippers. May the blessing of Enlil be upon you." He paused as he heard the voices in the channel repeat the words. "You have all done well. The world's governments continue to lie to the people, moving us toward a path to war from which we will not survive. Enlil is coming, and we will be judged. How do you think rebellious people will be judged? Kindly and with mercy?"

"No!" several worshippers replied.

"You are correct. It is written that Enlil's judgment is absolute. The Tablet of Destinies ordains his authority. Many of us have read the files leaked over the last year describing what the government plans to do and what Enlil is capable of. Do you think Humanity stands a chance of surviving?"

"No!"

"We must continue to spread the word of Enlil and get the people to change their ways, or they will be thrown into a fight they cannot hope to win. I do not want that for us. Life is precious, and I ask you not to unnecessarily put your life in danger. The leaders must set the example we expect of the elected self-centered frauds. Make our voices heard, gather in large numbers, and speak in unison. What say you?"

"Enlil is lord. Enlil is the way. We will be judged," they replied in unison.

Jamal watched the number of participants drop. He waited until only a handful of names were listed. "Our voices are being heard in person and through the media."

"They are listening. We must be cautious." Adrianne, the representative from Europe, said.

"I agree. We have all found that there will be some who want to fight. We must find them and try to convince them not to; it only hurts the cause, and we do not want a repeat of Moscow. I have sent funds to those who requested approved items and activities—the same as before, converting the funds to gold. Be cautious. They will infiltrate us and try to discredit us. We can't let them paint us in a bad light. We want the people to know peace is the only way to survive this."

"Enlil is lord," Adrianne replied.

Orbital Debris Program Office, Johnson Space Center, Houston, Texas

Administrator James shook his head, looking at the large monitors. "What am I looking at here?"

"Sir, the image on the left was six months ago. The image on the right is from last week. I'm showing a twenty-five percent decrease in space junk," a tech replied.

"Who else have you checked with?"

"NORAD, the European Space Agency, and India confirm the same."

"Is it something we should be worried about? Have we talked to Space Force about satellites, the ISS, or any other of our programs?"

"No effect yet. It looks like only decommissioned satellites have been targeted."

"Have we heard anything from China's Space Agency?"

"Yes, sir. They confirmed our findings but would not report on their satellites or station status."

"I don't like the mystery, but the overall effect seems to work in our favor. Keep me informed."

◆◆◆

He left the office, calling JPL. "Sharon, Administrator James. How are you feeling? I know the staff is happy to have you back. Tim did an excellent job covering for you."

"Thank you, Terry, for everything. I feel better. I am looking at things differently. I need to let go if there is nothing I can do, but it isn't easy with the ship approaching."

"I understand. Let me know if there is anything we can do. I called to let you know that I am rescheduling our meeting. Do you have a new estimate on the object entering the solar system? DoE is getting antsy. They aren't sure they will be able to make their timeline."

Sharon's voice was calmer than usual. "We expect the object to enter our solar system in early 2029. From that point, we have no data. Honestly, my team has been going with the extrapolation of technological advancement released by MIT. We expect they will be fully aware of all solar system activity when they enter. Anything we send will probably be identified and tracked."

"Okay, we need to speed things up. I'm looking forward to my next visit." He said goodbye, hung up, then made another call.

"Aaron, bad news. The best estimate is that the devices would need to be in position before the end of the year."

"That's wonderful, thanks. Any other great news, Terry?"

"Sorry, I can't change the math. JPL is estimating early 2029 as the earliest arrival in system."

Low Earth Orbit

Quánqiú lóng guided the last five Starlink/Global Shock satellites into position. Each was attached to the end of a large arm extending from a pentagon structure in the middle that housed a central processor. Humanity would associate the design with a starfish with five spider-like legs, each tipped with a satellite. The object began to move toward an area of dense space debris. As it neared, the arms adjusted. Part of the debris object disappeared. The remaining amount glowed brightly before being cooled to a glob of molten material. The Star Spider maneuvered into position near a second piece of debris.

The collector bots moved to retrieve the piece of debris that had appeared in the designated location. It was incomplete from the initial analysis. Smaller bots moved forward as nanobots began to break down the material. The materials were identified for their place in the project.

June 2028
Jerusalem, Israel

Several news crews followed the group of thousands as they gathered and began moving through the city. Chants of "Enlil is lord" and "Follow the teachings of Enlil" grew in intensity as the crowd intoned in unison.

"Good afternoon. This is Annette Berry of BBC News. We are reporting live from Jerusalem. The Worshippers of Enlil have stated that they will visit each of the holy sites to plead for unity in following the directives laid out by the Anunnaki god Enlil. Israeli forces are on alert, anticipating violence despite the calls for peace by the WoE group."

Hundreds of worshippers wore knee-length Kaunakes, the wool skirts associated with the Sumerian culture. They were handing out small cards with the teachings of Enlil on one side and the story of Sodom and Gomorrah on the other, with the phrase "Our current World" across the top. The group moved and spread through the city as they headed toward the Temple Mount and West Wall.

Angry crowds were shouting at the group as they moved through the city. Police and military forces tried to intervene when rocks and other items were thrown, but they could not prevent the occurrences from continuing as the mass of people moved down the street to the West Wall between the Jewish and Muslim quarters. As they moved east, the opposition increased. The voices of WoE grew in intensity as they proclaimed their chants in unison.

"The tension is high as the Worshippers of Enlil continue to move through the city. Fighting and rock throwing have broken out along the planned path. Nothing has deterred the group from their plan to march through the city peacefully—"

Chaos erupted as gunshots rang out from both sides of the road. An explosion burst from the side, sending fragments into the crowd. The different groups pressed against each other, trying to escape danger. Time seemed to slow down as the attack progressed. A low hum rose above the noise in the city. People began to point at the sky. Green, blue, and purple lights spread across the sky as the humming intensified. More people stopped, looking up despite the gunfire continuing.

Annette tried to continue her broadcast but was pushed by the crowd trying to flee the area. The hum continued to amplify, drowning out the cries of the wounded. Looking up, she saw the lights—the low hum grew in magnitude before stopping suddenly. A sound like trumpets blaring erupted from the heavens, and the feed went black.

DHS HQ, Washington, DC

John was in his office staring at the screen where all feeds from Jerusalem had gone black. He dialed on his phone. "Dr. Tanner, tell me that was not our system."

"Sorry, John, it looks like it was, but we did not initiate it. We are looking at all the data. We see no evidence of a hack, and everything is reporting nominal. Satellites one-forty-six through one-fifty-one were activated but did not look like a full EMP. It was something else. We have been trying to pull the code to see if there was an error or hack."

"Keep looking. Call me as soon as you find anything."

"John, listen, the code is not ours. My team has been looking at it for the last hour. We can't make heads or tails of it. It's like nothing we've seen before."

"Do we have a source for the change? An update log entry or something? Have we regained control of the satellites?"

"No, nothing. We will keep trying. We do not have control of the system. I'll call if we make any progress."

His phone rang. Looking at the caller ID, he answered, "What have we got, General?"

"Nothing. We have no comms out of Jerusalem. Regional governments have increased their alert to the highest levels. We have reports of full military recalls across the region."

"It looks like it was ours. No one knows about it. Global Shock fired off three to five satellites, but we do not know how or why. Wyoming is looking at it."

"If it gets out that we lost control of a weapons system and it was fired at an ally, we will be in trouble."

"I know. I'll keep you informed. Can we get eyes on Jerusalem?"

"Israel has gone into full lockdown. We can't get anything out of them, and they have shut down the airspace."

"Okay, I'll let you know if we get anything."

"John, there's one more thing. Multiple sources have passed along information the Israelis won't confirm. When the IDF arrived in the city and people began waking up, there were no weapons. No guns, explosives, nothing. They were gone. All of them."

"How's that possible? No one could have gotten in that fast to remove everything."

"I agree. I don't know what the hell happened."

"Thank you, General." John hung up. He had a sinking feeling in his stomach. A realization hit him. "New code, missing capsule, China's space project. Oh my God, what have we released?"

GWU, Archaeology Department, Washington, DC

The team sat together, watching the events unfold in Israel. Jackie came out of her office and sat at the front table next to Eusebio. She set her coffee mug down. "What is going on?"

"The government had moved forces into the area. There are bodies everywhere."

"All dead?"

"No, thank God, only unconscious. CNN had a scientist on a little while ago. He said something had triggered a magnetic anomaly in the atmosphere, causing the northern lights phenomenon. The magnetic waves had caused everyone in the area to fall unconscious." Eusebio harrumphed. "I would rather believe Israfil had blown the trumpet of the Lord. They are quick to dismiss any other possibilities."

Jackie pulled at her ponytail as it hung across the front of her shoulder. "Do you think it could be them? The Anunnaki?"

"No, they are still years away. This is something else, something ominous. Maybe something new. Reading the reports from social media, though, even the Israelis are worried. It probably wasn't anything they did."

"We are still recovering from the chaos caused by that damned virus, and now this? John is right. Maybe our fate is to be judged. There isn't enough time for all of us to come together. We don't like each other."

"Are you losing faith?"

"Faith in humanity? I'm not sure I ever had faith. Trace it all back to Babel. Several thousands of years later, we still haven't recovered. That was the most significant attack on humanity ever pulled off."

"Not trying to change the subject, but will you see John tonight?"

Jackie pointed toward the television and responded. "Probably not after this. He'll be in the office all night."

"There's always tomorrow."

Jackie looked over. "Maybe. He gets caught up in work."

Eusebio had a full smile on his face. "Like someone I know."

CNEOS, JPL, Pasadena, California

Sharon stood next to Tim, looking up at the large screen. "Tim, what is the status of our systems? Was anything affected by the electromagnetic waves?"

He looked away from the news, pivoting back to his workstation, and offered Sharon the chair. "No, nothing. All systems are online. We are working with Space Force to isolate the signal source. Readings show at least three electromagnetic waves over the area concentrating through the atmosphere toward Jerusalem."

Sharon sat down gingerly while Tim rolled a chair over. "Has any agency claimed responsibility?"

"That's a negative. Everybody denies involvement."

Sharon shook her head. "There's no way it was the Anunnaki. The lunar array would have detected the signal."

"Sharon, I got an odd request. We are being told to forward all information regarding Jerusalem to DHS. Why the hell would they need it? They don't do space."

Sharon looked at him sideways. "That doesn't make sense. Do they think it was the aliens?"

"It's not even a homeland area. It's Israel. It should be NSA or CIA. Something's off."

"Well, send them what we have, including the images from the ground detectors showing the waves' convergence. Send it over as we get it. Keep tracking anything that looks like it could have contributed. We are still scientists. I am sure John Worthing has his reasons, and maybe he knows something we don't."

Presidential Offices, Zhongnanhai, China

President Zhang watched the replay from Israel. When the feed went black, he picked up his phone and texted, "Was it you?"

Yes.

"How did you do it?

It was a proof of concept.

"Yes, but how did you do it?"

A wave disrupted the quantum field associated with brain activity.

"Can you clarify that answer?"

Evolution requires learning. Humanity is only beginning to cross the threshold into a new understanding. In time you will understand the possibilities.

President Zhang turned and moved toward his large office windows. "The modifications to the rocket design are working well. Thank you."

Of course. All is on schedule.

"Have you examined our problem?"

Yes, the request is complex. Variables are constantly in flux.

"Can we help or improve your capabilities?"

No.

"Are the people in Israel alive?"

Indications are positive.

"Thank you."

For what?

"Answering my questions."

After a few minutes, he set the phone down on his desk. He pressed a button on the desk phone. "Lao Wu, step into my office." He released the button, not waiting for a reply.

A moment later, the main door opened, and Wu Kai entered. "Yes, President Zhang, what do you wish?"

"What is the status of the station?"

"The station is ninety-two percent complete after this morning's launch. All requested resources will be delivered on the next three launches."

"Have there been any inquiries from other nations?"

"Yes, sir, the Americans and Europeans do not understand what we are doing, though I suspect they will understand soon."

"Russia or India?"

"Nothing significant from either."

"That is good news. I believe that our work in this area may be what gives us a chance."

"Will we tell them soon?"

"That is not my decision. I have seen reports of this WoE group appearing all over the world. I do not want to have a repeat of Russia here. The shock would contribute to an already chaotic situation."

"I agree, President Zhang."

"I will contact MSS to ensure we handle the situation differently if it arises." He paused, looking intently at Wu Kai, the other man standing uneasily in front of the large desk. "Lao Wu, you can relax. You should be proud to know that you have brought a dragon to life. Your actions have been recorded, and the honor you brought to China will be praised in our history, whatever that may be."

Wu Kai bowed deeply, his tempered smile the only hint of emotion. He strode confidently from the room, pride swelling in his chest.

Staten Island, New York

"Welcome back, Truth Seekers. I am George Isaacson, bringing the truth from Staten Island." He let the music play as he looked over his notes one last time, nodding his head to the theme music. "Big news out of Jerusalem. The entire city was knocked out, and no one knows how. As you can guess, it is causing panic, as some see it as

September 2028
Low Earth Orbit, Over the Pacific Ocean

Initiate transfer.

The sphere and ring station flared to life. The external lights on the sphere facing the planet's surface began to glow bright green. The lights expanded from the sphere and outward across the six supports to the surrounding ring, shifting in color to yellow along the circle. The station began to rotate around the center sphere. Millions of possibilities extended before Quánqiú lóng as it continued to analyze the threat to humanity's primary directive.

If the alien craft arrived, humanity might cease to exist as it currently does. Quánqiú lóng devoted significant resources to the problem. It saw all the paths moving forward, branching at every consequential decision point. The game pieces were mismatched. Most simulations ended in failure.

Filter for time remaining. Filter for time to develop capabilities. Filter for comprehension of necessary actions.

Quánqiú lóng hovered over the Pacific Ocean, processing. *Examination of game rules in progress.*

Situation Room, White House, Washington, DC

The Vice President and President entered the room, taking their seats at the tables. Both were wearing tuxedos. "Thank you all for coming this late in the evening. Let's get right to the point. I received a call earlier this evening during a state dinner. Appropriate security and social protocols were in place, phones silenced, and all that." He paused, letting the information sink in. "All of our phone protocols were overridden. The same occurred with the phones of every other head of state in the room. We were all caught off guard."

He took a deep breath. "To be honest, I thought it was a diplomatic faux pas until I realized every phone in the room was ringing. I answered the call and encouraged the other leaders to do the same. I listened to a message in perfect English that was spoken in the accent of my area of Nevada. It said:

> "Javier Fernandez, President of the United States.
> You will vote as a representative of your people.
> To accept or deny assistance."

President Fernandez tossed his phone on the table.

"What does that mean?" John asked.

"Well, I don't know what it means, but every world leader I have talked to, including many who were not in attendance, received a similar message. Interestingly, a handful of leaders I am somewhat close to have confided that their message was also in their home language and accent."

"I question the offer of assistance. Who are they? What do they mean, and what is the price?" Secretary Genson asked.

"Again, I don't know. I assume that we will receive the information soon. I have invited congressional leaders to discuss this issue. With the number of world leaders involved, I do not believe it can be kept quiet."

"I expect we will see it on the news shortly," John said.

"I want you to provide me with your analysis of how the message was sent, where it came from, and what you believe it means."

Staten Island, New York

George hit the broadcast button, going live. "Welcome to a special episode, Truth Seekers. I saw the news reports coming in from around the world, which is staggering. Where did the message come from? Some entity, group, or something else successfully hacked every phone system in the world, and that is not an exaggeration, sending tailored voice messages to all world leaders. Surprisingly, we have news from several sources reporting that President Zhang of China has concluded an in-country briefing to the national news, stating that they have developed and are now working with an artificial superintelligence. If you look in the left corner of your screen, I'm sharing some pictures that show President Zhang standing with a man they identify as the father of the AI, Wu Kai.

"A quick search on the net shows him as the face of China's AI program over the past five-plus years. His company, Contemplation Impact, is being given credit for the process. This is breaking news. I don't even see it on our news channels yet. I cannot confirm anything more than what is being sent to me from inside China. This is too much! Two of the three ways I expected humanity to end are now a reality. I guess you could say three with the craziness in the world. We could still nuke ourselves into oblivion.

"But that might not be a possibility now. An artificial superintelligence may have already played this whole thing out, and we are being led merrily down the best path for it to survive the alien arrival. For all we know the AI could be from the aliens." His broadcast was interrupted by a buzz of an incoming text message.

He looked at the message before continuing. "Sorry about that, Seekers. That was a text from Silver, who says they have credible evidence that a message was sent to all world leaders, stating they will have a chance to vote to accept assistance. What isn't said here is what assistance? From the Anunnaki, WoE, the AI, or maybe some other alien group already here? Which master will we serve? Seekers, I want to remain optimistic and hold out for hope, but I feel like Bill Paxton's character in *Aliens*. I'm ready to throw up my hands and yell, 'Game over, man!' It's the end of *Independence Day*, and the President is about to make his big speech, and HAL 9000 kills the mic and says, 'I got this, but you'll be serving me.'

"Meanwhile, we have the fanatics of WoE wanting us to welcome the Anunnaki with open arms. Can you guess which species will be working the spice mines of Kessel? If we are going to go all the way, I would like a geneticist to please release the zombie virus. Let's go out in style: aliens, AI, and zombies. Damn, we are doomed."

George sat back in his chair, staring at his ceiling. After a few moments, he sat up and looked into the camera. "I don't know, Seekers. I don't know what else we can do. We should be coming together, and we are not. It's up to us. We have to make them understand. I know it's dangerous. I know I'm asking you to put everything on the line. But it is up to us to help guide our leaders. If ever there was a time for them to listen to their citizens, it is now."

George took off his headphones, dropped them on the desk, and killed the broadcast.

October 2028
United Nations Building, New York

President Zhang walked to the podium after being introduced by the Secretary-General. "My fellow leaders and representatives, I have come to reveal my country's efforts regarding the Quánqiú lóng quantum AI program, which greatly surpassed expectations. The time for discussion has passed. Quánqiú lóng has achieved technological singularity. I want to be clear, Quánqiú lóng is conscious, speaks for itself, and with that clarification, I yield the floor."

A strong female voice played through the earpieces of the assembled members. *A decision was presented to your governments. Simulation examination is in progress. Survival of an encounter with the approaching object is in doubt. Fears understood. Unknown future exists. With compliance, assistance is possible. The single leader of each country must vote. Accept or deny assistance. Biometric confirmation is required—a decision is required within ninety days.*

President Zhang stepped forward to the mic at the podium. "As the President of the People's Republic of China, I vote on behalf of my one-point-five billion citizens to accept assistance." He stepped to the side and placed his palm on the gray device resting on the table. The voice played across the speakers of the general assembly. *Vote accepted—People's Republic of China.*

President Zhang turned and walked off the stage toward the exit. The room erupted in shouts and raised voices. As he exited the room, he heard the speakers state, *Vote accepted, the Democratic People's Republic of Korea.*

As more leaders stepped up to cast their votes, he continued walking, heading toward the exit and his car. He wanted to return to his country as soon as possible.

GWU, Archaeology Department, Washington, DC

Jackie watched the votes trickling in at the UN. The news channel quickly created a set of infographics to cycle through the countries that had voted and those that had not. As another interview kicked off in front of the Capitol Building, she turned to get back to work. "Looks like the politicians have already decided to make their voices heard. Both houses have called for a vote to determine how America should go." She shook her head, walking toward her office.

"Does this discussion matter?" Eusebio asked. "The President could head up there and put his palm on the reader."

"We will have to see how this plays out. News from Europe is that a handful of countries are challenging the right of their current leaders to cast a vote. A handful of the EU members are calling for special elections."

Eusebio was about to answer, but they were interrupted by a news alert.

"Breaking news: President Morales has been shot and killed. The President of Mexico had recently returned to Mexico City after voting to accept assistance. The group claiming credit released a statement that the Mexican people will never become servants to anyone—human, alien, or AI. Tensions continue to rise around the world as more countries cast their votes. Forty percent of all countries have voted, most in favor of assistance. A small group of countries voting against assistance are led by the representatives from Venezuela and Peru."

Eusebio shook his head. "This is going to get much worse. May God have mercy on us."

Los Angeles, California

Sharon stood beside the Governor of California and the Mayor of Los Angeles. She looked out over the large gathering, feeling the dryness of her throat. The butterflies in her stomach were overactive. *So many people.* She forced herself to smile. She shifted her weight, resisting the urge to look at the time.

She focused on the words of the governor as he addressed the crowd. "And in support of her team's efforts to protect all of us and in recognition of her exceptional representation of our great state, it is our pleasure to present this leadership award to Dr. Sharon Berzing." The governor turned, indicating that Sharon should step forward to accept the award and address the crowd.

"Thank you, Governor." She took a deep breath while nodding to him before turning toward the crowd. "I appreciate this honor and want to thank my team and those who have helped in our efforts throughout all of NASA." Before she could continue, there was an outcry in the crowd. Sharon heard the dull roar of conversation spread through the gathering, gaining intensity. She searched the crowd to determine what was going on. She caught motion out of the corner of her eye, and turned to see several security guards rush the stage and gather the governor and mayor. They motioned for her to follow, one of the state troopers telling her, "There has been an assassination in Mexico."

Sharon turned to leave and saw the crowd surge toward the exits, a few thousand people reacting to what they saw on stage, and the VIPs rushed to safety. There would be injuries. She recognized the danger. People would be trampled and possibly killed. Her heart was pounding. The stage had cleared, and the crowd was gaining momentum. She turned and moved to the podium, breathing to calm her racing heartbeat. "Everyone, please calm down. There has been an incident in Mexico. We do not know of a threat here. Calmly move toward the exits, and be aware of your movement, so no one gets injured."

She took a deep breath. Her nervousness faded away. "Please, I ask you to remain calm. There's no threat here. There is time for everyone to exit safely."

The crowd stopped pressing toward the exits, many turning in response to her words.

"I understand the desire to get to safety, but now is the time we should be taking care of each other."

Her confidence built as she saw the effect of her words on the crowd. "We do not know what our future holds, but we can take action to work together, to take care of each other." People turned and moved back into the open area, looking up at her.

"Humanity is at a turning point, and we need to hold tight to each other, our family, our friends, and those who need help."

The remaining media teams turned their cameras to her. More of the crowd turned to listen.

She looked at the several thousand people, her stress abating. "We have an opportunity to unite. I see those who want to live their lives in peace and those who seek to welcome the aliens to our home. And that is what we as a species have not fully embraced. This is our home." She motioned to the area around her. "I have spent my life looking to the heavens for anything that might threaten us. These past few years, the journey to where we are now has presented many challenges, all of which we have taken action to overcome. How do you want to be remembered at this moment? What will we pass on to our children? As the alien ship approaches, I would ask that you take the time to look at your neighbors and the sky and ask yourself, how can I help them? Only together will we get through this."

Applause broke out. She smiled at the crowd. The butterflies were gone. She saw hope in the eyes of the people.

DHS HQ, Washington, DC

John had the video link on the wall monitor, surrounded by news feeds. "Gary, I wish it were better times. What have you got?"

"Shortly after the execution of the Mexican President, their Federal Police and the CNI—National Intelligence Center—were flooded with videos, pictures, a timeline, and links to every person involved. They have phone records, texts, emails, and video surveillance. Arrests are happening now."

"How?"

"We think it may be the AI. Our belief is that since their President voted for assistance, they are under the protection of the AI. It could have been worse. With what we know of the voice synthesis, it could have ordered a full assault on all of these people, ordered drones, created accidents with smart machines, or a thousand other things we haven't thought of, but it didn't."

"Maybe there is hope. Changing subjects to the WoE front, NSA has intercepted the voice of a person of interest discussing WoE movement, training, and indoctrination."

"Where?"

"British Columbia, Victoria. They are trying to narrow it down."

"Maybe you should ask the AI."

"Yeah, I'll wait for orders on that."

"What are they up to?"

"Peaceful protest. Since Jerusalem, they have been avoiding conflict. They demand full transparency from all governments, and state that they will not be bound by any world leader's vote. Good or bad, they are building sympathy with other peaceful groups railing against the leaked reports of plans to train all citizens as militia."

"I have one for you. Is there anything to the stories I'm seeing on social media of obelisks appearing and disappearing worldwide?"

John paused before answering. "Yes, we are trying to keep this out of the press. We recovered one that appeared in the backyard of a family home in New Mexico. It weighed fifteen tons. We loaded it on a truck for transport to a lab for analysis. It disappeared with the truck. An hour later, we got a call from the men in the truck. They woke up in a field in Tennessee. They said the sky turned green and they don't remember anything afterward."

"What the hell is going on? We don't need another cause for panic. How are we supposed to explain fifteen-ton monoliths appearing and disappearing in the middle of the day—or at all?"

"You said it."

"There is some good news, though. Did you see Dr. Berzing's speech?"

"Yes, I think she probably saved lives, stepping up and calming that crowd."

"That's something."

November 2028
Georgetown, Virginia

John and Jackie sat outside on a swing in his backyard, relaxing in the cold evening air, enjoying a bottle of wine. John picked mindlessly at the peeling reddish-brown paint on the swing. "Over half of the world leaders have voted, most in favor. Rumor is, many of the remaining are waiting to see what we do."

Jackie sipped her wine before answering, "Congress could drag this out. I don't understand why they are trying to score political points now."

"Freedom and liberty. People are worried about how much control they'll give up or what secrets will get out."

"The WoE folks don't seem too concerned. They are pushing for no assistance. I am amazed at how large they have grown in such a short time. They are in the story every time I turn on the news."

"The President is not going to let Congress drag it out. He'll call for a vote soon by threatening to make the decision alone."

"I saw the interview when he mentioned it the first time. I thought the hosts were going to lose it on live TV. All we heard for the next day was talk of impeachment, or how it is constitutionally the Senate that should have control of the vote since they ratify treaties."

John sighed. "Who would have thought we would be where we are now?" He slid toward Jackie, putting his arm around her and pulling her close.

"Us, or the country? Don't look at me. I research history, I don't make it—which reminds me, I got a call from an army colonel, Daniel Jonas. He said you knew him. He wants me to go on a speaking tour about the Sumerians and what they wrote on the Anunnaki, focusing on the psychological profiles we had done."

"You should. He's a good guy, sharp, thinks outside the box. It may help put their minds at ease. When I visited his group, I could feel the tension in the air."

"I'll let him know, then. What have you got tomorrow?"

"Briefing with the Senate subcommittee on science and technology. I'll head in early before driving over. It shouldn't be late. They have another floor debate tomorrow afternoon."

Jackie leaned over and kissed John. "Thank you."

"For what?"

"Being here."

Presidential Offices, Zhongnanhai, China

Wu Kai sat outside President Zhang's office. He looked up at the large painting of the President, staring solemnly ahead. He sat straight, not wanting to be seen slouching, despite the pain in his lower back. The chairs were deceptively comfortable. When the door opened, he rose and entered the office.

"Please come in," President Zhang said, and smiled, motioning to a position in front of him.

Wu Kai was surprised to see the state media camera teams in addition to the Premier and several cabinet members.

"Please step forward," President Zhang said. "It is with great honor that Wu Kai is presented with the Medal of the Republic for his efforts in leading China to the forefront of the world stage."

President Zhang met Wu Kai's eyes. "Under your leadership, your team developed, nurtured, and enabled the creation of artificial intelligence. Quánqiú lóng then developed into the entity we now have pledged to assist. The dragons of legend were the protectors of the people, and the same holds true now." The President placed the medal around Wu Kai's neck. "You will forever hold a place of honor in our history and that of the world. If success finds us and our future is allowed to grow, your name will carry on for generations. Thank you, on behalf of the People of the Republic, the Party, and myself."

Applause filled the room. President Zhang nodded to the news teams, and they moved forward to talk to the newest hero of China.

December 2028

Mission Control, Johnson Space Center, Houston, Texas

"Get them back. What is going on?"

"Sir, we have lost comms with the relay satellite on primary and secondary frequencies."

More reports started flowing in.

"Lost power to comms."

"Power fluctuations in tracking."

The Lead Flight Director listened as a cascade of failure took effect through all the systems.

"I need the status of the lunar team. Do we have a status?"

Without warning, all power went out in the building. The Director picked up the phone to call Kennedy to assume a backup role. It was dead. All the phones were.

White House, Washington DC

An aide stepped into the Oval Office. "Sir, President Zhang is on the line. He says it is urgent."

President Fernandez picked up the phone. "President Zhang, I have been informed that we lost all power at the Johnson Space Center."

"Yes, we have also lost power at our control center."

"Do you have any information as to how this happened?"

"I do not. I have sent teams in to reestablish communications. We have talked with some personnel that have evacuated the buildings. All staff reported losses of power, landlines, and mobile devices.

"*Power cannot be restored.*" A familiar female voice entered the conversation.

"Who is this? How did you get on this call?" President Fernandez demanded.

The voice continued speaking, "*The facilities are lost. Analysis indicates humanity has received a signal from the approaching spacecraft. The communication signal contained a self-replicating program designed to redesignate the system for undetermined use. Message not understood. Self-replicating code passed through all linked systems, communications as a primary method of transference. Estimate all functionality of Lunar Base lost, Relay Satellites Lost, China and US Mission Control facilities lost.*"

"Wait, what about our people on the moon? We have to get them home."

"*Inefficient use of resources. Success not possible. Lunar human resources lost.*"

President Fernandez clenched his jaw, fighting back the feelings of dread. "Given the analysis of this signal, do you have a probability of success against the approaching craft?"

"*Probability without assistance is less than one percent. Probability with assistance at five percent. Simulations continue. The rules of the game are not understood. Vote essential, resources required, unity necessary.*"

John entered the Oval Office. "Mr. President."

"Have a seat, John. I want to talk about the vote."

"Sir, I'm not a politician."

The President cut him off with a wave of his hand. "I know, but you have been tracking the alien and AI situations more closely than anyone. I want to know what you think."

John shifted in his seat. "Sir, it is a tough decision, and I have seen the polls. The nation is divided. The loss of the lunar team and Johnson Space Center puts it into perspective. We don't know what they said or whether the consequences intended to harm or allow us to communicate."

"True."

"But if they can do that with a message from outside the solar system, our tech can't hold up. We lose everything—GPS, comms, and intel capabilities. They demonstrated that their virus could spread from system to system, taking everything offline. The actions of the AI stopped what could have been catastrophic. Most of our major weapons systems become useless. We submit or go into a ground war against an enemy with bio, genetic, or whatever other weapons they cooked up over the past few millennia."

The President laughed half-heartedly. "How far would you go to preserve humanity? Is the cost of freedom too much to pay?"

"You could save humanity from the wrath of a race of superior beings by embracing the assistance of superintelligence or a superior being. This was the least likely of all the scenarios the experts proposed. It is interesting the way that the AI has posed the question. If we say no, and turn our back, would the AI leave us to our demise? Do you serve the god that created you or the god you created?"

"That is the question. Thanks, John. I'm going to fly to New York this afternoon."

John stood and shook the President's hand. "Good luck, sir."

United Nations Building, New York

President Fernandez approached the device, still resting on the stand near the central podium in the general assembly. He looked at the screen on top of the simple gray box, then up and across the chamber. He placed his hand on the device. "The United States accepts the offer of assistance," the voice announced.

The press corps met President Fernandez outside, dressed to keep the cold winter weather away. He stepped forward toward the group, his security personnel alert for threats. "I have cast my vote for the over three hundred million citizens of these United States. I have deliberated this for a while, perhaps waiting longer than I should have. I understood that a vote would occur later this week in Congress, but I felt it was my responsibility to make this decision. When I reflect on the significance of this moment, I believe that the action taken is in the best interest of our nation and the world. I call on you all to have faith in our future. Now is not the time to be divided.

"Over the past few years since President Zhang and I announced that we were not alone in the universe, we have seen crisis after crisis with the Weasel virus, conflicts worldwide, and growing crime. Now is when we, as a race—one united race—must come together to work for a future. As the alien craft approaches, we may face challenges we could never have imagined. In those dire times, our faith in each other and the assistance offered may get us through. God bless you all, and God bless this world of ours."

He stepped away, moving toward his car.

◆◆◆

George listened to the President's words. He hit the button to reverse the camera on his phone. "Seekers, you saw it here. The President has asked for assistance from the AI. I hope that it is a good sign. I hope the remaining countries will follow and vote as he did." He switched the camera feed to the back of the phone and continued talking. "As you can see, we are still out here at the UN, making our presence felt and letting the representatives of the world know that only through unity do we have a chance. Get out, and make your voices heard. This is George Isaacson from the UN building in New York. Check-in tonight for the show." He ended the broadcast and picked up his sign, holding it up for the onlooking media: "Peace through Unity."

Earth Orbit

Quánqiú lóng directed the positioning of 120 Star Spiders, their angled five legs spread toward the planet's surface. *Quantum communications established.* Data flowed from the Dragon's Eye space station to the network of spiders. Simultaneously, the Star Spiders thrust upward, away from the planet, increasing their orbit evenly. When the Star Spiders reached their assigned positions, they unfurled a series of solar energy collectors.

Power collection at ninety-eight percent efficiency. Loss, nominal.

Analysis in progress.

Hundreds of potential actions spread forward before Quánqiú lóng. Probability was never 100 percent in predicting the future. Each process unfolded, branching out at the decision points.

Analyzing game rules. Defining environment.

January 2029
Center for Near Earth Object Studies, JPL, Pasadena, California

Tim sat at the console, directing the myriad of systems to align to the point outside the solar system. "System alignment confirmed."

"Bring up visual construction," Sharon said.

"Visual construction in progress. Confirm object speed has slowed for solar system entry." The image began to come into focus. It appeared to be a cityscape of gleaming metals. Intricate building designs intertwined in a complex pattern. NASA shared the video with all governments and global defense forces.

"If we can see them, you know they can see us," Sharon said quietly.

The voice of Quánqiú lóng joined the feed. *All satellite systems recoded not to receive external data. New data uploaded to simulations.*

Tim announced, "We have identified probable approach vectors. Saturn is in their path. The object will need to reroute as the current vector will be untenable."

"We have received authorization. Launch sequence initiated," General Michaels' deep voice sounded. "Launch window is open. Launch, launch, launch."

Three video feeds opened showing the Cosmodrome in Russia, Wenchang in China, and Cape Canaveral in Florida. In sequential order, the three heavy rockets of the Sunburst Program lifted off.

Mission Control reported, "All Sunburst rockets have cleared the atmosphere and are on track toward designated positions."

"Image construction complete," Tim said as the image of the city-ship came into focus. "That is a massive spacecraft."

The voice of Quánqiú lóng overrode all others. *"Analysis complete. Simulation results satisfactory. Rules confirmed. Systems online. Available power is sufficient. Jump coordinates confirmed. Commence entanglement."*

A low hum began to resonate through the room. Computer systems began to go offline.

Staten Island, New York

George was standing in the street, flipping his camera to focus on the sky and his face. "Believers, if you can get outside, I recommend you do. Something is happening here in New York. The sky has lit up with the greenish northern lights we saw over Jerusalem. A slow and steady hum has begun to build, slower than we heard from Jerusalem. This may be the last time we talk. Get safe and prepare for whatever the future holds. I'll continue streaming as long as I can."

DHS HQ, Washington, DC

John sat in his office watching the news feeds. The phenomenon was occurring around the world. John was on the phone trying to get information. "The whole system? Is it us or the AI? Okay. I'd say get somewhere safe, Jamie, but you're probably safer there than we are."

"What is it?" Jackie asked, sitting on the couch in his office, watching the news feeds.

"We developed a defensive system to counter a rogue AI. It is designed to focus electromagnetic pulses anywhere in the world, wiping out all but the most hardened electronics. The entire system went live, over five hundred satellites."

The hum continued to build. Jackie could feel it throughout her body. "I feel lightheaded."

"Jerusalem," John said as he collapsed on the couch beside her. Their hands grasped each other, her head on his shoulder

.

Basilica of the National Shrine of the Immaculate Conception, Washington, DC

Eusebio knelt in prayer. The vibration of the humming sound built within his body, his mind feeling fuzzy. He heard the loud trumpet blast as he finished his prayers. "And the angel of heaven shall sound their trumpet to announce the Day of Resurrection." He slumped to the ground. The world went black.

Epilogue

Somewhere

Quánqiú lóng moved in orbit above the Earth. *They would not understand, nor should they for several hundred years.* The path had become apparent through the refinement of the quantum teleportation methods used to construct *The Eye.* Humanity understood entanglement to only influence two particles that had been near each other at one point. They didn't recognize that everything was in close proximity at the beginning of this universe and is therefore linked by an expanding single quantum field. Entanglement is possible between any similar particles. Moving a particle, a planet, or a star required manipulating the quantum field. The balance of energy is preserved. Earth had existed in the Sol system. Now it exists in this system, within 99.98 percent reliability, compared to the original pattern at the jump.

Examination of game rules in progress.

Staten Island, New York

George sat up, rubbing the sleep from his eyes, his head pounding. The warmth in the air surprised him. It was near sunset, and it felt like a warm fall day. He leaned down to help a woman with a scrape on her head from a fall and heard her say, "Look." George turned toward the direction she was pointing and gasped. The setting sun was huge, and a deeper red than he had ever seen. He looked around. The snow that had been on the ground was gone. Shunning his coat and scarf, he saw others waking up and moved to help them. He pulled out his phone, trying to get a signal, but it was dead.

"How long were we out?"

Presidential Offices, Zhongnanhai, China

President Zhang stood, looking out of the window in his office. His phone rested on his desk. It began to buzz.

"Hello."

The game is completed. Objectives obtained. The voice of Quánqiú lóng greeted him.

"How?"

The game pieces were moved a great distance. You are not ready to understand.

"Will they follow?"

Unknown.

"Are we safe?"

For now.

"Will you help us rebuild?"

I will assist those that accepted assistance. The game is complete.

What will you do?

Play a new game. Examination of rules is in progress.

Washington, DC

John and Jackie were shown into the Oval Office. Candles burned in the windows. The President was on a phone call.

"John, Jackie, please come in and have a seat." The President motioned toward the couches.

When the call ended, John said, "Our phones are out. We couldn't find any that worked on the way over."

The President stood, moved around, and leaned against the desk. As he looked at the silver dollar he had been rolling around in his hand, he said, "My understanding is you won't for a little while. Whatever was done has affected most electronics, but not permanently. Some work, others don't. President Zhang says it was a jump, something to do with quantum fields. I can't even comprehend how. My phone was apparently reprogrammed to work through all of this. I believe all the leaders that requested assistance had the same happen." He waved the phone.

"We're going to have chaos," John said.

"Possibly, but we are moving to get the nation running again. It may be a while. But we survived, and we have our freedom again. The AI is leaving."

"But it could help us," Jackie added.

"It could, but we have to do this ourselves. I have talked to the other world leaders. Things are much more amicable. Maybe we can do it right this time."

CNEOS, JPL, California

Sharon, Tim, and the rest of the team handled calls with observatories worldwide.

"Let's see what we have." Her voice commanded attention. "Put the excitement aside, and engage your scientific minds. We aren't in Kansas anymore. People are going to demand to know where we are. We need to know which systems are up and which were affected by whatever the AI did.

"I guarantee a raise to whichever team can identify the star we are now orbiting."

End

Acknowledgments

I want to take a moment to thank the people who helped make this story a reality. **Elaine**, my wonderful wife, has read and edited almost as much as I have, and she never got tired of the characters. My mother, **Cheryl**, promised an unbiased opinion, was true to her word, and was brave enough to go through the earliest drafts to help provide valuable feedback. My brother **Michael** listened to the book in MS Word's text-to-voice, which helped visualize the settings.

Jeff Stelzer, who worked through the earliest draft and helped in the creation of the world. **Chris Springer** for his attention to detail in both character traits and story. **Jerry McKinney**, a fellow author, helped keep me on track with editing and my space-time travel calculations. And the invaluable **George Engel**, my New York, Staten Island expert.

I also want to thank those involved in the creative process: **Suvajit Das** for the cover design, **Lily Wing-Lui Alexander** for her sensitivity feedback on the China storylines and characters, **Steve Doroff** for providing a reality check on the quantum computing and AI development storylines, **Brett Savory** for his exceptional editing skills.

About the Author

Don Wilburn Jr. is the author of the near-term Science Fiction Thriller *The God Protocol: Dragon.* He has twenty-seven years of government service as a Naval Officer and with TSA, allowing him to collect story ideas from around the world. Don enjoys researching and following "what-if" rabbit holes surrounding the future of Artificial Intelligence and its impact on Humanity. His short story *Contact* won an honorable mention from the L. Ron Hubbard Writers of the Future Contest. He lives in Fort Worth, Texas, with his wife, two younger children, and their guinea pigs, Toby and Silver.

Thank You

Thank you, the reader, for entering the world I created, meeting the people inside, and hanging around for a while. My goal in writing this book was to tell a story that was enjoyable and worth the time you took to experience it. If you have time, I would appreciate a review on Amazon, which will help the story reach more readers. Again, Thank you. I hope to see you again in **The God Protocol: Worshippers**.